PigT
By Boone Lock

PigTrail

Boone Lockhart Wilford

Published by Boone Lockhart Wilford, 2023.

PIGTRAIL

First edition. July 6, 2023.

Copyright © 2023 Boone Lockhart Wilford.

ISBN: 979-8223366607

Written by Boone Lockhart Wilford.

CHAPTER ONE

T he first two volunteer firefighters got out of their pickup trucks and stared in amazement. An attractive young woman was sitting cross-legged in front of the still burning hulk of an automobile. Greasy black smoke billowed from a bunker-like building set back into a hillside. What was once a metal garage door was now twisted and torn scrap metal hanging from the building entrance. The woman's clothes were scorched, and her hair was singed. Soot clung to her tear-tracked cheeks. She rocked back and forth, cradling the head of an apparently dead man while the lights of the fire trucks illuminated the twilight scene in slow motion flashes of red.

The volunteer battalion chief, Clinton James, pulled up and clambered out of his brush truck in full turn-out gear and started walking toward the young woman. An enveloping pall of smoke swirled across the scene and as it briefly cleared, he could see that she was gone and only the dead body remained. He could hear the sound of an engine racing through the nearby woods. Perplexed, he approached the door of the building where the battered and bloody body lay. He pulled the radio from his belt clip.

"County, 941."

"Go ahead 941." The emergency dispatcher replied.

"Advise the SO that we have a probable homicide. Tell 'em to get a deputy out here right away. I think the suspect just tore outta here on a four-wheeler or a dirt bike."

"Affirmative, 941. Clint, do you need EMS?"

"Negative. Just the coroner. One DOA so far but I'm thinking there's gonna be more. Stand by." Clint spoke tersely into the radio. He was edgy, not knowing what he and his men were walking into. The first rule was to ensure the scene was safe and it looked anything but safe.

"County standing by." Clara was certainly going to be standing by. This was more excitement than she'd had all day.

Clinton motioned for the other four responders to join him.

"Bring a line and get your gear on." Clint was already moving to the entrance of the building. Each man donned his Scott air-pack as they moved toward the smoke-filled building. Two of the men pulled an inch and a half hose with them as they moved cautiously and methodically through the large open room carefully examining the structure for signs of impended collapse. Clint pointed out the few smoldering places for them to hose down.

"Hit that trash pile over there." Clint pointed to a clump of debris with dark yellow flames licking the edges.

After a quick dousing, the lead man turned back to Clint.

"That ain't no trash, Clint." The firefighter's words were muffled by the full-face mask he wore but the words had a chilling effect on Clint. The blast of water revealed an image of soot-stained teeth which he would not soon forget. Clint put his radio against his own face mask.

"County, 941."

"Go ahead, Clint."

"We're gonna need more help, Clara. I can see at least two more victims."

TWO MONTHS EARLIER, Chet Farmer threw the last armload of dirty uniforms out through the back door of his step van. The stench of body odor mixed with pungent smell of greasy shop rags was overpowering. The uniforms landed on a small mountain of stinking, dirty laundry in a large, wheeled canvas cart.

The wash boy grumbled, "That it?"

"Yeah, that's all," Chet replied as he wiped beads of sweat from his brow with his forearm. He leaned against the door of his truck to catch his breath.

The wash boy pushed the cart into the dimly lit washroom where he began dumping the clothes into the open drum of a huge stainless-steel washer. Filthy wash water pooled on the floor and tendrils of steam issued from the many leaky pipes. Washers creaked and groaned as they sloshed the heavy loads of laundry. The entire building shook with the vibration of the extractors as they spun thousand-pound loads of wet uniforms. Centrifugal force slung as much water out of the loads as possible before they were laboriously hand-loaded into the gas-fired dryers. The massive dryers roared as they sucked air and gas into the combustion chambers, blasting the garments with searing heat to dry them. Flames occasionally slipped through the seams and cracks in the decades-old equipment.

Chet observed all this from the back door of his truck. He didn't know what Hell looked like, but that washroom couldn't be far from it in his opinion. He pitied the kid who worked in those conditions.

Chet stepped down and closed the doors of his truck. Parked next to him was another sweating route man, Larry, who was just finishing his unloading.

"Hey, Lar, let's get checked in and go down to Pete's. You owe me a beer."

Larry only nodded. It was the last day of a long, hot, frustrating week of dealing with hateful customers. Larry was continually amazed at the incredible pettiness that a small problem with someone's uniforms could bring out. He'd literally had customers throw their dirty laundry in his face over a missing button.

Larry watched Chet park his van in its customary spot. He'd been Chet's friend since they had started to work for this company. Chet could be difficult sometimes, but Larry always knew he could count on Chet. They had each other's back and that meant a lot in this world. Chet was also pretty damned quick to share his opinions with Larry or anyone else within earshot. Larry didn't mind and he hurried to finish his unloading and final paperwork of the day.

An hour or so later, they walked into the dimly lit bar that was their habitual hangout.

"A little attitude adjustment," Larry said over the first long neck.

"I need more than a little adjustment," Chet said.

"I've noticed. And so has Bob."

"Fuck Bob," Chet replied. "He's been on my ass constantly."

"You better clean up your act, Chet. Your review's coming up and he'll screw you out of your raise."

"Supposing we didn't have to worry about supervisors, raises or asshole customers?" Chet wondered aloud.

"What now, Chet? Another get rich quick scheme?"

"No, but just suppose. You know, just... what if. That's all."

"I'm tired of supposing, Chet. Just finish your beer and let's go. Karie's expecting me home early tonight."

"Listen, Lar. I've been thinking about this for months and I think I've got something."

"What have you got?" Larry snapped; his patience worn thin.

"If there were a way, we could each end up with a hundred thousand bucks or maybe more, would you be interested?" Chet asked.

"Give me a break, Chet. You've always got some sort of harebrained scheme. I'm going home. I'll see you at the sales meeting Monday morning." With that, Larry stood and set his empty beer bottle on the table.

"Sit the fuck down," Chet commanded and slammed his beer on the table with a withering glare at Larry.

Something in Chet's voice struck home with Larry, and he impatiently sat back down.

Chet leaned forward and said, "Just listen for five fucking minutes and then if you're not interested, we'll just forget the whole goddamned thing. Okay?"

"Okay. Five minutes and then I go home," Larry agreed skeptically.

Chet began speaking in low, earnest tones that kept Larry's attention. He glanced over his shoulder periodically to make sure no one was listening. Larry almost laughed at the absurdly serious way Chet was acting. He had the impression that Chet was trying to act like some underworld spy. Nonetheless, Larry continued to listen to Chet's plan.

Considerably more than five minutes later, after outlining the basics of his plan, Chet sat back in the chair and said, "So, what do you think?" For several moments Larry said nothing. Then he said, "You really have been thinking about this haven't you."

"Yep, but it takes two. You're the only one I'd even consider. Besides I know you need the money as bad as I do. By the time I pay MasterCard, Visa, the utilities and food, there's nothing left and the land payment's still due. I'm just glad we didn't have any kids. It was bad enough for just me and Josie. I don't see how you guys make it with a little one on the way."

Larry couldn't argue with him. He had just as many charge accounts to pay and now Karie wasn't working since the baby was due. There just didn't seem to be any way to get ahead. Every time they started to catch up on bills, something broke, wore out or went wrong. Karie deserved better, he told himself. Hell, for that matter, he deserved better himself, Larry thought bitterly. He was tired, frustrated and angry with Chet for always bringing up these schemes. They never worked. Never had, never would.

"You're so big on supposing. Suppose something goes wrong? Suppose we get caught? What then? What then, Chet?"

"Well, there's a risk. I admit that. Just keep your fuckin' voice down," Chet replied. Two guys across the room were watching and Chet was getting nervous.

"A risk, huh? I'll tell you what the risk is. The risk is about ten guys will hold you down while your fellow prisoners assault your rectum. The risk is my wife not waiting for me to get out. The risk is..."

"Okay, okay. Forget I ever said anything about it. Just forget it," Chet interrupted.

Larry stood, reached for his wallet and dropped a five on the table. "I gotta get home," he said and walked out leaving Chet sitting alone at the table. Chet made no effort to stop his friend. He was bitterly disappointed, but he figured if Lar wasn't up for the deal, fuck him, he didn't need him. He'd studied up on successful criminals and the one thing they had in common was a healthy distrust of their partners in crime. No doubt, they had good reason. Everything he read about crime revealed the criminal's downfall usually resulted from the fault of one or more of the partners. The really successful criminals worked alone. If Larry wasn't committed to changing his life for the better, well...just screw him. He deserves to live the way he does. Chet had thought about every way there was to pull off this job by himself, but he knew the odds were better if he had help. In fact, he wasn't sure if there was any way for a lone robber to accomplish what he planned to do.

Chet motioned to the bar girl with his empty bottle. She brought him another and later, still another.

CHAPTER TWO

L arry walked through the door of his house expecting a sharp reprimand from Karie, but she just looked up from her needlework and said, "Dinner's on the stove. I got tired of waiting so I already ate."

There was no warmth in her words, and he knew she was angry, but she wouldn't say so for several hours yet. It was a familiar routine. Anytime she got mad, she'd stew about it for two or three hours and then explode in tears and hurt indignation. Larry sighed and walked past her to the kitchen. He filled his plate and popped it in the microwave to warm. While he waited for the microwave to beep, he glanced at the mail. "Bills, just bills," he muttered. He looked at the cell phone bill and sighed, almost a hundred dollars. She'd gone way over her minutes again.

"What?" Karie demanded from her comfortable chair in the living room.

"Nothing. Just looking at the mail." He gritted his teeth and said nothing more. It had been a long, hot week and he just wanted to relax tonight. The prospect of another fight exhausted him.

He sat at the small kitchen table to eat his meal. The only time he and Karie ate together was when they went out. He always ate breakfast alone because she liked to sleep in. Dinner was a hit or miss proposition because most days he worked late. Karie didn't like to cook much, so many of their meals were defrosted and microwaved.

Typically, when they ate out, there was no cash in the checking account, so they charged the meal to American Express. At least,

Larry ruefully mused, they did eat at a better class of restaurant that way even though they couldn't afford it.

These thoughts reminded him of their financial situation and of his conversation with Chet that afternoon. He had been excited by the venture that Chet had outlined. He was no criminal, he told himself. In fifteen years of driving, he had never gotten so much as a speeding ticket. Who better to pull off a crime, he asked himself. Who would ever suspect a straight guy like good ole, steady Larry? He became aware that Karie was standing in front of him.

"Where have you been?" she asked.

"Oh, uh...just thinking about work."

"I bet. More likely thinking about your girlfriend," she said in a disarmingly playful manner. He had fallen for this type of ploy before. She was fiercely jealous and often tried to trap him into an admission of infidelity.

"No hon, you're my only lady."

She smiled and walked past him to the refrigerator. Correct response, he congratulated himself. He fell back to his revelry, thinking about what life would be like with a cool hundred thousand or so, tax-free.

CHET FINISHED HIS SIXTH or was it his seventh beer. No matter, what's one beer more or less, he thought. The bar girl came by his table. "Doing alright?" she inquired.

"Yeah, bring me another one," his words were slurred.

She smiled and walked toward the bar, aware that his eyes were on her the whole way. She recognized him as a regular, but she had never seen him drunk before. Probably a fight with his old lady, she thought. While opening the beer, she looked at him speculatively. Medium build, thick dark hair, brushy mustache - not bad looking in a rugged sort of way she decided. Strong broad hands, she noticed. The sort of hands that make you feel secure when they hold you, she thought. Forget it, she commanded herself. He's just another married man and that's nothing but trouble.

"Here you go." She set his beer on a napkin in front of him.

"Thanks," he mumbled.

"Where's your buddy tonight?" she asked.

"Went home to his wife."

"Well, this is last call. We'll be closing in a few minutes."

She started to walk away, hesitated, and turned back to him.

"Uh... are you okay to drive? I mean, the cops have really been cracking down lately... I could run you home."

He looked up at her intently for a few seconds. He wasn't so drunk that he couldn't recognize an invitation.

"I can drive just fine," he said bluntly. As soon as he spoke, he regretted the words because he saw a look of disappointment flash across her face.

"Okay. Goodnight," she said with a strained smile and walked away.

He finished his beer quickly and mentally kicked himself for not prolonging the conversation with her. She was a nice-looking woman, and he didn't want to go home alone to the empty trailer. He felt slightly disgusted with himself, so he got up, dropped some money on the table and left the bar.

The air outside was muggy and oppressive. The pavement still radiated heat from the broiling sun which had gone down hours before. His black Ford pickup sat alone in the deserted parking lot. Seeing it sitting by itself only increased his sense of isolation. He got behind the wheel, carefully drove out of the parking lot, and pulled onto the main street that led toward the outskirts of town. He passed darkened businesses, garishly lit liquor stores and at the edge of town, two black and white police cars sitting in the Wal-Mart parking lot. He could just feel them watching him. He drove steadily and did not look at them as he passed. He watched the patrol cars in his rear-view mirror. They didn't pull out to pursue him. By some stroke of luck, the officers were more interested in their conversation than they were in Chet. He breathed a sigh of relief and continued to focus on staying in his lane, holding a constant speed and trying to look sober. Ten miles outside of town he turned off onto the dirt road that led to his shabby travel trailer and ten wooded acres. It was just after two a.m. when he wheeled into the dusty yard and his headlights illuminated the tiny trailer where he lived.

"Home sweet home," he bitterly muttered as he climbed out of his truck. Chet stumbled across the dark yard and yanked on the door of his trailer. It took two tries because the door had been jammed since he parked the trailer there almost two years before. "Gotta fix that door sometime," he said aloud. The door finally opened, and he lurched inside and flipped on the light. Max, blinking in the light, stretched and came forward to greet his master. With typical catty affection, Max wound himself between Chet's legs and tripped him. Chet fell headlong into the cramped living room. Max narrowly missed being fallen upon and he deftly avoided Chet's angry swat at him.

"Damn cat. Oughta get rid of him." Chet crawled up on his couch and almost immediately fell into a deep, alcoholic sleep. Max guarded the still open door, which swung fitfully in the night breeze.

CHAPTER THREE

Saturday dawned cloudless and hot. Chet raised his head from the arm of the couch and winced, "Ow, my head."

He had a whopping headache and a kink in his neck.

"What's it to ya?" Chet yelled at Max who was looking down from the dining table. As usual, Max chose not to reply. Instead, he turned and began to groom his shiny black coat, as though to say, "You should take as good care of yourself." Max was a Manx, and he carried his bobtail pointed skyward with pride. No fluffy plumes for him. Since Josie had left, Max had become Chet's confidant, companion, and worst critic. Chet roused himself from the couch to shower, shave, and prepare for his day of self-imposed labor. He had bought the ten acres with the intention of building a house on it for himself and Josie. They had been living in an apartment in town and he yearned for the freedom of the country. She didn't. She was strictly a city girl, and she made no bones about it. Many of their squabbles had been about the property. She had no intention of living in "...some shack in the sticks", as she said, and Chet was just certain she would love it. "You just gotta give it a chance," he'd said. Josie had been gone over a year now and Chet had worked on his place almost every night and weekend. He had nearly completed the reinforced concrete basement which he planned to move into while he worked on the rest of the house. He had to admit it didn't look like much and even he doubted that Josie would have agreed to move into the stark concrete box while they finished the upper level.

Chet showered and quickly toweled off. He was anxious to begin work. Work took his mind off Josie, at least for a while. He pulled on some cut-off jeans and a camo t-shirt and set about fixing breakfast. It was a ritual that he forced himself to perform. In the days that had followed Josie's departure, he hadn't eaten much. In fact, he didn't really remember much about those days at all. He'd consumed a lot of booze. Sometimes he drank so much that he was unconscious for hours. No amount of alcohol seemed to ease the torment, though. The reality of her absence was always there to greet him when he awoke.

He was better now. Most days, anyway. He usually did some calisthenics, didn't drink as much and he had quit smoking – several times, in fact. He was presently a non-smoker but that was always subject to change. He was eating pretty regularly, too. This morning it was a bowl of milk and dry cat food for Max and cereal and coffee for himself. Chet munched thoughtfully and watched Max primly lapping his milk. "I wonder if it would have worked, Max." Max mewed softly and continued to drink.

"I think it just might," he continued. "If Larry had come through, I think we could have pulled it off."

As if summoned by Chet's thoughts, Larry pulled up outside the tiny trailer in his Bronco, followed by a cloud of dust. The trailer, scrub brush and trees were all coated in a thick layer of the fine dust from a hot, dry summer. It hadn't rained since early July, and it didn't look promising any time soon. Chet peered out the window and hurriedly sat back down. He didn't wish to appear overly excited to see Larry. Mentally he was deciding how to react based on whether Larry was there to discuss the proposed robbery or something else.

Larry tapped twice on the door and stuck his head inside.

"Come on in," Chet beckoned his friend inside.

"Morning."

"Coffee's hot. You know where the cups are."

Larry stepped into the tiny trailer and found a reasonably clean cup in the miniature kitchen. He poured a cup of strong black coffee and suspiciously eyed the oily film floating on top. It didn't look lethal, so he seated himself on Chet's couch, coffee cup in hand. He wrinkled his nose at the dust that flew up from the couch. The layer of cat fur clinging to the couch wasn't a surprise. Chet wasn't much on housekeeping.

"How late did you stay at Pete's?"

"Late enough. Was Karie pissed when you got home?"

"Isn't she always?" They both laughed at this, Chet grimly and Larry, philosophically. Chet wished he still had a wife to be mad at him. They settled back into looking at their coffee.

Larry broke the uncomfortable silence by bringing up the subject that Chet was dying to talk about.

"So, you think you could actually pull it off?"

"No. I *know* we could ...together," Chet replied with emphasis on the word *we*.

"What if someone got hurt? I mean, what if we shot somebody?"

"We won't have to shoot anyone if we follow the plan I've made out."

"I don't want to shoot nobody, Chet. Not for money. It ain't worth it."

"We won't have to hurt anyone. Not even if we have to shoot 'em."

"Come again?" Larry said incredulously.

Chet didn't reply but drained his coffee cup and reached for a shotgun standing in the corner. It was a Remington 870 with a folding combat stock, extended magazine and a gray Parkerized finish.

"Here," he said, handing the weapon to Larry.

Chet booted the reluctant door open. "Let's go outside for a while." He led the way to a deep ravine several yards away from the trailer. They crunched down a gravelly path bordered by briars and sumac bushes. In the bottom of the gully, hidden from prying eyes, was an elaborate firing range. Chet looked at Larry to gauge his reaction.

Larry whistled slowly and said, "You have been busy."

At the far end of the range were a variety of targets. Man-shaped plywood targets, some match bulls eye targets and a few plate-steel spinning targets. The near end of the ravine held a firing point with a bench rest table, sandbags for prone shooting. Everything was carefully arranged under an open-sided, tin-roofed shed.

"Let me see that, Lar," Chet said as he reached for the riot gun that Larry held. He handled the weapon with easy familiarity and jacked a round into the chamber. Chet selected a man-sized plywood target and fired once from the hip. Larry was expecting a thunderous blast from the twelve gauge, but instead, he heard only a heavy whump and a dull thud as the projectile hit the target. Larry looked downrange at the target expecting the typical damage that a shotgun should do at such close range. Instead, he saw a gray, irregularly shaped blob momentarily clinging to the board. The blob dropped noiselessly to the rocky ground below the still quivering target.

"What was that?" Larry asked.

"Silly Putty."

"What?"

"Silly Putty. You know, the stuff you used to play with as a kid. It's just a ball of Silly Putty on top of a small charge of powder. It hits hard but won't do any serious damage. Of course, its range is limited, and you wouldn't want to hit someone in the face with it."

Larry couldn't help laughing at the absurdity of Chet's invention. Chet looked hurt at Larry's chuckles.

"Well, it works, don't it?"

"Yeah, Chet. It works alright. What else have you got?"

"Well...," Chet hesitated, still stinging from Larry's laughter.

"A concussion grenade. It's designed to stun someone long enough to be able to overcome them." Chet looked Larry in the eye as though daring him to laugh. Larry didn't crack a smile this time; he only said, "Show me."

Chet walked over to a footlocker that was chained to one of the posts of the firing shed. He unlocked the heavy padlock securing the footlocker and took out an army surplus ammo can. From the can, he removed a cardboard tube that looked like a large firecracker with electrical contacts sticking out of it. Chet also removed a hand-operated generator and spool of wire. Chet took the device downrange and set it against the base of one of the plywood targets. He attached two wires to the binding posts which protruded from the sides of the tube. He retraced his steps to the shed and carefully attached the opposite ends of the wires to the generator. The generator had been purchased from a scientific catalog and was no larger than a pack of cigarettes. Chet gave the lever of the generator a hard squeeze, resulting in a blinding flash and a shocking concussion which shook the ground. Larry involuntarily gasped and then shouted, "You son of a bitch... why didn't you warn me?"

"That's the whole point. It was unexpected, and it shocked you enough that I could have had the advantage because I was expecting it." Chet didn't bother to explain further that it also evened the score for Larry's derisive laughter before.

"Let's check out the target," Chet said and led the way to where the blast had taken place. The tube had completely disintegrated and there was a scorched circle on the ground. The target itself had been flattened. Larry bent over the plywood target to examine it closely.

"Look at this Chet." Larry pointed to several jagged holes where the blast had penetrated the tough plywood.

"Yeah, I know. Maybe you can come up with something that won't hurt anyone," Chet answered defensively.

"What did you use for explosive?" Larry asked, ignoring Chet's rancor.

"Firecracker powder. I bought about a thousand of 'em last month. I split 'em open with a razor knife and dumped out the powder."

Larry was impressed by the practical use of available materials and the simplicity of it all.

"The main thing is," Chet continued, "we shouldn't have to use any of this stuff. If we plan it and execute it just right, there won't be any law enforcement to deal with."

Larry nodded thoughtfully and said, "Let's sit down and go over it all again...from the very beginning."

Larry started to lead the way back to the trailer.

"This way," Chet said to cut Larry off. He headed toward the spot where he had built the basement for his house. They approached the basement from the low side. Larry noticed that the walls were constructed of poured concrete, and there was a heavy concrete cap on top that formed the roof. A single steel door opened on one side and a garage door was located on the other. There were no windows, only a couple of turbine vents that turned slowly in the light breeze. The structure had the appearance of a fortress rather than the beginnings of a home.

"Watch your step," Chet said as he carefully navigated a line of boards laid across the clinging red clay mud that still lingered in spite of the hot summer sun. Chet's excavation had left some low spots in front of the basement.

Larry followed closely behind Chet, teetering occasionally on the unsure footing of the planks. Chet unlocked the heavy door, and a musty, dank odor met them.

"Needs a little more ventilation," Chet explained. Larry nodded in agreement but said nothing. Hanging just inside the door was a Coleman lantern which Chet set about lighting. Even though it was a bright sunny day, the interior of the building was pitch dark. Larry felt the icy fingers of a chill run down his spine. He wasn't sure if it was the coolness of the damp air or the sense of foreboding that he was experiencing. After several moments of pumping, Chet lit the lantern which burned brightly with its characteristic hiss. The yellow light revealed a large empty room. A row of steel pipe columns supported the concrete roof overhead; otherwise, the space was entirely empty.

"This way," Chet said as he held the lantern aloft to light the way. I haven't hooked up the electricity yet."

"So I gathered," Larry replied with heavy sarcasm.

Chet led him to the center of the room where a trapdoor was built into the concrete floor.

"It'll be covered by flooring later, so it won't be so noticeable," Chet explained as he opened the door. A steep ladder led to the bottom. Chet descended first, followed by a somewhat reluctant Larry. Once inside the room, Chet hung the lantern on a hook in the ceiling. For a few moments, the only sound heard was the hissing of the lantern as Larry looked around. The walls of Chet's hidden room were lined with shelves containing cases of canned foods, various tools, a rack of firearms and miscellaneous supplies. The center of the room was dominated by a table supporting a scaled relief map carefully molded of *papier mache* and painted with trees, buildings, water and various pertinent landmarks and terrain features. Larry instantly recognized it as a representation of Carbontown, a small coal mining village some fifty miles south of their current location.

Chet motioned for Larry to sit on the bar stool at the edge of the map table. As Larry sat, Chet walked over to a compound hunting bow hanging on the wall and removed an arrow from its quiver. He used the arrow as a pointer to indicate certain items on the map.

"There are several problems to overcome when you decide to rob a bank," he began. "First, you gotta find a bank with enough cash to make the risk worthwhile. Lotsa banks got a bunch of cash. It's just knowing which ones have the most and when it's there. The second requirement is that the bank must have very lax security systems. Very few banks meet that one," he concluded. Larry nodded in agreement and continued to study the elaborate mockup.

"What do you notice about the Carbontown bank?" he asked Larry. Larry looked at the tiny replica of the bank building. It was nestled in a draw at the base of the foothills of the Boston Mountains of Western Arkansas. There were few buildings near it as it was a new branch of a large Fort Smith bank. Larry remembered driving through Carbontown several months before and noticing the new construction.

"Well, it's new and on the edge of town," he finally said.

"That's right. It was built just after the coal mines reopened. It wasn't until the last couple of years that Arkansas coal was worth mining again. Them mines now got over fifteen hundred people working in 'em from all over this area," Chet said.

"Rotten kind of job, I'd say. Working in them strip mines, I mean."

"Couldn't be much worse than the uniform business. Everybody's dirty, stinking laundry. Sick of it. I'm just plain sick of it," Chet said morosely, momentarily distracted from his presentation.

"Pays the bills, Chet. Most of 'em, anyway. I guess these miners prob'ly feel the same about their jobs."

"No where else for them to work, Lar. Carbontown's a little place, and them mines are the only employer for fifty miles around or better unless you wanna work at the rendering plant." Larry was well acquainted with the stench of the rendering plant. He used to run the route that picked up uniforms and shop rags from that account. The poultry processors hauled truck loads of chicken guts, feces and feathers to that plant to be processed back into chicken feed. During the summers, the smell and the flies were unbearable.

"So, the bank would have to have a large payroll to cover each week?" Larry brought the conversation back to the bank job.

"Right, it has a large payroll but the mines only pay twice a month so that means a lot of money every other week. I've been watching their routine at the bank so I can tell you which week is the big week for cash."

"Okay, so it has cash. What about security. Wouldn't a new bank have the latest high tech security systems?" Larry asked.

"I reckon it does. But systems are only good if they can be used in time and if there are people to respond to them."

"Go on. What's your point?"

"The point is to isolate the bank and then shock and surprise the internal security people," Chet said. "Now look again at the bank. There's one street that passes in front of it. The street loops back into the draw and comes back out again. There is no back way to get to the bank. It's just a series of rocky, brushy hills behind it, right?"

"Right," Larry nodded in agreement. Chet had glued bits of cedar branches to the map to make miniature scrub brush and trees. As far as Larry could remember, the land in that area looked just like Chet's map.

"Well, there's also a railroad track that crosses the street and closes off the loop. Suppose a long train just happened to be stalled or broke down on the track. No one could get to the bank, except on foot, until the train moved, right?" Chet placed the arrow across the tracks to represent a stalled train.

"Okay, I'm with you so far," Larry agreed.

"My idea is to stage a diversion, maybe two diversions on the other side of town. Something that would draw the cops away from the bank area." Chet picked the arrow back up and stabbed at a couple of blank spots on the map board. "The diversions would be timed to happen just before the coal train passes in front of the bank.

As the train reaches a certain point, we'd derail it and that would isolate the bank."

"How do you plan to make all this happen?" Larry asked.

"We'll watch it all right from the bank lobby."

Larry looked at Chet incredulously. He started to say something skeptical, but he bit his tongue instead. What he had seen so far had convinced him that Chet might be crazy, but he was definitely serious about his plan, and it was well researched.

Chet waited for the expected remark and when it failed to come, he continued, "What do all route men have in common, Larry?"

"Underpaid and overworked." Larry responded.

"Besides that, shithead." Chet snapped.

"I dunno, Chet. What?"

"We're invisible. Completely inconspicuous. So long as we wear a uniform, drive a van, and carry something, we go unnoticed. Right?"

"Well, I reckon that's true. I feel like a non-person most of the time." Larry answered.

"Also, being in the uniform business, we have access to any costume we want. The phone company, for example."

"Okay, so we go in as phone men. Then what?" Larry asked.

"Well, first off, that gives us access to their phone system which we can disable before we enter the bank. Everybody'll be watching the diversion instead of watching what we're doing. Before we pull this off, we'll try to find out if their security system has a dedicated line. If it does, then we don't want to cut it. Some systems are set up so if the dedicated line goes out, an alarm signal is sent. The second advantage to being phone guys is that a phone van is easy to duplicate. The Carbontown vans are plain white with a ladder on top and a phone symbol on each door. We can make our own magnetic signs to go on the doors. Finally, the phone man's equipment and tools can come right out of the Radio Shack catalog or off the internet."

Larry nodded agreement and Chet continued. "After we're inside and we're sure the diversions have worked and the train is off the tracks, we'll get the tellers under control, and we'll clean out the cash. We'll have to be sure to prevent anyone from hitting a duress alarm before we disable the phone system."

"Hitting a what?" Larry asked.

"Duress alarm. Sometimes it's a foot switch, but it could be a button under counter or anywhere. It's basically just a silent alarm, Lar. The best thing is to get everyone away from their workstations immediately, and then we don't have to worry about it."

"Then what?" Larry asked.

"Well, I think we'd be better off using one of the tellers to gather the cash. One of us should take care of that while the other controls the remaining employees," Chet said.

Larry brought up a subject about which Chet had been concerned. "What about customers? That could be a problem."

"It's something we need to work on. Maybe you can come up with some ideas and I'll think about it also. Then we can get together and discuss the various options."

Larry shifted uncomfortably on the hard stool. He was experiencing mixed emotions. At once, he was excited about the prospect of pulling off such a crime and also feeling as though he had fallen into a situation that would lead to disaster.

Chet seemed to read the uncertainty on his friend's face. He, too, was uncertain about the whole thing but something drove him to mask these feelings. Up to this point, he had forced himself to exude confidence and enthusiasm. Now he said, "It's not too late to back out, Larry. Just say the word. Are you in or out?"

Larry looked up, startled by Chet's perceptive comment. "I'll let you know," he said crossly.

Chet shrugged and pulled a canvas cover over the map board.

"Let's work on this some more later. I need to finish wiring in here today."

"Yeah, I gotta go, too. Karie wants me to take her to the mall to look for baby stuff."

Larry climbed the steep ladder out of the hidden chamber. Chet followed him up with the lantern in hand. He walked with Larry to the door.

"No pressure, Lar. Think it over and make your decision. We'll talk about it some more next week. If you're in, that's great. If you're out ...well, all I ask is you keep your mouth shut. No hard feelings if you're out, okay?"

Larry nodded his assent and walked slowly back to his Bronco. Thinking deeply, he drove slowly away from Chet's place. The suspension of the old Bronco creaked in protest as he bumped out of the rutted driveway onto the dusty red clay of the county road leading back to town. He felt a surge of excitement at the thought of such an adventure. He was thirty-five years old, and what had he done with his life, he asked himself. Nothing, he quickly concluded. Just worked and sweated to make a living. If it worked and they didn't get caught, it'd be a long wait before they could spend the money. Six months at least, maybe a year. But after that, a new car, remodel the house, vacations...

"Shut up, stupid," Larry said out loud to himself. "You're just fantasizing about something you don't have the balls to pull off."

But he continued to think about what it must be like to have money. For once, to not be constantly broke. The miles melted away, and he found himself pulling into the driveway of their cramped two-bedroom duplex. He paused for a few moments to concoct a suitable story for Karie. She was sure to interrogate him as soon as he walked through the door. He decided to tell her the absolute truth, which, of course, she would never believe.

CHAPTER FOUR

By 5 o'clock Chet had completed the wiring of his basement. He stood facing the circuit breaker box and said out loud, "Here goes."

He pulled the main disconnect switch and nothing sizzled, popped, or exploded, so he took that as a good sign. One by one he flipped the individual circuit breakers to the on position. As he did so, the basement was flooded by the harsh glare of four incandescent bulbs hanging from the ceiling. He grunted with satisfaction and set about gathering his tools to quit for the night. The concrete was still relatively fresh, and it exuded moisture. The high humidity would condense on his tools with the coolness of the coming night. Chet could never really understand the concepts of dew point, humidity, and temperature but he definitely understood rust. He still remembered his father's words about a craftsman and his tools. "Chester," he would say, "you measure a craftsman by the care he takes of his tools. If you take care of your equipment, it'll take care of you." Old Chester Farmer had been a practical, no-nonsense kind of man all his life. Chet remembered many of the old man's maxims such as, "If a job's worth doing, it's worth doing right." Or "Idle hands are the devil's workshop," and on and on. He seemed to have an unarguable quote for every situation. The old man had believed in the sanctity of work, and he had worked himself into an early grave at forty-three. He left behind a penniless wife and child of twelve. Chet had never forgiven the old man for dying that way. Nonetheless, the work ethic that he learned from his father had helped him through life. Now he wondered what the old man would have to say about this scheme.

Chet finished collecting his tools and placed them in his large tool chest. He had crafted the tool chest from solid red oak planks. Chet had cut down a tall, straight oak tree in the dead of winter. He'd used his chain saw to cut the tree into thick slabs that he stacked under his shed to dry. He cut the rest of the tree into firewood-size pieces to heat his workshop. Chet waited patiently for the moisture to slowly seep out of the fibers of the clear, strong wood. It took a year before Chet was satisfied that the oak was ready to be worked. He took the roughly sawn slabs to a friend's workshop where he ran it through a planer to smooth out the imperfections. He planed it down to a thickness that was just right for building his tool chest. This was one project that he wasn't about to rush. He measured, drew plans and carefully started building the tool chest. Its corners were dovetailed together, and each hand tool Chet owned had its own special niche created for it in the box. His father would have approved of that sort of workmanship.

Now, as his final task for the day, Chet took a circuit tester and checked each receptacle. The tester light glowed brightly each time he slid it into the receptacle. Chet felt good about having done it right without help from anyone. He also felt the familiar pain of not having anyone with whom to share the satisfaction.

The last electrical item he checked was the exhaust fan. He had installed it so fresh air entered through a filtered vent on each end of the building. An exhaust fan on the opposite end pulled air out resulting in plenty of fresh air. He left the fan running to remove the mustiness from the dank basement. As he left the basement, out of force of habit, Chet locked the heavy steel door. It was unlikely that anyone would try to break in. In fact, it was pretty unlikely that anyone would be foolish enough to even trespass. Chet's property was remote, and local convention was to shoot trespassers. At least the locals liked to claim that anybody snooping around wasn't likely to live long. The fact was that no one had been shot for trespassing in Benton County for quite some time. Most violent crime revolved around the burgeoning drug trade, mostly pot and meth.

Chet gave the heavy door a tug just to be sure. He sauntered back to the trailer. The sun was setting, and he had a huge appetite. As he walked along, he savored the sensation of having worked hard with good accomplishment.

Max greeted Chet with a sleepy meow when Chet entered the trailer. Max had been sleeping in the window ledge as usual. Chet ruffled his fur and said, "We'll be moving out of here before long, 'ole boy. I wonder how you'll like that concrete pillbox. No windows for bird watching, you know." Max stretched luxuriously and returned to his window seat. Max was destined to spend the rest of his life indoors. Josie had insisted that he be neutered and de-clawed. Despite his considerable size, he wouldn't be able to defend himself or climb a tree to escape danger. Chet had often pondered the idea that Josie would have preferred to have had him fixed as well.

Max watched with interest as Chet cleaned up after his day's work. Chet stripped off his grimy clothes and stepped into the tiny shower. Max jumped down from his perch, bounded into the bathroom where he sat at the edge of the shower seemingly enjoying the fine mist that landed on his shiny coat.

Chet scrubbed away the day's dirt and thought about his options for the evening. He could read a book, continue working around the place, work on the plan, or go into town. The latter option appealed to him. He realized the need to get away from the place which constantly demanded his attention. He also realized that his thoughts had strayed to the dark-haired waitress at Pete's.

CHAPTER FIVE

C het rolled into the parking lot at Pete's and stepped out of his pickup with a sense of anticipation. Mentally, he chided himself for thinking like a schoolboy. She probably wouldn't even be working that night, and if she were, she'd probably not look as good as she did after several beers.

A heavy back beat and the twangy sounds of country music emanated from the low block building. As Chet approached the door, two drunks stumbled out, and he glimpsed a packed, noisy room full of tobacco smoke and rednecks. After a moment of hesitation, Chet turned on his heel and walked back to his truck. He didn't want the noise and confusion after all. The Ford started easily, and he rolled out of the parking lot and headed down the main strip with its garish neon lights, fast food restaurants, and bars. He pulled into the drive-thru of the nearest liquor store.

"Fifth of Jack Black," he said to the boy at the window and handed him some cash.

. His mind raced at a dizzying pace as he waited for the whisky and his change. He felt frustrated by his attempt to go to Pete's. Was it an aversion to crowds or was he afraid that the waitress *would* be there after all. Josie had hurt him so badly. Why take another chance, he asked himself?

"Sir...sir, here's your change." The boy at the window was holding out the money.

"Thanks." Chet realized that he'd been in a daze, thinking about Josie. He pulled back out into traffic and headed home. He was sorely tempted to take a swig of the sour mash whiskey, but he reminded himself a DWI would cost him his job and probably the opportunity to pull off the bank job. The street he was on led past the area where she was living now. Some morbid desire to feel the old familiar pain compelled him to turn into her subdivision. He'd done it before, late at night when everyone was asleep. Tonight, in the houses he passed, he could see lights over dinner tables, TVs, and children playing. Families sharing and enjoying life. "So alone, I'm so damned alone," he muttered with a hard lump in his throat.

House on the corner. Both cars in the driveway. Figure framed in the window. Her? Yes...damn.

Chet continued down the street, cheeks aflame with embarrassment that she'd seen him. He'd taken the divorce hard, real hard. He had called her at work a couple of times. Followed her around a few times. Not stalking her, you know. Just seeing what she was doing. The judge didn't see it quite that way. Slapped him with an injunction, whatever that was. Chet had to stay at least three hundred feet away from Josie. No phone calls, nothing.

Now she had seen him drive by, and technically, he'd been closer than three hundred feet. Bitch would probably call the cops. "Don't mean nuthin'. Not a thang," Chet muttered. He was finding it hard to see. Something in his eyes, he guessed.

He broke the seal on the bottle with his thumbnail and headed toward home, thinking about the past.

They had met when Josie was a twenty-two-year-old senior business major at the University of Arkansas. She was everything that Chet was not. Josie was a popular sorority girl with some very definite ambitions. Her plans included a business career, a cute red Porsche, and just maybe, but only maybe, a husband and family somewhere in the distant future.

Chet, on the other hand, was a boisterous young man, fresh out of the Army, with only two particular ambitions, beer and pussy. Not necessarily in that order, of course.

Dickson Street in Fayetteville was the home to a number of establishments that catered to the college crowd. Chet and his buddies frequented these bars in the hopes of encountering some horny college girls. Neither Chet nor his friends had ever been to college, but that didn't stop them from telling the girls that they were also members of the student body. Naturally, the student body was exactly what interested them.

Josie was a petite five-feet-two with a closely cropped Dorothy Hamill haircut. The night they met, Chet was smitten instantly, and he fell all over himself asking her to dance.

Chet was playing pool with a couple of his friends when Josie and her roommate entered the bar.

"Would you look at that," Chet murmured to his friends when the girls walked past the pool tables. Every male head in the bar turned to watch. Josie was completely aware of the effect she had on the young men in the room. It was the same effect she'd cultivated since she was old enough to understand the power of that furry little place between her legs.

Chet summoned up the courage to talk to her. Her ditzy friend giggled when he walked up to them. They had chosen seats at the ancient, scarred, and stained bar and were ordering drinks when he walked up.

"Hi."

Josie looked up, prepared to fend off another unwelcome come-on. Instead, she found herself looking into the most intense eyes she had ever seen.

"Hi'ya," she replied.

"I'm Chet." He held out his hand and she took it. To her, he seemed to radiate strength and warmth through his firm grasp of her small hand. He held her hand for just a second and released although she made no effort to remove it.

"Josie. Oh, and this is my roommate, Suzie."

"Hi, Suzie." Chet smiled at the girl sitting beside Josie. Suzie giggled again.

The juke box was playing a Stones tune, and Chet took Josie's hand again to pull her to the tiny dance floor. No one else was dancing, and she blushed bright red.

His friends whistled, and Suzie giggled again. Oblivious to it all, they danced to song after song.

Their relationship was tumultuous from the very beginning. Josie had some very ordered ideas about what Chet should and should not do. Her expectations included limiting his alcohol and pot intake, actually getting an education, and ultimately finding a job.

Chet found his time better spent hanging around with his buddies, getting high, and generally just getting into trouble.

Somehow Josie decided to take Chet on as a project. She even confided to a sorority sister that she could turn this guy into something worthwhile. Her parents didn't know she was dating Chet until it was too late. She knew they'd never approve, and besides, she wasn't all that sure about him either. He did bring an element of excitement and unpredictability into her life that she'd never experienced before. He might show up in the middle of one of her classes on some pretext, and then whisk her off to his apartment for an afternoon of frantic lovemaking. Sometimes he'd wait for her to step out of a door, and he'd shove a bouquet of flowers under her nose. Other times he wouldn't show up for days only to reappear unshaven and in need of a shower.

"Where have you been? You didn't call or anything," she snapped at him on the first unexplained absence.

"Well, I had stuff to do. You know, guy stuff." In fact, he'd been in the county jail for drunk and disorderly. He didn't have money for bail, and he wasn't about to call her for help. God knew his poor mother didn't have any money.

"Don't you ever do that again, Chet. I mean it. Never." She half turned away from him and pouted.

He put his arms around her in spite of her mock attempt to pull away. "Let's go to my place and get reacquainted," he said. She flipped her hair in a sideways motion meaning no.

Chet kissed the back of her neck and tingles ran all the way down her spine. His bristling beard was scratchy, but she found it so exciting.

Eventually they ended up at his place.

"Take a shower, Chet. You stink," Josie commanded. Chet meekly went into the cramped bathroom and stripped down. He had only been in the shower for a few moments when Josie slid back the shower curtain and joined him.

He rubbed the shampoo away from his eyes and appraised her wet, nude body. Her breasts were round and high on her chest. Pink nipples pointed upward in a definite pout. Tiny beads of moisture clung to the narrow patch of dark fur between her athletic legs.

He took her in his arms and kissed her deeply. He caressed every inch of her tight, firm body.

Chet awoke from his revelry to the shrill warble of a police siren and undulating blue and white lights in his rear-view mirror. He was miles outside of town with the safety of his place still in the distance. Chet tensed every muscle in his body as the state police cruiser grew large in his mirror. The car was approaching so quickly, he knew he had no chance to hide the bottle of whiskey.

His worst nightmare seemed to be coming true as the officer closed to within feet of the rear of Chet's truck. Chet instantly resigned himself to the certainty of a DWI with its associated costs. He braked hard and swerved to the shoulder of the road, not really caring if his actions forced the officer to brake hard as well.

The officer did have to brake to avoid Chet, but he was only waiting to pass. The oncoming traffic whizzed past them, and the trooper floored his accelerator and flew past an astonished and relieved Chet.

"Sonofabitch," Chet exclaimed. His hands were shaking from gripping the wheel so tightly and from the huge rush of adrenaline. "Son of a bitch," slower this time and with relief.

The side road to Chet's place was a welcome sight and for once he didn't mind the bumpy dirt road that led to his lonely little camper.

CHAPTER SIX

Monday morning was just a faint glimmer in the eastern sky when Larry pulled his step van out of his parking spot and backed in his Bronco. The other drivers were straggling into the yard one at a time. Larry pulled his truck alongside the dispatch office and parked. He noted, with faint satisfaction, that he was first in line again. Always one to start as early as possible, he was at work by 5 o'clock each morning and rarely left by 5 o'clock each evening. Chet was nowhere in sight as Larry walked into the dispatch. Bob, the supervisor, looked up from some paperwork.

"Morning, Larry."

"Morning, Bob," Larry replied. It was the same exchange every morning for the past eight years. Larry got his stained coffee cup out of his cubbyhole, noted that there were no messages for him, and drowsily poured a cup of scalding hot coffee from the pot. The coffee was bitter and strong, but he needed the caffeine jolt to get going. He sat down in one of the hard, metal folding chairs and patiently waited for the meeting to begin. The other drivers greeted him as they entered, dome with a cheerful good morning, others with just a nod.

The six o'clock bell rang, and Bob started the meeting as he had every Monday morning since he took over as the supervisor.

"Morning, gentlemen. Let's get started." He looked over his notes and began talking about new accounts to be delivered, truck maintenance, and customer service problems. Larry found his mind wandering back to the weekend and to Chet's scheme. Chet was late for the meeting again, and almost as if summoned by Larry's thoughts, he walked through the door.

"Glad you could make it, Mr. Farmer. We're not interfering with your sleep, are we?" Bob made no attempt to disguise the sarcasm in his voice.

"Sorry," Chet mumbled and sat down. Everyone looked around at Chet in disbelief that he didn't have his usual smartass comeback for Bob. Even Bob seemed surprised.

"Well, as I was saying...," and he droned on in his monotone voice.

Chet unbuttoned his shirt pocket and took out his spiral notebook and began jotting down notes on the meeting. Larry sat at the back of the room and thoughtfully sipped his coffee. During the seven years that Chet had worked for Pinnacle, Larry had never seen Chet pay any attention during a sales meeting, much less take notes. Larry came to the obvious conclusion that Chet was cleaning up his act to avoid any difficulties that would interfere with his plans.

The sales meeting lasted a brief half hour. The drivers were accustomed to the routine and had long since given up protesting the uselessness of it. After the meeting had been adjourned, Larry noticed Chet walking back through the plant toward the warehouse where new uniforms and emblems were kept. On a whim, Larry followed him toward the back. Larry walked quietly in the shadows and took up a position on a desk where he could watch Chet without being seen.

In the warehouse, Chet looked over his shoulder once or twice but failed to notice Larry sitting on the edge of the purchasing agent's desk. Chet walked up and down the aisles and finally selected two shirts and two pants in dark blue. He then went to the orderly rows of embroidered emblem storage cabinets and chose two telephone company emblems and two name emblems, Tom and Harry. As Chet headed out of the warehouse Larry said, "Which one am I, Tom or Harry?"

"What the hell, Larry? You scared the crap outta me?" Chet shouted in response.

"You look like a kid caught with his hand in the cookie jar, Chet."

"These are just samples for a sales lead I got," Chet answered as he positioned a shirt under the heat seal press to apply the emblems. He carefully laid the phone company emblem on the shirt and pressed the button. A hundred pounds of air pressure slammed the superheated head of the press down onto the shirt and the adhesive backing bonded the emblem to the fabric. "What did you think they were for, Larry?" Chet had recovered from the surprise of being caught and he now wore his typical smirk.

Larry chose to not rise to the bait but merely smiled and walked out of the plant. He got into his waiting step van and began his day's route.

CHAPTER SEVEN

The alarm went off with its usual infernal racket jarring Chet awake and jangling his nerves. He slammed his meaty fist on the offending clock and lay back. In the early morning darkness, he felt a certain sense of serenity that never lasted for long. For now, though, he felt good, and he took a moment to enjoy the sounds of the woods. The crickets and tree frogs kept up an unending serenade. He could hear the occasional hickory nut or acorn fall, and somewhere close by, a small animal scurried through the undergrowth. As he began to fully awaken, he became aware of his other senses. His coffee maker was equipped with a timer, and it clicked on, sending the inviting aroma of freshly brewed coffee wafting through his trailer. The warm lump at the foot of his bed stretched and audibly yawned. Jet black Max was invisible in the dark room, but Chet smiled because after so many years he could tell exactly what Max was doing without seeing him. Somewhere in the distance, the faint sound of a train horn reached Chet's ears and he bounded out of bed and into the shower. The train reminded him of how much he planned to do this day.

After a quick shower, Chet wolfed down his breakfast and managed to scald his mouth on the hot coffee in his haste. He uttered a dark oath under his breath and stormed toward the door. As usual, the door stuck, and he nearly plowed into it head-on.

"WELL, I'LL BE DAMNED," he groaned through clenched teeth. "It doesn't look like it's going to be my day." Nonetheless he kicked the door open, stepped out into the early morning darkness, and got into his truck. He had a list of things to do in his pocket, and he planned to finish his route early. The old Ford rumbled out of his drive and down the washboard dirt road with its myopic headlights casting a dim glow ahead. The old truck had given many years of faithful service to several owners. By the time it came into Chet's possession, its faithful years were long since past. Chet drove with his mind wandering, and he failed to notice the deep pothole ahead. The right wheel dropped into the hole with a sickening thud and the old truck shook to its very frame. Almost instantly the engine died, the lights went out and the truck lurched to a halt in the middle of the road.

"Shit, shit, shit!" Chet shouted, pounding his fist on the steering wheel. He sat for a moment shaking with rage. After a final thump on the steering wheel, he opened the glove box and felt around for a flashlight. Sure enough, his old angle head military light was there. "Can't believe it. Now let's see if this works." The flashlight glowed brightly. Satisfied with that, Chet grunted and got out of the truck to locate the trouble under the hood. He fumbled for the latch and lifted the hood with some effort. A strong sulfurous smell of burning wires assaulted his nose. "Well, shit," Chet swore again. The battery, which he had been meaning to fasten in place, had fallen from its platform. One of the terminals had landed against the frame and the resulting electrical short melted the terminal completely in two.

That same morning Larry was on time as usual. He sat flipping through the day's invoices, sipping his coffee as usual. He was waiting for his first customer of the day to open. Six o'clock came and went with all of the drivers present except Chet.

"Larry, where's Chet?" Bob asked.

"DUNNO, BOB. HE'LL be along soon," Larry responded. Bob did not reply and continued fussing over some papers on his desk. He looked up as Tim, the extra man, came in. Tim's unenviable job was to fill in for drivers on vacation or who had days off and to do any little chore that Bob came up with.

"Tim, I want you to stand by in case Farmer don't show up. You may have to run his route today," Bob said.

"Okay, boss. I'm ready," Tim said eagerly. He was young, just out of high school and anxious to prove that he could do the job, so he could get his own route someday. At 6:30, Bob was fidgeting and finally could stand it no longer.

"Tim, get the invoices for route seven and get going."

"Yessir." Tim jumped up and grabbed the paperwork from Chet's cubbyhole along with the truck keys.

Larry looked up at Bob with eyebrows raised.

"Well, if he was going to be late, he should have called. You know the policy. Any driver more than an hour late gets docked a day's pay," Bob said in defense of his actions.

"I never said a word, Bob. But you know he'll be here. He always is."

"Larry, don't you have a route to run?" Bob snapped. Wordlessly, Larry got up and went out to his van. His first stop on Tuesdays didn't open until 7:30, so he drove to a nearby cafe to drink coffee and wait.

CHET SET THE BATTERY in place and propped his elbows on the fender of the old truck to survey the situation. Finally, he decided on a course of action and began by holding the battery cable in place against the broken terminal. Sparks flew with a pop and crackle, but the lights came on and Chet knew the battery was functional.

"Now if I can just wire the two parts together long enough to get to a service station," he said to himself. Chet rummaged through the toolbox he kept behind the seat looking for pliers and some sort of wire. He found the pliers but had to settle for a rusty coat hanger he found in the cluttered truck bed. After several minutes of work, Chet stood back and examined the result. The two terminal pieces were wired together. He had twisted the coat hanger, so it held the pieces securely. If not elegant, it was at least serviceable.

"Here goes nuthin'," he said as he climbed into the cab of the truck and turned the key. The cranky old engine came to life with a roar and idled smoothly.

"Improvise, adapt, and overcome," he said out loud. It was his standard slogan for every difficulty.

Chet congratulated himself for his ingenuity as he slammed the hood shut and headed toward town. He drove slowly over the rutted dirt road and came to a service station without further mishap. The station attendant was just opening when Chet rolled into the drive.

"Morning," the lanky teenager greeted Chet.

"Morning. I need a new battery terminal. Got any?"

"Sure," the kid replied. "Post or side mount?"

"Post type. Battery tipped over and broke one," Chet explained.

AFTER ANOTHER 15 MINUTES, Chet was on his way to the plant. He pulled into the parking lot at 7 o'clock, exactly one hour late. He looked for his step van in its accustomed spot, but the parking lot was empty.

"Oh, hell," Chet muttered as he pulled up to the dispatch office.

Bob was standing in the doorway waiting for Chet. His pock-marked face was flushed with anger, and he fairly snarled at Chet.

"Farmer, I'm writing you up for this. You've screwed up for the last time. You're on unpaid disciplinary suspension for today, and if you come in late one more time, you're through here. Understand?"

"Yeah, I understand," Chet replied levelly. He knew Bob was itching for him to blow up so he could fire him on the spot. "I'll be on time tomorrow."

"See that you are," Bob answered and walked back to his desk.

Chet got back in his pickup and drove out of the industrial quarter where the plant was located. He headed toward the center of town. Strangely, he felt no anger at Bob, even though he had been given no chance to explain why he'd been late. He felt a certain release. He was certain that now he would pull off the bank job, and one way or another, his current existence would change.

CHAPTER EIGHT

At the cafe, Larry sat in a booth near the window, so he could keep an eye on his truck. He remembered that just the previous week a truck had been stolen while the driver was inside a garage making a delivery. A flustered waitress came over to him, brushed a trailing wisp of lank hair from her face and said," Morning, sir. What can I get for you?"

Larry looked up and saw Helen penciled on the cheap nameplate pinned to her smock. With a friendly smile he said, "Well, Helen. I'd just like a cup of coffee. Black."

"Thank you, sir. I'll be right back with your coffee," she said with lackluster enthusiasm.

After she returned with his coffee, Larry sipped and watched the girl work. She flitted from table to table taking orders, carrying food, refilling coffee cups. All the while, she managed a thin smile or pleasantry for each customer. Her situation reminded Larry of his own dead-end job and of all the crap he had to put up with from customers. His mind wandered back to the weekend and to Chet's scheme. He and Chet usually met at this cafe for coffee on Tuesday mornings and Larry wondered if Chet would make it this day. Within moments Chet's rattletrap Ford rumbled into the parking lot and stopped beside Larry's step van.

Chet got out, still wearing the light blue shirt and navy-blue pants of the Pinnacle Uniform Company. Larry motioned to the waitress as Chet walked toward the door.

"Helen, would you bring another cup of coffee. A friend of mine is coming in."

"Yessir. Just one moment," she replied.

CHET STRODE INTO THE cafe with his cap tilted at a cocky angle, and he greeted Larry with a bright, "Good Morning." Chet's normally ruddy complexion was flushed even more than usual. He was smiling and seemed enthusiastic.

"Morning, Chet," Larry said. He was surprised at what appeared to be an abnormally good mood for Chet.

"Lar, this is going to be a good day. I've got a million things to do and now I've got the whole day to do 'em." Chet plopped down on the other side of the table from Larry.

"I take it you've seen Bob already?"

"Yeah, he was pissed, but that's nothing new. I had a battery connection break this morning." Chet slurped the scalding hot coffee.

"He's going to write you up for this, you know." Larry looked at Chet earnestly. "He really means to get rid of your ugly ass."

"I know. But it won't matter soon, anyway."

"Chet are you still serious about it? I mean really serious?"

Chet looked Larry straight in the eye and said, "Larry, I've never been more serious about anything in my life. Are you in or out?"

Until this moment, Larry had only been toying with the idea. Now it was time to decide. He'd pondered the whole proposition for days now. His finances were getting worse as were Karie's mood swings. Sometimes he actually thought about taking the money and just leaving. Leaving his job, the bills, and especially leaving Karie but there was a baby on the way. Those were the thoughts he pushed to the back of his mind. Getting divorced had never been an option for him, but he had to admit that he didn't love Karie anymore. He was pretty damn sure she didn't care that much for him either. Their relationship had deteriorated day by day since they got married. Now she was pregnant, and for the life of him, he didn't know why he'd ever agreed to that. He'd seen the torment that Chet had gone through when Josie left. As painful as his marriage was, he didn't think he could stand to be alone. Guys with money, though.... seldom alone.

"Chet, I'm in. Let's go for it," Larry said and offered his hand which Chet shook warmly.

"THINGS TO DO," CHET said and walked out the door leaving Larry to pay for the coffee as usual. Larry continued to sip his coffee as he watched Chet drive away. He made a few notes in his notebook regarding his part in the plan. Today his activities mainly involved collecting information. He glanced at his watch and realized that it was time to begin his route but first he had a call to make. The pay phone was outside on a pole near his truck. He could have used his cell phone, but Karie was very particular in checking the numbers he called. Her suspicions were completely unfounded but right now he didn't want to answer any questions about his calling habits.

He paid his bill and left a small tip for the waitress. He caught himself wondering what the hell he was doing. Nonetheless, he walked to his van, got in and drove up to the pay phone. He slid a quarter into the slot and dialed information.

"What city?" was the bored response.

"Uh...Fort Smith, I guess," he stammered.

"What number?"

"The railroad office."

"Sir, which one? I have numbers for Burlington Northern, Kansas City Southern, and Union Pacific."

"I don't know. Which one goes through Carbontown?"

"Sir... do you want the numbers to all three?"

"Sure. All three," Larry said and proceeded to write down the numbers as the recorded voice pronounced them. He then called all three using his long-distance calling card. Each time he said, "Good morning. I'm uh, John Jones with the Carbontown street department and I need to check your train schedules for the upcoming Friday. We're planning to do some road work, and we don't want to get in your way." The first two had no trains going through Carbontown. On the final call, he was referred to the dispatch manager for whom he had to repeat his story. The manager seemed somewhat suspicious. "What did you say your name was?" he demanded.

"Jones. John Jones." Larry responded sheepishly. He hadn't thought through his speech.

"WELL, MR. JONES WE'RE not in the habit of giving out our schedules. Could I call you back at your office?"

"No. I mean, no I'm going to be out with the crews for the rest of the day."

"I see. Well, hold for just a minute and I'll see what we've got going through there." The manager put Larry on hold and turned to one of the dispatchers, "Say, Wally. Do you know a John Jones down at Carbontown street department?" Wally looked up from his paperwork, thought for a second and said, "No. Can't say that I do. But then I haven't been down there lately."

After another moment's hesitation, the manager punched the flashing light on his phone.

"Still there, Mr. Jones?"

"Yes, I'm here," Larry said, thinking about his long-distance bill.

"We've got one train building for Friday. It should be 112 cars going through at 11:58 a.m. Does that give you what you need?"

"Yessir. That's just fine. We'll be done long before then. Thanks." Larry said with relief and hung up.

"Damn, that was easy," he said to himself and started his truck to begin his day's route.

Back in the railroad office, the manager was jotting down notes on the conversation in his day planner. He was a very methodical man.

CHAPTER NINE

C het left the cafe and headed straight for Radio Shack. Ever cautious about attracting attention, he had been making small purchases over the last couple of months. First, he had bought a couple of tool belts, then pliers, cutters and screwdrivers. Today's purchase was to be a butt set; the peculiar looking phone set commonly seen hanging from a phone man's tool belt.

Chet pulled up to the store, briefly rehearsed his lines to himself, and then walked briskly in and up to the counter.

"Hi."

"Good morning, sir. How may I help you?" the chubby, red-faced manager replied as he looked at Chet's name tag.

"Well, I'm thinking about puttin' in a phone extension out in my shed, and I need one in my chicken house, too."

"I've got just what you need, sir. A portable cordless phone, or better yet our line of cell phones is right over here. Now for just..."

"Excuse me," Chet interrupted. "I don't want no portable phone or no cell phone. What I was trying to tell ya is I want one of them phones like the linemen carry. You know, so I can plug it in anywhere."

"Oh, well. We don't carry those in stock. But the portable system weighs jus..."

"Can you order one for me?" Chet interrupted again.

"I can order it, but it'll take at least two weeks to get here."

"Okay. Order me two while you're at it," Chet said.

"Two?" the man questioned.

"YUP. THAT'S WHAT I need. Name's...Smith. I'll check back with you in a couple of weeks," Chet said as he turned and walked out the door.

"Damn," the manager muttered as one of his assistants walked up. "I didn't get his phone number. See if you can read his license. Just in case it's a bogus order." His caution was the result of being stuck with several special orders that had never been claimed.

"Yessir," the boy responded and ran for the door. He spotted Chet's vehicle as he pulled out of the parking lot.

"That's KZW559. Black Ford pickup. Probably about a '62. My dad used to have one just like that."

"Just the license," the manager said as he began filling out the order form. He carefully wrote, Chet Smith, KZW559..."

Chet left Radio Shack and drove toward the edge of town. This was the newly developed strip where car dealerships, discount stores, and quick-stop stores popped up almost overnight. He felt a slight gnawing apprehension about his exchange with the guy at Radio Shack. The fellow had noticed his name tag, CHET, on his uniform shirt. Chet had nearly made a major *faux pas* by giving a false first name. Fortunately, he had noticed the man looking at his name tag.

He passed several car dealers and came to a Honda motorcycle shop. The marquee proudly announced, "Zero down on new four-wheelers with approved credit." He pulled into the parking lot, got out and walked past the motorcycles on display. He was speculatively eyeing a large four-wheeler when a voice behind him said, "She's a real beaut', ain't she?"

CHET TURNED TO FACE the salesman who had spoken, "Yeah. Not bad," he replied.

"Would you like to test drive it around the lot?" the salesman asked and held out a helmet for Chet to wear. "Yeah, I would," he said and donned the helmet.

"I need something for the deer woods."

"Yessir. Deer season is just around the corner."

Chet fired up the engine and motored carefully around the lot. After just a few moments he felt comfortable enough to try the field in back of the shop. The field had a trail established with several sharp curves, dips and a couple of low mounds to jump. He brought the now dusty four-wheeler back to the front lot after several minutes of pure enjoyment.

"How do you like it, Chet?" The name tag again.

"I like. How much my monthly payments be?" Chet asked.

"Well, let's go inside, and I'll work it out for you. Do you drink coffee?"

"No coffee. Figure it up for two and sharpen that pencil. I want 'em in camo, not red like this 'un."

Just over an hour later, Chet backed his truck up to the loading dock. Two of the men working in the service department pushed Chet's gleaming new four-wheeler up a ramp and into the back of his truck. Chet had purchased a rack to go behind the seat, a front rack and a handlebar gun rack.

"I'll be back to pick up the other one."

"No problem, Mr. Farmer. It'll be here waiting for you.

After a final handshake, the salesman wished Chet luck and watched him drive away.

Chet drove down the main strip in town feeling a strong need to show off his new toy to someone. At the same time, he felt the familiar pain of having no one with whom to share anything. He adjusted his mirror, so he could admire his purchase as he drove. He was almost past the Wal-Mart store when he remembered one final purchase he had to make. He wheeled into the parking lot and had the good fortune to find an empty spot near the entrance. He walked purposefully in, said hello to the girl who was greeting customers, and headed straight for the sporting goods department at the back of the store. In the bow hunting section, Chet found what he wanted. Camouflage tape in two-inch-wide rolls. Chet picked up four rolls and headed for the checkout counter. He stood patiently in line waiting to pay. The girl ran his purchases over the scanner and gave him the total. He paid in cash and left the store feeling exhilarated as though he were embarking on a great adventure. On the way home, he decided to try to catch Larry at work and talk him into coming out to discuss the operation. Chet pulled into his drive and rolled to a stop in front of his travel trailer. After dropping the tailgate, he propped two 2x12 timbers against the tailgate as a makeshift ramp. Chet decided to ride his new four-wheeler down the ramp. He took it out of gear and let it roll slowly down the steep incline. The big machine rolled down the ramp on its soft tires and settled on the ground. Chet brought the engine to life, and it purred smoothly. He enjoyed the feel of the powerful engine beneath him and the smell of a new machine. He dropped the transmission into gear and roared out of the yard and down the logging trail that bordered his property. He rode carefully at first and then he increased his speed and began to learn the quirks of his new machine. Soon he had discovered just how fast he could go around corners, how much slope he could cross, and he had a good feel for the center of gravity of this particular four-wheeler. All too soon, the gas gauge built into the cap of the fuel tank showed that it was nearly empty, so Chet started back to his trailer. He had been running through the national forest which bordered the back of his property. Now he motored right up to the door and killed the engine. He got off reluctantly, wishing he could spend the rest of the day running free through the woods.

As he yanked open the door, he noticed Max sitting in the window checking out this new item.

"You wouldn't like it, Max," Chet said as he patted the cat fondly on the head. "It's much too noisy for a peace-loving fellow like yourself."

Max purred his assent or perhaps just a response from the welcome attention.

Chet washed up in the tiny bathroom and noticed that a low hanging limb or briar had ripped his uniform shirt in two places. "Bob will probably charge me for it," Chet muttered out loud. He changed into camo shorts and a black sleeveless T-shirt. He took a moment to admire the new tattoo that adorned his left biceps. It was an ornate Celtic band that went completely around his arm. It had cost him almost two hundred bucks, but he figured it was money well spent. Chet slid his feet into a worn pair of hiking boots and stuck his battered old Lite beer cap on his head.

"IT'S LUNCH TIME, MAX. What's on the menu today?" Chet said as he peered into the refrigerator. "Bologna and cheese or perhaps cheese and bologna?" Max abstained, so Chet made his own choice. He sat down with a sandwich and a Corona with lime. Max jumped up on the table, something Josie never permitted, and waited while Chet poured a thimbleful of Corona into a saucer. Max preferred his beer without lime. Chet reached for the phone and dialed the familiar number.

"Pinnacle Uniform. May I help you?" Chet recognized the receptionist's voice.

"JoAnn, this is Chet. Is Larry in yet?"

"No, Chet. I haven't seen him. Can I take a message?"

"No. Well, yeah. Have him call me at home, please."

"Sure thing, Chet. Bye, now." JoAnn politely did not quiz Chet as to why he was at home instead of on the route. Chet hung up the phone and finished his meager lunch. He grabbed another beer from the fridge and went outside to work on his four-wheeler. He first used a shop towel to clean away all the dust and grime from all the chrome and the painted surfaces. He began applying strips of camouflage tape over the chrome handle bars and other shiny areas. The head light would be needed so he left a small rectangle exposed that would allow a narrow beam of light to project out. Just as he was finished taping, he heard a vehicle approach. He had no close neighbors, so it was unusual to have vehicles traveling his road. The vehicle turned out to be Larry's Bronco. Larry waved as he pulled up beside Chet's Ford.

"What's this?" Larry asked and pointed to the Honda.

"What's it look like?" Chet responded.

"A new toy."

"Nope. It's high adventure, Lar. High adventure. We're going to use this as our getaway vehicle. There's another one just like it for you down at the dealership."

"I THOUGHT WE WERE GOING to use a phone van," Larry said.

"Yep, at first. Then these'll take us where no one can follow. We'll leave the van down there," Chet said with a mischievous grin.

"By the way, why aren't you at work? I just called and JoAnn said you hadn't come in."

"I got done early, ...and don't change the subject. I'm beginning to think you haven't told me the whole story," Larry said crossly.

"Nope, I didn't. Because I couldn't be sure you were going to go through with it."

"Okay, I told you I'm in. So, what else haven't you told me?"

"Just small details. There's still a lot of things to work out before we'll be ready."

"Like what?" Larry responded.

"Well, as you know, there are three major events that have to be timed perfectly. That's the diversion, the train derailment, and then our entry into the bank. Do you want a beer?"

"Sure." Larry never turned down the offer of a beer.

They left the four-wheeler and walked together into the trailer. Larry tousled Max's ears affectionately as he entered. Max disdainfully ignored Larry and hopped up to his window perch.

"Thanks," Larry said as he took the ice-cold Corona from Chet. "Lime?"

"No. This is fine. When did you decide to get four-wheelers?"

"It's always been part of the plan. We'll load the money into bags, toss 'em over our shoulders and head for the hills behind the bank. We'll stash the four-wheelers in the woods the day before the operation.

"WHAT HAPPENS IF SOMEONE finds them?" Larry asked.

"No one will find 'em. I bought this for 'em a long time ago." Chet produced a small cardboard box that held a nylon camo cover.

"We'll put this cover over 'em, and no one will see unless they accidentally stumble onto them."

"What other goodies have you collected, Chet?"

"Well, these bags are the ones we'll use for the money." Chet held up two black rectangular bags made of heavy-duty nylon.

"They have shoulder straps for carrying them and they're exactly the right size to fit the racks on the four-wheelers. I've got a similar pack that one of us will wear on his back. That should give us enough carrying capacity for the kind of money we're talking about," Chet concluded.

Larry took a long swig of beer and thoughtfully examined the stiff nylon bags. The whole operation was starting to seem real. Now, for the very first time, it occurred to him that what they were proposing to do was wrong. Morally, ethically and legally wrong.

"Don't get me wrong, Chet. I'm not backing out, but have you thought much about the morality of this thing. I mean, it's stealing, Chet. I've never considered myself a thief."

"It may be wrong but living the way we do ain't right either. If you can tell me another way to get what we need, I'll be glad to listen," Chet responded with a hard look.

"I don't know any other way. Let's get on with it. What else have you got?" Larry said with resignation in his voice.

"LAR, I'VE PUT TOO MUCH into this to quit now. I've gotta know you're with me all the way. No reservations." Chet fixed Larry with a piercing gaze that was all business.

"Sure, man. No problem. I told you I wasn't backing out."

"All right, let's see how these bags are going to attach to the racks," Chet said in his usual, good-humored way. By all outward appearance, he had forgotten any doubts that he may have had about Larry. They walked out to the Honda and set the bags into the racks.

"They fit good, Chet, but we need some bungee cords to hold 'em down. I can pick some up tonight."

"Good idea, Larry. Why don't you do that?" Chet was pleased that Larry was showing some initiative. He chose not to tell him that he had already bought the strong elastic cords.

"Larry, can you get away this weekend for awhile?"

"Prob'ly. What's up?"

"I think it would be a good idea if we went fishing more often. Don't you?" Chet asked.

"Sure. You mean go check out the location?"

"Right. Tell Karie that you're going fishing and get her used to your being away occasionally." Larry nodded and thought for a moment.

"We need to find a good spot to hide the four-wheelers and we could also look for potential diversions. Maybe we could check out the fuel storage tanks or something," Larry said.

"Right," Chet agreed. "We also could load the packs full of paper to simulate the weight and see how we do."

"SURE. BUT WE'D BETTER not be seen around the bank, right?"

"Yeah, but we'll do it on Saturday when the bank's closed. What did you find out about the train schedule?"

"The guy was real hesitant about giving out information, but he said the regular ore train would go through there with 112 cars."

"We'll need to find out how fast the train goes through town. I suppose it won't have the same number of cars every time?"

"I guess it depends on how many loads they book. This train hauls more than just ore," Larry explained.

"How long is a train car, anyway?" Chet asked.

"Never thought about it. Sixty feet, maybe? We'll have to measure one to be sure or better yet I'll just Google it." Larry said.

"I think the key to this whole operation is backward planning. What I mean is, we should start here and work our way backwards through the plan, timing as we go."

Larry nodded in agreement. "Right. For example, we'll leave here this weekend and time how long it takes to get to the place where we'll hide the four-wheelers and then how long it takes to get from the four-wheelers to the bank."

"Right. But we'll need to add a certain amount of time for screw ups and the unexpected." Chet could not have foreseen just how much of the unexpected they were to encounter.

"Yeah, best laid plans..." Larry said thoughtfully. Gloomy thoughts started to intrude on his mind. He needed something to get his mind off the potential problems.

"Mind if I take it for a spin?" Larry asked and indicated the four-wheeler.

"SURE, GO AHEAD. BUT don't go too far, the tank is almost empty."

Chet leaned against Larry's Bronco and watched as Larry carefully piloted the unfamiliar vehicle up and down the country lane.

Since Larry's question about the right and wrong of the operation, Chet had been having nagging doubts about Larry's reliability. He began asking himself questions such as, "What if Larry backs out at the last moment? What if he refuses to use a weapon in a have-to situation?" With a shake of his head, he decided that he would have to handle any such situations as they developed, for there was no way to predict Larry's behavior.

The engine on the four-wheeler sputtered once and then died. Larry took it out of gear, and it coasted to a stop only a few yards away from Chet. Together they pushed it back into the yard.

"Whew. Heavy bugger, ain't it?" Chet said, wheezing.

"Yeah, but it'll sure get up and go," Larry replied enthusiastically. "I've got some things to pick up in town, so I'll see you tomorrow."

"Okay, Lar. Let's plan to leave about four Saturday morning."

"Four? You mean a.m.? When do you ever get up that early?" Larry asked, incredulously.

"When there's something really important to do."

"Obviously, work isn't something you consider really important," Larry chided him.

"Okay. Okay. I'll be on time tomorrow," Chet replied.

"Later," Larry said and climbed into his Bronco.

Chet watched him drive away, and he still had mixed emotions. He walked to his trailer, got another beer and sat on the doorstep. Max rubbed seductively against his back and purred. Chet picked up the heavy tom and sat him on his lap.

"Don't stand on my balls, Max." Chet shifted the cat's considerable bulk forward. Together they watched the afternoon sun drop behind the nearby hills. It was a glowing orange ball visible among dark, stormy clouds.

"Days are getting shorter, Max. September will be over before you know it." The end of summer always left Chet with a feeling of dread, sometimes even a knot in his throat. Even as a child he had hated fall and winter. Partly because of the cold, but mostly because of the impending return to school. Now he felt a similar dread and recognized that it was the upcoming operation that created this tension. October was the planned month of the operation, and they were in no way ready.

"So much to do, Maximilian, and so little time to do it," he said as he put Max back in the trailer and walked toward his old truck to go get the other four-wheeler.

CHAPTER TEN

The driving rain had found the leak in Larry's windshield. Now with each clack of the wiper blade a few drops of water splashed down on his knees. Larry peered through the misty windshield and drove carefully down the muddy lane toward Chet's place.

"I'll bet he's still in bed," Larry muttered aloud. He glanced at the luminous dial on his watch and noted that he was, as usual, early. It was just then a quarter to four on Saturday morning.

"Christ," he muttered aloud again. "I must be outta my fuckin mind." His lights penetrated only a short distance in the rain and fog. He leaned forward and switched on the amber fog lamps mounted low on the front of the Bronco.

"Better," he said as the fog lights helped illuminate the treacherous, muddy road. During the entire drive to Chet's place, Larry had not seen another vehicle on the road. This merely confirmed his suspicion that only a fool would be up at this hour on a rainy Saturday morning.

Larry pulled into Chet's yard and the beams of his lights shone full upon a dripping figure in a camo rain suit. It was Chet and he had just finished loading one of the four-wheelers into his truck bed. He snugged down the straps holding the nylon cover and turned to Larry who had rolled down the window on his Bronco.

"You're crazy," Larry shouted.

"Yep. A little bit," Chet responded affably. He seemed unaware of the rainstorm.

"Are you sure you still want to do this today?" Larry asked.

"Yep. We'll do the job rain or shine, so we need to practice rain or shine."

"Okay, let's do it and say we did," Larry said with mock enthusiasm. He parked the Bronco by Chet's trailer and donned his rain jacket before getting out.

"What else do we need to load? Where's the other one?" Larry shouted above the noise of the wind and rain.

"NUTHIN'. WE'LL RIDE double today. Let's go," Chet shouted in reply and got into the old truck. He fired up the engine and waited while Larry climbed in and got himself situated. Chet let out the clutch and the old Ford lurched forward, its wheels spinning in the mud, seeking traction. Chet reached across Larry and popped open the glove box. He fumbled around amidst unidentifiable clutter and produced a small spiral notepad which he handed to his partner.

"Here. You keep the log. Put down our mileage and time at each point. Let's see, the odometer just turned 96385, and I got 3:55 a.m. Right?"

"Right," Larry dutifully replied as he struggled to write clearly in the bouncing truck cab. Chet took the main highway and drove through the town of Springdale and passed through Fayetteville a few miles later. Both towns were quiet at that time of the morning. Only the unlucky ones were up and about heading to work in the poultry factories. Chet and Larry were both accustomed to the stench of the poultry business. Each of them serviced one plant or another on their uniform routes. Some were so-called kill plants, where live birds were trucked in and slaughtered by the thousands every day. Other plants were called by various names, but they all processed the chicken or turkey in some fashion. Regardless of the particular function of the different plants, they all shared a commonality. They reeked. The whole town smelled of poultry processing.

Neither man so much as noticed. The smell was familiar and unremarkable to them, since they smelled it every day of their lives.

Chet drove hunched over the steering wheel. He had to use considerable effort to see through the sheets of rain. He had to slow to a near crawl to navigate the deep, standing puddles of water on the roadway. Larry just stared out the side window and wished he were home in bed with Karie. He saw the occasional light in someone's kitchen or bedroom. It all seemed so domestic and, well...tranquil.

They drove in near silence for the next two hours. Their route took them south through the Boston mountains. The winding, steep road was known as the PigTrail because of the many switch backs and unexpected turns. Their adventure would soon resemble the PigTrail.

Larry followed their progress on a topographical map. Chet handed him a well-worn Army penlight with a red lens to examine the map. During his military training Chet had been taught that the red lens would save their night vision. He related this interesting tidbit to Larry who merely grunted in response. His interest in trivia was minimal at that hour of the morning. Larry noted various landmarks and intersections as he peered through the fog and rain. He ticked off those points on the map with a pencil and made corresponding entries in his log carefully noting the time. Highway 23, known as the Pig Trail, made a circuitous path through some of the most remote terrain in Arkansas. Larry looked at the map and tried to imagine what obstacles lay between them and success. As they neared their destination, Chet pointed out numerous side roads that intersected the PigTrail and Larry noted each one on the map. He made special marks for those which they considered possible alternate routes. As the two men proceeded farther south, deeper into the Boston Mountains, the terrain on both sides of the highway was covered in dense forest with sheer bluffs overlooking deep valleys. The lush vegetation encroached upon the road. In places, the trees arched over from both sides and formed a canopy that blocked the sun's light, even at mid day. Now in the darkness of early morning, the overhanging trees seemed eerie, and Larry stifled an involuntary shiver of apprehension.

"Cold?" Chet asked.

"Maybe a little bit."

"Kinda spooky at this time of morning," Chet observed.

Larry mused wryly at Chet's uncanny ability to read people. Sometimes he seemed to have ESP, and at other times he could be so damn dense.

The miles wore on as Chet negotiated hairpin turns, blind curves and steep hills.

The old truck rumbled across a bridge, and Chet slowed to a halt near the middle. Both men looked out their windows to the scene below the bridge. Dawn was just beginning to lighten the sky, and in the early morning light, the water running underneath looked cold and deep. It was the Mulberry River, a popular paddling river.

"Looks cold, Chet. I never cared much for canoeing, did you?"

"Some," Chet answered quietly. In fact, Chet and Josie had spent many hours on the water. It was one of the few activities they shared and enjoyed together. The Mulberry had been their favorite river because of its many moods. It could be calm and placid one day and then a raging torrent the next.

Chet shook the ghosts out of his head and slipped the shifter into first gear. He didn't talk about Josie to Larry or anyone else, and he sure wasn't going to start now.

They climbed out of the river valley and labored up a particularly steep grade.

"This hill reminds me of basic training," Chet said just to make conversation and to get the images of Josie out of his head.

"Oh, yeah. Why?"

"Well, at Fort Knox they have these three hills, see. They call 'em Agony, Misery, and Heartbreak. Each one steeper than the other. This hill reminds me of Heartbreak, the steepest of them all. I'm just glad to be driving up it instead of humping a pack up it."

Just as they crested that summit, Larry said, "I think this is the one we want." He pointed to a side road leading into dense forest. Chet eased the old truck into second gear and pulled off the road onto the trail that Larry had indicated.

"Looks like an old logging trail," Larry observed.

"Yeah. Muddy as hell," Chet said as he struggled to keep the wheels of the truck from slipping down into the deepest ruts which were filled with gooey, red clay mud. At his first opportunity, Chet pulled out of the trail and stopped the truck.

"Lar, I'm afraid we'll get stuck for sure if we go any farther." Chet looked disgusted. Larry reached for the Thermos bottle and poured a cup of steaming hot coffee.

"Here, Chet. Drink this and we'll figure something out." Chet sipped his coffee pensively and rethought his plan. The rain slowed to a light drizzle and the sun lightened the sky.

"Let's take the four-wheeler down the trail and see where it goes," Larry suggested what seemed obvious to him.

"Okay, we'll try it."

Together they unloaded the heavy machine and cranked it up. The engine purred smoothly as they motored down the trail. Chet drove with Larry hanging on for dear life. Within a hundred yards, they were both covered with the clinging red clay mud. Larry had brought the map, carefully folded, in a zip lock bag. They stopped at intervals to check their progress against the map. The trail petered out at a small clearing deep in the woods. Chet hit the kill switch and the engine died instantly. The woods were completely silent after the noise of the engine. Chet and Larry sat silently for a moment, just listening. Soon a tree frog croaked, crickets began to chirp, and the woods returned to its natural rhythm complete with a blue jay who scolded them from high in his treetop perch. The forest floor here was carpeted in damp pine needles and soft moss. Their feet made no noise as they dismounted from the vehicle. They had both worn their camo rain suits, helmets and goggles. Larry laughed as Chet removed his goggles.

"Man, your eyes are the only clean place on you."

"You think you're any cleaner, Lar?"

"Guess not," Larry admitted.

"Let's see that map," Chet said. He took it out of the bag and spread it on the forest floor. Previously he had coated it with Stormproof, a waterproofing compound for maps. Now the rain dripping from the trees beaded on the map's surface. He traced their progress with his finger on the map.

"I'd say we're less than ten miles from the interstate, as the crow flies," Chet said. "This would be the best place to hide the truck." He indicated a small grove of cedar trees near the clearing where they knelt. Larry nodded in agreement.

"According to the map, we've got two possible routes to the interstate. The rest of the terrain looks way too steep."

"Let's try one on the way down and the other on the way back," Larry suggested.

"Let's go," Chet said.

"I'll drive for a while," Larry said as he climbed on the seat. Chet nodded his reluctant agreement.

Larry started the engine and drove carefully through the thickly wooded terrain. Chet sat behind Larry and fretted at Larry's driving. Chet referred to the map periodically and Larry made course changes at Chet's direction. The last two miles of their journey took almost an hour, but they finally arrived at a steep embankment overlooking I-40 with its thundering traffic.

"Now what?" Larry asked. "How do we get over the highway?"

"We don't," Chet replied without explanation. Larry sat waiting for the answer. He knew that Chet was dying to enlighten him with some brilliant explanation, but he wanted Larry to ask. Larry was tired, wet and muddy. He had no patience for Chet's head games, so he refused to rise to the bait. Finally, Chet could stand it no longer.

"Well, don't you want to know what we're going to do?" Chet asked.

"Nope," Larry replied and dismounted. Chet stepped off as well.

"Oh, all right. We're going under the interstate, not over it."

"Where?"

Chet looked up and down the interstate to get his bearings. "Well, I think we're just a little west of it, so let's go this way," he said as he pointed to the east.

They remounted the vehicle with Chet driving this time. Chet headed toward the large culvert he had spotted on a previous trip. They arrived at the mouth of the cavernous box culvert and stopped. A small, sluggish stream flowed through the culvert which ran directly under the highway. Chet negotiated a steep, gravelly slope down to the water. There he stopped long enough to cut a willow branch with his heavy survival knife.

"What's that for?" Larry asked.

"Spider webs."

Larry knew that Chet's one weakness was a severe case of arachnophobia. Chet eased the four-wheeler into the culvert and began waving his willow wand in a circular motion. The willow was rapidly festooned with the wispy threads of spider silk. The light from the four-wheeler's headlamp illuminated the dank walls of the culvert which were covered with graffiti. The tires of the vehicle crushed old beer cans, bottles and trash as they slogged through the filthy water. Overhead, the men could hear the thundering of tractor trailer rigs.

"Glad to be outta there," Chet said over his shoulder as they broke out into the gray daylight.

Chet maneuvered the four-wheeler down the creek bed without speaking again. The tiny stream ran through a steep valley, heavily wooded on both sides. Chet killed the engine as they came to the edge of a clearing. There, not a hundred yards away, stood the Carbontown bank on the edge of the stream bed.

"Chet, it's just like the map board," Larry observed.

"Yep." Chet favored one-word replies.

They stepped off the four-wheeler and clambered up the muddy bank of the stream. They sat down in the pine needles just inside the tree line to observe the bank. The gully containing the stream continued right past the bank, and the edge of the stream bed was within ten yards of the bank parking lot. The stream disappeared into a small culvert at the far end of the asphalt parking lot.

"Is this where we'll park the four-wheelers?" Larry asked.

"Prob'ly," Chet answered absently. He was absorbed in studying the bank and the various approaches which were possible.

"Long way to run," Larry noted.

"Yep."

"Especially carrying all that weight," Larry persisted.

Chet did not answer. Instead, he stood up and began slogging downstream toward the bank. He noted mentally that the gully gave excellent concealment due to its depth. Equally, because of its depth, it became a deathtrap if the police could direct their fire into it. He knew there was no way to ascend those muddy banks in a hurry.

Chet stopped and peered over the top of the gully at the bank. There appeared to be no one present so he took his time and studied every detail. He noted where the underground utility box was located. The phone company had been kind enough to post a sign indicating where not to dig. Chet pulled his small notebook out of an inner pocket and sketched the location of the utilities, external power receptacles and the distance from the bank to the gully. He would transfer this information to the map board in his basement when they returned. He replaced the notebook in his pocket and rezipped his jacket. After one final look around, he pressed a small button on his watch and sprinted back up the gully toward Larry. He arrived, winded, almost one and one-half minutes later. He pressed the button on his watch again to stop the timer.

"Whew," he panted. "Too much beer drinking."

Larry shook his head at his red-faced friend.

"Maybe we should park closer," he suggested half serious, half poking fun at Chet's poor condition.

"I guess you could do better," Chet snapped.

"On one leg, old man," Larry snorted.

"So do it," Chet said, "I'll time you from here."

Larry nodded his assent and began working his way down the stream bed. He noted the large rocks, mucky places and other obstacles to avoid. He reached the same place as Chet and took a moment to observe. Larry raised a hand signaling Chet to begin timing. Despite his advantage, he discovered that it was indeed difficult terrain to cover quickly. He slipped and fell once, bruising an elbow.

Chet snapped his stopwatch off as Larry finally arrived.

"One minute, forty-five seconds," Chet called out.

"All right, you won," Larry grudgingly admitted.

Chet stifled a snide comment and thought instead about his concern for their ability to negotiate the gully with the heavy packs.

"I wonder how we'll do with those packs," Larry wheezed as though he had read Chet's mind.

"We'll do fine, but we're both going to have to get into shape," Chet replied. Together they stood up and remounted the four-wheeler.

"Let's find the spot where we'll hide these things," Larry suggested.

"Okay. Where?" Chet replied.

The stream bed was relatively shallow at the place where they spoke. Larry stood on the foot pegs of the four-wheeler and looked around.

"See anything?" Chet queried.

"Well, there's a clump of small pines about twenty yards away. It's pretty dense."

"Let's take a look," Chet said.

Larry regained his seat, clawing for the handrails just as Chet gunned the engine taking them up the stream bank and into the woods. The trees were indeed densely packed, and they provided ample concealment for the four-wheeler.

"That ought to do it, Lar. Why don't you get off and I'll see if this thing will fit." Larry dismounted and watched Chet maneuver the machine into the deepest part of the pine grove. Chet used his heavy Buckmaster survival knife to hack down a few limbs and saplings so he could go just a little deeper into the trees.

"Let's cover it and see what it looks like," Chet said as he dismounted. Together they spread the camo net over the four-wheeler and secured the edges to nearby foliage. They walked all around the clump of trees and found their work to be entirely satisfactory. For all intents and purposes, the four-wheeler was invisible.

"Good enough," Chet said as he entered the clump of trees. Larry followed and they removed the camo cover and packed it back into its pouch. Chet backed out and Larry remounted the muddy vehicle.

"Not so fast," Chet motioned Larry to get off. "We gotta get them branches outta here." Chet pointed imperiously at the pine branches he'd hacked off. Larry looked at him blankly. "Well, you gonna get 'em or do I have to do everything," Chet snapped.

Larry gritted his teeth and started gathering the pine limbs. He was seething underneath at the indignity of doing Chet's bidding. "Who the hell does he think he is?" Larry asked himself mentally. He continued gathering the branches until he had an arm load.

"Toss 'em in the ditch," Chet commanded and pointed toward the stream. He knew they'd wash away long before the time of the bank robbery. Larry did as he was told. The branches swirled on the surface of the slow-moving water. He watched them for a moment. A moment too long, because Chet shouted, "Can we go now?"

Red-faced, Larry strode back to the ATV and climbed on behind Chet. He didn't say anything. Chet was oblivious to Larry's consternation. He started the engine, and they retraced their route to the interstate and passed uneventfully through the culvert. Chet paused to examine the map after they were through the first line of trees past the culvert.

"Let's find an alternate trail to the east," he said.

Larry nodded and pointed to a line of valleys on the map.

"We could try there," Larry suggested.

"Let's do it and say we did," Chet answered good-naturedly, and this time, he clipped the map to his handlebars with two large alligator clamps. In this fashion, he could then drive and navigate simultaneously. He was completely past his earlier frustration with Larry. Larry, on the other hand, was not, and he continued to seethe as they rode along.

The new route took them through thick scrub brush smelling of sumac bushes, cedar, and all the other aromatic plants of late summer. They arrived at the beginning of the line of valleys Larry had pointed out on the map. The entrance to the valley was a narrow opening shrouded by scrub saplings and bushy cedar trees. Chet nearly motored right past it, but Larry spotted the nearly hidden opening and tapped Chet on the shoulder.

"On your left, partner," Larry shouted over the engine noise. Chet stopped abruptly and wheeled over to the valley entrance. He killed the engine and they dismounted for a closer look. The valley sloped upward toward the Boston Mountains which stood off in the shimmering distance. Behind them they could hear the highway sounds. Around them was the whir-buzz of the grasshoppers flying from bush to bush. Ahead of them was the inviting cool of the shaded valley with its mix of pine and oak trees.

"Chet, this looks perfect. If you didn't know it was here, you would go right past it."

"Yeah. Let's get on up the hill," Chet responded.

Their journey north proved the alternate trail to be as good as the primary one they had traveled down. They found Chet's truck just as they had left it. The broiling sun had obliterated almost all evidence of the morning's rain. Only the mud in the ruts remained. Exhausted and mud-caked, they dismounted from the four-wheeler.

"I vote we use the trail we just came up," Chet said as he opened the tailgate of his truck.

"Yeah, same here," Larry agreed. Together they set the sturdy boards in place and Chet rode the heavy machine up into the truck. They lashed it down with the nylon straps and peeled off their rain suits, securing them in the back of the truck.

"We can wash all our stuff once we get back to my place," Chet said.

"Let's go. I'm still keeping time," Larry replied as he checked the elapsed time on his watch. Chet nodded wordlessly and unlocked the truck.

The ride back to Chet's place was a quiet one with each man lost in his own thoughts. Larry continued to think about Chet's demeanor during the day. He accepted Chet as the natural leader, but he didn't like being run over.

Not a word was spoken during the entire trip through the mountains. Larry was surprised at Chet's reticence. Typically, Chet would have been bubbling over with enthusiasm. As they pulled into Chet's driveway, Larry checked his watch. They had departed at 4:30 a.m. and it was now after four in the afternoon. Their journey had taken much longer than it should have. They had spent considerable time finding trails to and from the bank.

Max greeted them with a baleful look, disturbed from his mid-afternoon nap.

"Wanna beer?" Chet asked.

"Sure," Larry replied as he swung a leg over one of the chrome and plastic dinette chairs. He sat facing backwards on the chair with his elbows propped on the chair back and his chin cupped in his hands. He watched Chet getting the beers from the tiny fridge.

"Chet, tell me how we get a phone van to use. Are you planning to steal one?"

"Nah, you don't want to steal something and take a chance of blowing the whole deal. We'll just rent a van and put some temporary phone company signs on it," Chet responded.

"You realize, of course, you have to have identification and a credit card to rent a vehicle." Larry took a long pull at his beer after posing this problem to Chet.

"No problem at all, I've got both," he said as he leaned against the kitchen counter and swigged his own beer.

"Did you buy a fake ID or what?" Larry quizzed.

"Nope. Look here," Chet said and from his wallet he produced a current driver's license and a VISA credit card.

"Chet, that ain't your picture on the license, and that guy was born at least ten years before you were."

"Everybody takes a bad drivers license picture. Besides, how often does anyone ever really check ID?" Chet replied levelly.

"It'll never work. Where did you get those anyway?" Larry asked.

"Yes, it will work, and I got them out of customer's uniforms."

Larry shook his head, "Now you're stealing from customers."

"The guy shouldn't leave stuff in his pants if he wants it back," Chet said with a slight edge to his voice. "Listen," he continued, "when I was in the military, we were assigned to go from post to post, checking security. We found 90 percent of the time, we could get into any facility, even classified ones, with an ID that had somebody else's picture on it."

"No shit?" Larry asked incredulously.

"No shit. We wore officer's uniforms and rank. The guards perceived us to be something we weren't. Perception is reality."

"Perception is reality. I like that," Larry mused.

"Well, it's true. Those people in the bank will perceive us to be phone company employees. At least they will long enough to allow us to control the situation." Chet took a swig of beer and looked for Larry's reaction.

"What if the guy's already turned in his credit card as missing?"

"No problem. I'll just pay cash, so they don't actually have to get an authorization code." Chet was hoping they didn't need an authorization code, but he didn't know for sure.

"Okay, so where do we get the phone company signs for the van?" Larry asked.

"I've got some sheets of magnetic stock I got from a sign shop. I painted them myself." Chet reached behind the couch and pulled out a manila folder. He produced two magnetic signs with credible phone company logos painted on them.

"Pretty good, Chet, but I gotta get going."

"All right. Think about things and let's get together after work tomorrow." Chet put his large hand on Larry's shoulder and squeezed firmly. Larry nodded and headed out the door. He hadn't forgotten the rough treatment earlier in the day and he wasn't that easily charmed. He stopped long enough to give Max a quick pat as he went.

CHAPTER ELEVEN

"Hi'ya. What can I get for you?" the girl asked. Chet looked up to see the cocktail waitress from before.

"Hello. I'll have a Corona, with lime."

"Be just a minute." She smiled and went to the bar and placed his order. The bartender, a sallow young man with greasy black hair, pulled a Corona from the cooler. He expertly quartered a lime and halved the quarters. He slid the resulting wedge into the mouth of the bottle.

"Here you go," he said as he handed the beer to the girl.

"Thanks, Pete."

She walked briskly to the table where Chet sat alone.

"That'll be two-fifty, please."

Chet handed her three crumpled ones and said, "Keep it."

"Thanks. I haven't seen you in here much lately, Chet," she said, eyeing his name tag. He looked uncomfortable for a second and then realized how she knew his name.

"Been busy. You know, no rest for the wicked."

"You don't look too wicked to me. My name's Bess." She stuck out her hand. Chet took her outstretched hand and squeezed it gently. He noted underlying strength in the responding grip of her cool hand.

"Bess, I'm Chet Farmer. Pleased to meet ya."

"Nice to meet you, Chet. I've seen you in here before, haven't I?" she confirmed.

"Yeah, I've been coming here for years. You're kinda new, aren't ya?"

"About a month. Just moved here 'cause I heard there's plenty of work in this area. Gotta go." She smiled at him and moved to another customer.

Chet lifted his beer to his lips and allowed a stream of the icy liquid to pour down his parched throat. Bess had stirred feelings in him he had not expected. Recently, his only concern had been planning and preparing for the bank job. Females had ceased to be a part of his life since Josie had left. He watched her as she served another customer across the room. She wore her chestnut hair cropped rather short for his taste, too much like his ex-wife's. She wore a white blouse made of that shiny fabric that always felt so smooth and cool to the touch. He could see her breasts straining against the fabric. They didn't move much, those breasts. Must be pretty firm, he mused. Her skirt was denim and short. She had long legs, sun-browned and no stockings. As she walked, he could see muscles flexing in her calves. Runner? Tennis player? He didn't know, but he thought she sure looked self-assured as she moved with the grace of someone in excellent physical condition.

He looked up at her face and found her watching him watch her. He blushed and looked away. She approached his table.

"Did you need something, Chet?" she asked.

"I, uh...well, I was just watching you work," he stammered.

"I know," Bess replied with an encouraging smile.

"Wondered if you'd care to join me for dinner sometime?" Chet said as he looked up into her green eyes. He hadn't really planned to ask; it just sorta came out, to his surprise.

Bess hesitated for a moment, "Well, we're not supposed to date the customers but...sure, I'd be delighted. When?"

Chet breathed a sigh of relief and surprise, "Uh, well...how 'bout tonight?"

"Chet, I'd love to, but I don't get off until eleven."

"Ok, how 'bout breakfast when you get off?" he persisted.

"Pick me up a little after eleven," she said and walked away.

He wiped a bead of perspiration from his brow. He shook his head as he mentally cringed at the unpolished performance.

"Feel like a damn teenager," he muttered to himself. He drained the beer and checked his watch. Larry should be arriving soon, he thought. He motioned to Bess with his empty Corona bottle, and she brought him another. As she set the bottle on his table, Larry appeared in the doorway. The setting sun silhouetted his lanky form.

"Here's your friend," Bess murmured.

"Bring him the same, would you?" Chet said.

"Sure," she replied and went to the bar. Larry pulled out a chair and, characteristically, turned it around to straddle it.

"Tough day, partner," Larry observed with a sigh as he settled on the seat.

"Yeah, me too. I'm still...," he stopped as Bess approached with Larry's beer.

"Chet, you wanna start a tab?" she asked while methodically positioning the beer on a napkin.

"Naw. We won't be here that long," Larry said and pulled out his wallet to pay. As she left, Larry looked her over.

"On a first name basis, are you? Not bad looking. Is she new?" he asked.

"Yeah. Been here a month she said."

Chet continued with his previous thought, "Like I was saying, I'm still tired from trompin' around the woods. How 'bout you?"

"Sore as hell, buddy. I feel like an old man," Larry responded. They laughed together the laugh of two conspiring boys. Their friendship had grown with the adversity of the past few days in spite of Chet's abrasive treatment of Larry. As they lifted their beers to drink, Chet clinked his bottle against Larry's for a toast.

"Here's to those who wish us well...,"Chet began "...and all the rest can go to hell." They finished together. Again, they laughed the little boys' laugh until Chet had to wipe tears from his eyes. The laughter subsided and Larry looked Chet straight in the eye.

"So, what's next?"

"I'm taking a couple of days of vacation this week," Chet said.

"There's an armored truck that delivers just before the pay day at the mine. I've watched it twice before, and I need to watch it just once more to make sure. We don't want to hit the bank before the money's there or after the employees start cashing their checks."

"Want me to go along?" Larry asked.

"Nope," Chet said shortly. He noticed a look on Larry's face he perceived to be hurt or insult.

"What I mean is, we don't want to be seen together down there. It'll be harder to tie us together later if something should go wrong."

Larry said nothing, but he didn't like the reminder that something could go wrong. It was a fact with which he was well aware.

Eleven o'clock seemed an eternity in coming. Larry had left at nine and since then, Chet had nursed his beer slowly. He was determined not to be drunk by the time Bess got off work. She cruised by his table at a quarter of eleven.

"Last call, Chet," she pronounced.

"Nope, nothing for me. I'm done."

"I can't believe you waited here all this time, Chet." She was flattered that this man would be interested enough to spend his evening waiting for her.

"Nothin' better to do," he said.

Her ego boost evaporated with his candid comment. If she had known him better, she might have snapped back a sarcastic comment. Bess pursed her lips instead and moved to the next table to take any "last call" orders.

Mentally, Chet kicked himself. "That was about as charming as a grease rag," he thought.

Bess finished serving her last customers and disappeared into the back of the bar to count her tips and clean up a little. She really didn't normally date customers, rules or no rules, but this guy had some appeal she couldn't quite resist. Besides, she hadn't had a decent date since she got out of prison. That fact of her history was never far from the surface of her memory. She'd been out for a few months, and she hadn't wanted the complications of a relationship. There'd been a few one-night-stands, but no one she wanted to hook up with long term. She'd moved to Springdale just because. Just because she didn't have anywhere else to go, and the bus had stopped there. She'd bought a Greyhound ticket with the money they'd given her at her release. "Don't leave the state. See your parole officer next Monday." Those were the words spoken to her by the matron that did her out-processing from the penal farm. The fact was, Bess had no intention to see her parole officer and absolutely no intention to stay in Louisiana. She'd walked straight to the bus station and got on the first northbound bus. No doubt there was a warrant waiting for her in Louisiana, but her plans did not include ever returning to that state.

Bess came out of the back room and took a quick look at Chet as he sat waiting at his table. He'd long since finished his last beer, and he looked a little nervous. She was amused at his apparent discomfort. What a strange man, she thought.

"Ready?" she said brightly as she walked past him to the door. Pete was right behind them to lock up.

They left the bar together. Bess took his arm as they walked toward his truck. He was surprised. "Hope you don't mind ridin' in my ol' truck," he said.

"Of course not. We...I used to have a pickup," she said as they walked across the still hot parking lot. The significance of the I-we slip was not lost on Chet. Obviously, Bess had a past, just as he did.

Chet opened the passenger door, and Bess sat down and demurely swung her legs in, knees primly together. He slammed the door and the latch failed to catch, as usual. A second, more thorough, slam did the job. Bess did her best to not visibly flinch.

"Sorry about that door," Chet said as he entered the driver's side. The old Ford groaned as Chet slid his hundred and eighty pounds behind the wheel.

"We can go to the waffle place. If that's okay with you," Bess suggested.

"Sure," Chet replied. He would rather have said, "How about your place instead", but he reminded himself to take it slow. As his mother used to say, "Patience, Chester. In time the grass becomes milk." Mrs. Farmer had been a simple woman who died when Chet was a young boy, not long after his father's death. He vividly remembered her gentle green eyes and her comforting voice. His earliest childhood memory was of his mother taking him by the hand to walk up the hill to the neighbor's house where she bought fresh okra and other vegetables.

"Earth to Chet," Bess said jokingly.

"Uh...Oh, Bess I'm sorry. I was a million miles away."

"I noticed. What were you thinking about so deeply?"

"Something reminded me of my childhood I guess," he replied sheepishly. At that moment, he noticed Bess had the most striking green eyes. Not like his mothers. No, these eyes had a hardness to them. These eyes had seen things of which his mother had never dreamed.

The ride to the restaurant was a short one. As he drove, they spoke of the trivial things strangers talk about. The weather, of course, and how she liked working at Pete's.

Waffle House was packed with customers when they arrived. Chet held the door for Bess to enter. The aroma of fresh coffee, bacon frying, and maple syrup hit them as they walked into the brightly lit restaurant. All the tables were taken, so they had to stand at the doorway to wait for seats. In the past, Chet would have been painfully self-conscious standing in such an exposed position. This time, however, he was aware that he was rather proud to be standing with this fine-looking woman. It occurred to Chet that he had often fantasized about Josie seeing him with just such a woman and now, here he was, but Josie wasn't here to see it.

"I hate waiting, don't you?" Bess said quietly.

A spot finally opened up, and they slid into the booth just as the waitress was wiping down the table. The room was laden with cigarette smoke and Bess was desperately

craving nicotine. "Mind if I smoke?" she asked.

"Of course not. Go right ahead," Chet detested cigarette smoke since he had quit the habit himself, but he wasn't going to let that deter him from enjoying the company of this woman. Bess lit a cigarette and drew the smoke deeply into her lungs. The tired-looking waitress finished wiping down the table.

"Coffee?" she asked with an order pad at the ready. Chet and Bess ordered, and the waitress called out the order to the cook. She rushed off to help the next customers. Bess watched her and shook her head sadly; she knew exactly how the other girl was feeling.

"Man, it was a long night. I gotta find a day job, you know. Waitressing's a bitch."

Chet nodded sympathetically, "Yeah, my job's not too much fun either. Pickin' up other people's dirty laundry ain't the most glamorous job you can have."

"You'd think there'd be a better way, wouldn't you?" Bess mused speculatively. Little did she know that Chet was actively planning his version of a better way. She rambled on about work and some other trivialities while they waited for their food to be delivered. Bess was happy to talk to someone and just to relax a bit. Chet, on the other hand, was not relaxed at all. He was fascinated with this woman, and he just stared at her as she spoke.

"Chet?" Bess was beginning to get the idea that this guy wasn't a very good listener.

"I'm sorry. Deep in thought again. Something you said," Chet said apologetically.

Bess just smiled and the waitress slid their orders down on the table just in time to keep Chet from having to explain. As he ate, he wasn't too sure he wouldn't have shared his plans with this woman. It was amazing how much he had needed to have a confidant and he still didn't.

For her part, Bess wasn't looking for a confidant. Her story was her own, and she planned for it to stay tucked away just where it was. In fact, she was just getting to the point that she didn't take it out and think about it too much. But it was always there. The story, that is. Her last few years hadn't been spent as a homemaker, waitress or anything like that. In simple fact, she'd been a very unwilling resident at a women's correctional facility in southern Louisiana. She had no desire to share that information with Chet and she didn't have a clue as to how she would ever deal with her past if she happened to stumble into a serious relationship.

Tonight, though, she wasn't feeling serious about anything. Bess just wanted to have a nice time with a decent guy that she kinda liked.

Chet had no idea what kind of woman she was or could become.

CHAPTER TWELVE

"Good morning, sir. How may we help you?" Chet stood gaping, for a brief moment, at this stunningly beautiful woman. The tiny, gold nameplate identified this person as Robin. Her auburn hair flowed over her shoulders in waves, and her eyes were a piercing blue. Definitely too blue, must be contacts, Chet surmised. The Rent-A-Car company logo was emblazoned on a neat, royal-blue blazer. Obviously tailored, her clothes fit to perfection.

"Sir?" Robin's smile was firmly fixed in place, part of the image.

"Oh yeah, I need to rent a van. I got some stuff to haul."

"Will this be local?"

"Yeah, Robin. Just for a day or so," Chet did his best to be charming. She wasn't impressed.

"Okay sir, you need to fill out this form and I'll need a major credit card for the deposit." She spoke with a polished but obviously canned style. She drummed her highly polished nails on the counter as Chet busied himself with the form. He used the address and name from the driver's license he had acquired.

"You know, why don't I just pay cash for the rental and deposit." Chet yanked his wallet out of his back pocket. She shook her head at him as he started digging in his wallet for cash.

"No, sir," she began with a slight edge to her voice. "I have to have a major credit card. You can certainly pay with cash, but you still have to provide a major credit card. It's company policy."

When it became apparent she wasn't going to compromise, he produced the VISA card. He held it out for her. Chet felt a bead of perspiration trickle down between his shoulder blades. So far, this was the most risk he had taken. If the owner of the card had already called it in as lost, Chet knew he was in big trouble. The young lady took the card from Chet and slid it through the scanner behind the counter. She stood with her back to Chet, waiting for the authorization code to appear on the machine's display. She drummed her long, manicured nails on the counter again. She turned and smiled briefly at Chet to fulfill her customer service requirements.

"Sometimes it takes a little while."

Chet swallowed hard and nodded silently. He had decided to run out the door if the card was rejected. Larry was outside waiting in Chet's pickup for a quick getaway, if needed.

Robin turned back to the machine. In spite of his apprehension, he found himself appraising this young woman. "What kind of man gets this girl," he asked himself. "What would it take? Money, good looks, fancy car?" Probably all the above and more, he supposed. She was the kind that just oozed money, so why was she working as a rental car agent? Chet couldn't begin to guess. Robin continued drumming her expensive looking nails on the countertop. The noise reminded Chet of a dog's toenails clicking on a tile floor. Finally, a confirmation number glowed in the display window of the box.

"All right, Mr. Edwards. You're all set," she said brightly.

"Great," Chet replied with considerable relief.

"Here are the keys. It's the blue one out front."

Chet had not counted on receiving a blue van. Several white ones usually set on the lot, and he had made the assumption that white was the only color they had.

"Is there a problem?" she asked after noticing his hesitation.

"Oh, no. I was just thinking about something else I need to do today," he said and turned away. He was unwilling to draw attention to himself by requesting a different color of van.

Larry was looking worried as Chet approached the truck.

"How'd it go?" Larry asked.

Chet dangled the keys in front of Larry, "No problem. Just follow me out to my place." Chet replied confidently. He paused a moment, "On second thought, I need to stop at Wal-Mart, so why don't I just meet you out there a little later?"

"Right. See ya in a bit," Larry agreed and started the old truck. Chet watched him drive away as he walked toward the blue van. Neither man noticed Robin peering out the window and noting the license number of the black truck. She entered it in the computer along with the fictitious information Chet had given to her on his rental application.

Chet drove to the Wal-Mart store, and once inside, he proceeded directly to the hardware department. He grabbed four rolls of masking tape and a dozen cans of white spray paint. He paid for his purchases in cash and headed for home. He found Larry pacing up and down in front of the little trailer. Chet drove past the trailer to the garage door of the basement. He motioned for Larry to follow.

"Hey Lar, how about opening the door for me?" He tossed a separate ring of keys to Larry.

"Sure," Larry agreed and proceeded to enter the dark structure. Moments later the heavy steel garage door screeched up its track on rusty wheels. Chet turned the van around and backed into the building.

"Chet."

"Yeah, Lar."

"It's blue."

"No shit, Sherlock."

"The phone company vans are all white. What are we going to do with a blue van?" Larry asked. Chet handed Larry the bag with the paint and masking tape.

"This way the rental company will have the police out looking for a blue van instead of a white one, see?" Chet said.

"I see. Was this part of the plan all along?"

"No," Chet responded, "but it's going to work out even better this way."

Chet began applying tape to the chrome and glass areas of the van. Larry taped newspaper over the wheels and large areas of glass. Within an hour, they had the van ready for paint. Chet rattled the agitator ball in the first can of paint and began methodically painting. He stopped after a few moments.

"What's the matter?" Larry asked.

"It ain't sticking. Must have wax on it," Chet replied in disgust. The paint had indeed formed numerous fish-eye spaces where it did not adhere to the original finish.

"No problem, Chet. We'll just get some acetone and wipe it down," Larry suggested.

"Don't have anything like that, Lar. I'll run back into town and get it," Chet answered as he moved to leave the building.

Larry watched him go and then sat down on an upturned concrete block to wait. Time slowed to an imperceptible crawl as Larry sat waiting. He replayed many scenes of his life and found it wanting. Always, he played it safe. Always the reliable, steady one. He looked back at so many opportunities for excitement and adventure. Always, he'd said no to anything outside his narrow comfort zone.

As an only child, he'd been probably overprotected. His middle class, suburban parents had carefully screened his friends and, of course, guided him to do the safe, the right things. Larry had gone through school with no particular ambition or success, and rather than go to college as his parents wanted, he'd gone to work. That had been a source of disappointment to them which they had never let him forget. He mused for a moment on the idea that all his life he'd played it safe for someone else's approval. Approval, which was conditional upon his meeting someone else's expectations. Was this adventure his ambition or was he again trying to meet someone else's expectations?

He heard Chet's truck approaching on the bumpy dirt road. He realized he'd been sitting and thinking for almost an hour. He knew he had needed the time to think through his feelings about the bank job. Right now, he felt sure he was going to go through with it. Damn it if he was going to take the safe road this time.

The old black Ford bounced into the yard, its rusty springs screeching in protest. Larry could hear Chet slam the door. Soon after, he strode through the door of the basement in a fizz.

"Sorry it took so long, Lar. The damned traffic around here just gets worse every day. These damned old hillbillies drive like they got nuthin' better to do," Chet muttered, not accepting that he fell into the same category.

"No problem. I enjoyed the break. You've got a great place here, Chet. It's so quiet compared to livin' in subdivision," Larry replied.

Chet grunted in reply.

Chet took the cans of acetone from a paper bag along with some paper towels and began wiping down the van. The acetone cut through the wax and soon the van's shiny surface took on a dull luster.

"Try that, Lar," Chet suggested impatiently.

Larry vigorously shook the first paint can until the ball rattled annoyingly. Chet gritted his teeth until Larry finally began spraying. He flowed the paint on in smooth, even strokes. It adhered to the vehicle's surface with no problem. Impatient with Larry's methodical application, Chet took over and gave Larry a break.

"Take a break, buddy," Chet reached for the can Larry was using. He shook it twice and started spraying a thick coat. Soon there was a fine mist of white paint floating in the air and Chet found himself having to step outside to breathe. Larry was sitting on an upturned concrete block in the sun as Chet walked out.

"It's looking good, Chet."

"Yeah, not much longer now. You wanna paint some on the other side?" Chet replied.

"You bet. Catch your breath. Or are you getting high?" Larry looked at Chet quizzically. Chet's eyes were red, and he looked a little dizzy.

"No. I'm fine. I'll just get a little air for a while."

Chet took Larry's seat on the concrete block and focused on remaining conscious. For the life of him, he couldn't understand what these kids got out of huffing paint. All it gave him was a blinding headache.

Inside the building, Larry rattled cans and sprayed paint while Chet recovered. He also developed a whopping headache and walked back outside after painting the driver's side of the van.

"Gotta take a breather, man." Larry's nostrils were bright white from the paint he'd inhaled.

Chet finished the painting and together they carefully peeled away the masking tape and paper.

"I'm going to get the signs while you finish that, Lar."

Chet briskly walked the short distance to his camper trailer. Max tolerated an affectionate pat from Chet when he entered. The phone company logo signs were behind the couch as he had left them. Chet grabbed two beers from the fridge. Max watched as Chet opened them. The cat jumped smoothly to his window perch.

"Max, old buddy, it looks like it might just happen."

Max made no reply. He sat in the window and ignored Chet.

"Should have got me a damned dog," Chet muttered as he struggled out the door with the signs under his arm, and a beer in each hand.

"Thanks," Larry said as Chet handed him the cold Corona. Chet went into the basement and prepared to mount the door signs. He eyeballed the signs, then the door, then the signs again. He placed the top edge of the first magnetic sheet against the door and let the rest of it slap into place. He did the same on the other door.

Larry lifted his bottle in mock salute as Chet pulled up a block and sat down beside him.

"Well done, old man. Well done," Larry said approvingly.

They sat quietly and watched the sun set through the limbs of the tall oak forest. Only a month had passed since they first had spoken of the operation. A chill wind blew from the west and Chet shuddered involuntarily.

"Be winter, soon," he said.

"Yeah, but we'll be living fine by that time," Larry answered.

"Wrong. We ain't touching that money for at least a year. Maybe more. We agreed on that already," Chet said sternly.

"Right. I just meant we'll be doing fine knowing it's there," Larry hastily corrected himself. Chet said no more. He watched as the sun disappeared behind the distant hills. A feeling of dread sat like a lump in the pit of his stomach. Had he chosen the right partner, he wondered.

He pondered this question for several minutes with no clear answer. Another dark question lingered in his mind. What would he do if Larry failed him? Just accept a prison sentence and spend the better part of the rest of his life behind bars? No, Chet concluded, he was already living like a rat in a cage. Going to prison was not an option. If it came down to it, Chet knew he had the strength to do whatever had to be done. If that meant someone got hurt; well, so be it. As long as it wasn't himself, Chet chose not to care. Larry might be a friend, as far as that went, but he was only a tool for Chet to use. Like any other of his tools, if it broke or didn't work then Chet would get rid of it.

He just hoped Larry would come through when the going got tough.

CHAPTER THIRTEEN

C het watched the heat waves dancing on the hot pavement. The air was laden with the late summer smell of pine trees baking in the scorching sun. Occasionally the scent of near-molten asphalt wafted into his hiding spot. The heat of the midday sun kept most animals in their burrows or dens, but the odd beetle or two scurried through the dry pine needles where he lay.

In the distance, Chet could hear the steady rumble of heavy trucks on the interstate. At this time of day, few people traveled the side road which he observed. The road Chet watched was a county road that led from the interstate to the village of Carbontown. In fact, it was the only road that led to Carbontown.

Chet was waiting for one particular vehicle. Today was Thursday, and it was the second Thursday of the month. If his information was correct, a heavily loaded armored truck would be in route to the Carbontown bank. The bank would be receiving a large cash shipment to handle the demands of the miners who would want to cash their paychecks.

Chet glanced at his watch for the umpteenth time and made a mental note to get one of those camo watch bands with a cover to prevent telltale reflections. It was nearly two o'clock, and he expected his quarry to be approaching shortly. He wiped a bead of sweat from the tip of his nose and pressed the eyepieces of his binoculars against his brow. In the shimmering distance he saw the armored truck approaching. As it drew near, he could distinguish the outline of the driver and guard through the darkly tinted glass. If there was anyone else in the vehicle, he could not tell.

The truck rumbled past him, close enough he could smell the diesel smoke from the engine and hear the whine of the gearbox as the driver shifted to make the sharp curve at the base of the hill.

Chet collected his equipment and walked back into the woods where the four-wheeler waited under its camo net. The air here was cooler and Chet looked forward to riding briskly to let the rushing air cool his sweat-soaked body.

"Too damn old for this crawling around in the bushes," he muttered to himself. Methodically, he folded the camo net and replaced it in a niche in his pack. He unhooked the bungee cords holding the cooler on the back luggage rack. The cooler held bottles of Gatorade on ice, one of which he gratefully gulped down. Ever mindful of security, he replaced the empty bottle in the cooler to be disposed of later.

The big Honda engine started with a touch of the switch and Chet eased the vehicle into gear and rode through the woods to the logging road. The ground was still heavily carpeted with pine needles and the wide soft tires of the ATV rolled across them smoothly. He was careful to take a different route to the road. No sense in wearing a path to his observation point, he thought.

The logging road wound its way through the scrub brush left after the forest had been clear cut. His old pickup was undisturbed where he left it in a small stand of pines. Chet dismounted, leaving the engine running and opened the tailgate of his truck. With practiced hands, he set the ramps in place to ride the four-wheeler up into the truck bed. Chet remounted the Honda and eased it smoothly up the ramps. He killed the engine and used the nylon tie-down straps to secure the machine to the truck bed. He gave each ratchet buckle an extra tweak for good measure.

Chet sat down on the tailgate of the old truck and opened another Gatorade. He contemplated the situation as he flipped through his pocket notebook. He nodded with satisfaction. He had gathered considerable information during his recon missions in this area. Today had been his third surveillance of the armored truck, and it established that the driver followed a set routine and route each trip. Chet considered this to be very bad security but very good for his purposes.

Chet perused his notebook and allowed his mind to travel back to the trips recorded there. His first trip had been to the bank. The bank was well chosen. The physical layout was just perfect for the plan. The entire facility would be isolated by the train wreck and the old bumpkin guard would be no problem. Chet had driven right up to the front of the bank and walked in, bold as day. Funny how your mind plays tricks, he thought. He wasn't doing anything wrong, and still it felt like every eye in the room watched him. The videocameras were inconspicuously located in corners and behind glass where Chet could feel them focused directly on him. He'd stood at the little counter and filled out a check for cash. His hands actually shook.

The young lady behind the counter was cheerful and happy to assist him. She asked for his driver's license and cashed his check without question. He walked out of the bank sweating.

The second trip was to tour Carbontown itself. He drove slowly through the old railroad town. There was an old-fashioned town square with a typical small town courthouse. Chet saw the police station was located in the basement of the courthouse. The only police car he saw was a five-year-old Crown Vic that he was pretty sure his old Ford pickup could outrun. He rolled past the fuel depot just at the edge of town. It was old and in disrepair. In fact, the whole town had an air of being behind the times. So why this bank? He asked himself that question several times. When he'd summoned up the courage to ask his silent partner the same question, the answer was a curt rebuke. Chet never asked again, and he focused instead on the details of the plan.

Now his last trip was complete, and he'd seen just about all there was to see in Carbontown. He could find no gaps of information or inconsistencies to be reconciled. Finally satisfied, he got up from his seat and closed the tailgate. He looked about for any telltale evidence of his presence there, found none, and proceeded to get in the cab of his old truck to head toward town for some additional reconnaissance.

CHAPTER FOURTEEN

Bess didn't seem at all surprised to see Chet stride into the bar. His features were sun bronzed, and he moved with a spring in his step that hadn't been there for years.

"Hi'ya, Bess. Gimme a Corona."

She smiled and nodded. Chet sat at his customary table and waited impatiently. He drummed on the table with his blunt fingertips.

"Chet, you seem wired," Bess observed as she set the icy cold beer on a coaster. Beads of sweat had formed on the glass, and they ran in rivers of coolness down the sides of the bottle.

"Yeah, I guess. How are ya?"

"Good. I enjoyed our visit the other night," she said.

"Me too. Maybe we could go out for dinner or something. You're off Sunday aren't ya?"

"Sure. We could do that," she replied with a sweet smile.

Chet smiled back and nodded. He wanted to share the excitement of his impending adventure with her, but he knew that was impossible. He had to maintain absolute security about their plan, and the fewer people who were in on it, the better.

Bess glided away to check on another customer. She knew with certainty where this was leading, and she was ready. It had been a long time since there had been someone special in her life. There'd been plenty of guys, but no one special.

Larry walked in the doorway some minutes later, and he sat down at Chet's table.

"So, what did you see?" he demanded without so much as a hello.

"Well, Lar, I saw the exact same thing I saw last time."

"So that's good, right? Predictable is what we want," Larry confirmed.

"You bet it is. I also drove into town this morning and walked along the tracks. There's a good spot to unbolt the track just west of the bank."

"Can we get to it without being seen?" Larry asked.

"Yeah. I think so. The gully that runs past the bank goes underneath the tracks. There's a small wooden trestle. We can break the track just before the trestle. They've got these wires screwed into the tracks. I'm betting it's so they can tell if there's a break in the track. We'll need to make up some jumpers to wire across the place where we unbolt the track joint."

"When the train derails, is anybody going to get hurt?" Larry asked with a frown.

"How could I know that, Larry? I really just don't know. The train always seems to move pretty damn slow every time I've watched it," Chet replied.

Larry nodded speculatively. He wanted guarantees on every risk. Of course, there were none, he realized.

"Did you look at the fuel tanks while you were there?"

"Yeah. It's pretty much just like I described. The tank we want to hit is at the edge of

the fuel yard. If they have any firefighting ability at all, they should be able to keep it from spreading. They've got dirt dikes built around each tank as a confinement dam, you know. The dams are supposed to hold the contents of any one tank, so I don't believe the fire will do too much damage."

Before setting up his observation post for the armored truck, Chet had driven to the bulk fuel yard and watched the operation for a while. He sat in his truck on a small hilltop some hundred yards away. Through his small binoculars, he viewed the train as it uncoupled a tank car and also saw several tanker trucks come and go. The local delivery trucks filled up from a manifold system near the office. As far as he could tell, no one ever really approached most of the storage tanks. The filling and delivery operations were handled remotely.

He carefully scanned the entire premises for evidence of any security system. There were no cameras or any apparent surveillance equipment in sight. The yard itself was surrounded by a six-foot-high chain link fence topped with barbed wire. He felt certain he or Larry could cut through the wire, place the explosives, and retreat unseen. There were several mercury vapor yard lights on utility poles, but if there was actually no security system in place, then there would be no one there to see what was taking place.

"No Lar, I don't think we'll have any problem at the fuel depot. We'll still plan to enter

through the back fence around 3 a.m., place the device, and leave. From there, we'll move to the railroad track, unbolt it, and pry the rail out a few inches."

"Where are we going to park the van?"

"I've decided to use the van to do each job. We'll wear our phone company coveralls to the bank, a railroad jacket to the railway and just our Fuel Depot shirts inside the fuel yard. I'll make up magnetic signs for the railroad and Fuel Depot to stick on the van."

"I don't know what Fuel Depot uses, but the railroad uses yellow trucks, not white vans," Larry pointed out.

"That's true, but we're counting on not actually being seen. The signs and uniforms are just back up props in case someone happens to be around," Chet countered in defense of his plan.

Larry nodded slowly. He knew it was pointless to argue with Chet when Chet's mind was already made up.

"All right, Chet. I see your point, what's next?" Larry asked in a resigned voice.

Chet detected the sullen tone of voice, and it struck a chord in him that he had to control with supreme effort. His impulse was to attack and start a fight. He was already feeling the demands of keeping his job and doing almost all the leg work for this bank job. Larry's lukewarm acceptance of his plan left Chet feeling frustrated and angry. In his coolest, most controlled voice, he said, "I've got some work to do on the device. I'll see you at work tomorrow some time. All right?"

"Sure, you bet."

Larry lifted his beer bottle in mock salute as Chet walked briskly out of the bar. Once again, Larry was left to pay the bill. He flashed a wry smile at Bess when she raised a questioning eyebrow.

CHAPTER FIFTEEN

She was lost when first she saw herself in the mirror. She really preferred cocaine when the money was good but lately, she'd been lucky to afford crank.

Bess had come from a typical upper middle-class family. Typical-three-bedroom house in a nice neighborhood, typical two cars, typical dog in the backyard and one very atypical teenager.

The date with Chet had been a struggle for Bess. He had been relatively quiet during dinner. He offered few glimpses into his own life and had asked too many questions about hers. She resisted the feeling that he had been prying, preferring to think he was simply making conversation. It was painfully obvious to Bess that Chet was unpracticed in the modern art of dating. She assumed, rightly, that it had been some years since he had dated anyone. Aware of his discomfort, she kept the conversation light and easy. She didn't share any details of her sordid past, nor did she delve into his personal history. She learned of his years as a route man, and she told him she had grown up in Memphis, a city girl you know, never been a housewife and worked as a waitress from time to time.

After they ate, he took her home and in a sort of quaint gesture, offered to shake her hand goodnight. She laughed and used his hand to pull him close. She kissed him lightly on the lips and went into her apartment. He stood quietly on her step and watched her close the door. Bess peeked out her window and watched him drive away. She knew she'd see him again, and she felt a warm dampness begin when she contemplated the result of their next date.

As he left the parking lot of the downtown apartment complex, Bess sat on the hard couch in front of the glass-topped coffee table. She pulled an aluminum foil packet from her purse and carefully tapped out a small pile of snowy white powder onto the glass.

Some days she could wait until she got home. Most days found her dipping her long pinky nail into the powder for a quick toot to get her through the day. She'd picked up the habit in Memphis, of course. Her former lover was a Beale Street blues player. His name was Tony Shea, and he'd play in any smoky club that would have him. Over time, fewer and fewer clubs would have him due to his rather unconventional tastes, unconventional even for Beale Street.

He was pure adventure and excitement to a rebellious Germantown high-school girl with a fake ID. Late one night, he sat down at her table during a break. She was there with a would-be lover from Memphis state. Tony had dark black hair tied back in a tight ponytail. He talked to her as though she was an adult, and he completely ignored her date. She was enthralled with the grown-up attention. She was sick of being treated like a little girl by her parents, private school teachers, and family. The frustrated college boy stormed out of the bar after a few minutes, when it became apparent Bess was fascinated by the slick musician. Tony affected a certain style by wearing dark Armani-style suits with black T-shirts and gold everywhere. Heavy nugget rings, gold loop in his left ear and a gold Rolex replica on his wrist.

After his next set, Tony moved to her table again when the band took their break. He had watched her constantly from the stage. Tony's intense dark eyes were set below heavy black eyebrows, and his angular features made her think of him as a European mystery man. If fact, as she was to discover much later, he was the belligerent son of an alcoholic truck mechanic from nearby West Memphis.

She was thrilled when he again chose to sit with her during his last break before the end of the night. Half a dozen men had tried to pick her up or dance with her while she sat alone during his previous set. She fended them off hoping he would come back to her. Now he sat close, smelling a little too strongly of cologne, beer, and cigarettes. He talked constantly, trying one practiced line after another. Finally, just before the end of the break, he asked her to step in the back with him. Alarm bells went off in her head, but she went anyway. He took her by the hand and led her through the crowd to a door marked "No Admittance". A small office was behind that door along with the liquor storeroom.

He pulled her into the office and closed the door. The tiny office had a one-way mirror looking onto the crowded and smoky bar room.

"Beth, how would you...," he began.

"Bess. My name is Bess, not Beth," she interrupted.

"Sorry, baby. It's loud out there you know."

"It's all right, Tony."

Bess was beginning to have her doubts about this guy, but the adrenaline and hormones still surged through her body. She tingled with anticipation of what was to happen next. He released her hand and pulled a small leather case from his inside jacket pocket. He sat on the edge of the cluttered desk and opened out the neatly organized little set. The case had a small mirror attached, a tiny brown glass vial under a leather loop, and under other loops, tiny silver spoon and a short glass straw with a large wooden bead at one end. A single edge razor blade was nestled in its own slot. She gaped, for a moment, at the contents and then she understood. Bess had grown up exposed to drugs, especially pot which she and her friends regularly sneaked out of class to smoke. She had yet to be introduced to the world of the powders until that night.

Tony looked at her, and she slowly nodded. He opened the bottle and tipped out a portion of the contents onto the mirror and using the razor blade he deftly arranged two small lines. He placed the beaded end of the straw against his nose, bent down and powerfully inhaled one line of cocaine. He wiped his nose, sniffed twice and handed the straw to her.

As he placed the tube in her hand, the rush of excitement was nearly as strong as she would come to crave from the drug. Without hesitation, she bent over the desk and placed the tube at the end of the remaining line. Briefly she looked into the mirror and saw the eyes of innocence. She would never see them again.

Bess inhaled all the powder and tried to look cool as she handed back the tube.

"First time, huh?" Tony inquired.

She shook her head and touched her nose.

"Uh, huh. The tingle will go away after awhile," he informed her.

He pulled her to him and kissed her deeply. She vaguely noticed the taste of cigarettes and beer as his tongue probed her mouth. She hardly felt his hands as he fondled her breasts.

"Tony, damn it. Get the fuck outta my office."

The manager, known only as Kincaid, was a heavy-set black man. His bulk filled the doorway as he stood impatiently waiting for Tony and Bess to leave.

"Sorry, Kincaid. We're going." Tony held up both hands in mock fear. He took Bess back out into the throng of people, and they threaded their way toward the stage. The other band members were starting to assemble, and they busied themselves checking amps and tuning guitars.

Tony sat her down at the side of the stage nearest where he played. The bar was packed, and the tiny table where she'd been sitting now held two tourists, obviously from out of town.

He got her a beer from the bar and found his seat just as the three other band members began to play. Tony picked up his bass guitar and laid down the heavy back beat without missing a stroke.

J.J., the drummer, a Rastafarian sort, leaned over to Tony and shouted over the din.

"Jailbait, mon."

Tony looked at Bess and nodded.

"Yeah, ain't it great?"

After the set was over and the bar was closing, Tony took Bess up to the stage and introduced her to the band.

"Beth, this is J.J. on drums, Clive is on brass and lead guitar and Gerry here does vocals and harmonica."

"Hi, guys," she said brightly and grinned at them. They each responded with a nod and smile. They'd seen plenty of very young girls being introduced in just this fashion. Tony's taste in females ran on the young side, usually resulting in big trouble.

Bess pulled Tony aside.

"What, babe?"

"I told you my name is Bess. If you forget it again, I'm outta here. Okay?" she snapped.

"Whoa, babe. I'm sorry. Let's go out to your car. You do have a ride, don't ya?"

"Sure, I do," Bess responded in her sixteen-year-old's voice. What did he think she was, a kid or something?

She led him down the still-crowded street to the paid parking lot where her mom's new black Beemer sat. She found the alarm remote in her purse and aimed it at the car. Two annoying chirps announced the alarm system had been disabled.

The windows were tinted as darkly as possible, and no one could see inside when she and Tony got in and closed the doors.

"Nice ride, Bess. Your dad's?" he asked.

"Mom's," she said after a moment of hesitation.

She turned the key to accessory and slid a B.B. King CD into the Blaupunkt sound system. As the music started, Tony produced his special leather case, and together they did two more lines of coke. He put the case away and leaned over to kiss her. She responded warmly to his touches and kisses. He slid his hands all over her young body, touching her breasts and stroking her legs. She wore a short cotton skirt and to his delight and amazement, nothing underneath. She had felt deliciously wicked going without panties. Bess had planned something special for the Memphis State boy, but this was so much better. Tony's fingers nestled into the curly fur between her legs. She responded by opening her legs ever so slightly and he let one probing finger find its way into the dark, wet place. She boldly reached for him and unzipped his trousers. His penis was swollen and erect even before she touched it.

Chapter Sixteen

Their romance continued at a feverish pace for some weeks until her parents found out. Her father was furious, and her mother was, as she put it, simply devastated. It just would not do for an underage, Germantown girl to be consorting with a Beale Street player. There were recriminations and screaming arguments. Finally, under threat of prosecution for statutory rape, Tony disappeared. Bess was lost. She went through a period of intense depression and one night tried to kill herself with her mother's sleeping pills and her dad's scotch. Unlike many teenage suicide attempts, this one was not a cry for help. She really meant to accomplish it, and it was only because her parents came home early from a social function that they found her in time.

After a dreadful night in the emergency room having her stomach pumped, Bess convalesced in her room at home. Her parents came into her room late the following day.

"Bess, we have to talk," her father began. She didn't answer. He was red-faced and angry. Her mother stood beside him, wan and despondent.

"We've had enough of your behavior. I've found a school for you in Birmingham. They specialize in... well, in situations like yours."

He waited for her usual smart-mouthed reply, and when one was not forthcoming, he took it an assent.

"You'll be starting there in about a month. You'll like it there. Plenty of girls your age, you know."

She nodded bleakly, and he forced a thin smile in return. They left her room without further comment. As she watched them leave, it occurred to her there had not been a word of encouragement, love or support. She knew her mother's social circle was buzzing with gossip, and her father simply wouldn't tolerate anything that interrupted business.

That night she packed a small bag and crept downstairs. She was weak and sick, but she wouldn't stay there another minute. She found her mother's purse and took what money there was along with an ATM card. She turned off the elaborate alarm system and walked out into the warm Memphis night. She never looked back.

Bess went to see if Tony was at the club where they met. He wasn't. She walked to several other clubs he frequented. Hadn't seen him, was the answer. He had vanished from the Memphis night scene.

The ATM maxed out at $600. She could get more the next day but there was a limit on what she could get a one time. Bess was afraid if she used it again, her parents would have the cops waiting for her.

After walking the streets for hours, Bess rented a grimy downtown hotel room complete with a dripping air conditioner and a full complement of cockroaches. She paid cash, and the clerk didn't ask any questions. Bess climbed to the second floor and found her room. The door looked like it was just barely hanging on its hinges. Bess unlocked it and tentatively reached in to turn on the light.

"Oh, my god!"

The roaches scattered immediately when the light came on. Bess swallowed hard and entered the room. She was horrified at the stench and the filth, but she had no where else to go, so she slid a rickety chair under the doorknob. The prospect of sleeping in the bed turned her stomach, so she curled up on the armchair and tried to sleep. The old hotel echoed with sounds of domestic disputes, rhythmically creaking bed springs, and the quiet sobs of one very lonely and very scared young girl.

The next morning, she hid in the filthy room until check out time which was at eleven. A different clerk was on duty when she left. He looked her up and down speculatively. She shuddered involuntarily at the thought of what he must be thinking.

After leaving the hotel, she walked for hours and finally sat down on a park bench. She was accosted repeatedly by men and sometimes by women passing by. There didn't seem to be a moment she wasn't under scrutiny or near assault. Exhaustion was overwhelming her, but she got up and left the park. Bess walked the mid town streets until dark. As the sun went down, the streets began to fill with the outcasts and scum of the city. Countless men leered at her and offered all sorts of deviant suggestions. She ignored them all. She walked and walked until she realized she didn't know where she was anymore. Bess turned down a side street that looked familiar. She thought it would lead toward a club that Tony played in from time to time.

"Hey, baby. Wanna fuck?"

She jumped, startled. The voice was from a white man, filthy with scraggly hair and an unkempt beard. He leaned out of a broken-down old car and followed her down the street right next to her. She refused to look at him, and he honked and shouted more obscenities. Bess obstinately looked down and kept walking.

"You fucking slut. You think you're better than me. Don't ya, bitch?"

Bess tried to remain stoic as she hurriedly walked toward the nearest store. Tears welled up in her eyes, and she was more frightened than she had ever been in her life. She couldn't think, and her legs seemed to be moving in slow motion.

"You're gonna suck my cock, you cunt." The guy was literally screaming at the top of his lungs at her. No streetlight illuminated the section of street where she walked. The local gang kids had shot them out so often the city workers gave up and stopped replacing the bulbs.

Bess was feeling trapped with no where to go. The sidewalk was narrow and there was no place for her to duck into. He was leaning even farther out of the car window as he drove down the wrong side of the street. He was so close she could smell his fetid breath as he described what he was going to do to her. An oncoming car honked and swerved. He raised a finger and honked back.

"Fuckin' asshole," he shouted at the car as it sped around him. He was momentarily distracted, and she dashed into a small neighborhood shop before he knew it.

The clerk was a large black woman whose name tag said Doris.

"Honey, what are you doin' on this street?" she demanded in alarm as Bess rushed inside. White girls didn't last long on her street, black girls either for that matter. Doris had good reason to know. Bess breathlessly pushed the glass door shut behind her and leaned back against it. Tears began flowing down her cheeks.

"I...I don't know. I'm looking for Tony, ...my boyfriend, and I can't find him." The words tumbled out in between sobs.

"Come here to me, child."

The woman came out from behind the counter and held out her arms, and Bess didn't hesitate to rush into the protective bear hug.

"Girl, you could have been killed or raped or...girl, where are your parents?"

Bess didn't reply. She leaned her head against the ample bosom of her new friend and simply sobbed. The older woman had seen so many lost girls on this street; there was a time she'd been one herself. Doris stroked her hair and wondered what to do. There were so many kids in trouble. Now Bess was just one more, and she looked like a rich bitch kid at that. Doris didn't have to think about it for very long.

"You come with me, child." She led Bess by the hand and took her behind the counter and through a door into the tiny apartment where Doris lived. She sat the girl down on the threadbare old couch.

"I'll be right back, honey. Don't you worry your head about nothing." Doris picked up an old ball bat and strode to the door. She peered out and looked for the girl's stalker. He was no where to be seen.

"Damn good thing for him," Doris muttered. "I'd whup his ass. Don't care who he thinks he is."

She shuffled back to the apartment and checked on Bess. The girl was sound asleep, curled into a near fetal position on the couch.

Doris leaned down and smoothed her hair. "Always the pretty ones. Just can't stay outta trouble." Her voice was soft and understanding. "Just can't stay out of trouble..." she repeated sadly.

Bess stayed with Doris for almost a week. Doris was kind but demanding. She had Bess up at dawn and doing chores after the first day. In all of her life, she never had to work so hard. Doris had her cleaning the bathroom, taking out trash, unloading shipments, and stocking shelves. Bess spent every waking moment thinking about Tony.

Before she'd been in the apartment for a whole week, Doris figured Bess had been there long enough.

"Bess, honey. You got to go home. I'm real proud you spent time with me, and you can come back any time to visit. But right now, you got to go back to your folks. They got to be worried sick about you."

"I'll go. But not back to them. Not now, not ever."

"Bess, ...honey." Doris was distraught. She remembered her own youth and all the mistakes she'd made.

"No. I mean it. Never." Bess fussed with her few possessions and prepared to leave.

"Doris, thank you so much. You saved my life, and I'll never be able to repay you." Bess walked out of the door and headed for Beale Street.

She avoided the Memphis police officers, fearing they would have her description. That night she found Tony as he left a bar.

"Tony," she fairly screamed his name.

"Bess, dawlin', what the hell are you doing here?"

"I came to be with you," she said quietly, tears welling up in her eyes.

He took her back inside the bar to a corner table where they could talk. She told him how she had left home and how she'd looked for him everywhere. She told him about Doris and even told of the suicide attempt.

That night they made plans to leave together for New Orleans, and for what she thought was to be a better life. Tony was more than ready to leave Memphis. He'd worn out his welcome at almost every nightclub and he had some people looking for him. They were the sort of people that Tony didn't want to see again. He didn't bother to mention to Bess that he had a small problem with some of the local gentlemen who ran the drug trade. Tony made a little side income by dealing coke on a very small-time basis. Unfortunately for Tony, he'd been dipping into the profits, as well as the product and his bosses had decided Tony was more of a liability than a benefit.

The last person who'd stolen from them washed up on the banks of the Mississippi with his hands wired behind his back with a coat hanger. They hadn't bothered to kill him before they pushed him off the bridge; they let the muddy water do that for them. Tony wasn't planning to experience a similar fate, so the opportunity to leave town with Bess came at a perfect time. He knew Bess was good for some money and she was pretty good in the sack. Tony figured it was a win-win deal for him. He'd use her money to get out of town, and then when he got tired of her, well...he'd dump her ass on the street and find another bimbo to keep him happy.

CHAPTER SEVENTEEN

Chet sat on the stool in one corner of his hidden subterranean room. An odd assemblage of items lay strewn across the bench in front of him. Plumbing parts, reloading supplies and hobby craft parts.

Working slowly and methodically, Chet picked up a twelve-inch section of galvanized pipe. The pipe was two inches in diameter and threaded on both ends. He lightly screwed a cast iron pipe cap on one end. On the other end, he assembled a series of pipe reducers that ended with a spring-loaded cylinder. The spring-loaded cylinder had been drilled out to hold a forty-five caliber, phosphorescent, tracer round. A firing pin was poised above the bullet primer. A small cotter pin held the firing pin in its retracted position. Chet attached a compact electronic timer to the firing apparatus with two stainless steel hose clamps. The timer was wired to a small servo motor which, when activated, would pull the cotter pin out and allow the firing pin to strike the bullet primer.

When he had the entire clumsy looking contraption assembled, he set the time for five minutes and waited. Five minutes later, exactly, the timer beeped, and the servo motor whirred, pulling the cotter pin out. The firing pin slammed home on an empty chamber.

Chet smiled and decided he was ready for the live fire test. He took a regular forty-five round from one of the many boxes on his ammo shelf and prepared to carry the explosive device to his makeshift firing range outside.

He climbed the steep ladder out of his hidden room in the fortress-like basement.

The summer days were winding down and he felt a sense of urgency to complete preparations for his upcoming adventure. He walked past the little trailer on his way to the firing range. Max occupied his usual perch in the window. He seemed to be sleeping soundly with the sun's rays glinting on his coat. Chet wondering what would become of Max if something went wrong. He could, after all, get shot, arrested or both. Chet hated to think of Max ending up in a shelter, waiting to be euthanized or worse yet, being left alone in the trailer to starve to death. Perhaps Bess would like a cat, he thought. They'd never spoken of such things, but maybe when he saw her again, he'd mention Max and see what her reaction was. Probably allergic or something, Chet mused ruefully.

He continued thinking about Bess as he walked to the firing range. He imagined taking her away to some tropical destination and wowing her with his newfound wealth. There would be moonlit walks on the beach, those silly drinks with parasols stuck in them, and the water. The water would be so blue and there'd be so much water. Such fantasies occupied his mind until he parted the sumac bushes and walked down into the narrow ravine that held his much-used gun practice area. He carefully distributed his materials on the shooting bench. Chet swung a leg over the stool attached to the bench and he carefully began sorting out his paraphernalia.

Chet removed the pipe cap from one end of the apparatus and dropped it into his pocket. He unscrewed the firing mechanism from the other end and fitted the forty-five caliber bullet into its chamber. When fired, the slug would exit the now open end of the pipe and fly downrange. Carefully, he reattached the firing mechanism and pulled the firing pin back until he could push the cotter pin into place. Chet gingerly released his grip on the firing pin. It didn't discharge. The cotter pin held the firing pin securely.

His plan was to pack the tube with as much smokeless gunpowder as he could get into the tube. The forty-five tracer round would, theoretically, ignite the powder resulting in a powerful explosion. The resulting blast would, again theoretically, shatter the valves and pipes on the gasoline storage tank and a massive fire would then ensue. Chet had examined a number of valves over the last few months, and they all were made of cast iron, brass or occasionally, stainless steel. He felt certain that his bomb could smash a brass valve but it the tank had a stainless valve, well...things would get really complicated.

Chet kept his finger on the cotter pin. He set the electronic timer for thirty minutes and then set the device on the ground. The business end of the pipe pointed downrange toward the dirt backstop that had already absorbed so many practice bullets. Chet placed two heavy sandbags against the pipe bomb to hold it in place. He didn't want a wild round to hit something or somebody.

Using his blunt finger to manipulate a tiny button, Chet set the stopwatch function on his cheap Timex sports watch. He wanted to gauge just how closely the timer would match his watch.

Now with thirty minutes to wait, Chet trekked back to his camper. Max was awake and watching as Chet approached. Chet bumped the reluctant door open with his knee.

"Max, I need a beer. How 'bout you?" Chet ran his fingers down Max's shiny coat creating a crackle of static electricity. Max didn't seem to mind the tiny jolt of electricity that popped between his fur and Chet's hand. He purred and stretched extravagantly.

Chet opened a Corona and found a dried-up piece of lime to put in it. He swigged the beer and sat in the doorway of his camper to wait. Max sat patiently beside his master and waited too. Chet now had some time to reflect on the state of his plan. There were myriad details to be handled and his anxiety level increased as he thought of every tiny item that needed to be checked and rechecked. He drained his first beer within a few minutes and started on a second one. He continued to fret about Larry and his level of commitment.

Chet felt a hollow sensation in the pit of his stomach when he thought about Larry too much.

Chet's timer approached thirty minutes and he listened expectantly for the blast. At thirty minutes and some twenty seconds, a muffled pop echoed across the landscape. Chet held up his beer bottle in mock salute.

"Right on time, Max. Let's hope it works that well for real."

CHAPTER EIGHTEEN

B ess could hardly contain herself as the bus rumbled toward New Orleans. She'd been there with her parents a time or two as a child, but she didn't remember much except for them arguing in the car.

This was different, way different. This time she was on her own and about to experience life as an adult with a man she idealized. She was totally infatuated with his looks, his lifestyle and the sex. The sex was incredible, and she trembled every time he touched her. She didn't have a huge amount of experience to compare with, but she just knew Tony was the best lover she would ever have. She'd had the usual awkward teenage romances in the back seats of cars, under the bleachers at school and even a threesome once at the dorm room of an older girlfriend but nothing compared to a night of coke and sex with Tony.

They'd boarded the smelly Greyhound at six that morning. Tony immediately fell asleep and snored loudly the entire time. Bess was fidgety and wanted to talk about the new city and all the fun things they'd be doing together. She kept her mouth shut after her first attempt to rouse him resulted in a sharp rebuke. Tony had never spoken harshly to her before, and her feelings were bruised.

She spent the time watching the pine forests of Mississippi slip past the window. Bess decided not to spend much time looking at the other occupants of the bus. The majority of whom seemed a little scary to her. In fact, a couple of the seedier men kept staring at her and that made her extremely uncomfortable. The diesel engine droned on and finally lulled her into a half-sleep, half-awake revelry.

She imagined walking the quaint, deep south streets of New Orleans with Tony. They would have a great apartment in the French Quarter, and she'd watch him play at the best clubs.

Eventually, the bus arrived at the New Orleans Greyhound terminal after interminable stops along the way to pick up and drop off other passengers. Tony woke up grumpy and irritable and she began to get a picture of her future life.

In fact, life with Tony turned out to be a hellish nightmare for Bess. He was usually too drunk or too stoned to work, so she did. Some nights, he beat her when he felt particularly bad about himself.

He played with a few bands but never achieved any measure of success. Bess worked as a waitress in a crowded, smoky restaurant on the corner of Jackson Square called Pierre's. She generally made good tips from the tourists because of her looks and eager-to-please manner. The owner of the restaurant liked her and was exceptionally friendly. So friendly, in fact, he kept putting his doughy fat hands on her arm, leg or any other available body part. His name was Jesse Boudreau, and he enjoyed the power of being able to manipulate most of the waitresses into some particularly degrading sexual favors. Jobs were scarce, and he made it plain that if they didn't want to take care of Jesse, well, why should Jesse take care of them?

Bess avoided him whenever possible, and on the occasions that she couldn't, she told him to leave her alone. He always laughed and slapped her on the bottom.

"No problem, ma Chere," he would say in his best Cajun accent.

"You'll come to Jesse. Someday soon, you will."

One night after work, Bess made the mistake of telling Tony how uncomfortable this made her feel.

"You're coming on to him, aren't you?" he demanded angrily.

"No, Tony. I swear I didn't."

"You slut. You're fucking him, aren't you?" He slapped her hard across the mouth. She fell to the floor, whimpering. He unleashed a vicious kick to her midsection. It knocked the wind out her and she gasped for breath.

"Tony. Tony, no," she screamed, and he kicked her again.

"I'll teach you to cheat on me, you whore." He slammed the door and left her alone and crying.

Tony walked through the Quarter until he came to the restaurant where she worked. He sucked on a bottle of Cuervo tequila and wiped his mouth with the back of his hand.

Lights shone from Pierre's windows. They were not yet closed, so Tony leaned against a bench on Jackson Square and watched as the closing crew cleaned tables and swept the floor. One by one, the employees left for the night. Tony was waiting for one man in particular to come out, the owner.

The night wore on, and Tony grew impatient. He had consumed most of the bottle of Cuervo, and as he drank, he worked himself into a frenzy. He visualized this fat, rich bastard touching his woman. Sticking his greasy hands in her pants, and the slut probably liked it. On and on, he imagined what had transpired when he, Tony, had been working. You know, taking care of bidness. The bitch. The ungrateful slut.

Tony continued to drink and wait and watch. Sometime after midnight, the front door of Pierre's opened, and Jesse stepped warily out. He looked up and down the sidewalk, and then he turned back to lock the door. Tony lurched out of the shadows of the park.

"Hey, you. Yeah, you're the one. You're fucking my old lady, ain't ya?" Tony's voice was slurred from the alcohol, but the vicious, resentful tone still came through.

The restaurateur turned quickly to face his assailant.

"Who are you? What do you want with me?" he asked in a frightened voice. His heavy jowls quaked with fear. He had been robbed many times in this town.

"You stupid, fat fuck. You're screwing her, I know you are." Tony teetered on his feet but managed to look menacing, nonetheless.

"I don't know what you're talking about. I'm not screwing anybody." Beads of sweat had popped out on the man's forehead, but his fear was turning to anger. He had been in business on this corner of the Quarter for many years. His father had started Pierre's and had passed the business on to him. He was tired of being robbed, tired of being scared, and he also realized Tony was exceptionally drunk.

"You stupid fat, fuck. I'm gonna kick your ass." Tony took a step forward and raised the near empty tequila bottle as if to hit the man.

"Thirty years, I been here," Jesse said. Tony stopped, surprised.

"Thirty years of drunks, druggies, whores, and every sort of human waste. And now you." Jesse reached in his back pants pocket and pulled out a Smith and Wesson snub-nosed, thirty-eight caliber revolver.

Tony stood rooted to the spot and watched as Jesse raised the weapon and carefully sighted on Tony's forehead. Now Tony was the one immobilized with fear. He wasn't too drunk to understand that he was about to die.

"Thirty years and now who is the stupid fuck?" With that, he squeezed the trigger, and the Smith bucked in his hand. The bullet made a smacking sound as it plowed through Tony's skull. A small dark spot appeared on Tony's forehead, and he slumped to his knees on the pavement. The weight of his torso toppled him over backward in an awkward sprawl. His blood pooled on the sidewalk and ran into the gutter with all the other filth and debris.

THE POLICE HAMMERED on Bess' door just after dawn.

She had cried herself to sleep after Tony left. Bess had no idea where he was or what he would do. Many times, he would leave her to go, "take care of bidness", as he said. Sometimes he would be gone all night and returned hung over or stoned the next day. She surmised that taking care of business involved selling drugs. He provided her with an endless supply of coke, but refused to discuss where he got it.

"Just takin' care of bidness," he would say and lay out another line for her to do.

She had learned to gage his moods within the first few minutes of seeing him. The first time he struck her, she was so shocked that she didn't know what to do. It was totally foreign to her previous way of life. There was no doubt that her parents despised each other, but there had never been a hint of violence.

Bess had held back the tears when he slapped her that first time. She concluded she must have deserved it. Why else would Tony have hit her? She'd try to do better next time, so she could be good for Tony. He really deserved better than her anyway and surely, she could help him become what he wanted. So went the thoughts of a confused young woman, alone in a strange city.

The problem was, she simply didn't know what she'd done wrong. And the beatings continued. Sometimes she'd end up with a bruise or a black eye. She went to work and tried to cover it with makeup, and she'd explain it as an accident. Her female friends at Pierre's tried to tell her to leave the rotten jerk, but Bess refused to listen. Besides, she was afraid. Afraid of being alone in a city, afraid he'd track her down but mostly afraid of losing the coke or crank which he supplied for her burgeoning habit. Bess had discovered that crank was cheaper and gave her a more intense, longer lasting high than cocaine. Tony had encouraged her to use it, and on some occasions, they would stay high together for two or three days and nights continuously. One morning she awoke with Tony snoring by her side. She didn't know where she was, how she got there, or how long they'd been wherever it was they were. She discovered they had slept in an alley in Metairie. They were some forty miles from their apartment. Neither of them had any recollection of the binge that got them so far from home.

Now, some ten months after moving to New Orleans, she was awakened by the insistent hammering on her apartment door. Her eyes were puffy and matted together. She rubbed the crusty matter from the corners of her eyes. Her lips felt bruised and sore from the slap she'd received from Tony. But her ribs were the worst. She moaned in pain as she tried to sit up in bed. Her ribs felt as if they were broken and every breath she took caused her to wince in agony. The hammering on the door continued. She gritted her teeth and sat up in bed. Bess had to sit still for a moment to let the dizziness pass before she attempted to navigate to the door. The pounding on the door commenced again and she struggled to her feet and gingerly stepped to the door.

"Who is it?" she called out in a meek voice.

"New Orleans police. Open the door, please." It was a very authoritative voice, and she found herself obeying automatically.

Homicide Detective Vincent Hebert and his partner Cameron Volk stood at the door.

"Miss Morris. Bess Morris?" Detective Hebert inquired.

"Yes. I'm Bess Morris. What's going on?"

Uninvited, the two detectives moved past Bess and into the tiny apartment. Detective Volk began looking around the room and in the adjacent bathroom and kitchen.

"Just a minute...," she started to protest, but Detective Hebert interrupted.

"When was the last time you saw Tony Shea?" Hebert had her cornered against the wall. His imposing bulk seemed to dwarf her diminutive frame.

"I don't know, last night, I guess. What's going on?"

"What time last night, and how did you get that bruise on your face?"

Before she could answer, Detective Volk moved along side of Detective Hebert

"So did you fight with Shea last night?" Volk asked and stared hard into her eyes.

"No. Well, not really. No. I mean, well...we might have. A little, I guess." Bess was stammering, frightened, and confused.

"You'll be coming with us, Miss Morris. Tony Shea was found dead this morning and you appear to be the last person he had contact with." Detective Volk took her firmly by the arm and guided her out the door. She let him move her down the stairs and over to their car.

She was in shock, just trying to process the information they had just revealed. Tony just couldn't be dead. No, they're mistaken. It's somebody else. But she knew it was true. Tony was really dead.

Something was horribly wrong, though. These police officers were treating her as a suspect. She started to resist just as Detective Volk was about to have her bend down and enter their sedan.

"Just a minute. Where are you taking me? I didn't kill him. Why do I have to go anywhere?" She pulled her arm out of Volk's grasp. He snatched her arm back and squeezed, just a little, so she'd know who was in charge.

"You're being detained for questioning. If you're innocent, you've got nothing to worry about, right?"

"I don't want to go. Don't I get to call a lawyer or something?"

By now, Volk had guided her into the back seat and bodily pushed her over with his bulk so he could sit beside her.

"You're not under arrest yet, so you don't need to call nobody. Just relax, we'll be at the station in a few minutes."

Detective Hebert expertly navigated the busy New Orleans traffic, and he reached the precinct in short order.

The interrogation that followed was intense and frightening. She was seated on a hard chair at a metal table in a small interrogation room. She half expected to have a bright light directed into her eyes but that didn't happen. The rest of it was pretty well right out of a stereotypical cop show.

The detectives sat in carefully designed positions. Hebert sat across from her, and Volk actually sat almost behind her. They fired questions at her in rapid succession. She was confused and scared. Each question came from a different direction, and she had to turn her head to see Volk. Every question seemed to incriminate her more. She felt guiltier by the moment, and she was sure it showed on her face.

Volk insisted that she tell him of her involvement in Tony's drug business.

"Bess, I need you to tell me how much meth and coke you and Tony were moving." Volk stood up from his chair and leaned over her. He asked the question again and blasted her with his foul breath, stinking of cigarettes and stale coffee.

"I don't know what you're talking about. I don't. I never knew..." Volk interrupted her with his fist pounded on the table. She jumped, visibly shaken.

"Don't fucking lie to me, you little junkie. I see your types all the time. You'll be so strung out by noon that you can't sit still."

She didn't respond, but she knew he was exactly right. Right then she'd kill or die for anything to settle her jangled nerves.

"Who was he buying from?"

"I don't know. I don't." She looked up at him with her green eyes filled with tears.

"Ever been in a prison, Bess?"

She shook her head, no.

"Those old hides like you fresh young cunts. Don't they, Vince?" Detective Hebert nodded in agreement.

Bess looked down at the table and shivered.

"You know what they're gonna do to you, Bess? First, they'll take a broom handle and shove it up you so far, you'll think it's coming out the top of your head. Then you'll get to lick and suck whichever old hide wants you. Anytime she wants it, and any way she wants it. Ain't that right, Vince?" Again, Hebert nodded and this time he laughed. A bulge was growing noticeably in his pants. He was becoming aroused at the thought of watching Bess perform cunnilingus on another woman.

She started crying, and her shoulders shook with her sobs. "What do you want me to say?" she sobbed.

CHAPTER NINETEEN

The proposed date of the robbery was upon them before they knew it. Chet fussed over last minute preparations, and Larry grew increasingly pensive. He couldn't shake a sense of impending doom. Chet, on the other hand, was buoyant and optimistic. Larry wisely kept his misgivings to himself.

"Lar, it's time to take the van down the hill. Can you get away tomorrow?"

Down the hill referred to the Pig Trail. The highway wound its way over and down the Boston Mountains. The following day was a Sunday, and Larry had promised Karie he would mow the lawn and do some other chores.

"Well, I guess I could. I've got some stuff to do," he lamely replied.

"Look, Lar. If this operation is getting in your way, by all means, we'll just put it aside." Chet used his most acidic voice to chastise Larry.

"Gimme a break, Chet. You don't have a pregnant wife to keep happy, do you?"

Chet really didn't need the reminder of his singleness.

"Whatever. Can you go or not?"

"Let's go early, so I can get back," Larry said.

"How about now, instead?" Chet asked. They were at Chet's place working on the four- wheeler and checking their equipment. Larry knew Karie didn't expect him back until dinner time.

"Let's do it and say we did," Larry responded with forced cheerfulness.

"How 'bout we do it and don't say nothing."

Chet tossed the van keys to Larry, and they walked to the basement where the vehicle was waiting. Chet opened the garage door and Larry climbed in the stark white van. It started easily and Larry drove it out as Chet lowered and secured the door.

"Chet, did you change the license plate already?"

"Yeah, I borrowed a plate from a van in the junkyard. All I had to do was glue the date sticker from the real license onto the borrowed one. That way, if some cop actually runs the tag, it'll show up as a van." Chet was leaning on the driver's door of the van as he spoke.

"Head on out, Lar. I'll follow you in my truck." Larry nodded his assent and drove briskly out of Chet's driveway. Chet followed in his old black truck.

It was an Indian summer day, early in October. The leaves were brilliant hues of reds, oranges and yellows. Vivid green pines and cedars were interspersed among the colorful hardwoods. Larry wasn't normally given to fall foliage tours and sightseeing, but on this day, he took in all the sights as though he might never see them again. His sense of foreboding pressed down upon him like a weight crushing the life right out of his body. At moments, he found himself struggling to breathe. Nonetheless, he kept driving and eventually turned south onto highway 23, the PigTrail. Chet followed and as he drove, he too absorbed the colors, the warm fall air and he reflected upon the preparations they had made. In his methodical way, he was certain he'd covered every angle. The only unknowns were the people in the bank, and the most worrisome, Larry's performance. As the operation drew nearer, Chet became more focused and more determined. Larry on the other hand, seemed more ambivalent, even sometimes refusing to talk about it. Chet watched and tried to evaluate Larry's level of commitment. "Are you in or out?" Chet had asked a dozen times. Every time, the answer was the same. "I'm in. I told you that already." Still, Chet kept asking himself the same question, "Is Larry going to let me down when I need him the most?"

Larry drove the stolen van with some trepidation. He had an overactive imagination and every car that he met looked like an Arkansas State trooper. None of them were. He drove with exaggerated care. "Man, oh man, all I need is to get stopped for speeding or something stupid like that," Larry thought to himself.

Chet was thinking about the operation, as he had come to call it. Larry was fretting about all the bad things that could happen. His nerves were jangled, and he was on edge. At any moment, he expected a police officer to pull him over in the stolen vehicle. Sheepishly, he realized he'd probably spill his guts about the whole plan if he were ever to be questioned.

They proceeded down the PigTrail until they came to the Mulberry River. Chet and Larry had previously scouted the banks of the river and found a secure spot to stash the van. They didn't expect anyone would likely stumble across a dilapidated old barn on an obviously deserted farmstead. It seemed like the perfect location to hide a getaway vehicle.

This particular fall day, there was very little traffic on PigTrail. An occasional truck ground its way up the mountain and a few tourists took in the fall foliage. School had started, and soon the mountainous byway would be busy on the week ends with students traveling back and forth to the university at Fayetteville.

Larry turned down the dirt road that led to the secluded farm. Chet dropped back to avoid the dust cloud that billowed up from the van's passage. No rain had fallen recently, and the normally turbulent Mulberry was a quiet babbling brook. Spring and fall usually found the Mulberry crowded with canoes and kayaks. The river offered challenging water for those adventurous enough to try it and there were several stretches of relatively mild class I and II rapids. Those same stretches and others could quickly change their complexion with the spring or fall rains. As of yet, the fall rains had not started, and the river was deserted.

Larry found the barn and drove around back to enter it. Chet stopped at the edge of the barn yard and got out. He grabbed a broom from the back of the truck and walked toward the dilapidated structure. The metal roof was rusted and torn away in places by some errant gusts of wind. The oak boards that sheathed the structure were twisted and curled. No doubt sawn in some wretched back woods sawmill and hammered up when they were still green and unseasoned. The overall color of the barn was a dusty gray. The wood had been bleached by the sun and rain and wind to the characteristic light gray of most of the older structures in the area. There was no evidence that these boards had ever seen paint. The bottoms of the boards had long since rotted away or been eaten by termites. The doors to the building were hanging by rusted hinges that screeched in protest when Larry opened them to get the van inside. Larry eyed the hinges suspiciously, concerned that the massive old doors might possibly fall right on him. The hinges were attached with rusty old nails that looked ready to give up their purchase in the ancient wood. The barn yard was grown over with tall skinny weeds that struggled to find nourishment in the poor soil.

"All clear, Lar?" Chet shouted.

"No problem."

Chet entered the barn as Larry finished wiping all the fingerprints from the vehicle. They had taken considerable care to avoid touching the van after they had painted it and now it was a simple matter to remove a few prints from the steering wheel and door handles.

"Is there a house around here somewhere?" Larry asked.

"Naw. I saw some rocks piled up on the hill over there. Prob'ly a house place there at one time. Don't nobody live around here now," Chet replied.

"Can't figure how anybody could live out here. Middle of nowhere. This old farm couldn't have made any money."

"Lar, they were subsistence farmers. Forty miles from town. Must have been real independent people," Chet mused.

As Larry finished with the van, Chet walked out behind the barn and began sweeping the tracks. He obliterated every mark that the van had made in the dusty barn yard. Larry had run over several of the tall weeds, so Chet yanked them up by the roots. He kicked dirt into the divots made by the roots. He swept over the spots until the soil was uniformly smooth. Occasionally, Chet stopped to look around for any intruders but by all appearances, they were alone. He noticed a few odd footprints in the dirt, but they didn't appear recent. Larry joined him, and together they brushed out the last of the tracks, Chet with a broom and Larry with a branch he'd picked up.

"Should be safe. Don't ya think?" Larry asked.

"Yeah. It won't be here that long and besides, it don't look like nobody's been here for awhile."

They walked to Chet's waiting truck and got in. Chet started the old Ford, and they began to retrace their path back up the PigTrail. The truck rattled over the bridge at Turner's Bend and the Mulberry flowed slowly and benignly beneath them.

As they drove north, dark storm clouds were building in the late afternoon sky. The roiling clouds foretold of much turmoil to come.

In the old barn, dust began sifting down between the boards of the hayloft. A solitary figure arose from the moldy hay and peered over the edge of the loft.

CHAPTER TWENTY

C het awoke slowly. It was not yet light, but he could tell it was nearly sunrise. A warm furry bundle was curled against the back of his knees. Max stirred and stretched as Chet slid out of bed. It was Sunday, and Chet had a busy schedule planned for his last day before returning to work. Disturbingly, the event most occupying his mind was his upcoming afternoon date with Bess. He planned to take her hiking on the Pigeon Roost trail in the hills overlooking Beaver Lake. The rugged hiking trail climbed and turned through the Ozark hills much like the PigTrail wound its way through the Boston Mountains to the south.

Chet had bought food for an intimate picnic on the bluff over a quiet cove. His backpack would contain a blanket, lunch, a bottle of wine and well...who knew what could happen.

Max blinked in the sudden light that Chet switched on. Coffee brewed as Chet showered and completed his daily rituals. Max waited on the bed for breakfast to be served. He was not a morning cat, and at the very least, he expected to be fed promptly after being awakened so early.

Chet completed his ablutions and took care of his hungry cat. Two cups of coffee and a light breakfast prepared him for a morning of preparations. He sat at the tiny dining table and methodically created a checklist of every item that would be needed for the bank job. This was Sunday and the plan was to hit the bank on the upcoming Friday morning. All the payroll money should have been transferred and the vault would be brimming with cash. His inside information had been very specific about the need to strike this

Friday and this Friday only. Chet had not seen fit to question the urgency; his silent partner was not one to be questioned lightly.

His checklist included weapons, ammunition, clothing, camo nets, uniforms, vehicles, fuel, lights and more. He played the mental video tape of the entire day in his mind, looking for any potential problems or missing details. He added checkpoints to his list as he thought through the plan. He'd played this mental tape a hundred times and it always started with their early morning departure from Larry's house for a fictional hunting trip and it ended back at Chet's hidden basement room, where they would count all the money. Everything in this movie worked like a Swiss watch. No screw ups, no problems, no worries. This time, though, he couldn't play the whole tape without getting distracted thinking about Bess. He'd get part way through the bank robbery and find himself thinking about her green eyes or her legs or...

"Focus. Focus, Max. I gotta stay focused on the plan." Max seemed perfectly focused on breakfast and was not the least concerned about Chet's inability to finish his checklist.

"Aw screw it." Chet stood up and kicked open the stubborn door. Max looked up briefly as Chet went outside and slammed the cranky door. He was torn between the need to work on his plan and the need to go see Bess. In the end, he was influenced by the primal need for female companionship. Chet jumped in his old truck and headed for town. Bess didn't expect him until almost noon. His watch indicated it was only nine a.m.

The drive into town usually passed with Chet thinking about the bank robbery and the many details that were involved. On this particular trip, he could think only of her captivating green eyes, firm body and warm smile. He hoped she wouldn't be angry with him for showing up early. The miles melted away and by ten o'clock, the old black Ford rolled into the parking lot of Bess' apartment complex.

The brakes screeched in protest as Chet slammed them on a little too hard.

Without thinking, Chet bounded up the stairs to her apartment door. He pressed the doorbell eagerly. Nothing happened. He waited and few moments and pressed it again. Silence, except for the kids screaming in the adjacent apartment.

Chet was puzzled. He knew she had worked the night before, so she must be sleeping really hard, he thought.

He stood outside her door and pondered the situation. Ringing the bell again seemed kinda rude, he thought. If she was really sleeping that hard, she probably needed her rest. On the other hand, he was dying to see her and get started on their adventure.

"Chet?" Bess asked from behind him.

He whirled around, startled. He blushed from head to toe.

"I...uh, well I guess I'm kinda early."

"I'd say about two hours early, Chet." Bess didn't look particularly glad to see him. "Well, come on in anyway. I've got some stuff to do this morning, but I'll fix you a cup of coffee, if you like."

Chet liked and said as much. He followed her inside. The living room was dark, and he got the impression that she hadn't been home at all the previous night. The air in the room was stale and musty.

She saw him look around, but she offered no explanation. He didn't know her well enough to ask and it wasn't any of his business anyway, now was it, he thought.

"Black?"

"Excuse me?" Chet was lost in speculation about her night's activities.

"Your coffee, do you like it black or what?"

"Black's fine."

Boy, she's a little testy in the mornings, Chet said to himself. Bess busied herself in the kitchen preparing the battered old coffeemaker. She could sense Chet's curiosity, but she'd be damned if she was going to start explaining herself to this guy. The plain truth was, she'd scored some high-grade coke from a bar patron and together they'd partied all night. She wasn't real clear on everything that had happened, but some things are best forgotten.

"Thanks," Chet murmured as she handed him a scalding cup of coffee. He sipped the bitter, black liquid carefully and watched her over the rim of the cup.

"Bess, would it be better if we postponed our outing? I mean, if you're tired or something."

"No, Chet. I've been looking forward to this all week. It's complicated, you know. I had to work really late, and then I had to get some things done this morning. So, I'm sorry if I didn't react well when I saw you here early."

She held her hand up when Chet started to apologize.

"It's all right. Why don't I take a quick shower and freshen up. We can go in just a little bit, okay?"

"Sure. As long as you're up to it."

Bess nodded in reply and walked to her bathroom. Chet sat down at the cheap dinette set and sipped his coffee. Complicated, he thought. What did she mean, complicated?

After several minutes, Bess returned looking bright and fresh. She wore a tight, black tank top that molded itself around her firm breasts. She had khaki hiking shorts and sturdy hiking boots. The outfit was that of a healthy, young outdoorswoman. Chet was instantly charmed.

"I'm ready. How about you?" She spoke lightly and with her characteristic smile. She slipped on a faded light blue chambray shirt and buttoned it only part way.

"You bet. I've got everything we'll need in the truck. You look great, Bess."

She smiled and opened the apartment door for them to leave. Chet scrambled up from the couch and together they walked down the stairs to Chet's truck. She took his hand in hers with an easy familiarity. He was entranced and so excited to once again be with someone.

Bess hopped onto the seat when Chet opened the creaky old door for her. "It's a beautiful day, Chet. I'm really looking forward to this. I haven't been hiking for years."

Chet opened his own door and slid into his seat. The old Ford actually started on the first try and he was relieved.

They drove out of town and toward the lake. The place he wanted to share with her was secluded and incredibly beautiful. The old highway wound through tree-covered hills and periodically offered them views of Beaver Lake. They chatted comfortably about small things. The scenery made small talk easy.

Chet pulled the old truck into a gravel parking space created for hikers. A carved wooden sign proclaimed this to be the head of the Pigeon Roost Trail. A few other vehicles were already in the other parking spaces.

Chet retrieved his sturdy daypack from its spot behind his seat. It contained all the essentials for a long hike or even a night out in the woods. He checked the contents earlier and knew that there were four liters of water, freeze-dried food, first aid supplies and numerous camping gadgets.

Bess had brought a fanny pack and she donned this while Chet prepared his pack. Her pack contained what she considered to be essential for a successful outing. Cosmetics, tissues, handi-wipes, condoms and her drug paraphernalia.

Chet shouldered his pack and smiled broadly at Bess. "Ready for adventure?" he asked.

Bess smiled back and nodded. She had a different sort of adventure in mind. Chet's plans were still a mystery to her, but she anticipated a very hot afternoon of sex and the prospect left her tingling with excitement.

Chet signed his name at the trailhead list of hikers. The local park management insisted on each hiker signing the roster so they would have a way of accounting for missing persons should someone not return as planned.

The trail was narrow and winding. Volunteers had hacked this path through the dense undergrowth that bordered the park. Shortly after entering the trail, the terrain opened out into the steep woodlands that were characteristic of northern Arkansas. The ground was composed primarily of rocks and stones. Chert, limestone and very little dirt. Oaks, hickories, sumac, and dogwoods proliferated in the poor soil along with the ever abundant and aromatic cedar trees.

Chet led the way with his long strides, and he only thought to look back after some minutes. He expected to find Bess some distance behind because of his rapid pace, but to his surprise she was keeping up with him. And apparently with little effort.

"Sorry, Bess. I tend to walk pretty quick."

"Me too. This is beautiful country. Is the lake very far ahead?"

"No. Just a mile or so. We'll walk right along a bluff overlooking it in a few minutes."

"Look at that, Chet," Bess pointed at a white-tailed deer and her fawn. The young deer had obviously been born late in season. Its spots were still visible, and it ran on spindly legs to keep up with its mother.

"Beautiful creature. But so are you," Chet said in a quiet, sincere voice.

"Thank you, Chet. You don't have to say things like that."

Chet turned and placed both hands on her shoulders. "I know I don't, and that's the best thing of all. You really are a stunningly beautiful woman." He leaned forward and kissed her soft lips. She responded to his touch and her lips opened for him. She pulled him to her and gripped the back of his head with her hands. His tongue sought hers and she quivered with excitement.

Chet pulled back and looked deeply into her brightly shining eyes.

"Bess, let's walk on a little ways. I've got a special little place I'd like to show you."

Bess nodded and took his hand. They walked together toward the bluff that Chet had chosen for their lunch. Their pace was now slow and considerate. Chet savored each sensation, and he knew with some certainty that they would consummate their relationship that afternoon.

The trail was littered with newly fallen oak leaves, and their steps were cushioned by the layers of leaves and humus. They walked up steep, twisting tracks and down into cool, dark hollows. The hill sides grew lush with sumac, dogwood and azalea. Overhead, the squirrels chattered incessantly and leaped from limb to limb.

The trail was deserted other than for an occasional lone hiker. Chet nodded and spoke to everyone they passed. Bess merely smiled in greeting.

Chet led them down a lesser traveled path that veered off from the main trail. The way was steep and littered with fallen limbs and brush. They picked their foot placements carefully because of the treacherously steep drop-offs that bordered the trail.

A panoramic view of Beaver Lake appeared as they broke through the final barrier of brush.

"Oh Chet, it's gorgeous," Bess exclaimed as she took in the scene that lay before her. A small grassy meadow clung to the hillside overlooking a quiet, secluded bay. Verdant green hills specked with fall color surrounded the crystalline water and their shapes were reflected in mirror images on the glassy surface of the lake.

"I thought this might be a good spot for a picnic," Chet murmured as she took in the view. He pulled the picnic blanket out of his pack and spread it out on the ground. Bess stood with her hands on her hips and watched him lay out the blanket. He looked up to see her watching him. "Is this okay?"

She turned and put her arms around his neck for an answer. Bess pulled him to her and kissed him deeply again.

"Lunch can wait," she said and kissed him deeply again sending him into a frenzy of sexual excitement.

"Let's lay down, Chet," Bess murmured and stroked his hair. She looked down and the blanket and then back into his eyes. Speechless, Chet could only nod, and he felt his legs quiver as he knelt before her.

Bess didn't immediately join him on the blanket. She bent and loosened the laces on her hiking boots. She grinned at him as she kicked them both off. Her toenails were painted a soft pink.

"Like pink, Chet?" Again, Chet could only nod.

"It' my favorite color," Bess said and grinned again, this time at his discomfiture.

After a considered moment, she languidly began to unbutton the light chambray shirt she wore. Chet watched every movement of her fingers with rapt attention. She moved slowly, deliberately but there was no hint of drama, just a deliberate slow sensuality that spoke volumes to Chet.

Bess' small strong fingers finished with the final button and her shirt fell away. Chet could see how the tight black top fitted closely to every contour of her breasts. Her nipples were compressed by the fabric, but they were outlined, and he could imagine how hard they would feel between his lips.

He was completely entranced by her body and didn't see her eyes watching him. Bess moved even more slowly now. She could see the hunger in his eyes, and it did not frighten her. In fact, his controlled lust excited her more than words could describe. She shrugged the light shirt off her shoulders and let it fall to the blanket at her feet. Her fingers now dallied with the silver buckle of the belt that encircled her trim waist. She delicately slid the tip of the leather belt through the buckle and let it fall open. Chet couldn't take his eyes away from her hands. Her finger's slow steady movements captivated him. He'd been in many strip clubs before and had seen some amazing erotic performances, but nothing had excited him so much. Those shows had been raw and unsophisticated. Bess' movements were elegant, languid and fluid.

She let her fingers twist the brass snap through the buttonhole at the top of her khaki shorts. The zipper slid down with agonizing slowness as she opened her shorts. They too fell to the blanket at her feet, and she gracefully stepped out of them. Now Bess stood before Chet in a black tank top and black lace panties. Chet's eyes started at her bright pink nails and moved up.

Bess' legs were long, slim and browned by the sun. Her waist was firm and small. Chet's eyes stopped at the provocatively small panties that she wore. They were cut high on the sides and covered very little. Small curls of dark hair peeked out on each side and Chet felt his blood racing furiously through his body. He let his eyes move a little farther up to her flat belly. Bess had a pink jewel in a belly button piercing. Chet took in a breath. The sun glinted on the jewel and Chet looked up at Bess in amazement.

"Like it?" she asked with a knowing smile.

"My favorite color, too. Pink, I mean."

Bess laughed and Chet was charmed again by the melodious tone her laugh. It was deep and full, and he couldn't wait to hear it again.

Chet squirmed in his position on the blanket. He started to rise toward her, but she stopped him with a sharp look. She pointed imperiously to the blanket.

"Sit, stay."

He sat and she watched him for a moment. This was her game, and she would be completely in control. Too many times she'd been the one controlled and that didn't turn her on at all.

Chet wondered if he'd angered her or scared her, he never could understand women.

"Just watch, Chet. Just watch," she said with a firmness that allowed no discussion. He nodded silently and did as she commanded.

Bess crossed her arms and grasped the hem of her tank top. She almost laughed as she saw Chet unconsciously lick his lips in anticipation. In one fluid motion, Bess peeled the tank top up and over her head.

Chet's entire body froze as he saw her breasts for the first time. They were full and very firm with large, erect nipples. A distinct tan line outlined her milky white skin against the deep tan of her torso.

Chet forced himself to look up at her eyes.

"Beautiful...just beautiful," he whispered.

Bess smiled a slow smile. She'd seen that reaction many times before. Some quirk of genetics had blessed her with a slender build and full breasts that needed no augmentation. Bess had one more tan line for Chet to see. She watched his eyes travel back to her midsection as she slid her fingers into the side of her panties. Slowly, deliberately, she slid her panties down until they fell to the ground at her feet. Chet didn't say a word. He stared with frank fascination at the dark, curly pubic hair that she revealed. He studied every fold of skin and he yearned to explore every crevice, but Bess had other ideas.

She stepped out of her panties and moved toward Chet. She held out her hands for his. She grasped his leathery hands and pushed him back on the blanket. She moved to straddle him as he lay back on the blanket. Her breasts were mere inches from his lips as she pushed him back. He tried to lean forward to kiss them, but she pushed a little harder and he reluctantly lay back. She pinioned his arms to the ground and leaned over him.

He was amazed at the strength of her arms as she held him down.

"I'm stronger than you are, Chet. Never forget that." Chet was caught off guard by the matter-of-fact statement. Physically, mentally or emotionally? Chet wondered for a second. He would never be sure.

She continued to hold his arms for a few moments more as she looked into his eyes. She seemed to be seeking something and Chet, in spite of his urgent sexual need, was disturbed.

"I'll never hurt you, Bess. Never," he said with quiet conviction.

Bess leaned down, kissed him softly and released his hands.

CHAPTER TWENTY-ONE

Monday morning started with rain pattering on the roof of Chet's old camper. Max snored quietly at Chet's feet. Normally, Chet would have found it difficult to get out of bed on a cool rainy morning when it would have been so easy to just turn over and snooze away the day. Today was not an ordinary day. It was, in fact, the Monday before the robbery. Chet and Larry had only four days to complete all preparations for Friday's attack on Carbontown and the bank. Memories of the weekend filled his head for several moments. He relived the time that he and Bess spent together on the blanket overlooking the lake. It was simply the most erotic experience of his life. She'd been an enthusiastic and imaginative lover. They'd exhausted themselves and then rested on the blanket in the sun. She curled up against him and rested her head on his chest. The sun and intense sex took its toll on Chet. He dozed off briefly. Bess lay awake, still with her head on his chest. She listened to him breathe and felt his chest rise and fall.

He awoke to find her looking up at him with those intense green eyes. He hadn't felt so good since he could remember.

Now, he shook off the memories of the weekend and rolled out of bed before the alarm had a chance to sound. He flipped the alarm switch to off and stepped into the tiny shower. Max chose to enjoy the sound of the rain on the roof by remaining in bed.

Chet donned his Pinnacle uniform and readied himself for the day. He had to make the six o'clock sales meeting and then hit his route hard. He planned to make all of his stops and be off work by three or so.

He put out food for the still sleeping Max and shrugged on his rain jacket as he shoved open the sticky door of his camper. No sign of light appeared in the early morning sky. Sheets of rain poured down and drenched Chet as he climbed into the old Ford. The old truck started without complaint and Chet roared out of his driveway, spraying mud in all directions. He was bound and determined to be early for the meeting.

The roads were deserted as Chet drove into town. He didn't see another vehicle until he turned onto the main highway that led to Springdale. A few other early morning travelers braved the darkness and downpour. Springdale was a largely blue-collar town, and many of the plants started work early, so Chet could deliver uniforms as early as he wanted, most days.

Chet arrived at the plant before anyone else and he had to wait in his truck in the parking lot. Drivers were not entrusted with keys to the building. Chet fidgeted in the cab of his step van. He shuffled through his invoices and generally got organized for his day. It occurred to him that he'd never been early before, and it might not have been such a bad idea to get around a little sooner. Not that it would matter in just a few days. Chet's uniform career would continue just long enough for the heat to blow over. Then it would be the easy life. Caribbean beaches, those fruity drinks with little umbrellas and all the pussy that money could buy. Actually, Bess was starting to fill that bill pretty nicely, all by herself.

Chet's fantasy ended abruptly as vehicle lights swung into the parking lot and halted right in front of the building. The occupant left the lights shining on the door as he jumped out and ran through the rain to the building. Chet could make out Bob's rotund figure as he unlocked the entrance to the plant.

Chet started his engine and began rolling toward the office. He saw Bob look up in surprise. Bob stood in the lighted doorway and waited to see which of his drivers was getting around so early.

"Farmer? Is that you?" Bob was obviously astounded to see Chet so early in the morning.

"Yessir. I thought I'd get around early today," Chet responded cheerfully as he jumped down out of his truck and ran into the driver's room.

"Chet, what kind of bullshit are you trying to feed me? You've never got your nasty ass outta bed before five in your life." Bob stared hard at Chet.

"Just give me a chance, Bob. I'm trying to get right with everybody. I told you I'd get serious about my job, and I meant it." Chet stood eye to eye with Bob and didn't flinch or look away. Bob continued to attempt to stare him down for a few seconds. Bob was the first to avert his gaze.

"All right, Chet. I don't know what you're up to, but I'll find out soon enough. I've known you for a long time, ole boy."

"I've changed, Bob. Really."

"People change...rarely. By the way, you didn't need to get here so early. I cancelled the sales meeting. You would have known that if you'd been checking your messages," Bob replied sarcastically and turned to walk into his office. He didn't wait for Chet to answer. Chet shook his head in disgust. Bob was right, of course. Chet had never been an early riser, never would be. The plain, simple truth was – he hated the uniform business. Hated being nice to customers. Hated picking up their dirty uniforms, nasty shop towels and above all, hated picking up those goddamned, maggot-ridden grill towels from restaurants. Why, the first time he'd gone in the back of a restaurant and had to count those filthy towels, he nearly gagged. There was just something about rotting food on a terry cloth grill towel. Just the most nauseating, sickening smell. Almost a cloyingly sweet smell, that clung to your nostrils. He hadn't eaten out at a restaurant for nearly a year after that. There hadn't been a day of his life since he started the job that he didn't ask himself why he was doing this.

The fact was, he had done it for Josie. He worked like a slave to make a decent income for her. It didn't help. She'd become bitter and resentful after she discovered that she wasn't pregnant. The realization that she'd trapped herself in a marriage with a man that she really didn't love was overpowering. Their marriage was over as soon as it started but Chet was in love and Josie...well, Josie just needed more. That was what Chet told himself. She was a smart girl. She needed lots of attention and activity. As it turned out, he'd been a little short on everything she needed. They'd fought over money. She bought nice clothes and hid them from him. He bought guns, beer and stayed out with his buddies.

She found a friend.

Chet hadn't known about the affair, until the day she left. She was in love, she said. He made her feel...well, something. Chet never was exactly straight on what this guy made her feel. He knew exactly how he felt, though. Cheated, alone and foolish. The guy she'd fallen for was a successful local businessman. He was able to give her the new car, nice clothes, jewelry and from what Chet heard, they traveled. A lot.

"Ah, screw it," Chet muttered and continued walking through the darkened plant. He had already loaded his garments for the day's delivery, so this morning all he needed to find were his late pieces and any new garments that had been ordered for his customers. Several racks had been set up to hold garments for the drivers. Chet's was full of late pieces, as usual. "Goddamned plant. Can't they get my route together?" Chet's mood was rapidly declining. He was always getting the shaft by these production people. They just didn't care how much extra work they put on the poor driver. It never occurred to him that he created most of his own problems. Chet grabbed the bundles of garments and headed back outside. The rain had abated somewhat, and he finished loading his truck just before the next driver arrived. It was Larry, of course.

Chet stood in the doorway drinking a cup of the rancid brew that the vending company called coffee. He greeted Larry with a raise of his cup, "Morning, partner."

"Good morning. I'm pretty sure I ain't never seen you here this early."

"Yeah, Bob was surprised, too. Not in a good way, of course. Just surprised," Chet grinned ruefully.

"So why are you in so early? You know they cancelled the sales meeting, right?" Larry asked and the hard look he got from Chet answered his question.

"We got four days, buddy. Four days, and I don't feel good about nuthin'," Chet replied morosely. Larry walked past him and grabbed his few late pieces off a rack and swung the bundles of garments up so they rested on his shoulder. It was the typical uniform route man's fashion of carrying clothes. He walked back to where Chet was still leaning against the doorway.

"Look at that fat bastard, Chet said bitterly. They could see Bob sitting at his cluttered desk with his feet up. He was talking animatedly to one of the other drivers, gesticulating with his hands.

"No doubt chewing that poor guy's butt," Larry answered.

"Yup, just happy as a pig in shit." Chet could almost taste the bile well up in his throat.

"I'd say he's pretty content, Chet. Got it made, you know. The old man will keep him around forever."

"Content, huh? I'll tell you something, Lar. Contentment ain't nuthin' but the absence of misery. Content don't mean shit to me. I'm gonna live life from now on. No holds barred. All it takes is money and we know where that comes from."

Chet looked at Larry speculatively, "You in or out?"

"I told you I'm in. I mean it so quit asking." Larry's voice came out weak and unconvincing.

"You scared, Lar?" Chet's question was more of a challenge than a query.

"Sure, Chet. I'm concerned, but we've been over the plan a hundred times. The gear's all packed. The van's at the barn. I'll recheck the train schedule tomorrow. I mean, what else is there? What are you worrying about?"

Chet looked out of the open door and watched the rain steadily falling. He drained the last of the bitter coffee from the paper cup and crushed it in his hand. "I don't know, Lar. Just a lot on my mind, I guess. You stopping by the diner later?"

"Yeah, if you want. I gotta make my first two stops and then I got some free time. Coffee at eight?" Larry offered.

"Yeah, eight is fine. I can make my in-town stops and get there 'bout then. The rest of my route is outta town." Chet raised his hand in a wave and walked out in the rain. He boarded his truck and began his day's route, still deep in thought.

Larry loaded the new garments on his truck and returned to the office to check his box for messages. He scribbled a few reminders in his pocket notebook and waved at Bob who was still sitting in his office.

"Larry. Come here a minute," Bob shouted from behind his desk, feet still up. Larry stuck his head in the doorway.

"Morning, boss."

"What's up with Farmer? You know him better than anyone," Bob snapped without the benefit of a good morning.

"Nothing I know of. Why do you ask?" Larry replied innocently.

Bob glared at him. "He's been acting funny. You know, different. What's going on?"

"Well, I don't know. Really." Larry didn't look him in the eyes when he spoke.

"Don't bullshit me, Lar. That no-good sonofabitch is up to something, and you damn well know it."

Larry bristled. "No. I damn well don't. You got no call to talk to me that way, Bob. I'm your best driver and you damn well know that don't you?"

Bob raised his hand in surrender. He shook his head impatiently. "You're right, Lar. I'm just tired of Farmer and all his shit. But you don't worry about it. He'll fuck up sooner or later. He just can't help it." Bob waved Larry out of his office. Larry shuffled to the doorway and watched the rain pour down. "He just can't help it," Larry echoed and walked out into the rain.

CHAPTER TWENTY-TWO

C het's first stop was the Tyson kill plant. It was into this plant that truckload after truckload of chickens arrived to die. There was a peculiar stench that permeated the air around a kill plant.

Chet allowed his step van to coast to a stop by the back side of the stark concrete block building. It was actually a huge complex that covered dozens of acres. He was allowed to enter the building from the service door, but USDA regulations prevented him from actually stepping foot inside the massive complex. That was completely okay with Chet. He saw all the poultry processing that anyone ever needed to see. He grabbed several dozen white smocks from the rails in his truck and ran through the rain carrying them into the building. To get to the employee locker room, Chet had to step over the blood gutter. Three or four times a week, the gutter ran brimming full of fresh, warm chicken blood. Chet always tried to time his arrival to avoid that mess but today he could smell it as soon as he stepped off the truck.

"Oh, God. Here we go." Chet took in a deep breath and strode rapidly into the building. He purposely did not look down at the dark, red river flowing beneath his feet. The concrete gutter terminated at an underground blood tank. The fresh blood entering the tank disturbed the rotting blood already in the tank and a fetid stench permeated the room. Chet couldn't hold back the gag reflex that knotted his throat when the smell penetrated his nostrils. He hurried toward the locker room. As he entered the room, several maintenance workers were changing for their shift.

"Hey, rag man. My pants don't fit. I told you that last week," the voice was from a belligerent, red-faced man who glared at Chet. Chet gritted his teeth and fought back an equally angry reply.

"Yes sir, you did. I got them pants ordered but you know how that stockroom is, they haven't come in yet. I'll get 'em to you next time."

"I don't fuckin' want to wait till next time. My pants don't fit now. What are you gonna do about it?" The man glared at Chet again.

"I told you...I mean. Look Billy, it is Billy, right? I'm doing the best I can. I can't help it if your pants haven't come in. You're just going to have to wait."

"I'm gonna kick your goddamn ass, rag man. I don't have to take no shit off a goddamn rag man." The guy stood up and put his hands on his hips in a threatening posture.

Chet balled up his fists and started advancing toward the man. The rest of the maintenance guys went dead silent waiting for the inevitable brawl. Chet stopped. He had another agenda to follow, and a fight today would ruin everything.

"Okay, you're right. I had no right to say that. I apologize." Chet forced the words out with seeming sincerity. The guy was so surprised by the apology that he was speechless.

Chet took advantage of the silence and walked out of the locker room. He could hear the men laughing behind him. His face and ears were burning bright red with anger and humiliation. He hopped over the blood gutter and walked straight to his truck. He sat for a few minutes considering his options. He hadn't completed his delivery, but as sure as the world, if he walked back into that room today there would be a fight. The last thing he needed to do was lose his job and the opportunity to rob the bank over a fight with some stupid redneck. The sound of the men's derisive laughter was degrading and on any other day, he would've kicked that idiot's ass but today was not like any other day. He wasn't afraid to go back in, he was afraid of what would happen if he did.

Chet continued to ponder his options as the rain continued to pound on the roof of his truck. He hated the rain. Seemed like every bad thing that had ever happened to him had happened in the rain. It looked like today was heading down the same path.

He forced himself to focus on the issues. The most pressing issue was to get the customer serviced without a fight developing. The easy option would be to just leave and come back later, but Chet was determined to get his route done quickly so he could focus on the more important issue – robbing the bank.

In the end, he did what he knew he was going to do anyway. He went back in.

He carried in the rest of the day's delivery, consisting of several large bundles of smocks and a few uniform shirts and pants. The new pants for Billy were not in the load. In fact, Chet had completely forgotten to order them.

The blood trench was still running sluggishly as Chet re-entered the building. He never could get used to that smell.

"Come back to get your ass whupped, rag man?" Billy was still in the locker room. This time, though, no one else was in the room.

"No sir. I'm just going to finish my delivery and get outta your hair." Poor choice of words, Chet realized. The maintenance guy was almost completely bald.

"You're just pretty goddamn funny, ain't ya? Rag man." Billy glared at Chet.

Chet walked slowly and with elaborate care to the racks where the uniforms were hung. He could sense Billy walking up close behind him. Chet methodically hung up each bundle with extra care. He could almost feel the man standing right behind him. He could hear him breathing and could smell stale cigarette smoke. Chet raised his right hand up to scratch his nose and then he stepped back suddenly. His quick back step put him right against the other man. Chet drove his elbow back with all his strength and he could feel it plow into Billy's soft belly. The whoosh of air exiting the man's

lungs was followed by intense retching and gagging sounds. Chet turned around and put his hand on the fellow's shoulder until the retching and gagging stopped. The man's eyes were red-rimmed and watery as he slowly and painfully stood up straight. He looked at Chet with pure hate in his eyes. He started to speak but Chet held up his hand. The man actually flinched as Chet moved his hand.

"No, you be quiet," Chet commanded quietly. "I been dealing with your types all my life and I've had just about enough. Here's what's gonna happen. You're gonna get your shit outta your locker and go home or go to work or go to hell for all I care. Mostly, you're gonna get outta my way. If you want some more, I'll be available next week. I just don't have time today or I'd really kick you ass. Do you understand?" Chet held up his hand again. "No, no. Don't speak, just nod your head for yes or shake it for no."

Billy nodded his head in agreement. He was holding his belly and trying not to retch again. His stomach muscles convulsed with painful spasms. All he wanted to do was leave and he said as much. "Chet, just let it go man. I'm hurt and I'm leaving." Billy turned, still holding his belly, to go.

"No. Not just yet, Billy boy." Chet tightened his grip on Billy's shoulder. Billy looked up in fear. Like most bullies, Billy was by nature, a coward.

"If you're thinking about reporting this, I wouldn't." Chet looked him directly in the eyes, unblinking. Chet's voice held a menacing threat of extreme violence and vengeance.

"No, man. It was my fault. Let's just let it go." Billy looked around the locker room. "Look, man. I just wanna get outta here before somebody comes in. I'm done, all right?"

Chet nodded. "As long as it stays that way, Billy. I ain't got nothin but my job so if I lost that, well...I wouldn't have much left to hold me back. Now, would I?"

Billy nodded and twisted free from Chet's powerful grip. He walked briskly to the exit, still hunched over his aching belly.

Chet finished carrying in all the garments for his delivery. He walked through the winding corridors with the invoices to the front office and got them signed without incident. He was prepared to be challenged by the building security force or to be confronted by his contact at the office. She was a belligerent old purchasing agent who could be very difficult. He had no doubt that she would blast him if she even suspected that he'd slugged Billy. For once, she was mild and distracted. She signed his invoice without comment.

"Thanks, Sue. How's them cats doing?" Sue was a breeder of cats and many of his visits had been slowed down by having to listen to cat stories. Today she must have been busy plotting against some other vendor.

"Huh? Oh, fine. Thanks."

Chet escaped out of her office and trotted back to his van. The rain was still steadily drizzling down.

Chet drove to his next couple of stops and serviced them without incident. The customers there were always easy to deal with. Chet glanced at his watch when he got back into his truck, it was nearly eight o'clock. He slid the door shut and drove toward the diner. He rolled through the middle of town in a drenching downpour and coasted to a stop in front of the diner. Larry's step van was already sitting there. He could see Larry through the rain-streaked windows sitting at one of the front booths, already drinking coffee.

Larry raised a hand in greeting as Chet blew into the diner. He was flushed and still angry over the confrontation with the Tyson maintenance worker.

"Lar, you just wouldn't believe the shit I just went through."

"Prob'ly would. What was it this time? Customer wouldn't pay loss charges?" Chet was notoriously bad about collecting money due from customers. Bob was constantly riding Chet about his lousy performance at getting contracts renewed and collecting A/R money.

"No. That stupid fucker at the kill plant kept nagging me about a size change that he doesn't really need. Just kept on and kept on bugging me. Finally, he comes up behind me like he's fixin' to kick my ass and..."

"You don't mean to tell me you got in a fight with him?" Larry interrupted.

"Well, yeah. What was I supposed to do, let him kick my butt?" Chet answered defensively as he slid into the cracked vinyl seat of the booth.

"If Bob hears about it, you're done. He'll can you so fast it'll make your head swim." Larry was genuinely shocked that Chet would do anything that could jeopardize the operation.

"He's not gonna hear about anything. That old boy isn't about to speak up. It was his fault and he'd get canned by Tyson for starting a fight. What'd you expect me to do? Let him beat the shit outta me? Where's the waitress anyway?"

"She'll be around in a minute. You gonna kick her ass too?"

Chet's face went beet red, and he started to push himself up out of the booth.

"Sit down, Chet. I was just screwing with you. What else are you planning to do this afternoon?" Larry asked in order to take Chet's mind off the confrontation.

Chet slid down in the booth and pondered on this for a few moments. "Well, Lar, I'll tell you this much, I'm going to collect some very important information." Larry was irritated at being left out of whatever Chet was talking about, but he knew it would be fruitless to ask. Once Chet had made up his mind about something, that was it.

A rotund waitress finally showed up and took their order.

"Just coffee. Black. And two pieces of that cherry pie." Chet was used to ordering for Larry. It never occurred to him that Larry might want something else. Larry didn't protest.

She returned in a few moments with a cup, a carafe of hot black coffee and two generous portions of cherry pie. After the waitress left, the conversation turned to Chet's encounter with Billy, the maintenance guy. Chet related the exact details of the encounter. He kept checking his watch during their entire visit. Normally Chet was the last person to want to leave the coffee shop. Today was a notable exception.

"Listen, Lar. I gotta get going. I really need to get this route done by three or so. Things to do, you know."

"Yeah, I do know, Chet. I'm going to go ahead and call the train office today after all. I'd like to get everything wrapped up, so I don't have to worry as much when the time comes."

Chet got up to leave the table. He pulled a crumpled five out of his wallet and tossed it carelessly on the table. Larry was watching him speculatively.

"What?" Chet snapped when he realized Larry was staring at him.

"You baffle me sometimes, Chet. I just don't think I know what I've got myself into. You hold all the cards, and you only show me the ones you want me to see. Ain't that right, Chet?"

Chet glared down at Larry. "That'd be right, Lar. I do hold all the cards and I aim for it to stay that way. Any more questions?" Chet continued to glare.

"Reckon not." Larry looked down at his cup of coffee.

CHAPTER TWENTY-THREE

C het left the diner at a near run. He trotted across the wet parking lot and yanked the step van's sliding door open. He climbed in and just as he was about to plop down on the seat, he saw the manila envelope. It was on his seat, big as day.

"Well, I'll be...who the hell got in my goddamned truck?" Chet muttered furiously. He looked around quickly to see if the intruder was still in his truck. The truck was empty but suddenly Chet knew who had been in his truck and the realization sent a shiver down his spine. He carefully picked up the nondescript envelope and sat down. Chet ran his fingers all over the envelope without being able to detect the actual contents. Probably just papers. He wasn't expecting a bomb, but he was feeling pretty skittish. The whole situation made the hair stand up on the back of his neck and he started looking around, trying not to be conspicuous about it.

The parking lot was busy with vehicles coming and going. Chet looked intently at each vehicle, and he strained to see the driver behind the moving windshield wipers. Cars splashed past him, and he recognized no one. He watched the traffic for a long time but to no avail. The mystery would continue as it had for several months.

Chet turned his attention back to the envelope. It was completely blank, addressed to no one. Chet knew who was intended to receive this package. He'd been expecting to get something this very afternoon. He hadn't expected for it to happen this way.

Chet eyed the seal for a few moments before he summoned up the nerve to open it. He looked around one more time to see if any passerby looked more suspicious than the next. No one did and Chet warily slid his thumbnail under the seal. He lifted the flap ever so slowly. He peered under the flap, looking for wires or some kind of detonator. Papers. Just sheets of paper with neatly printed information. The contents did not surprise him, but they did serve to deepen the mystery.

There was a train schedule. Detailed to the minute, number of cars, approximate tonnage of coal and even the engineer's name. It showed the expected departure time from the mines and an estimated time of arrival at the vicinity of the bank. A second sheet listed all the potential local law enforcement officers, their armament and there was a photocopied duty schedule for the entire week. Another sheet described the bank employees, their names and the hours they were expected to be working on the day of the robbery. The name at the bottom of the list was that of the security guard. He was sixty-four years of age, overweight, armed with a Smith and Wesson 38 caliber service revolver. He had not qualified with the weapon since becoming employed by the bank.

And finally, there was a detailed blueprint of the bank. It showed every detail of the construction including the dimensions of the vault. There were overlays that depicted the electrical, phone, HVAC and plumbing systems. There was even a page that showed the entire security network. Chet studied each page carefully. He'd have given his eyeteeth for this information during the initial planning stages of the robbery. After some minutes of careful examination, he decided that the layout and dimensions that he and Larry had used were pretty accurate.

Chet shook his head in amazement. Who in the hell would have access to this sort of information, Chet asked himself. Was it a contractor? For a long time that seemed like a pretty good guess but now...no contractor would have access to all that information. As always, he had no answers. His mysterious benefactor never allowed himself to be seen and seldom heard. In fact, Chet had only spoken to the man one time. It had been a disturbing phone call that had caught Chet completely off guard. The phone had rung, late at night. It was less than a month after Josie had left for the second and final time.

"Hello," Chet answered the insistent ringing.

"Is this Chet?" The voice was soft, almost a whisper.

"Yeah, who's this?" Chet was tired of the constant telemarketing calls and this call was starting out to be just another one.

"Never mind who this is. I need to talk to you about an important matter." It was a man's voice. Muffled, but discernable.

Normally, Chet would have hung up on such a caller, but something piqued his interest.

"All right. What do you want? What are ya selling?"

"I know some people that you know. I'm told you might be available to do a job. It'd be worth your time." The man spoke in measured, even tones. Not persuasive, just matter of fact. Chet thought through this guy's words carefully. The caller didn't sound like a crackpot or a telemarketer so who the hell was this guy?

"Listen, mister. I don't know who you think you're talking to, but I got a job, and I don't need no more work."

"I know exactly who I'm talking to. I know where you work, where you live, that you owe over twenty grand in credit cards and who your wife's sleeping with. I know more about you than you know about yourself." The caller's voice changed from soft and measured to authoritative and insistent.

"Now just a goddamn minute..." Chet started to protest.

"No. You just listen for a minute," the caller interrupted. "You've got an opportunity here if you're smart enough to recognize it. But you only have one chance. After that I'll just find someone else, and you can keep on living the way you are."

Chet's temper started to flare but he controlled it out of simple curiosity. Besides, the prospect of continuing to live as he was had little appeal. Every day he had to force himself to get out of bed and go into town to a job that he hated.

"All right, I'm listening. What the hell are you talking about?"

"I won't tell you any of the details until we have an agreement on a few things. Fair enough?"

"I reckon it'll have to be," Chet answered warily.

"All right. What I'm able to tell you is that there is a substantial amount of money to be acquired. By substantial I mean at least six figures for each person involved. There would be some risk and quite frankly, it would be strictly illegal." The caller let that sink in for a few moments. Chet didn't reply. In fact, he was simply stunned into silence.

"Mr. Farmer, do we need to discuss this any further?" The caller's question was again matter of fact and devoid of emotion.

Chet's mind was reeling. He'd been through so much emotional turmoil in the last months that he'd lost all sense of purpose. He'd told Larry once that he no longer knew who he was or what he was supposed to be doing. Fact was, he didn't much care anymore. He sure didn't care about his job, his customers or even what happened to him in the future. His answer was no surprise to the caller. There couldn't have been any other answer from someone in Chet's situation.

"I reckon we do. You know I ain't got much going for me right now, so I don't much give a shit about anything. I could use the money, if it'd get me outta that shit-hole job." Chet's words were a little slurred. He'd been drinking most of the night, as usual.

"All right, Mr. Farmer. We can talk some more. Here's the rules, don't ever break even one. I'm very serious about that. Understand?" The caller's voice was again imperious, even threatening.

"I understand you're serious but there ain't no need to threaten me." Chet was incensed at the caller's manner.

"Mr. Farmer, there is every need for you to understand the seriousness of the venture you may be allowed to embark upon. Let me put it in simple terms for you. If you screw up, talk to anyone about this or try to cheat me, I'll have you killed." The last sentence was delivered in the matter-of-fact tone that sent a chill right down Chet's spine. There was no doubt in Chet's mind that this guy wouldn't think twice about doing just as he said.

"I... I understand," Chet stammered. He was shaken and a little intimidated.

"Rules, Mr. Farmer. Very simple. You will never meet me. You will never try to find out who I am or what I do or anything about me. Agreed?"

"Agreed," Chet replied.

"You will follow my directions without question. Most of our communication will be accomplished by written notes and plans that I will have delivered to you. You will never copy, photograph or otherwise duplicate the materials I send to you. Agreed?"

"Agreed, but when are you going to tell me what's up?"

"Don't interrupt or question me again, Mr. Farmer. I don't like it." The stern rebuke was again delivered with the same cold, emotionless voice.

"Sorry," Chet replied. Why the hell was he even listening to this asshole, Chet asked himself?

"One final rule, Mr. Farmer..." The caller let the silence hang for several moments.

"Yes?" Chet could stand the silence no longer.

"If you contact the police, I will know about it instantly and you will die very badly."

Chet swallowed hard as a chill ran down his spine again.

"I understand," he said simply, and the phone line went dead.

CHAPTER TWENTY-FOUR

The second interlude in the meadow with Bess was just as intense and passionate as the first. Chet hadn't been with a woman since well before Josie had left. She had cut him off even before the affair started. Chet was not well adapted to a sexless marriage or a sexless life for that matter. They fought bitterly over Josie's decision to keep Chet celibate. He had to laugh when he thought about the whole situation. He'd been doing without and never gave a thought to infidelity. All the while, Josie had been getting all she wanted on the side.

He and Bess had redressed after their first lovemaking. Chet was uncomfortable being naked in the wide-open spaces of the meadow, but Bess enjoyed the feel of the sun on her skin. Nonetheless, she also slipped her clothes back on and together they spread out the picnic lunch that Chet had packed.

"This is great, Chet. I haven't been on a picnic...well, since I was a kid." In fact, as a child, she'd never been on a picnic. It just wasn't something her family would do. Stuffy dinners at the country club or perhaps one of the social clubs of her mother would have a catered luncheon somewhere but never something as informal as a picnic. The whole idea of a real picnic appealed to Bess in a quaint sort of way. She was truly touched by Chet's awkward attempts to be a gentleman and uncork the bottle of wine. She finally took the corkscrew out of his fumbling fingers and deftly uncorked the wine. Both laughed when Chet realized he hadn't packed any glasses for the wine.

"No problem, Chet. We can drink right out of the bottle," she laughed. And they did.

Bess turned out to be the fiery lover that Josie had never been. Chet was first taken aback by the aggressive way that Bess attacked him. He quickly recovered and found himself responding to her every move. After they finished eating, she pushed him down on the picnic blanket and landed right on top of him. He started to laugh but she covered his mouth with hers and stifled his laughter. She was all business and she meant for him to know it. Her scent filled his nostrils. It was a musky, exotic smell that he couldn't quite place. Her hard, small fingers probed his body while she kissed him deeply. Chet was so amazed by this wildcat behavior that eventually he simply lay there and didn't even try to keep up. Bess sat up abruptly and looked at the man she was straddling. She smiled slowly and began unbuttoning her shirt. Her movements were deliciously slow. Each button took an eternity to undo. He could see the cleft between her firm breasts as the shirt gapped open. She pulled the tail of the shirt out of her shorts and peeled the garment off her smooth, tan shoulders. The tight black tank top came off next. Chet's breathing was ragged and shallow. This woman excited him more than anyone before. She could feel the growing hardness pushing into her crotch and she swiveled her hips to grind against him.

Chet started to reach up and unfasten her bra, but she grabbed his hands and pushed them down to the ground and pinned him. "Not so fast. You just watch," she commanded. Chet let his hands lie limply on the ground beside him. Bess pulled the bra straps down off her shoulders and let him savor the view of her breasts spilling over the tops of the bra cups. When she was satisfied with his near frantic squirming, she slipped loose the front clasp of the bra and let her breasts fall free. "Oh, Bess. I just gotta..." Bess leaned forward and covered his protests with her lips. She pinned his hands down again. Her hard, dark nipples brushed his chest and she gasped at the tingling sensations. Bess pulled away from his lips and slid her body forward so that her nipples brushed against his lips. Chet lunged forward and captured each hard nipple between his lips to caress them with his tongue. Bess cooed and fairly purred with excitement. Once again, she pulled away and pushed him back to the ground. She stood up, still straddling Chet. He found himself gazing up at the two full breasts with nipples poking skyward. She languidly fingered the button at the top of her shorts. Still watching Chet's reaction, Bess undid the button and slid the zipper completely open revealing a dark, curly bush. "Oh, Bess..."

This time she didn't try to contain Chet's enthusiasm as he pulled her back down. The next few minutes were a blur of frantic groping, kissing, fondling and the resulting intercourse was intense and quickly done. They lay quietly together after the powerful orgasms subsided. Within a few minutes they began caressing each other and soon began moving together with increasing intensity.

Much later they lay side by side and enjoyed the feel of the afternoon sun on their naked bodies. A light breeze was blowing and the sensation of the wind on their skin was delicious. Chet drifted into and out of a light, dreamy nap. Bess didn't sleep. She lay awake and gazed up at the sunny blue skies. The woods were buzzing with insects and small animals. Occasionally birds flitted from limb to limb and Bess was content to watch them and the antics of the nervous gray squirrels that scampered from tree to tree. Occasionally, she would look over at Chet and she silently appraised the man with whom she'd just made love. She saw the strength in his hands and arms. The muscles were corded and heavily veined. He was lean. No fat around the middle to be seen. He was tough and hard all over. That bothered her a little. A woman kinda wanted a man with some flaws. She figured his were on the inside.

CHAPTER TWENTY-FIVE

Chet coasted to a stop in front of Larry's suburban home. No lights were evident, and Larry was not outside. Chet fidgeted behind the wheel for only a few seconds before the front door opened and Larry appeared.

It was just before midnight and raining again. The wipers on the old Ford clacked in a steady rhythm accompanied by Chet's fingers drumming on the steering wheel.

He was impatient to leave. Sleep had evaded Chet for the few hours that he'd spent in bed. Bess had fallen asleep on his chest, and he'd held very still to avoid waking her. It would have been so easy to just stay in bed with her. Just forget everything else in the world. He'd nuzzled her hair and breathed in the clean scent. So soft, he'd thought. She'd murmured in her sleep and snuggled closer.

Carefully, he'd disengaged himself from her arms. Ever so gently, ever so softly, he'd slid away from the warm soft body. It had been the most difficult thing he'd had to do for a long time.

Now, in the chilled darkness, he watched as Larry carefully and quietly pushed his front door shut. Chet could only imagine the turmoil that occurred when Karie found out that Larry was leaving at midnight for a hunting trip.

Larry pulled his jacket collar up and ran to the truck. He yanked open the door and jumped into the seat. His face was a mask of anxiety and apprehension. "Let's go," he said, without making eye contact with Chet.

For his own part, Chet was also anxious but now he was downright near panic. He was overwhelmed with feelings of foreboding and disaster. Not because of the inherent risks of the operation, but because of a certainty that he'd chosen the wrong partner. Chet was completely convinced that some how, some way, Larry would let him down when he needed him the most.

Nonetheless, Chet slipped the transmission into gear and let out the clutch. The old Ford rolled away down the wet street.

The drive out of town took only a few minutes. Springdale was nearly deserted at midnight. The second shift poultry plant workers were already gone, and the rain discouraged the usual casual traffic. They rolled out of town heading south on highway 265. Their path would take them through the outskirts of Fayetteville to highway 16 which led to the PigTrail, highway 23 south.

Chet and Larry were both silent as they passed through the little towns and villages that appeared through the rain-streaked glass. Each man was lost in his own imaginings of what lay in store.

After turning onto highway 23, few lights were to be seen. The farms and country homes were widely scattered and mostly unlit. They passed no other traffic on the wet, dark and treacherous road.

After thirty minutes or so of intense concentration on the road, Chet rounded a curve and saw the bridge at Turner's Bend. He slowed to a crawl as they passed over the river.

"Man, would you look at that," Larry exclaimed. The lights from the truck illuminated a river gone mad. Obviously above flood stage, the river pounded against the bridge abutments and threatened to engulf the outfitter's shop at the south end of the bridge.

"Yeah, the campground's history." Chet pointed at the swirling mass of water and debris where a scenic campground once occupied a quiet bend of the river. Indeed, the torrents of water had washed away the picnic tables and facilities that campers and paddlers had used during their float trips.

Chet drove on, awed by the incredible force of the flood waters. Larry looked pensively out the window, occasionally catching glimpses of small trees, brush and debris being carried away downstream.

The turnoff to their predetermined hiding spot was at the top of the hill that Chet had not too affectionately named, Agony. He turned the truck off the pavement and immediately the wheels started sinking into the gooey mud. Chet gunned the engine and the old truck bounced, jolted and spun its way to somewhat firmer ground. Chet drove slower now and spoke, "Okay, Lar. Let's do it just like we planned. We take the four-wheeler to the barn and get the van. You'll drive the van into town and park near the wooded hill. I'll meet you at..."

"I remember the plan, Chet. We've been over it a hundred times," Larry broke in.

"Okay fine, just don't fuck it up," Chet shot back and instantly regretted his words. The clearing at the end of the logging road came into view just then. Larry opened the truck door and hopped out even before Chet had fully stopped. Chet inhaled deeply to steady his nerves. Larry was standing, in the rain, red-faced with his fists clenched. The lights from the truck cast shadows on his face which only served to enhance his furious appearance.

"Aw shit," Chet muttered as he turned off the ignition. He climbed out of the truck and stepped toward Larry.

"Look Lar, we ain't got time for this bull shit. I'm sor..." Chet began.

"I'm sick of it. Sick of it, Chet. You're so God damned perfect. I'm gonna kick your ass," Larry sputtered.

In spite of himself, Chet laughed. The absurdity of the whole situation struck him as hilarious, and Larry looked so foolish standing in the rain shouting threats.

Larry charged. He literally lowered his head and charged like a bull. Chet was caught off guard and Larry's shoulder smashed into his midsection. Chet's breath whooshed out of his lungs and they both landed on the ground. Chet was gasping for air and Larry was kneeling on his chest with his fist cocked back ready to strike. Larry stopped, lowered his fist and stood up. Suddenly, his anger dissolved as quickly as it had flared.

"Chet. I'm sorry," he said quietly.

Chet finally caught his breath and propped himself up on his elbows in the mud. He looked up at Larry, "So, ready to go rob a bank or what?" Larry nodded sheepishly and said, "Reckon so." He extended a hand to help Chet get up.

They worked together for some minutes unloading the heavy four-wheeler. Larry set the ramps in place and Chet climbed up into the back of the pickup and mounted the four-wheeler. He pushed against the truck cab with a booted foot until the four-wheeler rolled down the ramps and the big, soft tires squished into the muddy ground.

Larry reached into the cab of the pickup and retrieved the shotgun. The heavy mist and humidity instantly beaded up on the well-oiled surface of the weapon. He slid it into a protective plastic cover and clipped it into the rack that was mounted on the handlebars of the four-wheeler. Meanwhile, Chet was adjusting the black nylon shoulder holster that carried his nine-millimeter Beretta. The weapon nestled under his left arm with a reassuring heft.

"Here, we're gonna need these for sure." Chet tossed Larry's camo rain suit to him.

They each donned the stifling PVC garments and began a quick, final check of the gear and bags.

The nylon bags which were to carry the money were carefully packed with all the essential equipment they would need. The front rack held the bag containing the wrenches and pry bar for unbolting the railroad track. A zip lock bag held two sets of stranded copper wire to use as jumpers. Electrical connectors were already crimped in place. These were bundled inside Chet and Larry's coveralls.

The bag on the rear rack held their phone company uniforms, phone company tool belts and assorted rolls of duct tape, cable ties, an entrenching tool and other handy items. The final bag was lashed onto the top of the fuel tank. This particular bag held the explosive device which would initiate the fuel depot fire. Chet had meticulously placed each component of that device in a zip lock bag and wrapped that in bubble wrap for protection. A separate bag held the remote triggering device. This was wrapped in multiple layers of bubble wrap and then surrounded by a waterproof plastic bag.

As they prepared to leave, Chet tugged on each of the straps holding this bag to the fuel tank. He couldn't and didn't want to imagine what would happen if that bag was subjected to the wrong sort of abuse.

Larry moved the truck into the thicket while Chet finished the last-minute checks. The old truck was nearly invisible among the cedars and young oak saplings.

Chet swung a leg over the four-wheeler and settled into the saddle. The engine came to life with a throaty roar and idled down to a quiet purr. Larry mounted up behind just as Chet yanked the machine into gear and they roared off down the trail. Larry grabbed for a hand hold to avoid being thrown off.

The trail was obscured by absolute pitch-black darkness and the steady downpour. Occasional flashes of lightning illuminated an unfamiliar scene. The trail they had scouted previously was now a dark and forbidding tunnel of overhanging branches and low hanging limbs that slashed at their faces. The rain rolled off the trees in blinding sheets and cascaded down the backs of their necks. They traversed rocky hillsides and descended into narrow defiles that ran with frothing streams of water. Their actual progress through the woods turned out to be painfully slow. The distance from the truck to the barn took only twenty minutes in daylight. Chet realized that the distance that they had covered in twenty minutes had been at full tilt on relatively dry ground. Now the headlight illuminated only a narrow path and he was constantly dodging low hanging limbs and brush. Their journey to the barn took twice as long as Chet had planned. Finally, they broke through the last of the woods and crossed into the open field adjacent to the old barn.

The dilapidated old structure loomed ominous, dark and forbidding. Larry looked over Chet's shoulder and couldn't suppress a shiver of apprehension. Mentally, he chided himself for such a childish reaction. Chet had no concerns for such issues. He was fuming over his lack of proper planning. How could he have underestimated the time required to cross that distance? Over and over, he beat himself up for such a blunder. He'd planned in a few extra minutes for each step of the operation and now he'd wasted much of his time cushion.

Chet raced across the barnyard and slid to a halt in front of the main doors of the barn. Larry jumped off and ran to open the doors. He pulled on the latch and the heavy planked door swung open. The blood drained from his face, and he stood stock still with his hands dangling at his sides.

"What? What's going on?" Chet demanded from his position on the four-wheeler. He couldn't see into the barn.

"It's gone. The van's gone," Larry shouted over the pounding of the rain.

Chet yanked the throttle open and nearly collided with Larry who quickly jumped out of the way. Chet drove right into the barn and the light from the four-wheeler shone on an empty room.

CHAPTER TWENTY-SIX

Bess and Chet's first romantic encounter occurred on the Saturday before the bank job. The days following that were a blur for Chet. He was torn between the conflicting emotions of a new and passionate relationship, and the overriding need to prepare for the robbery.

For her part, Bess wasn't conflicted at all. She enjoyed the sex, and she liked Chet well enough, but she had no intention of entering into a committed relationship so soon after getting out of prison. She had suffered miserably with Tony, and she had no plans to go through that sort of pain again. She wanted to take her time and find somebody that would treat her right. In fact, she wasn't completely sure she ever wanted to be with just one guy. Although Chet didn't know it, she had a couple of other guys she was seeing as well, one of whom was a lot better in bed. She kept that information to herself, knowing that Chet would be crushed if he found out. It wasn't that she wanted to keep secrets from him, but what was the point in hurting the guy, she reasoned with herself. His demeanor concerned her somewhat. He was showing signs of getting pretty serious and that was the last thing she was going to allow.

Chet took the week off as vacation, ostensibly to go fishing and to scout his hunting areas. During the days, he spent way too much time with Bess just messing around. They went for walks around her neighborhood and in the country. He took her to his place and introduced her to Max with favorable results and she thought his place was cool. Max showed an unusual receptiveness toward Bess, allowing her to stroke his shiny fur. Chet took that as a good sign because Max rarely misjudged people.

There was an awkward moment when he took her for a ride on the ATV.

"Chet, why the green tape? It looks kinda goofy, you know?"

Chet was at a loss for words for a few seconds.

"Well...hunting. It's for hunting during turkey season. Those critters are so skittish, you just gotta camo up everything."

She pondered that for a moment and nodded thoughtfully. Hunting wasn't a popular sport in Germantown, so she knew little about it. Something didn't seem quite right with Chet's explanation, but she just couldn't put her finger on it.

They rode through the woods and Chet loved the feel of this woman with her arms wrapped around him. Her firm breasts were nestled against his back and those sensations resulted in an impromptu lovemaking session on the four-wheeler deep in the woods behind his property.

Bess reached around Chet and found the reaction she was expecting. Chet grunted in surprise when her probing hand encountered his firmness.

"Just checking the indicator, Chet," Bess giggled as she groped him. She knew very well that the proximity of their bodies would ignite Chet's passion again.

"Don't you think we ought to stop and take care of that?" she asked over his shoulder. He did, indeed, think just that. He pulled the four-wheeler off the logging trail and into a secluded clearing in the woods. As soon as the engine died, Bess leaned forward and kissed his neck in a provocative way and continued her exploration of his most intimate areas.

"Chet, I'd say this seat is a pretty good height. Wouldn't you?"

Chet hadn't considered anything of the sort right up until that moment. He quickly concluded that the height of the machine was just right...

Later, Chet showed her the beginnings of his house and she appeared to be impressed with his skills. He was dying to have someone to share his life with and this woman made him feel things he hadn't felt for a long time. She enjoyed the attention and the company, but she was afraid Chet was falling in love. Chet was concerned as well, he had trouble concentrating on the plan and getting Larry up to speed. And Larry was a huge concern to Chet – huge. Bess worked nights at the bar, so Chet spent the evenings of the last week with Larry working on the plan and practicing various scenarios in his basement. Larry showed up with considerable resentment from the pressure from his wife. She didn't like Larry to be away, and his excuses weren't satisfying her curiosity.

"Chet, she thinks I'm screwing around. I've never been gone this much, and she's pissed."

"Lar, for God's sake," Chet replied in exasperation. "Figure something out, would you?"

"Chet, I'm telling you she's the most suspicious woman I've ever met, and I haven't done a damn thing wrong. It's probably a good thing we don't have another car, or she'd be out following me around."

Chet shook his head in commiseration and said nothing. In his mind, Chet wasn't sure if the problem was Larry's wife or Larry. He didn't like the idea of Karie showing up unexpectedly.

The practice sessions went okay but Chet was never sure Larry was on board.

On Monday, Chet started waiting outside Jake's to pick up Bess after work and take her home. When she walked out of the bar, she was surprised to see Chet waiting in his old black truck. Her apartment was within a few blocks, and she wasn't afraid to walk alone in Springdale. She was flattered, and more than just a little relieved that he hadn't seen her leaving with anyone else. It'd been a close call because she was giving serious consideration to going home with two local boys who'd been flirting with her all night. Nonetheless, she agreed to ride with him, and she invited him into her apartment. Predictably, he spent the night and to her surprise, each night that week. The two other guys kept calling her at work and she put them off. Somehow being with Chet just seemed right.

They slept late and made love each morning all week, until Friday. Her concern about Chet was growing. She could see he was head-over-heels in love, and she wasn't. Well, at least she didn't think she was, but it was awfully nice to wake up with someone every morning. When she awoke Friday by herself, she was miffed. Why hadn't he said something? Who did he think he was? Where the hell is he? No, I'm not in love, she concluded. I'm not, dammit.

CHAPTER TWENTY-SEVEN

"Chet, what are we..."

"Shut up. Shut the fuck up," Chet bellowed. He beat the top of his thigh with his fist. "I shoulda fuckin known better. Nothing's working out. Nothin." Chet was livid. Larry had never seen him in such a mindless rage. Larry shrank back into the shadows and remained silent. Chet got off the four-wheeler and began pacing back and forth in the empty barn. Larry could hear him muttering to himself, obviously unaware of Larry's presence. Chet paced and muttered and paced some more.

"Improvise, adapt and overcome. Improvise, adapt and overcome," Chet repeated the phrase over and over. He considered and rejected every conceivable option that he could think of. Finally, he stopped pacing.

"Lar. Larry, come here," Chet impatiently motioned for his timid partner to approach.

"Here's what we're gonna do." Chet left no option for Larry's input. He chose to assume Larry would do what he was told. Larry wasn't so sure he was inclined to do anything. In fact, he'd been pretty damn glad that van was gone. He'd assumed that meant the operation was off. Apparently, Chet didn't share his assumption.

"We'll take the four-wheelers right into town. Nobody's around at this hour anyway. I'll drop you off at the ditch that runs under the train tracks. You start unbolting the rails. Be damn sure you attach the jumper wires first. First, you hear me?" Larry nodded, speechless.

"After I drop you off, I run straight for the fuel depot. I'll cut through the fence at the back and set the explosives just like we planned before. As soon as I get the device set, I'll come back and help you finish up with the tracks. With me so far?" Larry nodded again.

"Okay, after we get the tracks pried out, we'll move the four-wheeler back into the woods just like we planned and later we'll just walk into the bank, bold as brass. Everybody'll be lookin' at the train wreck anyway. Nobody's gonna be checking to see if we've got a phone van or not. Right?" Once again Larry nodded his assent.

"Well, get on. It's already after two." Chet pointed imperiously at the back of the four-wheeler. Larry wanted to protest, he really did, but Chet was standing there pointing and he just didn't have the balls to say anything. He got on the back and waited. Chet mounted in front of him. "Got something to say, Lar?" Chet said over his shoulder. "No, Chet. I'm ready," Larry responded after a moments pause.

Chet started the engine, yanked it into gear and rolled the power on. The knarly tires spun and sprayed the loose dirt and straw of the barn floor into a dusty plume that hung in the still air long after they had roared off into the drenching rain outside.

Chet drove with absolute abandon. Their rain suits were ripped and torn by brambles and low tree branches. The powerful engine responded to Chet's insistent application of the throttle. After what seemed an eternity of insane driving, they came to the culvert where they had reconnoitered in the rain weeks ago. The usually sluggish stream was running full of muddy, swift water. Chet eased the four-wheeler down into the water which, although fast, was only inches deep. Chet applied power and the wheels spun again, seeking traction on the muddy creek bottom. The masked headlight pierced the darkness of the culvert as before but with the majority of the lens obscured by tape it illuminated only a narrow section of the pitch-black culvert. Instinctively both riders bent forward at the waist although the ceiling of the concrete tunnel was well above their heads. Chet grimaced as several newly spun spider webs wrapped around his face as they drove. He mentally steeled himself to hold the handlebars and focus on driving rather than imagining the creatures that had spun those webs. In spite of the rushing water and clinging webs, they proceeded through the tunnel without incident. As soon as they emerged from the other side of the culvert Chet raked his fingers across his face to claw away the hateful strings of sticky silk. After leaving the darkness of the tunnel, they could begin to see the beginning of the dawn. The heavy rain clouds were starting to dissipate and faint traces of the morning sun were beginning to appear through the broken clouds in the eastern sky. The color of the light was a deeply hued red. Chet couldn't help but recall the old sailor's rhyme, "Red sky at morning – sailors take warning." Rather than being a comforting thing, the dawn only served to increase their anxiety. Time was running out, and they would soon be caught in full daylight without having completed their preparations.

Chet pushed the limit of the vehicle and raced down the water-filled gully leaving rooster tails of muddy spray in their wake. They jolted over unseen rocks and potholes but each clung to their handholds without becoming unseated.

They passed the spot where they intended to hide the four-wheeler and the bank building came into view. Chet paused momentarily and surveyed the situation. The area was deserted at that time of morning. The bank and its parking lot were illuminated by the streetlights which cast an eerie glow in the early morning mists and ground fog. No one was around, and Chet felt confident to continue past the bank and on to the low railroad bridge. He increased throttle again and they rolled down the trench past the bank. Each man looked up at the structure as they passed. Only the fates knew what was in store for everyone involved with the bank on this day.

Chet did not want to attract undue attention, so he slowed their speed somewhat as they passed the bank and approached the low railroad bridge.

"You got the tool kit?" Chet asked Larry as they neared the heavy timbers of the bridge.

"Of course. I'm ready," Larry responded.

Chet rolled to a brief stop just under the bridge and waited briefly for Larry to dismount. Larry rolled off the back of the four-wheeler and nearly lost his balance on the slimy rocks of the stream bed. He looked up at Chet for guidance, none was forthcoming.

"I'll be back as soon as I'm done," Chet said tersely and gunned the engine as he continued driving down the gully. He did not look back.

Larry stood in the calf-deep, swirling water and watched Chet driving down the waterway. He was tired, scared and incredibly excited. He half expected to be arrested at any moment, but the adrenaline was flowing, and it gave him the confidence to do what they had planned.

Larry hefted the small black canvas tool set. It contained two wrenches, an extension pipe for leverage, a tapered steel punch, a short-handled hammer, a specially fabricated pry bar for removing spikes and a set of jumper cables to maintain continuity between the track sections. He had measured the nuts and bolts himself on an earlier trip so he would have the correct wrenches for the job.

He slogged to the edge of the embankment and clambered to the top by holding on to the rough timbers of the bridge. The angle of the embankment was steep and very slippery. He was covered in yet more mud by the time he reached the top where he paused and collected his thoughts. After carefully surveying the area, he was pretty certain that no one was around to observe his activities. So, he unpacked the wrenches and moved to a rail section well before the bridge. Their plan was to derail the train in such a fashion as to have the cars pile up across the incoming and outgoing part of the street that led to the bank. By breaking the track before the bridge, the train engine should stop before plunging the few feet into the water which would cause damage or death to the operators of the massive engine. Larry had insisted on that detail of the plan. Chet was less concerned but as long as it didn't interfere with the success of the operation, he didn't care. He knew Larry was highly concerned about people getting hurt and that reminded him of the likelihood that Lar might freeze at just the wrong moment.

As Chet plowed through the water heading toward town, Larry knelt by the tracks and attached the alligator clips of his jumper cable to each side of the rail sections that he planned to disconnect. He wiggled the clips to insure they penetrated the rusty patina of the steel and would make good electrical contact. When he was certain the clips were securely attached, he fitted one wrench to the bolt and a second wrench to its nut. He slid the extension pipe over the end of the wrench and tugged. He tugged again and still again. The nut was rusted securely on the bolt. "Well, shit," Larry grunted with exertion and tried again. The stubborn nut refused to turn. He repositioned the wrench so he could stand on it with all his weight. He stepped on the end of the wrench and applied his entire one hundred and eighty pounds. It still refused to budge.

"Dammit." Larry looked around sheepishly to see if anyone was watching his performance. The area was still deserted. "Now what am I gonna do?" Larry muttered out loud. He moved his wrenches to the bolt and nut on the other side of the rail section. He tried again without success to break the rusted nut loose. He and Chet had practiced unbolting and moving several sections of track on their previous trip. What they had not considered was this was a very old rail spur that had been laid over thirty years before when the mines were at their peak. The railroad, like the mines, had shut down and the whole system was long overdue for maintenance. These bolts and nuts had not been unscrewed since the day they were installed.

Larry threw his wrench down in disgust. He recalled Chet's motto, "Improvise, adapt and overcome." What would Chet do? Larry looked around and saw an old, discarded timber next to the bridge. He figured the heavy beam could somehow be used for leverage, but time was rapidly running out. Larry pried the long timber out of its muddy place and carried it over to the rail section he was trying to unbolt. He replaced the wrenches in their proper positions and tried to find an angle from which to pry. There was no place to put the timber that would give him any mechanical advantage. He looked around in growing desperation. The only place he could possibly lodge the timber to use it as leverage was against the low structure of the bridge itself. They had avoided breaking track anywhere near the bridge because they did not want anyone to get hurt in the derailment. Larry was frantic. The red light of morning was growing with each second he delayed and finally he made the decision to break the track right next to the bridge. Hopefully, he thought, the train will be moving slowly enough that the engine driver could bail out.

In the distance, Larry heard the sound of an approaching vehicle. Frantically, he grabbed his jumper cables and wrenches and moved them to the rail section next to the bridge. He placed the wrenches on the bolt and nut. The heavy timber fit under one edge of the bridge structure, and he was able to angle it right over the end of the wrench. He applied all his weight to the timber and the nut still refused to move. Nearly in tears, Larry repositioned the timber and literally hung from the end of it. The nut broke free with a screeching pop that sent Larry to the ground on his back. The impact knocked the wind right out of him. He gasped for air and nearly panicked. He scrambled back to his feet and repositioned the wrench and timber. Each turn of the nut required considerable effort and time. The vehicle sounds in the distance became more distinct. Larry worked frantically to loosen the stubborn nut until it finally loosened enough that he could thread it off with his bare hand. He realized just as he was removing the nut that he had not installed the jumper cables.

"Oh, shit." Larry grabbed the cables from the ground and quickly clamped them into place. He looked back over his shoulder and cringed as headlights appeared in the distance. Someone, probably an early morning worker, was heading down the street toward the bank.

Larry realized he had left the tool bag sitting on the edge of the tracks where he had first attempted to break loose the bolts. Now the car was approaching the area where he had been working and he desperately needed the steel punch and hammer that was in the bag. There was no way to drive out the rusty bolt without a punch, but he couldn't afford to be seen running back to get the bag. The car was less than a mile away now and he could see it flying around the curves of the road heading right toward him. With no other choice, Larry crawled back over the edge of the embankment and waited for the car to pass. As the vehicle drew nearer, Larry could see that it was a sedan with a light bar on top. The county deputy was making his morning rounds and his path would take him right past the section of track where Larry's tool bag was setting. Larry started shaking violently in abject fear. He couldn't breathe. He crouched even lower and watched as the deputy drove into the loop that led to the bank. The vehicle was equipped with a spotlight which the officer aimed at the bank and the surrounding area. He stopped in the parking lot and illuminated the doors, windows and bushes around the building. He also swung the beam of his light toward Larry who gasped and fell flat on his face. The deputy's inspection was only cursory, and he failed to notice the tool bag or Larry who holding his breath in anticipation. Larry released a huge sigh of relief after the vehicle rolled past him and on to his other routine check points. Larry watched the taillights of the car dim in the distance before he could summon the courage to get up. He scrambled back up the embankment and ran to retrieve the tool bag. With just a few taps from the hammer, he was able to punch the old bolt out of the track section. He struggled briefly with the second bolt and tapped it out as well. With the track now unbolted, he proceeded to drive the pry bar under the first steel spike. He used the wrench handle and the extension pipe to lever the spike loose from its home in the heavy cross tie. The spike proved to be just as stubborn as the nuts and bolts. Larry persisted and managed to loosen two more spikes which gave him enough freedom to then pry the rail itself loose. He slipped a broad steel wedge in the gap between the rail sections. He drove the wedge with his hammer, forcing the gap to widen. By now, he was sweating profusely from exertion and nerves. He was working in near daylight would be easily observed by any passersby.

CHAPTER TWENTY-EIGHT

Across town, Chet was also working at a feverish pace. He had driven the four-wheeler like a madman down the gully and had climbed out onto the bank of the streambed near the town square. He quickly sized up the situation and decided to risk traveling down the town streets. He switched off the headlight and moved out. There was no time for surreptitious, careful movement to the fuel depot. He had to get there quickly and get everything set up before full daylight caught him. In the back of his mind, he could only hope Larry was accomplishing everything he was supposed to do. Chet had his doubts.

With caution thrown to the wind, Chet pulled the throttle wide open and roared down the quiet streets of the small town. Most of the houses were dark and there was no one on the streets. He flew around corners and nearly drove right in front of a county deputy who was making his rounds. The deputy had his windows rolled up and he was looking intently into the windows and doors of the downtown businesses with his spotlight. Chet screeched to a halt and waited. The deputy continued slowly down the street, checking each business but never looking back toward Chet.

Chet waited until the officer turned a corner and then he shot across the street and headed for the back of the fuel depot property. Chet carried his own tool bag which included a heavy-duty set of wire cutters. He removed the cutters from the bag and dismounted. He looked in all directions and listened for any activity. There was none. Satisfied that he could work without interruption, Chet moved quickly to the chain link fence and began cutting links. The heavy cutters were designed to cut much thicker wire so he no difficulty in rapidly cutting a suitable opening. Once he had a man-sized gap, Chet grabbed the bag containing the explosives from its place on the four-wheeler. Again, he stopped to listen and watch but he was still alone, so he proceeded to one of the huge fuel tanks. On his previous reconnaissance trip, Chet had been unable to actually get near any of the tanks, so he had no way to know which one contained gasoline. He wanted the more volatile gas rather than diesel to have a better chance of actually igniting an inferno.

The first tank he approached was labeled number two diesel. So were the second and third tanks. Frustrated, Chet had about decided that this was only a diesel yard when he came to a somewhat smaller tank that was marked, GASOLINE-HIGHLY FLAMMABLE in dark, bold letters.

The tank was located near the yard office which had a light visible through the window. Chet watched the office but saw no sign of movement. He proceeded to unpack the components of his explosive device and he laid them out in order on the soggy ground next to the tank valve assembly.

Methodically, Chet began to assemble the parts of his device. He picked up the tube which was packed with smokeless gun powder. He inspected it carefully to make sure it hadn't been damaged or had gotten wet during the trip down. It was fine, he concluded. Next, he examined the firing assembly, checking the spring, firing pin, and cartridge chamber. Again, everything looked to be in perfect working order.

Taking a deep breath, Chet screwed the components together except for the bullet which he held for last.

The valve assembly on the tank appeared to be about four inches in diameter and quite thickly constructed. Chet began to have his doubts about the ability of his explosives to penetrate the metal of the valve. Nonetheless, he continued to assemble his device and to attach it to the valve body. He chose to attach the business end of the bomb to the valve body rather than to a section of pipe. He reasoned that the valve body was of cast iron construction and therefore would be, hopefully, more brittle.

Chet had brought an assortment of stainless-steel hose clamps of varying sizes. He chose one of the largest to bind the device in place. He secured it with a second band for good measure.

All of these meticulous preparations took valuable time, and Chet's anxiety level grew with each second. Finally, he set the timer for a short fifteen minutes. That would be cutting it very close, he thought. But it was essential for the fire and police departments to respond to this side of town before the train derailment took place.

With shaking hands, Chet inserted the forty-five caliber tracer round into its chamber. He screwed the firing pin assembly into place behind the bullet and carefully pulled the firing pin back and slid the cotter pin into place. The cotter pin held back the firing pin against the stiff spring that would propel it into the primer at the bullet's base. Chet attached the tiny cable that ran from the cotter pin to the servo which would be activated by the timer. He was painfully aware that the tiniest slip of his clumsy fingers could trip the mechanism and set off the fireball that would incinerate him. He didn't slip and the mechanism was set. He pressed the tiny start button, and the timer began to count down from fifteen minutes.

Chet collected up his tools and took a quick look around for any stray evidence he might have left behind. He expected there would be little evidence for anyone to find after the fire, but he wasn't taking any chances. He didn't spot anything that he'd left behind and so he ran in a crouch toward the opening in the fence. Just as he neared the last tank before the fence, he heard the door of the yard office bang shut. He froze. The yard attendant was standing in front of the little building stretching and yawning. The attendant was an older guy with little ambition to fulfill his security duties, he was simply out stretching his legs. Chet watched as the man started walking in his direction. "Shit, shit, shit," Chet whispered in exasperation. The guy was walking right toward the gasoline tank with the explosive device in plain view. Chet slid the Beretta out of his holster and crouched motionless in the shadow of the diesel tank. The Beretta's slide was well oiled and made little sound as Chet pulled it back to chamber a nine-millimeter round. The morning light was still weak, but Chet couldn't be sure the explosive wouldn't be discovered, and if it was...well, he'd come too far to let some stupid security guard screw up everything.

The bleary-eyed guard was cradling a hot cup of coffee in his hands and his attention was focused on not spilling the scalding liquid as he walked. He continued walking past the gasoline tank until he reached a spot twenty yards from Chet's position. The guard stopped and leaned down to place his coffee cup on the valve assembly of a diesel tank. After he was certain that the cup was securely perched on the valve, he turned, unzipped his pants and proceeded to urinate noisily against the base of the tank.

Chet was shaking with anxiety and adrenaline. He wanted to shoot the guard just for being so goddamned stupid. He remained crouched, waiting impatiently for the guy to empty his bladder. After an interminable period of penis shaking, butt scratching and a particularly loud fart, the guard zipped his pants, retrieved his coffee cup and ambled back toward the yard office. Chet released a sigh of relief and some disgust. He could well imagine the whole operation being blown by some slob just being in the wrong place at the wrong time. As soon as the office door banged shut again, Chet ran for the opening in the fence and leaped upon the four-wheeler which started easily, as usual, with just a punch of the starter button. Chet yanked the machine viciously into gear and roared back toward the side of town where the bank was located. He'd lost track of the deputy's whereabouts, and this concerned him greatly. All he needed was some small-town Barney Fife getting in the way. As he approached the populated area of town, he slowed down to a crawl and began watching for people.

The sun was beginning to break over the horizon as Chet motored carefully through the little town. He warily looked each direction before proceeding down the deserted streets. The gully that ran through town was bordered by fences and guardrails to prevent the unwary from accidentally falling or driving into the creek bed. These obstacles also prevented Chet from reaching the relative safety of the gully with its steep banks. Chet had never felt so exposed while he looked for a likely spot to enter the creek bed.

A small-town park spread out to the edge of the stream bed and Chet decided that would be his best point of entry. Unfortunately, the park was adjacent to the town's only early morning business, the donut shop. The cheerful donut maker, Bud, had been at work since three that morning, and he was now turning on his lighted sign. He stepped out on the sidewalk to assess the coming day when he spotted a muddy four-wheeler rolling down Main Street.

"Well, what the hell?" Bud muttered out loud. "Don't that ole boy know he can't ride that thing on the street?" Bud proceeded out into the street and started waving his arms and yelling at Chet.

"Hey, you. Hey. Hey, you can't ride that thing in town."

Chet was headed directly for the creek bed when he heard an angry voice shouting. Chet turned to look over his shoulder. A plump little man in whites was waving and gesticulating wildly. Chet waved back and drove right through the middle of the park. His tires dug deep ruts in the grass and mud splashed out in rooster tails behind him.

Bud ran back around the corner and was headed for the police station when a huge fireball erupted into the sky, illuminating the street with a brilliant light. Seconds later Bud felt, rather than heard, a deep booming explosion. The fireball mushroomed into a greasy black cloud of smoke that looked for all the world like a nuclear explosion. Bud couldn't see the actual location of the fire because of the buildings but he could tell it was billowing up from what could only be one place.

"Omigod. It's the fuel depot." He started running for the fire station, stopped, ran a few steps back to secure his shop, stopped again. "Aw, screw it," he said and ran straight for the fire station. Bud was the volunteer fire chief, and his sense of responsibility got the best of him, and he decided not to worry about his shop. Besides, who would want donuts when there was a fire to watch? All thought of the outlaw four-wheeler was forgotten in his haste to respond to the blaze.

Chet ducked his head involuntarily when the blast wave reached his location. He looked back in time to see a second fireball rise into the early morning light and then more black smoke blossomed up and merged into the already huge mushroom cloud. Shortly after the first blast, Chet could hear sirens wailing in the distance over the sound of his roaring engine. He guided the four-wheeler into the roiling stream and headed for Larry's location near the bank.

In the distance he could hear a second and then a third blast. He couldn't see what was happening, but he assumed that the gasoline had ignited a couple of the other tanks. That wasn't part of the plan, but it certainly didn't hurt the situation. The thought that the Fuel Depot guard might be toast didn't overly concern him.

Chet rode the four-wheeler as fast as he could reasonably negotiate the rocky stream bed. The muddy water obscured his ability to see big rocks and deep spots, so he was worried that he'd get stuck or damage the vehicle. He stayed in the lowest parts of the stream bed so he would be less likely to be observed. The trip back to find Larry took only a few minutes and Chet was certain that he'd not been observed by anyone other than the dumpy little man in the white uniform.

Chet rolled under the railroad bridge to find Larry packing up the last of his tools.

"Did you get done?" Chet asked tersely. Larry glared at him. "Did you think I couldn't do it?"

Chet resisted the impulse to dismount and check Larry's work or whip his ass. He couldn't decide which would give him the greatest satisfaction. Instead, he just shook his head and motioned for Larry to join him on the four-wheeler. Larry slogged down the embankment and climbed on behind Chet. He held his tool bag with one hand and grabbed the handrail with his other. "Let's go," Larry urged. Chet looked back over his shoulder at the rising column of black smoke. The inferno was growing in intensity and huge tongues of dark yellow flames shot into the sky. Chet was a little astonished at the destruction he had caused and more than a little excited. He could feel the adrenaline coursing through his body. He forcibly slowed his racing thoughts and reminded himself to proceed with control. He'd put together a good plan and by God they were going to follow the plan. In the distance, he could hear additional sirens approaching from the east and from the west. The additional emergency crews were not part of the plan, but Chet figured they would not be a problem so long as the train derailment occurred as planned.

Chet clicked the four-wheeler into gear and moved out into the stream bed. He navigated the waterway as carefully and as quickly as possible. The chaos taking place on the other side of town provided adequate diversion, so Chet and Larry were unnoticed as they motored up the creek bed in full morning light. Both men were covered in mud as was the four-wheeler. As they passed the bank building, they looked up at the structure. Larry gripped the handholds ever tighter. Everything about this was wrong. Dead wrong, but he couldn't think of a way out. He was now a full-blown accomplice and there was no going back. Larry wondered about the explosion and fire. What if someone got burned or killed? He thought about all the volunteer firefighters that could get hurt. That would make him an accomplice to murder. How in God's name had he gotten himself into this mess?

Chet was also absorbed in his own thoughts about the impending robbery. He was elated that their improvised plan had worked so far but so many things could still go wrong. Larry had performed his role without a hitch, so Chet was somewhat relieved about his partner's shortcomings. Chet still harbored reservations about Larry. Chet was no psychologist, but he had learned to read people and Larry's fear and misgivings were as plain as day.

Chet had brought them to the place at the edge of the woods where they could climb up out of the gully. He eased the four-wheeler up to the edge of the bank and let the big knarly tires pull them up the shallow incline. Once on top, he gunned the engine and scooted back into the dense brush where they couldn't be seen.

The woods were deathly quiet as Chet touched the kill switch and the engine died. The birds, crickets and tree frogs were all waiting for the disturbance to pass. Larry dismounted wordlessly and stood waiting for Chet.

Chet swung his leg over the saddle and sat pensively for a few seconds before speaking. "Lar, we got this far. I reckon you can quit now if that's what's on your mind."

Once again, Larry was startled by Chet's perceptive evaluation of his thoughts. He wanted nothing more than to quit and go home to Karie.

Chet continued, "I know you're worried about how this is all going to turn out and I don't blame you none. In fact, it could get real ugly. Its gone okay so far, you know. But...well, I don't know."

Larry stood there in the woods, caked in mud and thoroughly miserable. He looked at Chet and tried to decide if Chet really meant what he said. Larry had a secret worry that Chet would literally kill him if he backed out. Chet had been his friend for many years but during this thing, he'd seen a side of Chet that he hadn't known existed. The Chet that Larry knew was good-natured and affable, although sometimes quick to anger. This new Chet was so single-minded in purpose and so driven that Larry hardly recognized him as the same man. Larry couldn't summon up the courage to say what was really on his mind.

"Chet, I told you I was in. I never said any different," Larry spoke quietly and waited for Chet's reply.

"I know it, Lar. But it's fixing to get real serious. We got by with a good deal of luck this morning but that could run out. You gotta be sure, a hundred percent. Are you in or out? Last chance."

Larry looked up and found Chet's eyes boring a hole right through him. He met Chet's gaze for a couple of seconds and then looked down. He chose his words very carefully. "Chet, I ain't let you down yet. Have I?" Chet shook his head, no. "Well, I don't plan to let you down now. I know you don't have much confidence in me, but I can hold up my part of the deal. Is there anything you haven't told me? Anything at all?" He looked into Chet's eyes again.

There was plenty that Chet hadn't revealed. None of it that Larry had a need to know, Chet figured. He answered the question simply, "No."

"In that case, I'm in. What's next?"

"Let's get outta these filthy damn things," Chet said, indicating the muddy rain suits. They peeled off the slimy plastic garments and tossed them on the ground. Their phone company uniforms were still reasonably clean but wet from sweat and the soaking rain.

"Man, we're a mess," Chet observed. He glanced at his watch; they still had a few minutes before the train was scheduled to roll past the bank. "Let's get cleaned up and ready for action."

The two men gathered up the rain suits and trudged down to the little stream. The water was muddy from the heavy rains, but it served to wash away the clinging mud that caked the rain suits. Larry had a neckerchief that he used to wash the mud from his face and neck. He rinsed the mud from it and tossed it to Chet who followed Larry's example. They looked each other over critically and after some final cleaning efforts, decided that they could pass for hard-working, although somewhat dirty, phone guys.

The plan called for them to be in the stolen van at this point. They were to have driven right up to the bank, waited for the derailment and then they would do the robbery. The stolen van was to stay right where it was in the bank parking lot while they escaped on the four-wheeler...

Chet verbalized his thoughts, "The only real difference here is how we get to the bank. We already done everything else. The way I see it, we just walk right outta the woods big as day. If anybody's looking out, they'll probably be looking at the fire anyway."

Larry nodded in agreement. The woods provided concealment for them right up to the edge of the field that bordered the bank parking lot. Once they entered the field, they were completely in the open and would simply look like phone company employees out checking for problems. The only reason they wouldn't run through the field on their way out was the lack of cover. They'd be right out in the open and would make excellent targets for any law enforcement that happened to get around or under the train.

"I reckon that'd work just fine, Chet. Nobody's gonna be looking this way anyhow."

"All right, then. Let's get the gear unpacked, check our weapons and get ready. We got to get in place before the train rolls through."

They walked back to the four-wheeler and unloaded the packs. Larry sorted through the phone company gear and laid it out on the forest floor in order. He repacked the tool sets and rain gear into the pack that would remain strapped the fuel tank. The other packs would be carried into the bank.

Chet removed the plastic covered Remington 870 from its handlebar rack. The weapon's covering was plastered with mud and dirt. He'd slid the shotgun into a clear plastic sleeve before clipping it into its mount. The weapon was in pristine, dry condition inside the bag. Chet worked the action a few times to confirm that it was operating properly. He removed the shotgun shells from a separate pouch and began loading the weapon. The first rounds he loaded were double ought buckshot normally used for hunting deer or other large game. The last round he loaded was the lightly loaded, Silly Putty shell. He hoped they would never have to use any of them.

He leaned the weapon against the four-wheeler and checked his sidearm. It was a Beretta, nine-millimeter, semi-automatic. He'd loaded it the night before with rounds that he'd carefully hand-loaded himself. Chet had set up an ammunition reloading bench in a corner of his basement room. He'd studied the science of reloading and had good success at loading just the right combination of powder, primers and bullets. He could manufacture rounds for accuracy or for brute power. The rounds he made up for this robbery were designed to do just one thing – kill.

Chet loosened the canvas sling that was attached to the shotgun. He slung the weapon upside down across his right shoulder while he checked the other equipment. The shotgun was to be carried in one of the nylon packs until they approached the bank. Larry's job up to that point was to carry the extra packs and keep a sharp look out for problems.

"Belts are ready." Larry pointed to the phone company tool belts that he had loaded with official looking tools. Chet nodded and accepted one of the belts which he fastened around his midsection.

"Let's get walking. We've still got to cut the phone lines going out. That oughta put the security system outta bidness," Chet observed.

The two men began walking toward the edge of the wood line. Larry looked back and confirmed that the four-wheeler was well hidden in its brushy thicket. Their path took them across an open field behind the bank. The field was bordered by steep, rocky hillsides that were all but impossible to climb. At the edge of the parking lot, Chet and Larry stood motionless for a few seconds to listen to the wailing sirens, horns and the occasional low explosion that could be heard from across the little town. Dark smoke continued to billow up in angry clouds that darkened the sky. "Let's check out that box, Lar," Chet commented and walked briskly toward the black utility box that contained the phone lines. Larry hustled to keep up with Chet's suddenly hurried pace. A distant rumble had stimulated Chet to rush. Along with the sounds of the emergency crews fighting the diversionary fire, he had discerned the noise of a heavily loaded coal train. They knelt by the plastic box and Chet began unscrewing the box cover. He had no sooner removed the lid when a voice disturbed his concentration.

"Got a problem with the phone?"

Chet and Larry were both startled by the appearance of a young boy of about eight.

He was sitting on a battered old red bike watching the two men intently. "You fellers sure jumped. You ain't doing something wrong, are ya?"

Chet looked sternly up from his work, "You got someplace you need to be?"

The boy leaned over his handlebars and said simply, "Nope."

"Well, why don't you go there anyway?" Chet was becoming flustered at this unexpected intrusion. The sound of the approaching train was distinctly noticeable.

"It's a free country, ain't it? I can stay here all day if I want to." The boy was stubbornly determined to watch the men working. Larry walked over to the boy and stood blocking the boy's vision of Chet's activities.

"You're mighty curious, ain't ya?" Larry asked.

"Nope, I just wanna watch. That's all."

"Nothing to see, my friend. We're just making some small adjustments to the phone system. You probably wouldn't understand," Larry spoke condescendingly.

"Well, I might. My daddy's a big boss with the phone company. Say, where's your van? All you guys are supposed to have a van." The boy looked accusingly at Larry and peered around his shoulder to look at Chet.

"It's around back, son. Why don't you show him where it is?" Chet looked at Larry with the hope that Larry would pick up on his meaning.

"So, where's your ID badges? All my daddy's guys have to wear ID cards," the boy was persistent.

"They're in the truck, son. Take him around back and show him the truck and our badges, okay?" Chet said impatiently.

"Yeah. Okay, we can do that. Come on around back and I'll show you the inside of the truck. That's where we keep all the tools and stuff." Larry tried to sound convincing. "What's your name, son?" Larry continued.

"Tommy. You guys are weird. I ain't going nowhere with you." The boy started backing up quickly. Larry followed him, uncertain what to do. Chet hurriedly snipped all of the phone cables in the plastic box. No alarms sounded. Chet stood up rapidly and joined Larry in confronting the kid.

"Son, what is your problem? We're just trying to work here and you're getting to be a real pain in the ass." Chet moved along side the boy who was clumsily trying to get his feet on the pedals. "Hey mister, you leave me alone. I'm gonna tell. I mean it. You leave..." Chet clamped one hand over the boy's mouth and wrapped a powerful arm around the boy's shoulder. He lifted the boy off the bike as Larry caught it and together, they walked to the rear of the bank. Larry rolled the bicycle along behind Chet and his unwilling hostage. Chet half dragged; half carried the little boy. Remarkably, no one was looking out of the plate glass windows or the entire spectacle would have been plainly seen.

Tommy struggled, kicked and tried to bite Chet's hand. "Hey, you little fucker. I'll knock the shit outta you," Chet growled and lifted his hand as though to strike the boy.

"Forget it, man. He's just a kid. Don't hurt 'em." Larry leaned the bike against the back wall of the bank and grabbed the boy's legs.

"Zip tie 'em," Chet said in a loud whisper. Larry pulled out some of the heavy-duty nylon cable ties that he carried for the purpose of securing the bank patrons and employees. He bound the young man's legs together at the ankles and knees. Chet lowered the boy to the ground and held him down while Larry fastened his hands behind his back. "Duct tape," Chet said, and Larry pulled the roll of two-inch tape from his pack. The boy struggled ever harder when he realized that the men planned to tape his mouth shut. Together they held the bucking child until Larry could wind the tough tape around the boy's head, covering his mouth. Larry felt a pang of remorse when the boy quit fighting and lay, nearly fetal, at their feet. Tears rolled down his grubby cheeks and lefts furrows in the dirt on his grubby face. "Tommy, just lay still. It'll all be over soon, son," Larry spoke soothingly.

"Put one between his hands and feet," Chet commanded, and Larry stared at him blankly. "Hog tie him, man. He's a kid. He can still hop, you know." Larry shook his head and fastened another cable tie between the boy's hands and his feet, effectively preventing any hopping.

"I can't believe this is happening," Larry muttered and glared at Chet. "He's just a kid. What if he gets hurt?"

"Nothings gonna happen to him. He'll be fine right where he is. They'll find him plenty quick enough." Chet was obviously not too concerned with the boy's plight.

"Let's get ready. The money train's almost here." Indeed, the train was moments away from the impending derailment.

Chet and Larry left the boy where he lay on the ground. The youngster sobbed quietly but no longer struggled. The two men inched around the side of the bank building and watched for incoming bank customers. The bank had only been open for a short while so the usual payday traffic had not yet begun. The parking lot held only a few cars and most of those belonged to bank employees.

Larry leaned against the building wall and waited for the upcoming impact. Chet hunkered down and chewed his grimy fingernails. It was not commonly a habit of his to be a nail-biter, but this day had given him every reason to start chewing.

Larry looked back at the boy lying on the ground. He could see the slight frame convulsing with sobs. He turned back to watch the spectacle. The train was just around the corner and Larry's attention was riveted to the low bridge over the track. What he did not observe was the little boy wasn't sobbing, he was choking. The trauma of being tied up had terrified him so much that his stomach had ejected its contents into his throat. The duct tape held his mouth tightly shut and no matter how he squirmed or fought, it didn't release its grip on his cheeks. He was drowning in his own vomit and there was nothing he could do about it.

The train was moving slowly but inexorably toward the bridge. Chet and Larry watched in fascination as the first engine came into view, followed by a second. The train was a long one, about a hundred and twenty cars. Each of the open top hopper cars was heavily laden with the shiny black material that would be used to fire the turbines in nearby power plants. Chet and Larry could see the engineer in the cab of the first engine. He was looking ahead toward the upcoming road crossing. He sounded the train's horn for a couple of short blasts to warn unwary motorists of the train's approach.

Chet found himself shaking with anticipation as he watched the huge locomotive roll right into disaster. It wasn't that he wanted anyone to get hurt, it was just so damned exciting to be creating all this chaos after living such a mundane and boring existence for so long. Larry was equally agitated but not for the same reasons. He was furious with Chet over the handling of the little boy. He'd told Chet up front that he didn't want to be responsible for anyone getting hurt. The whole thing was starting to look like a disaster from Larry's point of view.

The front wheels of the lead locomotive slid into the gap between the rails and sparks flew. The massive weight of the machine drove the steel wheels through the ancient wooden cross ties, splintering the thick creosote treated beams like matchsticks. The air was filled with the high-pitched screech of steel against steel. Chet could see the shocked face of the train engineer who was taken completely by surprise. The man's expression was of complete disbelief and horror. The engine's huge horsepower was still relentlessly turning the drive wheels, pushing the train further into the gap. As the engine tilted crazily, the engineer fell away from the dead-man switch that disabled the throttle. The massive diesel engine dropped to an idle, but not before the damage was done. Behind the first engine, the second engine was still pushing and behind that the long line of coal cars. Each hopper car was mounded high with the dark coal. Even though the train was moving relatively slowly, the momentum of the incredible weight of all that coal pushed the following cars into the melee.

Some motion in his peripheral vision caused Larry to turn and look at the boy. "Ah, shit," Larry shouted and turned to run to Tommy. Chet remained focused on the train wreck. He was oblivious to Larry and the boy in distress. The activity that had caught Larry's attention was the awkward thrashing of the boy and the distinct blue color of his face. Larry immediately realized that Tommy must be choking, or the tape was cutting off his air supply.

Larry rushed to the youngster and knelt beside him. The boy's face was a mottled blue and he was no longer moving. Larry ripped the tape from his mouth and grimaced in disgust. Vomit drooled from the little boy's mouth, so Larry turned the limp body over and thumped him vigorously between the shoulder blades. More vomit poured out of the child and Larry thumped him some more.

"Larry, Goddammit, we gotta go," Chet shouted in a hoarse whisper. He needn't have bothered to lower his voice. The sounds of rending steel, breaking glass and devastating impacts continued to mask any sound he could have made. Larry ignored Chet and continued to work on the boy. The cable ties binding the boy's limbs made it difficult for Larry to perform a Heimlich maneuver, which he was vainly attempting. Finally in desperation, Larry draped the child's body over his own knee and pushed. A final gout of vomit shot out of the boy's mouth along with a whoosh of stale air. Larry flipped the child over and cleared his small mouth of the vomit with his finger. Hesitating for only a moment, Larry leaned over and pinched the tiny nose shut. He covered the boy's mouth with his own. The smell of vomit nearly gagged him, but he saw a young life ending right before his eyes and he overcame his revulsion. Larry blew gently into the boy's mouth several times and waited. Nothing happened. He pushed on the frail chest four or five times and blew into his mouth again. Still nothing happened. Larry sat back in despair. He had received CPR training at work, but they never said it would be like this.

Chet was standing over him by this time. "Larry, we gotta go. You've done all you can do. It was an accident."

"He's just a little boy. We've killed a little boy," Larry glared at Chet and returned to giving the child breaths of air and pumping his chest. Miraculously, the boy coughed.

"He's breathing, Chet. I think he's breathing." Sure enough, the small lungs were taking in rasping breaths on their own.

"Okay, fine. Now let's go," Chet replied. He felt remorse at the child's condition, but he hadn't asked the little shit to interfere, now, had he?

Larry rolled Tommy onto his side so any other fluids could drain out of his mouth without choking him any further. As Larry walked away, he watched the boy on the ground. There was no way he could ever forgive himself if that child died. He reluctantly joined Chet at the entrance to the bank.

CHAPTER TWENTY-NINE

The massive impact shook the ground. Coffee cups flew off the desks and the vault alarms started shrieking their shrill demands. Momentarily, everyone was frozen in place before the panic set.

One customer screamed, the bank manager spilled a cup of coffee, and everyone started shouting and asking what happened. The elderly guard, John Bailey, was the first to look out the window. "The train's going over. It's a derailment," he shouted in his shaky old man's voice.

Everyone ran to the bank windows to watch the spectacle. The unheeded alarms continued adding to the chaos.

"Oh, my god."

"Look at that."

"Somebody call nine one one."

The coal cars began a slow-motion accordion dance. The first car buckled under the force of all the remaining cars. It broke free from its coupling and pitched over into the ditch. Rivers of coal poured over the top of the car and filled the watery ditch. The second and third coal cars did the same. The patrons and staff of the bank watched in amazement. They were so close to the action that they could see the buckling metal and spinning wheels that were no longer in contact with the rails. The entire wreck lasted for only seconds but to the observers it seemed to last an eternity. The remainder of the coal cars stayed upright as the third car came to rest in the ditch. The only sounds were from broken air lines and pouring coal.

No one noticed as the two apparent telephone company employees entered through the front doors. Larry lagged behind Chet in order to close the pleated curtains across the doors. Both men pulled down the nylon stockings that were rolled up under their phone company caps. Their features were suitably obscured before they stepped forward into the room under the surveillance cameras. Chet unholstered his pistol in one smooth motion. He'd already cycled the action and a round was waiting in the chamber.

Larry brought the Remington 870 up and noisily jacked a shell into the chamber. No one noticed. They continued chattering among themselves, exclaiming about the wreck. Chet and Larry looked at each other, perplexed. The plan had been for that sound to get everyone's attention.

Chet nodded toward the security guard. Larry moved forward and gently placed the muzzle of the shotgun against the old man's check. Old man Bailey stiffened but did not panic. He slowly started to raise his hands in surrender. Larry pulled the Smith and Wesson service revolver out of the cracked leather holster that Bailey wore around his considerable waist. Larry hooked two fingers into the man's shirt collar and pulled him back away from the windows. Still, remarkably, no one noticed. The customers and bank employees were glued to the unfolding spectacle that was happening just outside the window. They remained oblivious to the equally remarkable events transpiring inside the bank.

Chet produced a thick, heavy weight nylon cable tie with which he secured the old man's hands behind his back. Larry quietly pulled the now helpless guard to a small office just off the main lobby.

"Lay down," Larry said. The guard carefully knelt down and lay on the floor. Obviously, the effort caused his joints some discomfort. He groaned but did not complain.

Together Chet and Larry moved back toward the windows where they selected their next victim. The bank manager was a ruddy-faced man of some fifty years. Perry Osten had been a banker for most of his adult life and a robbery was his greatest fear. Larry gripped the man's shoulder firmly to get his attention. Perry impatiently snapped his head around to see who had the audacity to actually touch him. He literally squealed when Larry placed the cool muzzle of the shotgun against his neck. Perry's high-pitched voice finally grabbed the attention of his employees and of the few customers in the bank.

"Nobody move. Just stay right where you are," Chet commanded in his most authoritative voice. No one moved. Larry wrinkled his nose at a familiar smell emanating from Perry.

"Oh man, this guy's pissed himself," Larry grumbled. Sure enough, a large dark stain spread across the banker's trousers. One of the tellers failed to completely stifle a giggle. Perry, more red-faced than usual, glared at her furiously. She looked down and restrained her mirth.

"All right, folks. This won't take long, and nobody has to get hurt. You customers move to the center of the lobby." Chet motioned the frightened bank patrons toward the open space in front of the teller line. He scrutinized each face, looking for a hero. There were none. The customers were two older women and a farmer in overalls. The women would offer no resistance, and the farmer appeared to be too sensible to get himself hurt. Chet relaxed slightly.

"Good. Now you folks just lay face down on the floor. Don't look up. Don't move." The trio did just as they were told.

"Now, you there," Chet pointed to one of the two tellers. "Who, me?" asked the girl.

"Yeah, you. You come over here too." She meekly nodded and walked toward the people on the floor. Her name badge was engraved with Kathleen. She moved with assurance, unafraid but not seeking a conflict. Chet decided to keep an eye on her.

The giggly teller was left by herself behind the counter. She nervously glanced down at the inconspicuous button located on the front of her station. Larry noticed her eye movements.

"She's looking at something," he warned Chet.

"Don't even think about it," Chet commanded and swung the Beretta to point right at her face. She gasped slightly and reddened.

"That button don't work no more, anyway," he informed her. When they clipped the phone lines, he was almost certain that all communication was cut off to the bank. Almost certain.

"All right, now. You're gonna help me make a withdrawal, Tracy." Chet noticed her name badge.

"I...,uh, I can't. I just can't. I mean, I don't have the key, he does." She pointed toward Perry, still in Larry's control. Once again, he glared at the girl furiously. This time she glared back. Chet almost laughed at the ludicrous exchange.

"Give it up. The key, give me the key," Chet shouted. Larry poked the muzzle of the gun into the man's neck for a little extra encouragement. The effort was unnecessary. Perry had no intention of performing any heroic acts. The money wasn't his and he saw no reason to get hurt for it. Besides, he was humiliated by his loss of bladder control and he just wanted this nightmare to end and end quickly.

He lowered one hand toward his pants pocket. "Careful," Larry advised.

"It's in my pocket, okay? It's on my key ring."

"All right."

Perry produced a bulging key ring. He sifted through the mass of keys and isolated a single specialized key. The shaft of the key was dimpled with small perforations for the tumbler pins to engage. The lock this key operated would be nearly impossible to pick.

"Go get it," Chet told the girl. She nearly fell over her feet in her haste to cooperate. Perry relinquished the keys with a distasteful look aimed in her direction. He had some very definite plans for that young lady when this ordeal was over.

Without being told, Tracy moved directly to the vault. The main door was standing open but access was prevented by a barred inner door. She slid the key into the door lock and opened the inner door. The vault alarm still sounded its piercingly high pitched alert. She punched a four digit code into the discretely mounted alarm pad. Silence.

"Thank God," one of the women customers muttered from her place on the floor. The shrieking alarm was painfully loud in her hearing aid.

"Quiet," Larry commanded. He produced another nylon cable tie and secured the banker's hands. Perry offered no protest as Larry guided him into the same small office with the guard. He grimaced in disgust as the sopping wet fabric of his pants clung to his skin when he knelt down. He hesitated to lay fully down, not wanting to be trapped in his own urine.

"Get on down. All the way." Larry prodded him with the Remington.

"Oh, all right." Perry complied sullenly.

The bank guard sniffed. "Shut up," Perry snapped at the old man.

"No, you shut up," Larry snapped back. "Don't either one of you two move. Not one inch." Larry backed out of the little office and checked out the situation. The customers and one teller, Kathleen, were still quietly lying on the floor. Chet was headed into the vault with the other teller. Larry looked around and noticed a small room off the foyer. He tossed the guard's thirty-eight special into the room. The teller on the floor, Kathleen, was watching. Larry didn't notice. Instead he walked over to where the patrons and Kathleen were laying. He knelt down beside Kathleen. She looked up defiantly, expecting trouble. Larry kept an eye on Chet's activities while he whispered to Kathleen in conspiratorial tones.

"Listen, there's this kid outside. He's gonna need help real soon."

Kathleen perked up as soon as she heard that a child was in need. She was the mother of three and she doted on her own children. She started to rise.

"No. Lay back down," Larry spoke urgently in a hoarse whisper. He could see Chet at the counter. Chet's attention was on Tracy and Larry didn't want him to notice the conversation with Kathleen. She lay back down without protest.

"He got sick, see. He's out back. When we leave, you go see about him. Okay?"

"Of course I will. What's wrong with him?"

"I told you; he got sick. I mean, he threw up and I guess got some of it down in his lungs."

"Problem?" Chet called from the teller's counter. He was watching Larry talking to Kathleen.

"No. I was just telling her to stay put. No problem." Larry's voice didn't sound convincing to Chet.

"Okay, fine. Come on over here and keep an eye out." Chet was starting to have some serious doubts.

"You do like I said and there won't be any trouble," Larry spoke sternly to Kathleen.

Kathleen nodded and Larry stood up to help keep watch at the counter.

Chet slid his weapon into its holster and produced the three nylon bags. He tossed one of them to the teller under his control. She caught the bag and turned to walk back into the vault without being told to do so. It was apparent that she knew exactly what they wanted, and she had no plans to get hurt. Chet stepped into the vault and followed her past the safety deposit boxes and through a second security door which she unlocked with Perry's key and into the main chamber.

Chet involuntarily gasped when he saw the stacks of currency on the shelves. Never in his wildest imagination had he pictured so much money. There were canvas bags of coin on the lower shelves and all the upper shelves were neatly stacked with bundled packs of hundreds, twenties, tens, fives and singles.

He regained his composure quickly. "Just the big bills. Fill up that bag and be quick about it." The young lady instantly started reaching for some cash when Chet stopped her. "Just a minute, Tracy." He squeezed the bicep of her right arm.

"What? What'd I do?" She was wide-eyed with fear and no longer had any impulse to giggle.

"Where's the dye packs? I know you got them hid somewhere." Chet fixed her with his most intense gaze.

"In the front. We don't have any back here. We just keep those in the teller's cash drawers. Okay?" Chet continued to stare straight into her eyes, but she didn't flinch.

"Okay, let's get this done." Chet nodded and released her arm. He watched her for a few seconds and then opened one of the other packs to start filling it. He moved to the farthest most set of shelves and began stuffing bundles of currency into his pack. He positioned himself so that he could watch the girl and see what activity was taking place in the front.

From his vantage point, Chet could see Larry standing with his back to him. Larry held the shotgun at the ready and watched for any sign of resistance. Chet had drilled him with countless possible scenarios over the last few days. Larry was sick of the rehearsals.

They'd taped off the floor of Chet's basement to represent the bank. Chet had entered the bank on a couple of his reconnaissance trips and sketched out the dimensions. The tape on the floor represented the front door, the teller's counter, a scaled down version of the lobby and the doorways to the offices across from the tellers. The only aspect of the structure that remained a mystery to them was the vault. There was no way Chet could reasonably gain access to the vault without attracting undo attention. He had considered renting a safety deposit box just so he could gain a peek into the depths of that inner sanctum, but it just wasn't worth the risk.

They'd practiced entering the bank, rolling down their masks and then following a prescribed set of actions. Sometimes the scenario included a resistant bank employee or guard. Sometimes it was a heroic customer or even an off-duty cop. Each event had been carefully worked through, time and time again. Several times, the events had been staged to force Larry to fire his weapon. Larry had resisted Chet's insistent demands that he become accustomed to firing the heavy shotgun.

"I know how to shoot a gun, Chet," Larry had protested but to no avail. Chet set up man-sized plywood cutouts behind the mock teller stations. He'd also posed some behind office doors, in the vault and he made one cut-out that was painted with a police uniform. During each mock run through, Chet had shouted some command that required Larry to fire. When the weapon was loaded for the robbery, the first round would be the silly putty, but the second round would be for real. It was to be a heavy load of buck shot that would kill or maim.

Chet loaded the weapon with very light birdshot for the practice sessions. He didn't want large chunks of lead flying around his basement. The tiny birdshot pellets flattened against the concrete walls if they managed to penetrate the plywood targets. He and Larry wore long sleeved jackets and safety glasses for protection. The roar of the shotgun in the confines of the basement was deafening so after the first couple of shots, Chet dug around in his storeroom and found two sets of ear plugs. He meant for Larry to become accustomed to the feel of a heavy recoil, the smell of burnt gunpowder and the stunning sound that the big twelve gauge would make. He had no plans for Larry to be shocked or surprised during the real event.

The practice scenarios usually resulted in a stubborn opponent that took two shots to take down. Sometimes the first round might be expended against a teller or guard only to have the police officer burst through the front door.

Finally, Larry had had enough. "Chet, I know what I'm doing. I think you just like shooting guns inside your house." Chet stepped back and considered his words for a moment. "Lar, I want this to work. Nothing can go wrong," Chet spoke in his firmest, most sincere voice. "I know you're tired of this, but it's no game. These people will kill us if they can. We have to be ready. Let's go through it one more time." And so they did.

Chet had timed each phase of the operation and they'd gotten it down to less than five minutes in and out. They were just guessing about how long it would actually take to gain access to the vault. It all depended on how cooperative the manager turned out to be. In this case, the helpful teller had shaved precious seconds off their allotted time schedule.

Larry looked carefully at each of his charges. The girl, Kathleen, was quietly watching him, memorizing every detail she could see. "Put your face down." Larry pointed the muzzle at her. She complied after holding her rebellious glare for a few more seconds.

The old farmer was breathing heavily, and Larry was concerned that the old fart would have a coronary or something. The two women were in no distress, although one of them kept whimpering occasionally. Larry glanced briefly toward the office where the bank manager and the old guard were bound. He could see the old man straining at his bindings in a futile effort to break free. Larry sidled over to the door while still watching the room. "Lay quiet, old man. You don't want to be no hero." Old man Bailey snorted in disgust and lay still. He couldn't look up, so he fixed his baleful glare on Perry.

Larry moved back to his predetermined spot at the counter and waited.

Chet finished filling his first pack before Tracy was even halfway done. "Hurry up, girl. We ain't got all day," Chet snapped. Tracy jumped in fear. She frantically began stuffing any bills she could reach into the bag. Chet failed to notice she was stuffing tens, twenties and even singles into the pack.

Chet stepped through the vault door and motioned for Larry. Chet tossed the pack to him, and Larry immediately shouldered it just as they had rehearsed. Chet popped open the other bag and returned to the vault. Tracy was stuffing the bag with the last currency it would hold. She looked up as Chet entered. "It's full."

"All right. Fill this up too and faster this time." Chet tossed the empty pack to her and snatched up the full one. He grunted in surprise. The pack was significantly heavier than he'd expected. He wondered how in God's name he would be able to run with that much weight. Nonetheless, he pulled out the pack straps and shouldered the bag. His knees nearly buckled under the weight.

Larry was growing increasingly nervous. He could hear sirens approaching their location. No doubt the authorities were struggling with the decision to split their ranks between two catastrophes, but they had dispatched at least one emergency vehicle for the train wreck.

Larry fidgeted. He shifted his weight from one foot to the other. The weight of the pack was overbalancing him backward and he could picture himself flat on his back with his feet kicking in the air. Finally, he could stand it no longer. "Che...I mean...how much longer back there. We gotta go."

Chet turned furiously toward his partner. "Shut up. We've been in less than four minutes." Larry blew out his breath in exasperation and turned back to watch the room. He was becoming frantic with fear. His nerves were strung as tightly as piano wire. Unconsciously, he shifted his weight from foot to foot. Larry could hear the sirens getting closer and closer. The warbling sirens sounded like they were just outside the door when they suddenly stopped. Outside the bank everything was silent except for the continuing sound of compressed air hissing from the ruptured lines on the locomotive.

"Oh shit. Come on, man. Come on," Larry shouted frantically. Chet glanced at his watch. They were approaching five minutes in. Time was up. He grabbed the bag from Tracy even though it wasn't completely full. He zipped it shut as he ran out of the vault.

"We're outta here," Chet said under his breath as he neared Larry. That was Larry's cue to make his final instructions to the people in the bank.

"All right, you people. Listen up. We'll be leaving here in just a second. I want everyone to stay right where you are." He swung the barrel of the shotgun around the room menacingly. "Nobody needs to get hurt and this'll all be over soon, so just stay put." Larry managed his well-rehearsed speech without stumbling over his words. Nobody moved as the pair ran for the door. Larry, as rehearsed, poked his head around the blinds on the door. He scanned the parking lot and surrounding area for activity. He was amazed by the twisted carnage strewn across the railroad tracks. Larry nodded to Chet, and they moved out quickly.

The teller, Kathleen, bounded to her feet as soon as Chet and Larry made it through the door. She ran first to the empty office where she retrieved the guard's weapon and then she rushed into the office where Bailey and Perry were tied up. "Kathy, get me loose. My hands are killing me." Perry's shrill demands went unheeded. Kathleen went to the desk and found a pair of scissors with which she cut Bailey's bonds. The old man rolled onto his side and painfully pulled himself up. Kathleen handed his weapon back to him. Perry thrashed around in frustration. "Cut me loose, woman. Now!" Kathleen bent down to free him. She slid the scissors between his skin and the nylon cable ties. "Careful," Perry warned. "Don't cut me." Whether intentionally or not, the scissors cut a neat little snip of skin from the fleshy part of Perry's thumb. He squealed in pain and anger. "Goddammit, Kathy you did that on purpose."

"No sir, Mr. Perry. You were squirming around and..."

"Oh, never mind," Perry interrupted. He scrambled to his feet and rubbed his sore and now bleeding hands. He looked at Bailey who was also rubbing the circulation back into his arthritic old hands. "So, what are you waiting for Bailey? I pay you to stop robberies. Go get those guys."

The old man checked his revolver and started out the office door. "Mr. Bailey, wait," Kathleen spoke to him. He turned to face her. "Mr. Bailey, ...don't. I mean, it's not worth it. Those guys, well, they could hurt you. It's not even your money..."

"Kathy, shut up. Bailey, you do what I say, or you're done." Perry was livid and his voice had risen an octave. The old man swallowed hard and strode to the exit. He held the worn Smith and Wesson in his tired old hands.

"Mr. Bailey don't go out there please. There's a little boy out back. He needs help."

Perry interrupted, "Bailey, I told you for the last time. Go do your duty."

Old man Bailey went through the front door with Kathleen close behind. Perry hung back and watched to see what would happen next.

Kathleen turned toward the back of the building, not knowing what to expect. She saw a pale little boy, bound hand and foot. Her heart melted instantly, and she ran to him. Kathleen instantly recognized the smudged face. She brushed the stray lock of hair from his grimy face. He didn't respond.

"Why Tommy, it's you. I'll get you loose and then we'll get your dad. Tommy? Tommy?" Kathleen's voice caught in her throat, and she quietly began sobbing. She knelt down by the small body. Tommy had died while the robbery was taking place.

CHAPTER THIRTY

L arry bounded out the bank door with Chet right behind him. They slid down the muddy side of the gully. The recent rain had created a quagmire in the normally dry waterway. Water no longer ran in torrents but had settled in deep pools leaving only the small mainstream running down the gully. The mud sucked at their boots and twice Larry fell within fifty yards. The safety of the woods was still another hundred feet away when the angry hornet sound whizzed between them and something spanged off a rock to their front. A fraction of a second later, they heard the report of a pistol.

"What was that?" Larry blurted and kept running for his life.

"A bullet, you idiot," Chet snapped and looked back to see the old security guard aiming his thirty-eight service revolver at them for a second shot. Chet dropped to one knee in the muddy water and pulled the nine-millimeter Beretta from its shoulder holster. A faint puff of blue smoke appeared at the muzzle of the old man's gun and a hundred and fifty-eight grain semi-wad cutter bullet slammed into the pack strapped to Larry's back.

"Oh shit, Chet. I'm hit. I'm hit," Larry screamed.

"Get down and shut up, would ya," Chet shouted and Larry scrambled for cover behind a rock outcropping. He was only partially protected from gunfire.

Chet thumbed back the hammer of the Beretta and carefully took aim. Purposely he disregarded the fact that the man was preparing for another shot. The Beretta was fitted with a luminous three dot sight system. Chet centered the dot of the front sight between the two dots of the rear sight and settled this sight picture on the security guard's throat. He expected the bullet to impact at mid-chest, considering the range.

The old man fired again. This time, perhaps unnerved by the image of Chet aiming back, the shot went wide and splatted into the mud. Chet momentarily lost his sight picture when the guard fired. He regained his composure and resighted. He took in a breath, let out half and held the rest. He squeezed the trigger ever so slowly and the gun roared. A tiny nine-millimeter slug raced toward the security guard. The 110 grain SilverTip smashed the man's sternum, mushroomed and lodged in his heart. He fell without a sound and slid headfirst down the muddy slope into the filthy water.

Chet immediately rose and went to Larry's side.

"How bad are you hit?" he asked.

After gingerly exploring his back, Larry sheepishly admitted, "I guess I'm not hurt. I don't think the bullet went through."

Sure enough, the guard's bullet had lodged in the stolen money.

"Clean livin', Larry. It'll save ya ever' time. Now let's get outta here." Chet pulled Larry to his feet, and they began slogging toward the safety of the tree line. This time, Chet peered over his shoulder every few minutes.

They arrived at the tree line winded and mud-soaked but alive. No other pursuers appeared behind them to give chase. Larry dropped to the pine needle carpet to rest for a moment.

"Hold up Chet. I need to breathe a little."

Chet hesitated momentarily and checked behind them one more time.

"All right, but just for a second. We won't have too much time," Chet replied tersely. He pulled out his small telescopic monocular and examined the bank building and the area surrounding it. He was looking for indications that the authorities were beginning a pursuit, but his attention was caught instead by activity behind the bank. Chet slid the zoom feature on the monocular and focused in on a pathetic scene. He could distinctly make out the form of Kathleen, the teller, bent over a small figure on the ground. She was in the act of performing CPR on the little boy. It would require little imagination for most people to understand the anguish that she was experiencing. Chet looked at the image without feeling the slightest remorse. Normally a reasonably sensitive guy, Chet was wired on adrenaline, and he wasn't feeling much of anything except elation. At some level, he knew he should be shocked and appalled at the death of the bank guard and the almost certain death of the little boy, but he wasn't. He watched the woman rhythmically pumping the little boy's chest. Periodically she stopped to blow air into the tiny lungs. Pessimistically, Chet knew it would be to no avail.

Larry pulled his pack off and stuck his little finger in the bullet hole. He located the slug buried deep in the bundles of money. He held it up for Chet to see.

"Pretty lucky, huh?" Larry grinned.

"Yeah, luck was all it was," Chet said grimly.

"You were supposed to have disabled the guard. That was your responsibility," Chet said.

"I did. I mean I thought he was under control. I taped his hands and feet just like we planned." Larry was nearly whining in his own defense.

"What about the gun? The plan was for you to throw it in the gully as we left. How did he get hold of it?"

"Well, I guess I thought he wouldn't get it from the room where I tossed it."

"You're the one who was so worried about somebody getting' hurt, right? Because you didn't do your job, somebody's dead. You get that Lar?" Chet glared at his partner. "Do ya? It could have been one of us just as easy."

Larry took in that information with a stricken look. He felt like he was going to vomit.

"From now on, you do exactly what I tell you to do. Got it?"

Larry nodded, still reeling from the realization that his actions had resulted in the death of the guard.

"I just figured it'd be okay in that room, Chet. I mean...I had no idea that he'd...," his voice trailed off and he felt the bile rise up in his throat.

"Somebody must've cut him loose. Don't mean nuthin' now. Let's get going," Chet said as he rose to leave.

Larry started to protest this chastisement, thought better of it and followed Chet to the thicket where the four-wheeler was hidden. They dropped the heavy packs on the ground and Larry leaned the 870 Remington against one of the packs. This action infuriated Chet. He snatched up the shotgun and savagely shoved it into Larry's hands.

"Don't ever leave your weapon. Sling it," Chet commanded. He had that principle pounded into him by his drill instructor during boot camp and he still believed in it.

Larry, red-faced, slung the weapon over his head and shoulder without complaint. He proceeded to move aside the brush and limbs that hid the four-wheeler. He had known Chet long enough to know when to keep quiet and let the man cool off. Chet was as good-natured as anyone, but when he lost his temper - look out.

The machine was just as they had left it. Chet carefully rolled and folded the camo net while Larry backed the Honda out of its hiding spot. Chet stowed the net in its pouch, and they strapped the packs on the luggage racks, fore and aft. Chet strapped the third, smaller, pack on the fuel tank. Wordlessly, Chet mounted and started the engine. Unbidden, Larry mounted behind him, and they began their return journey.

They proceeded through the woods and scrub without incident. As they approached the highway underpass Chet stopped and killed the motor to listen. Above the normal traffic they could hear sirens approaching from the west.

"Let's get across quick, Chet. I bet those are state police and Ft. Smith cops coming."

Chet nodded in agreement. He paused long enough to reach down and collect a long willow switch before proceeding through the tunnel. As before, he waved the stick in a circular fashion to collect spider webs. He tossed the stick to the ground as they exited the underpass and emerged into full daylight.

Chet let the big soft tires claw their way up the muddy bank of the gully. He turned right and followed the trail they had explored previously. Their route paralleled the interstate and from time to time they could see law enforcement vehicles speeding toward the area they had just left. Chet paused on a wooded knoll to survey the situation. He pulled the tiny monocular from the pocket of his pants and scanned the terrain ahead. Finally, he scrutinized the area behind them for any sign of pursuit.

"Looks okay, Lar. Our trail is just a couple hundred yards ahead."

"I think we're gonna make it, Chet. I gotta tell ya I wasn't always so sure," Larry blurted.

"We're not home yet," Chet responded. "But it's looking pretty good."

"Chet?"

"Yeah, Lar," Chet answered while still scanning the woods.

"Chet, I'm real sorry about that guard."

"Forget it," Chet snapped. He stuffed the monocular back in his pocket and restarted the engine. The reminder of the man's death had disturbed him. He would wonder if there were children, a wife perhaps or did this old man leave no one.

"Don't mean nuthin'," Chet muttered under his breath as he started the four-wheeler rolling. At that very moment four state police vehicles screeched to a halt on the interstate. Two of the troopers crossed the grassy median and set up a roadblock as did the two on the other side.

Chet pulled in the brakes and stopped instantly.

"I don't fuckin believe it," he groaned.

"What is it, Chet?" Larry asked.

"Never mind, I see what it is," Larry continued.

The troopers had established their easternmost roadblock directly adjacent to the valley entrance that Chet and Larry had planned to take. Their intended path would be easily observed by the trooper who would no doubt find it unusual for two phone men to be traveling that way.

As usual, Larry looked to Chet for guidance.

"What now, Chet?"

"I don't know what now, Larry. Why don't you think of something for a change?" Chet snapped back. Larry said nothing.

Chet pulled the map out of its place and looked for alternate routes. Another valley leading north, with what appeared to be good terrain, was indicated on the map just east of the one they had planned to use. This posed the problem of bypassing the state troopers who were now engaged in checking each passing vehicle.

"All right, Larry, here's our options as I see them. One, we go back west and use the first trail that we explored. The terrain's pretty rough and we're taking the chance of running into anybody who's picked up our trail. Option two, we go farther east and take this valley north." Chet pointed to the valley with his finger on the map. Larry looked over his shoulder and studied the area Chet was suggesting.

"That's on the other side of the cops, Chet," Larry pointed out.

Chet spat and rolled his head around to fix Larry with a piercing glare.

"You have an amazing grasp of the obvious, Lar. I don't suppose you noticed the box culvert we just passed at the bottom of this hill, did you?"

"No Chet, I didn't," Larry said in a resigned voice. Again, he knew that confrontation with Chet was useless. Larry chose the path of least resistance and allowed Chet to run over him.

"Let's do it," Chet commanded and he wheeled the Honda around. The cedar trees and sumac bushes cloaked their movement as Chet picked his way down the slope to the wash leading to the box culvert. This culvert was shrouded by bushy willows and small sycamore trees. Chet eased the machine into the gravelly ditch. No water flowed here except during the heaviest rains. The big soft tires crunched gravel instead of slogging through mud.

Chet stopped at a sheltering willow and pulled out his massive Buckmaster survival knife. The razor-sharp blade effortlessly lopped off the required wand. He replaced the knife in its sheath and proceeded through the tunnel. He slashed at the spider webs as he went. At the far side of the culvert, Chet stopped and dismounted. He motioned for Larry to stay put. Chet crept cautiously to the top of the gully and observed the roadblock activity. It occurred to him that it was extremely fortunate that the police were rather narrow-minded in their search. Another part of the plan was happening just as expected. They had a friend helping to divert attention away from them for the moment. This was a part of the plan that Larry was not privy to because he didn't have a need to know, and the third partner insisted on remaining a very silent partner. Chet returned to the ditch and remounted in front of Larry.

"What's going on up there?" Larry asked.

"Nuthin'. Just searching cars for bank robbers," Chet chuckled in wry amusement.

"What's so funny?" Larry asked in confusion.

"Nuthin', Lar. Don't worry about it, man." Chet fired up the engine and yanked it into gear. They followed the dry wash for a good quarter mile south and then turned east for another half mile or so. When Chet was dead certain that he had put plenty of distance between them and the roadblock, he turned back north again. Larry looked back over his shoulder constantly. No one was following. At least no one that Larry could detect. The terrain they were crossing was more open now and they both felt quite exposed. The land on both sides of the highway was wide open pasture with the occasional scraggly tree. When they came to the interstate itself, yet another problem became apparent. The terrain was so flat here that no large drainage culverts were needed. The only option available to them now was to cut the wire mesh fence and then scurry across the highway. Once across, they faced the prospect of a hundred yards of exposed fields before reaching the relative safety of the wood line. Chet had sized up the situation and made his decision within seconds of seeing the terrain. For once, Larry was in tune with Chet's thoughts. He pulled the lineman's pliers from his tool belt.

"I'll cut the wire, cross over and cut the other side. Don't try to cross until I signal," Larry said as he slid off the seat.

Chet was impressed with his friend's initiative. Larry had not shown such drive since the whole operation began.

Larry approached the fence in a crouch and when a vehicle approached, he dropped flat on his belly and low-crawled the remaining distance. He began snipping at the bottom of the fence wire and found the wire to be tough to cut. He worked furiously when there was no traffic. As vehicles approached, he dropped down and waited impatiently. After what seemed an eternity, he finished cutting a gaping hole in the fence. Chet would only have to move the panel aside to pass through the opening.

Larry now poised himself for the dash across the highway. Eastbound traffic came at regularly spaced intervals, no doubt a result of the roadblock. Westbound traffic was not so predictable. A westbound traveler would certainly report a man running across the interstate at an upcoming roadblock.

He made two false starts. Unexpected traffic caused him to drop back to the ground and wait. On his third start, no vehicles appeared. He ran with all the speed he could muster and landed with a thump at the base of the fence on the other side. Very little concealment existed so he stayed low while he worked. The north side fence gave way sooner due to Larry's improved technique. Within only a few minutes he had severed enough wires to create an adequate opening. He watched for traffic and finding the way clear, he stood and waved for Chet to cross.

Chet responded instantly. He drove hard against the gap in the fence, and it flew open allowing him to pass through. Chet pulled the throttle wide open and roared across the pavement. He bounced over the median, across the westbound lanes and through the gaping hole that Larry was holding open.

"Wonder what the hell them boys is doing?" the trucker murmured to himself. Seated high in the cab of his 18-wheeler, he could see a camouflaged 4-wheeler crossing the highway ahead. At the side of the road, he could see another man holding the fence open. As he passed, he saw them racing away toward the wood line north of the highway. He pulled the cable on his air horn and sent a long blast echoing across the landscape.

Larry looked back over his shoulder and saw the big rig westbound. A premonition caused him to shudder involuntarily.

"That trucker saw us, Chet," he shouted over the engine noise.

Chet looked back and saw the truck in the distance.

"Don't mean nuthin'," he shouted back over his shoulder in reply and then he continued concentrating on reaching the concealing trees ahead. The field had been cut, raked and baled at the end of the growing season so the grass stubble proved to be the smoothest riding they had encountered during the entire adventure. Chet kept the throttle wide open, and they made the crossing in short order.

CHAPTER THIRTY-ONE

"Don't mean nothin. Not a thang." Chet's habitual reply to every problem had a hollow ring to it on the day Josie left. As he and Larry raced through the open field and into the sheltering woods, Chet found himself thinking back to that awful day. He couldn't shake it and he couldn't figure out why that day popped into his mind when he was busy with their escape. Nonetheless, the images and words were overpowering. The robbery was forgotten, and he ignored the cedar branches slapping him and the brambles that tore at his legs. Chet was completely entranced by the past as they drove north.

He was sitting on the steps of his camper with Max at his side. Josie had left in the rain and Chet was staring at the water filling her tracks. It had swirled and eddied in patterns of mud and trash.

She'd chosen a thoroughly miserable day to leave. It was a cold, rainy Saturday in February. The sky that day was overcast and threatening to snow or maybe sleet. Chet had been working hard all day. He was clearing brush and saplings with his chainsaw to make an opening in the woods for the house he was going to build. The work was backbreaking, but it was satisfying to Chet because it would be their home. Josie drove into the muddy driveway at noon. She honked the horn of her car impatiently and waited. Chet trotted out of the woods with a bright grin in spite of the bone-chilling cold.

"Hi, lady. I'm so hungry, I could eat a bear." Chet leaned over her window and dripped water onto her jacket.

"Careful, Chet. I just got that back from the dry cleaners." Josie was not smiling. She hadn't smiled much for a long time. She handed him a brown paper bag through the open window.

"Sorry, hon. Let's go in the camper and eat."

"I'm not staying, Chet. I brought your lunch. I've got some things to do," she replied coldly.

"Jo, we never see each other anymore. Can't you just stay for a little bit? I wanted to show you all the progress."

Josie glared at him for a moment. "All right, Chet. I guess now is as good a time as any. I'm leaving you," she said flatly and waited for his reaction.

Chet put his hand against the car roof to brace himself. His stomach tightened into a tremendous knot. He was wracked by a sudden bone-deep chill.

"I don't...I don't know what you mean, Jo." Chet shook his head in disbelief. Sure, he'd known she wasn't completely happy lately, but who was?

"You heard me, Chet. I'm leaving and I want a divorce. We've talked. Nothing's changed, nothing ever will with you. I need more and I intend to find it." She held both hands on the steering wheel and stared straight ahead. Her knuckles were white.

"Jo, you can't leave. I...I won't let you. You come inside right now, and we'll talk this out."

"There's someone else," she spoke the words quietly and continued to stare straight ahead. "I don't mean to hurt you but I'm not going to live like this anymore."

Chet was stunned. It was like a sledgehammer had slammed into his stomach. He stepped away from the car and stood in the rain. He couldn't think straight. He'd heard the words, but they just didn't register. He stared at a pool of muddy water at his feet. He looked up at Josie, "I don't understand. "

Josie turned her head and looked right at him. "Your stuff will be under the carport. I'm going to change the locks, so don't try to come into the apartment."

She rolled up her window and turned her car around. Chet walked dejectedly to his little camper and sat in the doorway with the rain pouring down the neck of his Carhartt barn coat. He was in shock. Someone else? He felt sick at his stomach. How could there be someone else? His mind raced through denial, disbelief, anger and finally profound sadness. He experienced all the facets of grief in a brief few moments. He thought back to an incident that should have clued him in to what must have been going on for months. She'd been spending increasing amounts of time on the computer. Surfing the net, she'd said. No big deal, she'd said. One night Chet had walked quietly up behind her and read some of the words on the screen.

"Josie, what the hell is that?" Chet had demanded. She was in a chat room conversing with somebody with a screen name of Xcentrik. Chet read this person's comments about his feelings and how emotionally isolated he felt and his feelings for her. Josie was typing her reply as Chet walked up. She literally screamed when he put his hand on her shoulder.

"Chet, don't you ever do that again. Don't sneak up on me." She angrily shook his hand off of her shoulder. "Don't touch me." Josie was nearly hysterical. She quickly punched the power button on the computer and the screen went dark.

Josie had reacted so violently that he didn't have a chance to question her activities. She grabbed her purse and stormed out of the house. He could hear her tires squealing on the pavement as she left.

When she left, he tried to summon up the courage to reboot her computer and follow the history to see where she'd been. Maybe it was denial. Maybe it was just fear of what he'd find, but he never touched her computer.

Now she was leaving again and as her vehicle bounced out of their driveway splashing water and mud in her wake, he reflected back over their life together. They'd been married almost five years now. He could still recall the panicky sound of her voice during a frantic phone call all those years ago. He'd driven to her dorm room and picked her up. She was in tears, nearly hysterical in fact. They drove to his apartment to talk. She had refused to tell him what was wrong until they were behind closed doors. She stood looking out the window with her back to Chet. He was stunned by what she told him.

She was pregnant. Or so she had thought. Chet was shaken by the announcement but after considerable reflection, he decided marriage wasn't such a bad thing. Josie on the other hand was devastated. All her plans and dreams for the future were gone. She cried, she screamed and finally she sat and didn't cry or talk at all. Just sat.

"It's okay, baby," he said after a few moments. "We'll get married, build a house. You know, all that normal stuff. We'll be a family." He was thinking about how different it would be from his life as a child growing up without a father.

She glared at him.

"Chet, I don't want to get married. I want a career. I want to travel. I want..." She broke down in tears again.

Chet sat helplessly beside her on the couch in his ratty apartment. He simply didn't know what to do. He'd expected some sort of gratitude for his gesture but all he got was a rebuke.

She finally pulled herself together. "All right, Chet. But let's do it quick before I change my mind. I don't want to walk down the aisle with a big belly." She wiped her eyes with a tissue.

"Take me home, no take me ...oh, I don't know. I don't know anything right now."

He'd taken in his arms and held her while she cried.

She'd avoided telling her parents until the last possible moment. Her mother asked repeatedly, "Are you sure. You've been late before. Are you sure?"

"I'm sure, mom. Positive, I came up positive on the test." She had purchased a home pregnancy test when her period didn't start. They were shocked but didn't argue when she told them of the upcoming marriage. Her mother asked if she loved Chet. She supposed so and said as much. Her mother carefully pointed out that there were other options.

"Josie, you could put it up for adoption and, well...you know. There's always the other thing." Josie was stunned that her prim and proper mother would even consider abortion. Josie wouldn't hear of it, and the marriage proceeded.

Chet's mother was ill, and she tried to be supportive, but it was obvious that she was unconvinced of the wisdom of the marriage.

"Chet, honey. I know you want to do the right thing, but you hardly know this girl. Son, I want you to be happy and life, well...life can be difficult with the wrong partner." It was the only hint that perhaps his parent's life together hadn't been all it could have been. Chet had always assumed that his parents had loved each other right up until his father's death. Now there was a nagging doubt that surprised him.

Chet and Josie went to the marriage license office in the county courthouse, and they submitted to the required blood tests.

"Chet are you sure. Do you really want to do this?" Josie tentatively asked as they left the nurses office after the blood samples were taken.

"Of course, Jo. I love you." In his mind, he really did.

The marriage ceremony was quick and very private. A few friends and family attended the ritual which was held in her parent's stately house. After hugs and frantic goodbyes, the couple departed for a weekend in Little Rock. They arrived at the hotel and quickly went to their room overlooking the river to consummate their vows.

Josie went into the bathroom to freshen up.

"Chet," she screamed after a few moments.

He rushed to the bathroom door. "What is it, Jo. Are you okay?"

She slowly opened the door and faced him, "My period, Chet. It just started."

CHAPTER THIRTY-TWO

D ub Cato saw the huge plume of black smoke as he drove south on highway 71. He pulled a double horse trailer behind his four-wheel drive Dodge pickup. Inside one stall of the trailer was a wiry quarter horse with whom Dub had lived for some 15 years. The sturdy sorrel had taken him hunting every year in the hills of Arkansas and on more extensive trips to the mountains of Colorado. It was a rare occasion when they did not pack out a large whitetail buck or other large game. Reb stood fifteen hands tall and had a piss n' vinegar disposition, as Dub would say. Together they rode in Christmas and Thanksgiving parades and every year they did crowd control duty at the county fair. In addition to his job as a security guard at the chicken plant in Springdale, Dub was a deputy on the Washington County Sheriff's Posse. This was a group of reserve deputies who wore their uniforms and cowboy hats at every public occasion and generally assisted the real deputies when called upon. They were issued badges, guns and had peace officer status. Most were conscientious and professional, some were not.

On this particular day, Dub had called in sick to go scout out some of his favorite hunting areas in anticipation of the upcoming deer season.

Upon seeing the massive cloud of smoke, Dub switched on his scanner and tuned it to the public service frequencies. The scanner crackled with activity on the fire net and police channels. As best Dub could decipher from the radio traffic, there had been a fire, something had happened to a train and for sure there'd been a bank robbery.

He continued to monitor the frantic calls on the scanner and realized something unusually exciting was happening. In his ten years as a deputy, he had never worked a bank robbery or any other sort of robbery for that matter. There had been mostly drunks and domestic disputes. The occasional robbery or murder was handled by the regular deputies while he was at work. What the hell, he thought. Carbontown's on the way. I'll just stop by and see if they need a little help. He pulled another Budweiser from the cooler on the floor and turned up the volume on the scanner.

The trucker saw the cars backed up before he saw the blue lights. He shifted down a few gears and let the big Peterbilt conventional slow to a crawl behind the cars. He slipped the shifter into first and just let the powerful diesel idle. He noticed the westbound lanes were moving through much faster than the eastbound. As he neared the roadblock it became obvious that the troopers were doing only a cursory check of the westbound traffic. On the other side, he could see cars backed up for almost a mile. The troopers were looking under hoods, in trunks and questioning people. As he got closer, he took the zip lock baggie of white powder from his console and stashed it inside a pack of Camels. He put the cigarettes back in his shirt pocket, confident that the eight ball of crank would never be discovered.

When his rig rolled up to the roadblock, he pushed in the clutch and the truck eased to a stop. A young state trooper stepped up on the driver side running board. He peered into the cab through mirrored glasses.

"Good afternoon, sir. Have you observed any unusual activity in the last few miles?"

The trucker hesitated momentarily. He had a schedule to meet and a pocket full of trouble.

"What kinda activity? How come you 'all is stopping everybody?"

"Well, actually there's been a robbery and we're looking for the perpetrators."

"Well, I did see a couple guys a ways back. They were on a four-wheeler, and they cut through the fence to cross the interstate," he finally replied.

"Sir, would you pull your vehicle to the side please? We need to get some information and then we'll let you get on your way."

"Ah shit, officer. I gotta be in El Paso day after tomorrow. I don't make no money if these wheels ain't rollin.'"

"Pull over to the side, please." The trooper was very firm in his request, so the trucker chose not to argue. He pulled the truck off the road, set his flashers and waited as the first trooper was joined by a second. They quizzed him on time, location and descriptions of vehicle and men. Another trooper was dispatched during the interview to locate the breach in the fence. Within minutes he called to report the opening did exist and there were fresh four-wheeler tracks headed north. With his information corroborated, the trucker was allowed to continue his trip. Which he did with considerable relief and a long sigh. He shifted smoothly through the gears with the illegal drugs in his pocket weighing heavily on his mind.

Dub Cato arrived some moments later at the Carbontown Sheriff's office. Reports on the scanner indicated that the train was still stalled on the tracks with its engines and some coal cars fully derailed. The railroad company had vehicles and men already working on site.

Dub stepped down from his high-wheeled truck and swaggered toward the tiny office. A couple of deputies that Dub knew well were lingering outside the building, smoking cigarettes and speculating on the outcome of the case. They nodded to him as he walked up to the building. The Sheriff's office was buzzing with phone calls, radio traffic and a heated debate between the local sheriff and a tall blond man in a suit that probably cost more than Dub made in a month. Cato listened in from outside the room. The two deputies rolled their eyes and grinned at Dub.

"Sheriff Cowen, you will provide me and my men with the cooperation we require. This is under Federal jurisdiction as you very well know. Now, shall I rent a motel room for our command post or is this office available?"

Sheriff Cowen, flustered at this unaccustomed intrusion, acquiesced.

"All right, you can use the damned office," he sputtered and walked away. Dub intercepted him at the door.

"Howdy, Sheriff. I'm Dub Cato. I come to see if you might need some help." Dub held out his reserve deputy badge as he spoke.

"Don't ask me. I ain't in charge here," Cowen snapped. "You go ask thet feller there. He's the lord high agent-in-charge." Cowen pointed at the FBI agent who was now barking orders at his men.

Dub slid in the door and sidled up to the man Sheriff Cowen had pointed out.

"Excuse me, Mr. Agent-In-Charge. I'm Dub Cato, with Washington County. I thought maybe you need some help."

"My name is Agent-In-Charge O'Conner and I do not," he said flatly as he eyed Dub. Cato, in fact, did not inspire confidence by his appearance. Agent-in-charge O'Conner looked with distaste at Dub's beer belly, run-over cowboy boots and greasy Caterpillar cap.

"Well, sir. I got my horse here, and my tracking dog. I kinda figured you might need someone who can track," Dub persisted despite the agent's attitude.

"Thank you, Mr. Cato, no. As you can see, we're very busy here."

"All right. If you change your mind..."

"No. Thank you, anyway," Agent O'Conner interrupted.

Cato stepped out of the office and spat in disgust. He pulled the Copenhagen can out of his back pocket, knocked it against the heel of his left hand, pulled off the lid and pinched up a large dip which he carefully placed in his lower lip. He waited for the nicotine rush to kick in and then he spat once more. The two deputies chuckled at Cato's frustration. They'd already seen how the FBI treated locals.

"Fuck them people," he grumbled to no one in particular and walked to the back of his trailer. Now the two deputies laughed out loud. "Where you goin', Dub? Ain't you gonna solve the big case?" The older of the two was a hunting buddy of Cato's and he knew he could get away with the comment. The younger man didn't know Cato so well and he had a healthy respect for Dub's legendary fists.

Dub just shook his head and spat again. "Like I said, boys. Fuck them people."

He walked around his truck and went to the horse trailer to check on his passengers. He stood at the back of his horse trailer and looked inside.

"You reckon you can control yourself now?" Dub asked the creature inside. A throaty woof answered his question. The animal normally rode inside the cab of Dub's truck but on this particular day, she had a nearly lethal case of gas. The stench was overpowering, so Dub made her ride with the horse.

"What the hell did you eat, Tundra?"

Tundra had no answer, but Dub judged that she looked pretty sorry about the whole issue.

"All right, let's go," Dub said as he opened the tailgate with a loud screech of its rusty hinges.

A massive hundred and thirty pound, gray hybrid timber wolf bounded out of the horse trailer. The dog's shiny coat shimmered in the sunlight as she shook herself with pure delight at being outside the trailer.

Dub closed the gate and opened the driver's side door of the pickup. A hand signal was sufficient to guide the animal into the cab of the truck where she sat on the seat beside Cato.

"Tundra, if that fibber agent had half your brains, he'd be all right."

Tundra looked up with doggy devotion apparent in her crystalline gray eyes. A single white cast had formed in each eye giving her an oddly disturbing appearance.

"Fact is, the more I think about it..." Dub's voice trailed off as he pondered the bizarre actions of the FBI agent. Cato drove slowly through the little town and toward the bank. He observed the fuel tanks burning furiously at the south end of town and the train derailed across the access road to the bank.

"Pretty smart, Tundra," Dub observed speculatively.

He patted the wolf on her massive head. "Them fellers sure pulled off a good 'un." He pulled to the side of the street and got out to look around. Tundra exited the truck and stood expectantly beside him. Cato walked to the edge of the creek and perused the situation. He could see the four-wheeler tracks in the sticky mud of the creek bank. A county coroner was taking pictures of the dead bank guard who was still laying face down in the mud. The local news team from Ft. Smith had just arrived and a pushy young female reporter was asking questions of everyone in sight. Several local residents were crowding into the area to offer their estimate of the situation to the news crew.

Cato put a fresh dip of Copenhagen in his lip. He watched the activity surrounding the bank. The FBI flunkies were stringing crime scene tape around the perimeter of the area and shooing away curious on-lookers and reporters. The coroner and his helper finally slid the old man's body into a black body bag and loaded it into the local funeral home's hearse. Dub ambled back to his truck and leaned against the side of it. He spat every few minutes as he watched the drama unfolding.

After finishing with the bank guard, the coroner and his helper went around to the back of the bank. Dub couldn't see what they were doing but he could see a couple of women standing nearby. They were crying, blubbering and holding on to each other. Dub speculated that it must be something sadder than a dead, old bank guard. Nobody seemed to be blubbering over the guard although he did see one young woman standing at a bank window looking out. She looked pretty sad, Cato thought.

He sized up the damage to the train. The rails were pretty twisted up so he couldn't tell what happened. It looked pretty likely that somebody had fiddled with the track to cause the derailment. Dub didn't know much about trains, but he figured it couldn't be that hard to run one off a track. The lead engine had plowed a deep furrow into the muddy bank of the creek and now its diesel tanks were pouring a steady stream of fuel into the muddy water. Dub watched the metallic shimmer of the fuel oil as it coagulated on the water's surface. The volunteer fire fighters must all be across town. Dub speculated that the environmental guys would be having a regular shit fit when they found out about all that fuel oil screwing up the water. He didn't find the activities around the bank to be of much interest. He was more interested in the people who'd pulled off this robbery. It was apparent to Dub that a lot of foresight and planning had gone into this crime. He pondered on the type of men that must have been involved. Although he was pure Arkansas hick himself, he didn't delude himself about the level of sophistication of the typical hillbilly. "Tundra I don't reckon your average feller from around these parts could've pulled this one off." Tundra sat obediently by her master. She looked up at the familiar sound of his gravelly voice.

"Let's go, girl. I reckon we've seen all there is to see around here." She bounded back to the truck and jumped into her part of the seat with one smooth motion. She was a powerful animal, and she could jump higher than a man's head with little effort.

Cato started his truck and drove to the edge of town and entered the eastbound lane of the interstate. Almost immediately he encountered the traffic backup caused by the roadblock.

"Tundra, I don't believe them fellers is likely to be drivin' up and down the interstate."

Dub settled back to wait. He turned up the volume on his scanner and turned on his CB. He listened with amusement to the radio traffic. Apparently, the perpetrators had used a four-wheeler to make their getaway, according to a witness. Cato took in this information and continued to listen and ponder the situation.

As he approached the roadblock, he recognized the trooper who came up to his truck.

"Hey, Dub. What are you doing down here?

"Headed down to scout the deer woods and get outta town for a day or two."

"Well, take 'er easy."

"Listen, where'd them fellers get off to?" Dub asked.

"They cut through a fence about a half mile down. I expect they're headed north toward Springdale," the trooper answered.

"So why are you' all running a roadblock?"

"That FBI agent figures they're headed toward Little Rock. He don't believe they'd go through the woods."

Cato nodded and drove on through the roadblock. As he neared the area where the fence was cut, he slowed and pulled off the road. He and Tundra investigated both sides of the road, saw the freshly cut wire, knobby tread marks in the dirt and examined two different sets of footprints.

"Get a good sniff, Tundra," Dub said.

Tundra had already sniffed and cataloged the smells peculiar to both sets of prints. Tundra had a natural tracking ability that Cato had enhanced through many hours of training.

Dub and Tundra returned to the truck. They drove to the nearest exit, which happened to be a rest area. He had made his decision and he prepared to do a little different sort of hunting.

Reb backed out of the trailer and pranced sideways for a moment or two. He was skittish and high strung after the long trailer ride. He allowed Dub to pat his neck to settle him down. Dub brushed the horse's coat until it was shiny and smooth. He then put an Indian saddle blanket across Reb's back and then another for extra padding. He settled the old, worn western saddle on Reb's back and cinched it down. Reb accepted the bridle and bit without complaint. He stood quivering, anxious for a brisk ride. Tundra lay in the shade of the trailer watching the procedure. She and Reb had covered many a mile together. She, too, felt the stirrings of an adventure to come.

Dub Cato had always been a solitary man, and as such, had always gone prepared. He loaded his saddlebags with surplus Army rations, MREs, for three days, ammunition for his rifle, various camping necessities, his poncho and only the barest toiletries. He took out another set of saddlebags, smaller ones, and called Tundra with a short low-pitched whistle. She trotted obediently over to her master. Cato slung the bags over the wolf's back and secured them under her belly. The durable nylon packs held several days supply of dog food. The chore of carrying a pack came naturally to Tundra because Dub had trained her to it as a pup. She had carried her own rations on every outing and adventure they had taken. Generally, Tundra would hunt on her own and frequently come back to camp with a rabbit or squirrel to supplement the dog food that Dub provided.

A rack behind the pickup seat carried Cato's rifle. It was a gleaming stainless-steel Ruger Mini-14 with a matching stainless four power scope. Dub slid this formidable weapon into the scabbard attached to Reb's saddle. After securing the vehicle, Dub swung into the saddle and set off toward the area of the damaged fence with Tundra following Reb's heels.

Reb broke into a canter immediately on the grassy shoulder of the highway. They rode briskly past the sign forbidding bicycles, livestock or tractors. The speeding traffic did not spook Reb who was well accustomed to it from his many days of traffic and crowd control. They crossed the pavement with care to avoid the traffic speeding past. When they arrived at the openings in the fence, Dub dismounted and led Reb through. Tundra bounded through with no hesitation. Cato thoroughly examined the tracks and footprints. Tundra sniffed the tracks, snorted the air through her grizzled nose and sniffed again. She had refreshed the complex set of scents that would lead them to their quarry. She was salivating in anticipation of the hunt. Dub remounted and aimed Reb to the north. The chase began.

CHAPTER THIRTY-THREE

Chet and Larry drove through scrub brush, over small trees and around bigger ones looking for the location of the entrance to the valley they had observed on the map. The area had been clear-cut by loggers' years before and the undergrowth was thick and tangled. It was a mild introduction to the brutal path they would being following. Chet stopped the four-wheeler briefly to take a long pull from his canteen and to look at the map.

"How long do you reckon it'll take to get back to the truck, Chet?" Larry inquired.

"Dunno," Chet answered after a brief glance at the map. "This route looks pretty rough. The contour lines on the map are really stacked up on both sides of the valley. Very steep sides, in other words."

Chet shook his head. He was perturbed at his plans having been changed for him yet again. He had not set up a contingency plan for anything like this. Their journey back would now involve crossing two deep valleys and a raging river to get back to the old black Ford. Most of these valleys were rimmed with sheer limestone bluffs that were hundreds of feet tall. Worse yet, they would be hemmed in with no avenue for escape if the authorities actually were chasing them. Chet could just imagine the sounds of a helicopter beating down on them. He glanced back over his shoulder but there was nothing approaching them from the sky or on the ground.

"Let's get moving," Chet said. He eased the four-wheeler into gear and headed north again. They continued to weave their way up the valley following what passable terrain they could find. Chet had to lean forward in the saddle to use his Buckmaster to hack through vines and low branches. He would have given anything for a sharp machete. Their progress was frequently blocked by thickets of newly ripened blackberry brambles with wickedly sharp thorns. Cedar trees grew in abundance and their prickly, low limbs drooped to the ground creating impenetrable barriers. Huge boulders, fallen from the bluffs, littered the valley floor creating a frustrating obstacle course. Over and over again, they reached impasses and turned back to try other routes. Progress was painfully slow for the pair, and they questioned whether they would ever get out of the maze. The clouds had long since melted away leaving the hot sun to beat down on them in the sweltering valley. They were soaked with sweat from the heat and near one hundred percent humidity.

"Chet. Chet," Larry shouted over the roar of the engine. Chet backed off the throttle and left the four-wheeler roll to a stop.

"What?"

"Let's take a break, man. This thing is beating the shit outta me." Larry's backpack was slamming against him with every jolting bump that happened. He was hot, tired and scared.

"Just for minute. We gotta keep moving." Chet was hot and tired as well, but the sense of imminent pursuit hung over him like a cloud. He scanned the sky for the police chopper that he knew must be bearing down on them. None appeared. Chet continued to scan the sky, nonetheless. The hair on the back of his neck seemed to stand on end with the sense of someone watching them. He just didn't see anyone or anything.

Larry climbed down from the punishing seat and stretched his sore and aching muscles. Chet remained seated on the four-wheeler, vigilant. He fidgeted as Larry stretched and grumbled about his aches and pains.

They had stopped near some limestone outcroppings that were now baking in the afternoon sun. Larry noticed a trailing boot lace as he stretched and twisted. Chet watched as Larry shuffled over to the outcropping to put his foot up. He bent down to retie his boot when a bronze flash arced toward his hand. "Look out!" Chet shouted a moment too late. A thick bodied copperhead had been lurking in the cool shade under the rocks. Larry had stumbled into its lair and the animal was simply defending itself.

The reptile's strike happened so fast that Larry scarcely had time to flinch before the snake bit deeply into his boot and recoiled back under the rock.

Larry squealed involuntarily and jumped back. He caught his heel against an embedded rock and fell hard on his back. He recovered quickly and started scrabbling backwards on his hands and heels.

"Shoot it. Shoot it, Chet," Larry shouted in a high pitched, breathless plea.

Chet didn't do anything.

"Shoot it, shoot that fucker!" Larry demanded.

"You dumb ass. Just how stupid can you be? That snake ain't after you." Indeed, the shy reptile was frantically trying to crawl deeper into the crevices under the overhanging limestone. Larry had terrified the reclusive, normally passive creature.

Chet dismounted and asked, "Did it get ya?" He walked over to Larry who was back on his feet and looking all around for other snakes.

"They run in pairs, don't they?" Larry looked like he was finished with his break and plenty ready to leave.

"Nope. It was just minding its own business and you 'bout stepped on it."

Larry carefully examined his hands and arms. There were countless scratches and cuts but no puncture wounds.

"Take your boot off. Let's see if he got through the leather." Chet was only slightly concerned. He knew that a copperhead's bite was painful but almost never fatal. He also knew that most snakes could control the discharge of venom during the bite and that many times they didn't envenomate the subjects of defensive bites. Larry unlaced his heavy work boot and pulled off his sock. There were no punctures of any kind. Larry breathed a sigh of relief.

Chet laughed. "You shoulda seen your face. I bet you pissed your pants," Chet fairly cackled.

"Shut up. Just shut the fuck up, Chet." He glared at Chet with sincere hate. He'd come to see a cruel side of Chet that he just didn't like. Chet, on the other hand, had come to know a weak and whining side of Larry that he didn't much like. Chet quit chuckling and reseated himself on the four-wheeler. He stared straight ahead into the brush and waited for Larry to put on his boot.

Larry hopped around on one foot while he struggled awkwardly to put on his sock and boot. He looked furtively around for other snakes. He was burning with anger and humiliation. He'd have gladly left Chet alone in the woods if he'd been driving. Larry choked down the bitter anger and climbed back on the seat behind Chet.

"Okay, let's go," Larry said in an emotionless voice. Chet started the engine and resumed the journey without further comment. He hated the lost time, but he wouldn't have missed the show for anything. Fortunately for Larry, he couldn't see the broad grin on Chet's face as he drove.

During all their struggles to get out of the valley, the pressure was mounting on them as they knew that someone must be following them. Considering their pitifully slow progress, Chet and Larry knew the pursuers must surely be closing the gap.

They heard long before they saw the source of the rumbling roar. As they approached the Mulberry the sound of the engine no longer could mask the furious pounding and crashing of water.

Larry shouted at Chet, "What's that sound? Is that the river?"

"Must be," Chet shouted back over his shoulder. He continued driving and soon the source of the thunderous noise became apparent.

Normally placid, the Mulberry became a torrent during the spring and fall rains. The slopes of the Boston Mountains collected and funneled every drop of rain down into this waterway. Rain had been falling for days now and the ground was saturated. Typically, the rocky, porous soil of the area would absorb and moderate even a heavy rain. Now, though, the ground could hold not another drop and the Mulberry was rampaging out of its banks.

The paddlers that brought their canoes and kayaks to the Mulberry used a system for classifying the intensity of the white water. Class I water was considered mild. Class II and III were fun and required at least some experience and training. Class IV required considerable skill, experience and intestinal fortitude. Class V was challenging and definitely risky even for the experienced paddlers. The Mulberry was way off the scale, and not even the most intrepid paddler would have been foolhardy enough to tackle it.

The brown turbid water blasted trees and tore them from the ground. The oaks and cedars shot downstream colliding with each other and ramming into any obstruction in their way. Huge standing waves cascaded up from the heaviest boulders in the stream bed. Smaller, refrigerator sized boulders rumbled and crashed against one another as the relentless power of the water pushed them downstream. Plumes of frothy, foaming water sprayed Chet and Larry as they rolled up to the riverbank. Chet looked back over his shoulder at Larry who shrugged and rolled his eyes.

"Now what?" Larry shouted over the din.

"Get the map out. There's gotta be a bridge around here somewhere."

Larry dug the map out of a pouch and together they held it open.

"I figure we're about...right...there." Chet pointed with a stubby finger at a spot on the map.

Lar nodded in agreement and traced the river's course with his own finger until he came to a crossroad depicted on the map. "What do you think, Chet? Is it worth a try?"

"I dunno, Lar. That's a mighty small road. Prob'ly just a low water bridge in which case it'll be under water."

"Well, our only other choice is the highway 23 bridge and it's broad daylight. Pretty risky."

"Let's try the crossroad," Chet replied and started the engine. They proceeded east to attempt to find the small, unpaved road depicted on the map.

The terrain was brutal. The Honda crawled over massive rocks and dozens of fallen trees and stumps. After half an hour of steady work, the four-wheeler stopped with a jolt. Chet flew completely over the handlebars, and he landed hard on his side. Larry managed to stay in his seat by hanging on to the rear cargo racks. He climbed down and ran to Chet's side.

"Chet. Chet, are you hurt bad?"

Chet was slightly dazed by the impact and his side was badly scraped. He was otherwise unhurt.

"No. I'm...uh, I don't think nothing's broke." He gingerly felt his sore places and didn't discover any major damage.

Larry moved back to the four-wheeler to assess the situation.

"Stump, Chet. It's high centered on a big ole stump."

Chet stood up and fought back a wave of dizziness. He went to the back of the four-wheeler and pushed against the rear cargo basket. The heavy machine didn't budge.

"Come on, Lar. Gimme a hand." Chet crouched low and placed his shoulder against the basket. Larry did the same.

"Okay, one, two, three...push." Together they grunted and heaved to no avail.

"Leverage, Lar. We need a lever. You know, a big limb or branch."
Chet scrambled around the brush in the immediate area and found a
stout oak sapling about three inches in diameter. He hacked it down
with several strokes of his heavy Buckmaster knife. Larry grabbed
one end of the young tree and they carried it back to the
four-wheeler. Chet placed the butt end of the sapling under the
four-wheeler and against the stump.

"Lar, you push, and I'll pry." Chet hung off the bushy end of the
tree and pried up the back end of the four-wheeler, but it still refused
to move.

"Damn it Larry, take it outta gear," Chet snarled. Larry reached
forward and tugged the shifter into neutral. Immediately he could
feel the four-wheeler start to move. Larry strained and pushed until
the jagged stump released its hold on their vehicle.

"All right let's get going. We're burning daylight," Chet shouted
and dropped the sapling where it lay.

They mounted up and resumed their ride across the valley floor
looking for the road. Larry tapped Chet on the shoulder and pointed
ahead. The road they sought was just yards away. A barbed wire fence
and a muddy ditch stood between them and the road.

Chet drove straight for the fence. He slid to a halt with the front
tires actually touching the barbed wire.

"Cut it," Chet commanded, and Larry jumped down from the
four-wheeler. He pulled his lineman's pliers from his tool pouch just
as he had for the highway crossing. Larry stood for a moment and
looked up and down the road to see if anyone was watching. The
road was deserted and there were no fresh tracks in the mud.

Assured that they were unobserved, Larry began cutting the
wires. A figure watched and waited high atop the ridge that rimmed
the valley. He'd been watching their progress for some time. Now
they were approaching his territory and trouble was about to
happen.

Larry pulled aside the wires as he cut them and when the fourth and last wire was cut, Chet gunned the engine and roared through the gap. Larry watched expectantly as Chet plowed through the mud of the ditch. The tires spun and sprayed mud in all directions including right at Larry. Finally, the knarly tread of the tires gained enough traction to pull the machine and Chet out of the ditch and up on to the more solid roadbed.

Larry wiped the mud from his face and lightly jumped across the ditch. He mounted behind Chet who pulled the throttle full open and drove wildly toward the waiting river.

The figure on the hill continued to watch their movement toward his domain. An older man, he leaned against an even older white oak and watched them through a set of powerful binoculars. The rain had halted some time before and the sun had burned off all the clouds. The air was saturated with moisture, and it didn't take long for the sun to bring the temperature up to steam bath levels. Both men suffered in their heavy uniforms. Sweat poured down their faces, but Chet was reluctant to stop. In fact, the faster he drove, the cooler they felt. Larry tugged at the buttons of his shirt and felt some relief as the breeze blew across his now exposed chest. Chet was too preoccupied to worry about his personal comfort and he kept the throttle full open as he negotiated the winding country road. They slid around corners and hoped not to come face to face with another vehicle.

"Shouldn't be much farther, Chet. It was only a mile or so according to the map."

They rounded another corner on two wheels and Chet jammed on the brakes sending them into a spinning slide that carried them almost to the waters edge.

"Shit, Chet. You're gonna kill us," Larry swore.

"Don't mean nuthin'. Look at that water."

The Mulberry was running faster here than where they'd seen it downstream. The valley had narrowed and choked the furious water into a blasting torrent. The bridge was a sturdily constructed concrete structure. Four huge steel culverts ran under the roadbed. The mass of swirling water was being forced through the tubes resulting in fantastic plumes of water being shot downstream and into the air. The sun's rays refracted through the mist rising from these plumes and Chet and Larry were treated to a spectacular rainbow display. They had no time to marvel at nature's show.

"It's not that deep, Lar. Let's check it out." The men dismounted and approached the swift water. The majority of the flow seemed to be going through the culverts. Only a few inches of muddy water poured over the top of the roadbed itself.

"I don't know, Chet. That water's moving pretty fast."

"I tell ya, it's not that goddamned deep. Look," and with that, Chet tossed a rock into the middle of the bridge. The current carried it rapidly away but not before they could see it bounce on the concrete of the road surface.

"Maybe three or four inches. We can make it," Chet pronounced.

"You're outta your cotton-pickin' mind," Larry shouted over the river's noise.

"We're going. I'm telling ya we can do it," Chet shouted back. "What else we gonna do?"

Larry shook his head. They were out of options, running out of time and there was a nagging certainty that someone was following them.

"Let's do it and say we did." Chet punched Larry on the shoulder. Larry nodded his assent, and they walked back to the four-wheeler.

Chet started the engine while Larry tightened each of the pack straps. He carefully looked over the vehicle as he tugged on each strap. Other than many deep scratches and a few dents, it seemed functional in spite of the brutal trail it had just carved from the scrub valley.

Larry climbed on and grabbed the handholds with white-knuckle intensity. Chet eased up off the brake and the four-wheeler rolled down to the water's edge. He held it there for a few moments studying the best approach. He knew the current would pull at the wide tires of the four-wheeler but the distance they had to cross was relatively short. If he could start on the very upstream edge of the roadbed, he was sure they could make it across by the time the current pulled them to the deadly downstream side. If he was wrong, he'd cost them both their lives because no human could possibly fight against the tremendous force of the water.

Chet lined up on the opposite shore and visually plotted his desired path. Too far to the right, and the wheels would drop off into the upstream side and they would be drawn down and through the culverts. Too far left, and their chances of overcoming the current were reduced. If they didn't make it across before the current carried them over the edge, they would be lost in the pounding maelstrom downstream.

"Lar, I'm gonna back up a little and get some momentum going. If I go too fast, we could lose it, but if I go too slow, the water will push us over." Larry was simply too scared to answer. He retightened his grip on the baggage rack and waited. Chet held the four-wheeler in reverse and backed up about twenty feet. He swallowed hard, "Hang on," he shouted and poured the power on. As soon as the tires hit the water the machine seemed out of control. Chet forced himself to focus on the opposite shore. where you aim to go", his father had counseled him about driving on slick roads. "Look Chet had been too young to drive when his old man was alive, but he rode with him any time he could. Chet could almost feel the old man's disapproval right now. If there really was an after life, old Chester Farmer was frowning right now.

Chet cocked the handlebars to the right and concentrated on fighting the machine to stay on the bridge. Now they had traveled into the brunt of the water and Chet realized how truly helpless they were. In spite of the powerful machine trying to claw its way upstream, the current inexorably pushed it farther and farther down across the bridge. The big, deeply cleated tires sought purchase and found little. They slipped, caught and slipped yet again. Baseball-sized river stones rolled with the current across the bridge along with limbs and debris. The four-wheeler bounced and jolted over the obstacles. The river blasted against the tires and cascaded up into plumes of icy water. Chet and Larry were both soaked to the skin, but the adrenaline rush was so intense neither man noticed. Chet swiped at his eyes to clear his vision so he could attempt to steer. The tremendous and unrelenting power of the Mulberry was pushing them toward the boiling downstream edge of the road.

The engine was screaming wide open. The roar of the water blasting through the culverts was deafening and unnerving. Water flew up from the spinning tires and blinded Chet again. He tried to blink the gritty water from his bleary eyes so he could see ahead. They were just over halfway across when the left front wheel dropped into a hidden pothole. The four-wheeler tilted sickeningly, and the water instantly boiled up under them and threatened to push the heavy vehicle over onto its side. Later neither Chet nor Larry would have any recollection other than the memory of a desperate attempt for self preservation. Even as he felt himself being unseated, Chet lunged to the right and shifted all his weight to the right foot peg. Larry also realized what was happening and he leaned way out to the right. Instinctively, they were both hiked out much as racing sail boaters do in a stiff breeze.

Momentarily, the four-wheeler tottered in a struggle between the force of the water and the combined weight of Chet and Larry. Miraculously, the river relented for just a fraction of a second and the water swirled away from them. The four-wheeler plunked down on all fours with a mighty splash. Now Chet and Larry were way overbalanced as the still moving vehicle bounced down. Larry still had one hand tightly gripping the baggage rack, so he was able to grab Chet just in time to prevent him from being thrown. Chet regained his balance and stood on the pegs to drive. He applied full power and aimed upstream. The deep tread of the tires found sufficient traction to propel them forward toward safety.

The edge of the water was mere feet away. The flow which had relented moments before now seemed to redouble its efforts to wash them away. The tires lost their precious traction and the machine seemed to float to the very edge of the bridge.

Chet was still balanced precariously on the foot pegs, and he could see they weren't going to make it. The four-wheeler spun out of control and the unrelenting flow of water pushed it over the brink.

Both men gritted their teeth and clung tenaciously to whatever handholds they could grab. Each expected a shockingly cold dunking followed by an immediate and brutal death. Instead of the expected violent end, the four-wheeler flowed off the edge and landed in a relatively calm pool of backwater, sheltered from the main flow. They turned to each other incredulously. No words could express the combination of disbelief and joy they felt.

"I can't believe it, Chet. We really made it," Larry shouted.

Chet beamed with a grin from ear to ear. "Yeah we did, old buddy. We really did. Now let's get outta here." The engine had stalled, so with shaking hands, Chet attempted a restart. The starter spun the engine over and over ineffectively. The normally reliable engine refused to start.

"Get off, Lar. Let's push it out." Chet also dismounted and together they pushed the heavy machine a few inches until it came to rest against the steep shoreline.

"Try it again, Chet. We can't move it. Too steep," Larry shouted breathlessly. Chet remounted and once again engaged the starter. The engine stubbornly refused to fire.

The men had succeeded in reaching the relative calm of the water's edge, but they were still standing ankle deep. The river still blasted through the culverts with a deafening roar and small trees, brush and limbs occasionally floated over the bridge.

"I'm gonna see if the plug's wet or something," Chet shouted to Larry who was standing at the back of the four-wheeler.

Chet knelt down in the swirling water to look at the engine. He checked the air intake first; afraid the engine had gulped a lung full of filthy water. The air filter appeared wet but not soaked. He next traced the spark plug wire from the distributor back to the spark plug where he discovered the problem. Somehow during the slide off the bridge, the spark plug wire had become dislodged. He plugged it back in to place.

"Oh shit, Chet. Look!" Larry grabbed frantically at Chet's shoulder. Chet stood up in time to see a huge oak tree bearing down on them. The massive tree had been dislodged from somewhere far upstream and now it hurtled downstream, stump first. The tree was obviously headed straight for Chet, Larry and the four-wheeler.

"Get out. Go now," Chet shouted to Larry and swung his leg over the machine for one final attempt.

Larry scrambled through the briars and brush that lined the shore. He slipped and fell on the muddy bank where he watched helplessly. Chet cranked the damp and stubborn engine with no result. The massive tree trunk was approaching the bridge and still heading directly for Chet.

"Forget it, Chet. Get outta there," Larry's voice was lost in the roar of the water. Chet never heard the words at all.

Chet sensed more than heard the engine cough, sputter and finally start. He jammed the vehicle into gear and pulled the throttle full open. The tree impacted the bridge just as the engine started. A long tap root protruded from the stump and the end of it caught in one of the culverts. The tree's forward progress was momentarily checked by the tap root which was quickly sheared off by the massive weight of the solid oak. The current then swung the huge tree around broadside to the river's flow. A massive standing wave developed over the tree sending sheets of water cascading over Chet as he was frantically maneuvering the four-wheeler up the muddy bank. The tires spun globs of sticky mud out in all directions and chunks of rubber were torn out against the jagged rocks as the machine sought traction.

Chet topped the edge of the embankment after what seemed an eternity. He rolled to a stop beside Larry who was waiting at the top. The massive oak rolled slowly, inexorably over the bridge and thundered down onto the very spot where the four-wheeler had been stalled. The current pulled it out into the main stream and they watched it gaining momentum as it floated away.

"God, Chet. That was close. You shoulda jumped, man. That tree was gonna take you out."

"I didn't come this far to lose all that money. No way, Lar. No fuckin way," Chet pronounced grimly. He was tired, muddy and still shaking from the fear that had helped him overcome the river.

"Let's go, Lar. We gotta make up some time."

Larry climbed onto his accustomed spot and held on for dear life as Chet roared off into the brush.

Overlooking this scene was a threesome on the side from which Chet and Larry had just come and the solitary figure of the old man high on the ridge on the other side. The threesome was Dub Cato, Reb and Tundra. The threesome was focused on Chet and Larry and did not see the old man. The old man, for his part, saw everything and he waited.

"They done pretty good, "Cato mused out loud to his companions.

"Not bad fer city boys. Not bad by half." Dub had hunted this area many times and he realized quickly where his quarry was heading. He had also realized the old logging roads tended to follow the tops of the ridges that paralleled the valleys that Chet and Larry struggled through. No trace of these old roads was recorded on the topographical maps that Chet had purchased.

While Reb effortlessly carried Dub's considerable bulk down the shady lanes created by loggers of years ago, Chet and Larry's four-wheeler engine could be plainly heard below. Occasionally, Dub would wait at a rock outcropping or bluff line to watch. He used his compact binoculars to observe their struggles and painfully slow progress. Cato shook his head when he saw Chet hacking away at the brush. He chuckled with amusement at their poor choice of trail. He knew they must be worn out from all the brush cutting, entangling grape vines and loose rocks. The Ozark hills were brutal and unforgiving for the unwary or unprepared. When he tired of watching their struggles, he nudged Reb and they too, continued their journey. Instead of crossing the river as Chet and Larry did. Cato guided Reb a few hundred yards upstream to where an old railroad trestle crossed the Mulberry.

Reb eyed the railroad tracks and the spaces between the timbers with some suspicion.

Tundra, as usual, was way ahead, investigating each new smell. The tracks and widely spaced timbers posed no problem for her agile paws.

Cato dismounted and led his horse to the edge of the trestle. The river raged beneath them, adding to Reb's discomfort. Cato knew the horse would do whatever he asked of him. He also knew that one slip and Reb could break a leg.

"Take a look at it, boy," Dub spoke in an easy, soothing voice. Reb trusted Cato implicitly but the roar of the water and the daylight between the boards was unnerving.

"Let's take a walk." Dub lightly held the reins and stepped forward. Reb followed him without great hesitation. His steel shod hooves clattered on the worn oak timbers. Cato guided him with a steady hand, and he took his time to allow Reb to place his steps with care. The timbers were old and rotted in places. Early railroad crews had spiked and bolted the structure together. The timbers had been soaked in a toxic mixture of creosote and kerosene. The noxious solution warded off bugs and dry rot, but time was beginning to take its toll. Reb's left hind hoof found a soft spot which broke under his considerable weight. The usually steady horse was now terrified. Cato stopped instantly when he heard his horse whinny in fright. Reb's leg was trapped in the gaping hole.

"Whoa, boy. Let's see what's going on here." Reb's eyes were wide open in fear, and he was sucking air into his lungs frantically. Cato didn't try to hold his head but rather ran his hand along his horse's neck and shoulder. "Stand, Reb. Stand." Reb was familiar with the command, and he held still, quivering. Cato moved slowly and deliberately past Reb. He knew that if the horse panicked, it would be disaster. The least that would happen would be a broken leg for Reb. Worst case scenario would be Reb knocking them both off the bridge and into the torrent below.

Dub knelt down and ran his hand down Reb's trapped leg. The wood had splintered, and now sharp spikes of wood were digging into Reb's skin. Each time he tried to pull his leg out, the sharp splinters dug in and held him even tighter. Dub slid his hunting knife out of its sheath and began chipping away at the jagged edges of the plank. "Stand, boy. Just stand there." Reb continued to quiver but he stood still and let Dub help him. He turned his head and focused one eye on his trusted rider to see what was happening. There had never been a day that Dub hadn't been a part of Reb's life since he was a colt. Dub was a single man, and he spent his free time in the woods with his dog and his horse. There were few distractions that kept him away from his cabin in the lower part of Washington County every weekend. Reb received constant and particular care from Dub every day. Now, when he was hurt and frightened, Reb looked at his owner with trust built over many years together.

Dub was careful to avoid poking Reb with the heavy hunting blade. He pried out several large chips and then he carefully lifted Reb's leg. The big horse nearly bolted when he felt his leg pull free of the trap. "Whoa, boy. You ain't goin' nowhere yet," Dub chided his horse. Cato moved in front of Reb and held his reins firmly. Together they crossed the bridge without further mishap.

Dub stepped off the bridge and he dropped the reins on the ground. Reb stood stock still. He was well trained not to move when his reins were down. Dub carefully checked Reb's legs and then he stepped into the stirrup and swung his leg over the horse and settled into the saddle. The chase continued.

CHAPTER THIRTY-FOUR

By mid-afternoon, Chet realized they needed to turn west to arrive at the location of his hidden pickup. He stopped for a moment and scanned the valley slopes for a pass that would allow them to climb out of the now sweltering valley. No such land feature presented itself, so they continued their northward journey. Throughout the afternoon they climbed imperceptibly until finally they found themselves at the head of the valley. From this promontory, they looked back over an expansive view covering thousands of heavily wooded acres. Most of it was inaccessible to regular vehicles due to the sheer cliffs, deep ravines and massive limestone outcroppings. The forest was dense and green. The majority of the trees were old second growth oaks that had grown unmolested since the first loggers had cut down their ancestors around the end of the nineteenth century. Thousands of logs had been hauled out by mule power. The powerful and surefooted beasts had been the heavy equipment of their day and even now they would have an advantage over any mechanization.

Chet and Larry continued into a clearing that overlooked the valley. Chet shut off the engine and breathed a sigh of relief.

"Whew, I though we'd never get out of there," Chet exclaimed.

"You and me both," Larry agreed.

They dismounted and stretched their stiff and weary limbs. The animosity of earlier in the day had faded and they were once again friends and co-conspirators.

"Let's bury this stuff now, Chet," Larry indicated the tool belts, rain suits and uniforms.

"Yeah, this'll do," Chet answered after looking around the area.

Chet produced a folding camp shovel from one of his many cubbyholes on the four-wheeler. He began chopping at the rocky soil which was bound with roots and humus. The shovel was military issue with a serrated edge for chopping on one side. He made good progress and in short order they pitched their uniforms, rain suits and tool belts into the hole. They had carefully wiped their fingerprints from all smooth surfaces on the tools and equipment. Chet scooped soil and leaves over the evidence.

"Good enough," Chet wheezed.

"Are you ready to get outta here?" he asked Larry.

"Sure, but let me take a leak first."

"Okay, I'll look at the map for a minute." Chet pulled the map from its protected spot on his pack and plotted the final leg of their escape.

Larry walked to the edge of the clearing and relieved himself. He gazed absently out into the woods and then he noticed something unusual.

"Hey, Chet. Come here, man."

"What, you need help finding it?" Chet ribbed him.

"No. Get over here," Larry said urgently.

As Chet approached, Larry pointed to a tall, bushy plant, then at another and still others.

"Chet, we're in the middle of somebody's patch."

"Okay, okay. Let's get going now. This stuff looks ready to harvest. Those buds are huge."

"That's right, they are," a voice replied from behind them.

"Oh, shit," Larry muttered.

They turned slowly to face the man behind them. He wore faded denim bib overalls, no shirt and a greasy railroader's cap. His gray beard was unkempt, and his eyes glowed with dull suspicion. He carried a pump shotgun in his filthy hands and as they turned, he jacked a round into the chamber. Chet and Larry froze instantly. Chet's eyes glanced furtively at the shotgun cradled in its rack on the four-wheeler.

"Don't reckon you'll be needin' that no more." The old man had noticed Chet's glance at the weapon.

"You boys planning on doing some harvesting of your own, I reckon," he said speculatively.

"No. We're just out scouting deer sign for the season coming up," Larry volunteered.

"That right?" the marijuana grower said.

"Right," Chet agreed.

"We just stumbled on your patch here and realized we're in the wrong place. We'll just get outta here and forget we ever saw it," Chet said and moved as if to go toward the four-wheeler.

"Don't reckon you will, jest yet," the man said and leveled the twelve gauge at Chet.

"Whoa, no need for that," Chet said and raised his hands slightly.

"You boys with the DEA, ain't ya. Or is it county or whut?"

"No way. I told you, we're just out on our own," Larry responded.

"What you need a scattergun like that for, if you'uns was just scoutin?" he said. "And jest what is in them bags, anyway?"

"Just camping gear and food," Larry answered.

"Joe Bob, get out here," the old man shouted over his shoulder. A thin-faced teenager materialized from the woods. His footfalls were muffled on the spongy forest floor as he followed his father's direction. Lank hair fell over an acne-pitted forehead above the same dull eyes as his father's. He wore a sleeveless T-shirt smudged with grease and dirt. His ragged blue jeans hung loosely on his emaciated frame.

"Open them bags, son. See what kinda camping gear them fellers got."

Joe Bob obediently shuffled over to the four-wheeler and unfastened the bag on the front rack. His eyes bulged at the sight of so much money.

"Daddy, it's money. I ain't never seen so much money."

"Open up the other one, boy," the old man commanded.

The boy did as he was told and opened another bag.

"Same thing. More money, Daddy." The boy's dull wits were stunned by the wealth. He stood mouth gaping, with handfuls of the greenbacks.

"Let's work something out, buddy. We can make some kind of a deal, can't we?" Chet said to the old man.

"I reckon I got all the cards so I can make any kinda deal I want. Ain't that right?"

Chet had no answer for the man.

"Joe Bob, put thet money back in the bags and bring me thet scattergun." He held his shotgun on his hip, muzzle skyward, and scratched his beard thoughtfully.

"I been watchin' you boys fer a spell. I seen you uns racing up the valley like a couple of scalded dogs and then I seen ya bury somethin'. What did ya bury?"

Neither Chet nor Larry answered.

"You uns ain't so talkative no more, are ya? Bring that shovel too, Joe Bob."

Joe Bob brought the shotgun and the folding shovel. The old man examined the shotgun with a critical eye and pushed the slide release button. He saw there was a shell in the chamber, and he closed the slide again. He handed the weapon back to Joe Bob.

"Hold this on 'em, boy. Don't be afeared to shoot 'em if they move an inch." Joe Bob nodded and held the riot gun pointed at Chet.

"Thet gun won't be no account fer huntin, boy. But you can have it anyway. That barrel's too short," the old man observed.

He tossed the folding shovel at Larry's feet.

"Dig up whatever you buried," he said.

Larry bent to pick up the shovel.

"Careful," the old man warned with a gravelly voice that sounded more like a growl.

Larry methodically unfolded the shovel and walked slowly to the spot where he had buried the phone company uniforms and gear. He bent down and began shoveling the soil away.

"Let's see what he finds," the old man said and motioned with his shotgun for Chet to move. Larry unearthed the clothes in short order and put them on the ground along with the tool belts.

The old man motioned for Larry to back away from the pile of equipment. Larry took a few cautious steps backward and waited. He and Chet watched as their captor kicked the clothing and tools across the forest floor.

"You fellers don't look much like phone men," the grower commented dryly.

"I expect you uns stole thet money," he continued and watched for their reaction.

Larry still held the shovel in his hands. He was waiting for the opportunity to smash the serrated cutting edge into the old man's skull. Larry surprised himself with his willingness to kill another human. At that particular moment, he realized it was a kill or be killed situation.

"I reckon you can put that shovel back to work," the old man said.

"What?" Larry and Chet said in unison. The sinister implications of his statement stunned them.

"You heard me. Start diggin' and I'll tell ya when you're done."

Joe Bob snickered, and the old man turned on him.

"Shut up, boy. There ain't nothin' funny about dyin'," he said savagely.

"Get to it. I wish we could let you uns go but I got a family to feed, and I jest can't trust you uns to keep quiet."

Larry hesitated a moment and then began digging. The first couple of inches were composed of soft humus and soil but below that he encountered rocky red clay and tangled tree roots.

Chet stood ready to try to make a break for freedom if the opportunity presented itself. His mind was racing furiously, examining and rejecting ideas.

Larry paused for a second and spoke to the old man.

"Since you figured out that we stole the money, you must have realized that they'll be coming this way. The cops, I mean."

"Then I reckon you best dig quicker less you want some critter diggin' you up," was the old man's reply.

Larry continued to dig, using the serrated edge to chop through the twisted roots. For some minutes the only sound was the noise of digging.

Chet broke the silence.

"Let me give him a break, okay?"

"Alright, but don't try nuthin," advised the old man. He glared directly at Chet with a cold-blooded malice that sent chills down Chet's spine. He knew beyond a shadow of a doubt that the old man wouldn't hesitate for a second to kill both of them.

Chet nodded and began walking toward Larry. He moved deliberately and without haste. Suddenly, he lunged toward the old man. He tried desperately to grab the shotgun but the old codger deftly butt-stroked Chet across the jaw with his weapon. Chet dropped instantly to the ground at the old man's feet, stunned.

"Your friend ain't too smart, is he? Not very quick, neither" observed the old man. He looked down at Chet and spat a long stream of brown tobacco juice on the ground near Chet's face.

Chet sat up slowly, gingerly feeling the already swelling lump on his face.

"You still feel like diggin'?"

Chet shook his head, no.

"Didn't reckon you would. Get back to it boy," he said to Larry.

Larry continued digging and Chet stayed seated on the ground, his jaw swelling rapidly, already turning black and blue. Chet watched the old man. He held the shotgun in the crook of his arm while he used a rusty, yellow-handled jackknife to cut a fresh chew from a twist of tobacco. It occurred to Chet that he had seriously underestimated his captor, but it was hard to take this bumpkin seriously.

Larry dug with a sense of hopelessness. He could feel the old man's eyes upon his back, and he half expected a charge of buckshot to tear into his body at any moment.

Chet sat quietly on the ground watching the old man. He knew time was running out and that he must make his move soon if they were to survive. Joe Bob held the riot gun pointed directly at Chet. There was a single-minded purpose in his dull brain - to kill Chet if he moved.

Chet sank back on his elbows in a seemingly relaxed position. Joe Bob tensed at Chet's movement.

"Don't...don't you try nuthin'," the boy stammered. His quaking voice lacked the authority and intimidation of his father's.

"Don't fret yourself, son. I ain't goin' nowhere fast," Chet replied.

The old man observed this exchange without comment. He continued to watch Larry intently.

Chet slowly, ever so slowly, moved his right hand toward his side. Clipped to his belt was a small, inconspicuous container of pepper spray which neither the old man nor the boy had noticed. After some moments of surreptitious movement, Chet's hand was against the nylon holster that held the can of spray. Still, the old man continued to watch Larry.

Chet held his position for a few minutes while he marshaled his thoughts and prepared himself for what was to come. After a sideways glance at Joe Bob, Chet sprang into action. In a single movement, he thumbed the Velcro tab off the container, pulled it out and aimed it at the old man's face. Still somewhat dazed by the blow he had received earlier; Chet's aim was faulty, and his first stream passed harmlessly to the right of the old man's face. The second attempt caught the fellow full in the eyes as he turned toward Chet. With a screech of pain and rage, the old man dropped his weapon and clutched his face. Chet lunged for the fallen shotgun. As his fingers closed around the stock, Job Bob fired.

The Remington 870 sounded like thunder in the still woods. Chet felt the searing pain as a projectile slammed squarely into his back.

The blob of silly putty fell to the earth with no sound.

Joe Bob stood with his mouth agape for an instant then he began to jack another round into the chamber. Realizing the implications of that move, Chet brought the old man's gun to his shoulder and swung the barrel toward Joe Bob. Without hesitation, Chet fired, and all three men watched in horror. The double ought buckshot pellets grouped tightly together at that range, and they punched a gaping hole in Joe Bob's chest. Several pellets passed completely through his body, some lodged in his spine and ribs and others obliterated his heart and lungs. Joe Bob sunk limply to his knees, eyes already rolling up, and fell over backward. His legs were crumpled in that awkward tangle that only a dead body can assume.

Chet instantly jacked another round in the chamber and turned back to the old man. He needn't have worried; the fight was completely gone out of him. Tears streamed down the old man's face, whether just from the pepper spray or not, Chet was never to know. He stood over his boy's body with his shoulders slumped.

"My pore boy. What have they done to you?" he groaned and dropped to his knees. He cradled the boy's head in his lap and rocked back and forth.

Larry approached Chet's side.

"Chet, let's get moving. We don't have much time."

Touched by the tragedy he had created, Chet seemed almost in shock. His simple plan to rob a bank had already resulted in at least three deaths. He wasn't sure what had happened at the fuel depot, but the size of the fire was incredible and there was a distinct possibility that someone had perished there as well.

"Right. Okay, I'm ready," Chet answered but he did not move.

"Now, Chet. Now," Larry insisted.

"Okay, Okay, I'm going."

Larry snatched up the 870 that had fallen from Joe Bob's hands. He noticed that a pellet had splintered the stock. Chet walked warily toward the four-wheeler, watching the old man all the way. Larry joined him and they strapped the guns to the rack and secured their bags of money. Chet mounted the vehicle first and brought the engine to life. He motioned for Larry to get on board.

Chet sped through the woods with only a quick glance over his shoulder. The old man still sat cross-legged on the ground cradling his boy's head in his lap.

Larry clung tightly to the rack behind the seat. Chet drove wildly with little concern for the tree limbs and briars. As they neared the edge of the clearing, Chet noticed festoons of spider webs dangling from the tree limbs just ahead. Instinctively, he ducked down to avoid the webs, realizing as he did that something was terribly wrong. His mind seemed to shift to slow motion. He was aware of a sudden jolt and felt Larry being pulled from the seat behind him. Chet looked back to see Larry sprawled on the ground, his face covered in blood. Chet skidded to a halt and ran back toward Larry with the four-wheeler still running and in gear. As he did, Larry reached for his face and began a high-pitched scream. The scream was not from pain but from shock and horror at finding an empty, bloody socket where his right eye had once been. A rusted treble fishing hook swung above him on clear monofilament line. The wicked hook still dripped blood and traces of the tissue from the destroyed eye.

Chet saw that the apparent spider webs were actually a curtain of hooks hung at eye level to injure any unwary trespassers or drug enforcement officers.

Chet grabbed the first aid pouch from his belt and tore open the plastic cover. He pried Larry's hands away from his face so he could apply the gauze pad against Larry's eye socket. Chet tied it off with a few strips of first aid tape wrapped around Larry's head. All the while, Larry was moaning and shaking from the shock of the injury.

"Here, Lar. Hold pressure against your eye."

"I don't have an eye. I'm blind, damn you," Larry sobbed.

"I know, Lar," Chet said gently. "Let's get you to a doctor."

Larry sat on the forest floor, rocking back and forth.

"Never should have done this, Chet," Larry moaned.

"It's God's way of punishing me."

"I don't know that God had much to do with this," Chet answered. "But I'm thinkin real serious about finishing off that old bastard."

He put his hands on Larry's shoulders and lifted him to his feet.

"Chet, I'll never see again."

"I know, Lar. Let's get you to a doctor." He began guiding Larry to the four-wheeler which had rolled against a small oak tree after Chet had jumped off.

"Lar, I'm real sorry. I never expected anything like this to happen."

"Well, it did and I'm the one who'll pay for it for the rest of my life. I'm blind forever, Chet."

"You've still got one eye, Larry. It could have been worse."

Larry glared at him with his one good eye and said nothing. Blood and fluids drained from the wound in a steady flow down Larry's cheek.

Chet looked over his shoulder as he helped Larry to the four-wheeler. He expected to see the old man approaching but the woods were empty and silent.

CHAPTER THIRTY-FIVE

Dub stood in the stirrups to stretch his legs. He heard the familiar creak of the saddle leather and smelled the reassuring smells of horse and saddle. Reb snorted and shook his head in a way Cato had seen a thousand times. They rode slowly through the scrub brush and thin woods. Tundra ranged out ahead of the horse and rider. Her training had prepared her for just such a job. She had worked several missing person cases with Cato for the Sheriff's department.

The trail they followed was obvious and required little tracking skill. The knarly tires of the Honda had left deep impressions in the soil. Chet had driven over many saplings and bushes in his haste. He'd left a path of destruction that a blind man could follow, and Dub was far from blind. He'd learned tracking as a boy hunting in the Ozark hills and it was a skill he took very seriously.

Dub bent down from the saddle periodically to examine the tracks. The trail led north, up a twisted valley that Dub had hunted years before. Reb moved sure-footedly through the rough terrain. He picked his way around and through obstructions that thwarted Chet and Larry on their cumbersome machine.

Their progress was swift compared to the four-wheeler, but Dub knew the valley would continue to twist and turn its way north for several more miles. There it would come to a head with steep limestone bluffs and only one exit trail that he knew of. He guided Reb up a tight, steep path to get out of the valley before the bluff line began. He was his progress to be unobserved and if he stayed below the edge of the bluffs, he'd be channeled into the same funnel that his quarry had been forced into.

Cato finally dismounted and walked up the last few hundred feet. From his vantage point he could see most of the valley and in the shimmering distance, he could see the area where he thought his quarry was most likely to emerge. High on the slope of the valley, he and Reb moved without obstruction. Now Tundra had no trail to nose, so she trotted behind Reb and investigated the odd smell or interesting track that she came across.

As the trio moved northward, a thunderous shot echoed across the land. Dub reined in his horse and listened intently for a few moments. Another, louder, shot blasted across the landscape. This one was followed by complete silence. All the normal summer sounds of birds, crickets and tree frogs ended while all things listened to the disturbance.

No more shots followed, so Cato nudged his mount forward. He figured the shot was fired less than a mile away. To his experienced ear, it sounded like a large caliber weapon, possibly a shotgun.

"Let's go, Reb. Them fellers is up to something."

Reb picked up his pace and carried Cato rapidly toward the valley's end. Within minutes they arrived at the pass that Chet and Larry had driven through earlier. Cato reined Reb in and surveyed the area before he proceeded. He considered these men to be capable of anything. The death of the bank guard proved that. He pulled the mini-14 from its scabbard and pulled the bolt back. He observed the orderly stack of .223 rounds in the magazine and let the bolt fly home, chambering a round. Now satisfied that his weapon was ready for action, he laid it across his saddle and nudged Reb forward again.

Reb was a deep chested horse and the climb up out of the valley had not winded him at all. He moved with the grace and power of a much younger horse.

They emerged into the clearing where the confrontation had just occurred.

"Whoa, Reb." Cato reined him in and observed an old man and the dead boy.

The man looked up at Dub and blinked through his tears.

"They kilt mah boy," he said thickly to Dub.

"Now why would they do a thing like that?" Dub asked. He had already made several observations and he was interested in what the old man would have to say.

"Well, I dunno. We jest come acrost 'em burying them tool belts and clothes and they shot mah boy." The old man was recovering from the initial shock of his son's death and his innate caginess had returned.

"Why didn't they shoot you?"

"I, uh...I dunno. Jest didn't, thet's all."

Dub had noticed the *cannabis sativa* growing in ordered clumps around the clearing. He also noted the bright, splotchy redness of the man's face and neck.

"What's a matter with your face?" Dub asked.

"One of them fellers squirted somepin in mah eyes."

Cato felt as though he had a pretty good idea of what had actually transpired. He stepped down from the horse, keeping an eye on the old man. He dropped the reins to the ground knowing Reb would not move. Dub carried the Ruger balanced on his hip as he walked around the clearing. The old man made no move to get up. Dub stooped to pick up a spent shotgun shell. He examined the hull carefully, sniffed it, and the dropped it into a pocket. A few feet away he noticed a small blob of gray matter on the ground. He retrieved it and looked at the old man in puzzlement.

"What's this?" he asked.

"Couldn't tell ya," the old man answered. He gently laid his son's head down and stood with some effort. He eyed Dub's badge.

"What will you be adoin' bout all this?"

Dub did not respond. He continued to examine the crime scene. After looking for less obvious evidence, he picked up the tool belts and coveralls. The labels had been cut out of the garments and the tools and belts gave him no immediate clues. He wrapped them all together in one of the rain suits and tied it behind his saddle. As he did so, a glint of light caught his eye, and he followed it to the folding shovel lying in the pine needles where Larry had dropped it. Cato picked it up and looked it over closely.

"Them boys was diggin' a mighty big hole for such a little dab of stuff," Dub observed.

"I reckon they didn't want nobody to find it," the old man replied.

Dub gathered his reins and remounted Reb. He sat thoughtfully for a moment and then spoke to the old man.

"I reckon there's two ways to go. One, I can bring a lot of police and deputies in here and do a full investigation. That would mean a lot of explaining on your part. Or...," he paused for effect.

"Or you can take your boy home and report a huntin' accident. I reckon you got enough trouble right now without causing any more."

The old man knelt down and gathered his son's body into his arms.

"I'll be taken mah boy home. His pore mama's heart's gonna be broke for sure."

Cato watched as the man carried his son through the woods to a soon-to-be grieving mother. He nudged Reb into motion again. Tundra had sat quietly throughout the previous exchange. Now she sniffed the ground and located the trail immediately. Reb followed Tundra's lead and soon they came upon the grisly spectacle of a bloody treble fishhook swinging from the tree branch. Traces of tissue still clung to the rusted barbs.

Cato let out a slow whistle and guided Reb along side the swinging hooks. He noted the disturbed leaves on the ground where Larry had fallen, droplets of blood and the packaging from the first aid dressing.

"I reckon one of them boys is a hurtin," Cato said aloud. Now he was completely certain of what had occurred. No doubt the perpetrators had stumbled across the old man's patch and a fight had ensued. Dub figured the old man had planned to bury more than the tool belts in that hole.

Dub pulled a lock blade knife from the leather pouch on his belt and set about cutting down the fishhook booby traps.

CHAPTER THIRTY-SIX

Chet drove carefully through the woods. He tried to avoid jolting Larry any more than absolutely necessary, but the terrain was rugged with gullies to cross, fallen timbers and myriad holes hidden by the fallen leaves.

Larry clung to the luggage rack with one hand and held pressure against his eye socket with the other. The initial shock of the injury had begun to wear off and the pain had begun in earnest. He was racked by throbbing waves of agony that were nearly unbearable. He cried out several times despite his intentions to be strong.

"Chet. Chet, let's stop a minute. Let me rest just a minute," Larry implored. Chet relented and stopped the vehicle.

"I know you're hurting, Lar, but we've got to keep moving. You need a doctor soon and we've got to find the truck before dark."

Indeed, the shadows were lengthening, and Chet did not relish the prospect of riding through the woods in the dark. While Larry sat holding pressure on his wound, Chet looked at the map. He traced their route up the valley and located where he thought the marijuana patch should be. Their flight from the old man's territory had been so abrupt that Chet was unsure of their present location. Not lost, exactly. Just misoriented, as his old drill instructor would have said. Chet made his best guess of their present position and calculated the heading that would take them to the truck. He then took out a well-worn Silva compass and shot the proper azimuth.

"Larry, we gotta go."

"All right, Chet. But take it easy will ya?"

Chet set off on the compass course with little assurance that his calculations were correct. The responsibility of getting Larry to a doctor weighed heavily upon him and he found himself almost to the point of panic. Mentally he took control and steeled himself for the task ahead. His father had often counseled him to keep his head when trouble struck, and he'd be okay. Chet had to admit the old man was right most of the time. His wisdom had helped Chet through some really rough times. Right now, seemed to be one of those times.

He forced himself to put aside thoughts of what had happened, especially the tragedy of the lives lost and ruined. He knew he had to concentrate on getting back to the truck.

The course Chet had chosen took them across several steep gullies and through some very heavily wooded areas. Larry began slipping into shock as the afternoon progressed. He began shivering in spite of the heat and his body was covered in a damp, greasy perspiration. When Chet looked back at him, Larry's face was an ashen gray. Several times Larry felt so dizzy and disoriented that he forgot where he was and what had happened. The journey seemed an endless series of agonizing bumps and jolts.

They emerged from the gloom of the darkening woods to find themselves at the highway. Chet's dead reckoning had placed them close to their original departure point. Chet took stock of the situation and made a quick decision.

"Larry, I'm going to let you rest here a few minutes while I go find the truck."

"All right, Chet. How far do you think it is?"

Chet looked up and down the deserted highway for recognizable landmarks. There were none.

"I dunno, Lar. I'll just have to ride until I see something familiar. I believe we're north of the truck, but I can't say for sure."

Larry dismounted and walked feebly into the woods where he sat against a tall red oak tree.

"I'll be waiting here, Chet."

Chet produced a foil emergency blanket from his survival pack and tossed it to Larry who was shivering.

"Here, Lar. Wrap up in this."

Larry gratefully accepted the package. The nighttime mountain temperatures had already begun to drop now since the sun had set. It was early fall in the Boston Mountains and the air temperature could easily drop twenty degrees in just a few minutes.

Chet pulled onto the pavement and rode south. He constantly checked for traffic behind him because he had no lights and in the early evening gloom, the camouflaged four-wheeler would be difficult for a driver to see. He rode for nearly a mile before he came across a place that he recognized.

"Ah, shit," he grumbled. He realized that the truck's location was further north. He was going the wrong way.

In frustration and without looking, Chet wheeled the little vehicle abruptly across the two-lane road to head back north. Suddenly he was blinded by the lights of a south-bound car that pulled into the left lane to pass him. Chet had no time to react. The driver of the car urgently slammed on his brakes and began skidding toward Chet. Abruptly the tires gained traction and the car spun off the road, narrowly missing a stunned Chet who simply sat there with no time to react. The impact of the crash was devastating. Chet watched as the car slammed sideways into the low limestone outcroppings that lined the uphill side of the road. Dust flew into the air and there was a rending screech of metal against stone followed by the tinkle of broken windshield glass showering across the pavement.

Chet rode over to the battered vehicle. Inside there was a young man slumped over the wheel, unconscious or perhaps dead. His head had struck the driver side window with sufficient force to shatter the glass. The safety glass had held together with a spider web pattern of cracks, spattered with blood and hair. Blood covered the boy's face and Chet could discern no movement, not even the slightest rise or fall of his chest.

Chet was torn between the desire to render first aid and to escape. He glanced at the bags of money and chose the latter. He rationalized that a motorist would pass by soon and would help. Chet drove north on PigTrail at a frantic pace with the engine screaming. His guilt followed close behind.

In his wooded hiding place, Larry heard the engine as Chet roared past. He knew that Chet had gone the wrong way and was still looking for the truck's location. The sound of the impact had startled him out of his state of near unconsciousness. He fretted and worried that Chet had been hit and that he would languish in the woods, alone, until he died.

Silence fell over the woods as Chet's vehicle flew down the road. In Larry's mind, hours had passed, and he believed Chet was gone, never to return. His body was wracked by bouts of shivering which left him exhausted and weak. The intense pain in his ravaged eye socket washed over him in waves. Finally, he could wait no longer, and he determined to walk out of the forest and seek help.

Darkness had fallen completely by the time Chet located the logging road which was almost two miles north of where Larry should have remained waiting. Chet raced down the dirt road, ignoring the low hanging limbs that whipped at his face as he rode.

The truck was just as they left it, ramps in place. Chet slowed down and carefully drove up the ramps and killed the engine. He jumped down from the truck bed and slid the ramps between the four-wheeler tires. He slammed the tailgate shut and rushed to get the old truck moving. He breathed a sigh of relief when the engine started at the first try.

Chet backed out of his spot and drove recklessly down the logging road to the PigTrail. His tires squealed as he turned hard onto the pavement and headed back to where Larry waited. The soft suspension of the old Ford groaned, and the truck fishtailed across the lanes as Chet mashed the gas pedal flat against the floorboard.

Everything looked different in the darkness, and he stopped twice at the wrong spot to look for Larry. Finally, he located the place where he had pulled out on to the highway with the four-wheeler as evidenced by the tire tracks. He turned the truck around in a careful u-turn, watching for traffic this time, and parked just off the road. He left the engine running with the lights pointed into the woods. Chet jumped out and ran into the woods to the spot where he had left Larry scarcely 15 minutes before. He was gone.

CHAPTER THIRTY-SEVEN

In desperation and despair, Larry pulled himself to his feet. He held pressure against his eye socket and starting walking in the direction he believed was north.

The PigTrail was mere feet away from him, but he was actually moving away from it, deeper into the darkened forest.

His pain-wracked body shuddered in spasms of cold, fear and agony. Gradually his thought processes became clouded, and he no longer had any sense of direction, time or distance. It was all he could do to put one foot in front of the other.

In the ever-increasing gloom, shadows appeared to move, and he recoiled in fright time and time again. He realized, sheepishly, that there were no demons pursuing him. He had lost depth perception when he lost his eye. Many times, he reached out to fend off limbs which were actually several feet away. Other times he ran headlong into unseen branches and tripped over waiting grapevines.

Finally, his legs gave way and he slumped to the ground in exhaustion. He landed on a mat of decaying oak leaves and humus. It made a soft bed into which he nestled, strangely calm now. He laid his aching head on his arm and began softly sobbing with his body curled into the fetal position.

His level of consciousness dropped into a drowsy, sleep state. He was vaguely aware of his surroundings, but shock-induced hallucinations began raging through his mind. He felt that he was being stalked by unspeakably evil creatures. In his mind they lurked in every crevice and dark place of the woods. Closer and closer they approached until he could hear their steps. He knew they were coming to tear out his eyes.

Suddenly he felt a claw like hand dig into the meat of his shoulder. He lashed out with his fists and shrieked a high-pitched wail of fright.

"Lar. Larry calm down, it's me. It's Chet. I'm going to get you out of here."

Larry stopped fighting Chet and allowed himself to be helped up. He didn't speak or seem aware of his circumstances anymore. Blood and pink-tinged matter oozed from the dressing on Larry's face. Chet choked back a gag of revulsion at the gory sight. Larry's skin was clammy and ash gray. Chet flashed on a picture of his friend lying in a coffin, dead.

Chet levered Larry's arm around his own shoulders and began dragging him toward the road. Larry didn't resist. He followed along in a deep state of shock.

Chet had located him by following the sounds of Larry's sobs. The pathetic noise had echoed through the silent woods. Larry had, in fact, walked less than a hundred feet before collapsing. In his disoriented state, it had seemed like miles.

When Chet arrived at the spot where Larry was supposed to be waiting, he panicked and started shouting for Larry. In the darkness, there was no way he could even attempt to look for tracks or evidence of Larry's passage.

After some minutes of calling his name, Chet stood still and listened. He could barely discern a tiny sound that emanated from the woods. At first, he thought it must be a small animal that was injured. Perhaps a child, he thought. Then he realized the sound echoing through the night was most likely his injured partner. He rushed through the trees and brambles toward the sound. He used a tiny mag-lite to illuminate the ground and what he saw was Larry curled up into a tight ball, sobbing like a child. He stood, for a moment, torn between pity and disgust.

CHET REACHED DOWN AND touched Larry's shoulder resulting in the defensive reaction.

The trip to the truck took only a few minutes and during that time Dub Cato rode up behind them in the darkness. He got there in time to see Chet help Larry into the truck. Dub watched as the truck drove away, tires squealing.

Cato stepped down from Reb and examined the ground where Tundra was sniffing. The soil and leaves were still warm where Larry had been curled up.

"Just missed 'em, Tundra." Dub said.

"Don't mean nuthin'. Not a thang." He philosophically observed.

"Can't be too hard to find." Dub had added another piece of information to his stock of clues.

Cato retreated into the depths of the woods and set up his camp for the night.

CHAPTER THIRTY-EIGHT

Chet drove with a sense of urgency all the way to the hospital. He maintained his speed at the limit or just above. He couldn't risk being stopped for speeding.

Once inside the city limits, he was painfully aware of their muddied, battered condition. He tuned the radio to a local country station to listen for news reports. The broadcaster gave the weather forecast, sports results and local events but there was no mention of the robbery. Chet was expecting an all points bulletin announcing a manhunt for two bank-robbing killers.

Chet pulled under the canopy of the emergency department. Larry was quiet as Chet helped him out of the truck and together, they walked through the automatic door. A nurse in whites rushed to assist.

"What's happened to this man?" She demanded.

"Got hit in the eye by a tree branch when we were out four-wheelin'" Chet answered.

"Well, you'll have to stay and fill out paperwork before he can be admitted." She snapped. No bedside manner wasted on Chet.

The hospital staff enveloped Larry and wheeled him into a trauma room.

Chet slipped out the door while Larry was being attended. He drove out of the hospital parking lot in a somber mood. He was elated by the apparent success of their robbery, but a terrible price had been paid.

Chet drove through Springdale and found a self-service car wash. He fed quarters into the machine and began washing the old

Ford and the four-wheeler. He thoroughly blasted every square inch of both vehicles.

Finally satisfied, he slid the spray wand into its holder. He wanted every trace of the mud they encountered to be gone. As he was finishing the job, a black and white cruised past the car wash. The police officer took no notice of him, and Chet breathed a sigh of relief.

"Whew." Chet said aloud. He sat for some moments before leaving the car wash. His hands shook with tremors of anxiety.

"Get a hold of yourself, Chet." He commanded himself. He took several deep breaths to steady his nerves and then he began the drive to his place. Larry's condition occupied his thoughts for most of the trip. Larry's injury complicated things considerably. The story about the tree branch seemed a little thin but there was nothing else he could think of at the time.

He drove through the darkness with a blur of thoughts clouding his mind. Chet pulled into his drive and looked carefully around. He saw no evidence that anyone had been there or was waiting for him. He began to wonder if he'd spend the rest of his life looking over his shoulder and waiting for someone to appear.

Chet yanked open the door to his camper and stroked Max as he entered. He sat on the edge of his tiny couch and dialed the hospital's number on his phone.

"Springdale Memorial. May I help you?"

"Yeah, I'm calling to check on the condition of a..."

"One moment, please. I'll connect you." The operator cut him off in mid sentence.

"Information desk, may I help you?" An elderly voice inquired.

"Yeah, I'd like to check on the condition of a friend of mine."

"Name, please."

"Well, my name's..."

"The patient's name, sir."

"Oh yeah, right. It's Larry Chisum. He got hurt today."

"One moment, please." She put him on hold.

Chet listened to canned music while she looked up the information in the computer.

"Sir, Mr. Chisum is still in the trauma room. The doctor would like to speak with you. Hold please."

Chet hung up instantly. He did not want to answer any awkward questions tonight. He could only hope the hospital was not equipped with caller ID. He remained sitting on the edge of the couch and thoughtfully scratched his chin. Max watched from his perch on the window ledge, his piercing yellow eyes seemed accusing to Chet.

"Mind your own business, Max."

Chet went outside to unload the four-wheeler. He set the ramps in place and rolled it off the truck. The engine fired up easily and he rode it to the basement where he parked it for the night. Chet unfastened the nylon bags and carried them inside. He opened his trap door and dropped the bags down. Tomorrow he would recount the money.

As he locked the basement, he did not anticipate being able to sleep. Back in his camper he opened the first of many beers and he went outside to sit in a lawn chair to think. The night was cold, clear and silent. Normally a couple of beers would settle him down but tonight his soul was tormented and gave him no peace.

Sometime before dawn he forced himself to go to bed where he stared at the ceiling, stained from many leaks. Images haunted him and kept him from sleep. He mentally played the tapes of the robbery in his head, over and over again. He couldn't shake the image of the old man falling down dead during the breakout. The little boy's face was an image that he knew he would never forget. Sleep eluded him until after the sun was already touching the horizon.

CHAPTER THIRTY-NINE

Cato broke camp long before dawn and began moving cautiously in the half light of the early morning. Reb was frisky in the chill air and Tundra bounded playfully about.

"Act your age, Tundra. You ain't no puppy." Dub grumbled at the dog. Tundra paid no attention and continued to romp in the woods, investigating each new smell.

The trio traveled south, staying just inside the tree line of the highway right of way. They followed the PigTrail all the way to I-40. Occasionally, the terrain would force them to move to the shoulder of the road to avoid a drop off or gully. Dub kept a tight rein on Reb, and he whistled Tundra in close to keep her away from traffic.

Cato followed the four wheeler's tracks all the way back to the box culvert they had used to avoid observation by the troopers at their roadblock. He reined Reb back and leaned over the saddle.

"Well, now. Wonder what that was for?" Dub stepped down and picked up a freshly cut willow twig. It was covered in spider web strands.

"Curious. I guess I might stop to knock down some spidee webs but not if I was in some big hurry, would you Tundra? Tundra looked up but kept her own counsel.

Dub swung back into the saddle and followed the day-old trail. He observed how it paralleled the highway until it intersected the gully which led to the bank.

He followed the stream bed until it came to another box culvert. Reb shook his head as Cato reined him in again.

"There's another one. I'll be damned." This time Cato observed the willow twig to be considerably older than the first one he had found. He stepped down from Reb's back and gathered the reins to lead the big horse.

"Come on, shithead." Cato muttered at the horse when Reb balked. Reb had no special interest in entering the box culvert that Cato was leading him toward.

Tundra trotted again and began investigating the interesting smells that inhabited such a place. All kinds of interesting things, beer can smells, an old shoe with very faint human smells, and a fascinating dead thing. What an interesting smell that was.

"Tundra." She jumped, startled by Cato's gruff shout.

"You comin or not?" Tundra followed. Humbled by being so immersed in those interesting smells, she hung back and followed Reb's hooves.

Reb had settled and now meekly allowed Dub to lead him through the dark culvert.

Dub stumbled over debris and filth in the dank, moldy tunnel. Reb's hooves echoed hollowly when he kicked a rock or touched the concrete floor. Tundra gingerly stepped along beside them. She didn't mind the water, she just liked to see where her paws were going.

The trio entered the light and fresh air after only a few moments, but Dub was very glad to be out.

At the side of the stream, Tundra loped over to investigate another thing with human smells.

"I believe you found another 'un, Tundra." Dub reached down to pick up the third willow switch. It too was covered in spider webs and bugs, but it had been freshly cut. Cato pondered these clues for a moment or two.

"I speculate them boys has been here before. Most prob'ly less than a month ago." Dub stated out loud. "Why else would there be more'n two sticks, eh? One stick going in and one going out. Them boys must be mighty feared a spidees, you reckon Tundra?" As usual, Tundra wisely remained silent, and Dub nodded in agreement with his own deductions.

Dub once again swung into the saddle and nudged Reb in the ribs.

They arrived back at the truck by early afternoon. Cato had used the riding time to ponder the situation. He considered all the facts and clues that he had put together.

As he loaded Reb in the trailer, he decided his next step was a trip to Springdale. There he would begin the painstaking process of tracking down each lead. It never occurred to him to contact the Springdale police. He knew he could find these bandits by himself and for his own purpose.

He drove back to the PigTrail and headed north. In the bright light of day, the road was free of traffic and did not seem at all sinister. The night before, the twisted turns of the byway seemed to hold mysteries and danger for the unwary. Many a road-weary traveler had plunged to his death in the tree-studded ravines that lined the road. The PigTrail could be a deathtrap.

Dub made good time and he rolled into Springdale with Tundra sprawled on the seat beside him. She was equally at home in the woods or riding through town. Cato trusted her with his life, but no other human dared try to pet her. She was capable of producing a vicious snarl that would discourage the most avid pet-lover.

Dub drove down Sunset Avenue and located the Radio Shack store. The tool belts were in the back of his truck, and he took a moment to retrieve one of the telephone handsets from one of the belts before walking into the store.

"Good morning, sir. How may we help you." The salesclerk greeted Cato as he walked in the front door.

"I'm Deputy Cato with the Washington County sheriff's department." He flashed his badge.

"Yessir." The man responded in a guarded tone, obviously concerned. He had a couple of tickets that had been unpaid for some time. He wasn't sure who this deputy was after.

"I've got a piece of evidence here with Radio Shack stamped on it. Can you tell me if you sold it to someone local?"

The clerk hesitated for a moment, "Well, I dunno. I guess I could get the manager for you."

"I'd be mighty grateful." Dub answered.

The salesclerk retreated to the back of the store where he stuck his head into the manager's office.

"There's some kinda cop up front. He wants to know about that handset we ordered this summer. Remember when that guy came in and bought two?"

"Yeah, I'll be there in a minute." The manager was playing games on his computer and usually didn't like to be disturbed. This sounded like it might be more interesting than playing Leisure Suit Larry.

He waddled toward the front of the store. Cato was standing at the counter looking at scanners.

"Bill Keyes." He said and stuck his hand out, which Cato ignored. "I'm the manager, can I help you?" He finished saying after an awkward moment's hesitation during which he pulled his un-shook hand back.

Cato repeated who he was and what he wanted to know. He even flashed his badge again for good effect.

"Well, we don't normally keep that kind of information, but you know I suspected something fishy when that guy ordered two handsets. Is there a reward?" He pronounced the word with heavy emphasis on the first syllable of the word *re*ward. Cato ignored the last question, "So you remember selling two of these." He asked as he held up the phone.

"Yeah, so what did he do?" The chubby manager persisted.

"That's confidential at this point but I could let you in on some of the investigation later on. I can tell you'd keep it quiet, right?"

"You bet I would, deputy. You know, I always thought I'd make a right fine police officer. As a matter of fact..."

"Excuse me," Dub interrupted, "when did this feller buy these?"

"I'll look it up for you. Just take a minute. Wait right there."

Cato watched as the store manager hustled back to his cubbyhole. He suspected the man hadn't moved that fast in his whole miserable life. He heard keys clicking on the man's keyboard.

"Deputy, come on back." he shouted from his office.

Dub sauntered back to the office. The little man excitedly pointed to his computer screen.

"Look right there, date of purchase, name and even his vehicle license. Not everybody can recognize a suspicious character, you know." He proudly pointed out.

"Yessir, I realize that." Cato took out his pocket notebook and wrote down, Chet Smith, license KZW 559.

"Well, what did this Chet Smith do?"

Cato looked him in the eye, "Jay walkin'." he said and walked out the door.

Cato grinned slyly as he got in his truck and patted Tundra on her broad head. "Damn fool civilians." he proclaimed.

He idly scratched Tundra's head as he pondered his next move. He had examined every inch of the phone company uniforms. All the labels had been cut out including the size and manufacturer.

"So, where'd these come from?" he asked out loud. Tundra had no answer, she just looked at her master expectantly.

Dub drove out of the Radio Shack parking lot and across town to the Southwestern Bell office. He sat across the street and watched the service people come and go. Their uniforms were an exact match with the ones Dub had recovered. Dub got out and walked over to one of the men who was getting into his truck.

"Excuse me, partner. Where do you all get them fine looking uniforms?"

"I dunno, they're just here every week when I come to work." The man replied.

"Pinnacle."

Dub turned at the voice from behind him.

"Excuse me?" Dub said to the other phone man who had walked up behind him.

"Pinnacle uniform company. They deliver every Monday morning." he answered.

"Thank you kindly." Dub said and walked toward the phone company office. Once inside he consulted a phone directory and, in the Yellow Pages, he found the listing for uniform suppliers.

Pinnacle had a bold listing and Dub wrote down the address in his dog-eared notebook. He left the phone company and drove straight to the Pinnacle address.

The building was an older concrete block structure in the industrial section of town. It was in dire need of paint as were the step vans that occupied most of the cluttered parking lot. Various pieces of laundry equipment sat rusting along the side of the building and the grounds were littered with lint, trash and rags.

Dub drove slowly into the lot and observed that there was no black Ford pickup, license KZW559, present.

A dour looking man stood outside one of the roll-up doors smoking a cigarette. He held the cigarette between his thumb and index finger, cupped inside his palm. He pulled furtively at the cigarette from time to time.

Dub let his truck roll to a stop near the man.

"Howdy. Wonder if you could help me out?" Dub asked in his usual cheerful tone.

"Maybe. What do you want?" The man's expression was one of sour cynicism. His attitude was one of having seen all there was of this world, and he didn't like any of it.

"Well, I'm interested in getting some uniforms and I talked to a feller awhile back. He was driving a dark pickup, black Ford, I think. You know anybody like that?"

"We don't rent uniforms to individuals, mister. Just to companies."

"Okay, what was that feller's name anyway?"

"Don't know who you're talking about. If you want to leave your name and number, I'll have someone get back to you."

"Well, that's okay. I may stop by later and see if I can catch him." No pun intended, Dub thought to himself. Indeed, he would try to catch him.

Bob, the route supervisor, walked back into the plant wondering why someone would be looking for Chet. Probably screwing his wife, Bob surmised. He made a mental note to visit with Chet about it when he came back from vacation.

Dub drove slowly out of the parking lot. He knew the man was lying but he didn't know why. Dub just naturally expected to be lied to but he just liked to know why.

"Everybody lies, Tundra. But what does this feller have to gain from it." Dub got no answer from his canine companion.

Dub pulled out of the Pinnacle parking lot and drove toward the center of town. He had collected considerable information and he had one more stop to make before he went by the hospital. He figured there must be five or six different dealerships that handled four-wheelers, but he had no way to identify the brand of machine that his quarry had been riding. The Honda dealer was the one nearest the Pinnacle plant, so he tried there first.

He arrived at the cycle shop just before lunch time. The floor salesman was sitting at a cluttered desk munching a sandwich. He didn't get up when Dub entered.

"Morning." He said with his mouth full.

"Morning." Dub answered." I'm Deputy Cato with the Washington County Sheriff's department." His badge had been flashed more that day than on any previous year.

"What can I do for you, deputy?" The salesman didn't sound particularly eager to do anything but eat.

"We're looking for a feller that drives a black Ford pickup. I believe he may have recently bought a four-wheeler from you all. Name is Chet Smith, I think."

"What do you want him for?" The salesman asked after swallowing a bite.

"We just need to ask him some questions. Do you remember selling a four-wheeler to somebody like that?"

"I don't know a Chet Smith, but you might be talking about Chet Farmer. Chet's not in any trouble, is he?"

"Probably not even the same guy. But you say this Chet Farmer bought a four-wheeler from you recently?" Dub inquired.

"Well, it was back in the summer. August, I guess. Our biggest model, luggage racks front and back, gun rack too. He plans to take it to the deer woods, you know."

"Have you got Mr. Farmer's address and phone number handy?" Dub asked.

"Just a minute, I'll see what I've got. You could check the phone book you know."

"Yessir, but I'd appreciate it if you'd check if for me anyway." Dub replied in a good-natured way. He really wanted to wring this guy's neck, but more flies are caught with honey than with vinegar, as his dear departed mother would say.

The salesman produced a copy of the bill of sale along with the financing paperwork.

"That ought to do it." Dub said. "Can you make a copy of that for me?" He asked. His lunch already interrupted; the salesman was less than excited to help. "Secretary can make 'em for you." He jerked his thumb in the direction of the office. Dub nodded and headed back to the cluttered office. A frumpy clerical-type was pecking away at a keyboard. She didn't look up when he entered. Cato cleared his throat.

"May I help you?" She asked with little enthusiasm. "Yes ma'am. I'd be mighty obliged if you'd make me some copies of these here papers." Dub did his best to control his already ragged temper. Wordlessly, the woman took the contracts and copied them.

With his copies in hand, Dub returned to his vehicle. Tundra was patiently waiting on the seat, right behind the wheel.

"Well, git over if you ain't gonna drive." Cato spoke to Tundra through the open window of the pickup. She obliged and moved to her spot on the passenger side.

Dub looked over the copies of Chet's purchase agreement and financial statements.

"Uh huh, let's see here Tundra. I got his name, address, phone number, where he works, how much he makes and two personal references. Wonder which one of them references is his accomplice?"

He started his truck and left the dealership. He had succeeded in collecting every piece of information he needed in only a couple of hours. A phone call to one of his buddies at the Sheriff's office could have netted him the same information but Dub didn't figure anybody needed to know he was interested in this particular crime.

CHAPTER FORTY

Max stood squarely on Chet's chest and mewed plaintively. He was hungry and Chet had slept well into mid-morning.

Chet awoke to Max's insistent demands and to a whopping headache. His dreams had a demented quality about them. He dreamed of being pursued, captured and tortured. Actually, not too far from reality.

Chet stretched under the covers and for a moment it was like any other morning. Suddenly the memories of the previous day flooded his consciousness, and he sat up with a start. Max bounded out of his way and stood expectantly at the foot of the bed.

Grimly, Chet got out of bed and set about his daily routines. He purposely did not allow himself to think about Larry or the guard or the boy who died. The radio reports were brief and gave him very little information. There had been a robbery, an undetermined amount of money had been stolen and a guard was dead. The announcer was righteously outraged that a little boy had been killed during the robbery. Apparently, the local authorities were besieged by the citizens of the small community demanding that the child-killers be brought to justice. The suspects had fled on foot and were to be considered armed and dangerous. No descriptions, no vehicles, no nothing. Another story told of a train wreck and a huge fire, all of suspicious origin. Finally, the PigTrail was reported to have claimed another victim. It seemed that a young University of Arkansas student had been killed in a one-car accident on the PigTrail. Somehow the announcer made no connection among the events. Chet was shaken by the news that he was responsible for yet another death. He pictured the wreck in slow motion, and he could vividly recall the gruesome pattern of blood and hair on the glass. He could still hear the sickening impact with the sound of tearing metal and breaking glass. What if the boy had still been alive when Chet had left? Could he really have done something? The real question was, would he have done something if he'd known how bad the boy was hurt? There was no way to know. Never in his wildest dreams would he have imagined so much death and pain. This should have been such an easy crime. No one was supposed to get hurt. He had planned it so carefully and they had rehearsed the whole process, over and over. Chet thought back over every step of the day trying to pinpoint the moment that everything turned wrong. He concluded that, as with most problems, there had been a series of small things that had contributed to the disaster.

Chet decided to ward off his deepening depression by keeping to his normal routine as much as he could. He made coffee, fed an impatient Max and showered in the tiny shower stall. Chet dressed in his customary hiking boots, camo pants and sleeveless black t-shirt. He stood for some time in front of the mirror as he shaved. Chet could remember his old man shaving in front of the mirror in the old house where they'd lived on Cherry Street when Chet was a little boy. "Always live your life so's you can look yourself in the eye when you get up to shave everyday." Those had been old man Farmer's words of advice to young Chester. Chet had never really given much thought to those words until today. Now he stood and looked into the eyes that peered back at him from a lathered face. He wasn't too sure the liked what he saw. He didn't hold the gaze too long before a deepening sense of shame caused him to look away.

Chet sloshed water on his face and toweled off quickly without finishing his shave. He poured a cup of coffee and walked out into the sunshine. It was a warm, early fall day but he felt gloomy in spite of the beautiful weather. Chet had purposely forced himself to wait a little bit before running to check on the money and count it. He knew instinctively that he would struggle with waiting to spend so much cash.

Chet sipped his coffee as he walked to the basement. He turned the key in the dead-bolt lock that secured the heavy door. Chet pushed the door open, and the early morning light illuminated the four-wheeler resting exactly where he'd left it. Chet clicked the transmission into neutral and rolled the heavy machine off away from the hatch which led to his subterranean room. He bent down and pulled up the door with an appropriately sinister creak. A musty smell issued up from the darkness below and he half expected to find his money gone.

It wasn't. Chet clambered down the steep ladder and turned on the single light bulb and it cast moving shadows as it swung back and forth on its cord. The bags of money were heaped on the floor just where he'd tossed them the night before. In a near frenzy, Chet yanked open one of the bags and ran his hands through the bundles of cash. Suddenly Chet realized with a gut-wrenching shudder that he'd left the door to the basement standing wide open. Anyone could just walk right in.

Chet climbed back up the steep ladder and secured the basement door. As an added precaution against being disturbed, he dropped the heavy four by six timber into the stout steel brackets, effectively barring the door from being opened.

Excited now, he slid down the ladder again and impatiently swept his worktable clean. All his hours of work to create the mockup were gone with a single swipe. He dumped the bulging bags of cash onto the table and with shaking hands he began making neat stacks of the bundles of money. He stacked the hundred-dollar bills together, the twenties made a huge pile, even more fives and tens. Chet came across several bundles of one-dollar bills. "Bitch." he muttered. He realized the helpful little teller had sneaked in some singles when he wasn't looking. "Don't mean nuthin'" he grumbled. There was just so much money, he couldn't believe it. He stacked, counted and restacked. Finally, he started counting and making tick marks on a notepad. When he finished, there were two hundred and eighty-five tick marks. Each mark represented one thousand dollars.

"Lord, God Almighty." he exclaimed when he had finished. The sight of so much money staggered him. He restacked the piles again, this time into three even segments.

A tiny, wicked little voice in the back of his head nagged him with several unscrupulous possibilities. "Just keep a little more than a third." The voice urged. "What if Larry didn't live?" The little voice asked. Chet shook his head as if to clear it of such thoughts. Chet divided the money evenly among three of the nylon bags. Each bag contained an equal share of the loot. One bag for each partner in the crime. He positioned the bags on his worktable and turned out the light. In the semi-darkness, Chet climbed out of his subterranean room and stood above the hatch. There was an overpowering draw about money, he concluded. Even though he couldn't spend it right then, he still wanted to touch it, feel it, smell it. He'd never really noticed the smell of money before. It had a real distinct smell to it. With the smell of money still in his nostrils, Chet lowered the trap door and prepared to leave.

He slid a sheet of plywood over the trapdoor to his hidden room and rolled the four-wheeler on top of it. Chet slid the wooden planks between the wheels, and he locked the basement door as he left. He just had to talk to someone, and Larry wasn't an option right then. In fact, Larry might never be the friend he once was. Chet wasn't too certain that Lar would ever speak to him again. Couldn't blame him much. Chet trudged back to the little camper and perched on the edge of the couch. He dialed a phone number from memory.

"Bess, Chet here." She'd answered on the second ring.

"Chet. What's up? You sound kinda winded."

Indeed, he was breathing hard from his walk to the camper. He steadied himself and took a deep breath.

"Bess, can we talk? I mean, can I come see you and talk?"

"Of course, Chet. Is everything okay? I mean, you left before I woke up and well...I just thought maybe you were having second thoughts about... well, you know...us." She had fretted all day about his unannounced departure the day before. He hadn't even called.

"Yeah, no. I mean...I just need someone to talk to for a while. Someone I can trust, okay? Something's happened."

"I'll be home all day, Chet. I don't go to work until eight. Just come on by."

CHAPTER FORTY-ONE

C het drove into town in the early afternoon. This was Saturday and he wanted to visit Larry and, of course, see Bess. He coasted into the hospital parking lot. The Emergency entrance reminded him of the journey back up the PigTrail. Larry had moaned and complained the entire trip. Chet had tried to be sympathetic but instead he just wanted to hit him and make him be quiet. Didn't he know a man wasn't supposed to whimper? Chet wanted to shout, "Be quiet and take it like a man." But he didn't. Now he found himself white-knuckled, gripping the steering wheel and gritting his teeth in suppressed rage.

Chet looked around in embarrassment. No one had noticed him, and he massaged his jaw where it ached from gritting his teeth so hard. He stepped out of his truck and walked purposefully into the hospital. He hoped to not encounter any of the people from the night before when he brought Larry in for treatment. He didn't want to explain his sudden departure.

Chet failed to notice a vehicle had followed him all the way from the outskirts of town. The vehicle was a nondescript pickup that was carrying Dub Cato with Tundra sitting quietly by his side. Cato pulled his pickup into a parking spot at the edge of the medical complex. From his vantage point he could see Chet get out and walk toward the hospital. Cato watched Chet as he looked furtively around. Cato murmured out loud, "Tundra, even if he weren't guilty of nuthin', he shore acts guilty." Indeed, Chet felt as though the entire world was looking directly at him as he walked the short distance to the hospital entrance. He stepped quickly past the throng of smokers who were banished from the hospital corridors. No one paid any attention to Chet as they drew in great lung-fulls of smoke before returning to work or ailing relatives. Inside the hospital lobby, a blue-haired lady in a pink smock directed Chet to Larry's room. As he walked toward the elevator, she logged an entry into the journal that she kept. She recorded a visitor to Larry Chisum's room at one forty three p.m.

Larry was alone and moaning in his sleep when Chet entered. He awoke at the sound of Chet's hiking boots on the glossy tile floor. Larry gasped with pain as he opened his one good eye. His drugged dreams had been filled with dark nightmares and terrible images of agonizing death. He raised his head long enough to manage to focus on Chet and then he let his head fall back to the pillow in disgust. Chet was the last person on earth he wanted to wake up and see. He was pretty sure he didn't much want to wake up at all.

"Hey old buddy, didn't mean to wake ya," Chet said with false cheerfulness. Larry made no pretense at good humor.

"I wish you hadn't. When I'm asleep at least I don't know I'm blind." Larry's words were harsh with a bitterness that struck Chet like a blow. He had not expected such anger from Larry.

"I'm sorry, Lar. I'd give anything in the world if things hadn't happened the way they did."

Larry glared at him with his one good eye. The other eye socket was packed and swathed with gauze. The bandages were wrapped around his head to hold the dressings against the wound. Chet felt slightly nauseated at the sight of the bandaged injury. Never the squeamish type, Chet simply couldn't stop picturing the swinging treble hook with the grisly remains of Larry's eye. The horror of it turned his stomach.

"Lar is there anything I can get for you. Something to eat? Coffee? Anything?"

"No," Larry said shortly. He didn't want anything but his vision. Karie had been there for part of the night. She'd been furious, of course. How could he have been so stupid? What was he doing on a four-wheeler, anyway? Here she was pregnant, and he was out playing in the woods. Didn't he see the branch coming? We're going to sue somebody. What about your job? How are we going to pay the bills? And on and on.

Finally, the pain medication took effect and he'd drifted into a twilight of numbness where Karie couldn't go. He vaguely remembered her yelling something at a nurse and stamping her foot before storming out of the room.

"Lar," Chet whispered and bent down toward Larry.

"What, Chet," Larry answered in a tired voice.

"Over two hundred thousand dollars, Lar. Actually, almost three hundred thousand dollars, Lar."

"I don't care right now, Chet. I can't see. I'm blind and if it was a million it wouldn't bring my sight back," Larry answered bitterly.

Chet nodded and stood back. He was unprepared for Larry's attack. Naturally he'd expected Lar to be in pain, upset maybe, but not like this.

"Why don't you just leave Chet? I don't think I want you here," Larry spoke through gritted teeth. He wouldn't look at Chet anymore.

"Lar, I'd really..."

"Just leave, Chet. Leave me alone," Larry interrupted.

Chet nodded, "All right, Lar. I'm going but I'll be back, and we'll talk when you feel a little better."

Larry didn't answer. He turned his head away and waited for Chet to leave. It was almost time for his pain medication and throbs of excruciating, white-hot agony were shooting through his face. He mashed the call button at his bedside for the nurse. He continued to hold it until he heard Chet leave the room.

A portly nurse swished into his room and reset the call button.

"How are we feeling, Mr. Chisum?" she inquired.

"Why do you people always say, we? We ain't hurt. I'm hurt and I hurt pretty God damn bad right now," Larry shouted and then put his hands to his face. The exertion had caused his wound to throb even more.

"Mr. Chisum, I understand you don't feel well but that's no excuse for vulgar language," she scolded him as she would one of her children. "I'm a Christian woman and I will not hear that kind of talk." She wagged her finger at him as she talked.

"You're not due for another injection for twenty minutes. If you think you can keep a civil tongue, I'll call the doctor to see if we can give it to you a little early, but just this once."

Larry nodded and kept silent as she left his room to call from the nurse's station at the end of the hall. He recognized that this woman held the power of pain over him, and she would use it. No angel of mercy, this one.

She returned a few moments later with a syringe and a small bottle of morphine that she'd logged out and removed from the secured cabinet. She drew a few milliliters of the clear amber liquid from the bottle and set the bottle on the bedside table. She expertly tapped the syringe to float any air bubbles and then she squeezed a tiny amount of the narcotic through the needle. Once she was satisfied that the dose was correct, she injected it into the port of the intravenous line that dripped steadily into Larry's arm. Within moments he felt himself gliding into soft, white puffy clouds of okayness. Everything was suddenly and completely okay.

Outside Larry's room the hallway suddenly erupted into chaos. A monotone recorded voice announced a code blue over the intercom and Larry's nurse bounded from the room. In her haste, she left the syringe on the tray beside the IV stand that held the steadily dripping medication. He noted that she moved pretty quickly for a big girl, and that was okay. She had turned out to be a real sweet girl, Larry decided just before he drifted off. Everything was just okay.

Dub Cato entered the room. He was wearing his official Washington County Deputy's uniform, and no one had questioned his presence on the floor. Cato had stood visiting with one of the nurse's aides he knew when he saw Farmer leave and the charge nurse go in.

"Fat old cow," the aide muttered sullenly. "She's been on my ass all day long. Clean this up. Dump that bedpan. You'd think I was her personal servant." The girl was a daughter of a friend of Cato's. He nodded sympathetically, "Yup, I know the type. Really likes to throw her weight around, don't she?" The aide tittered at Dub's observation. "How come you're here, Dub? Official business, I guess."

"Well, Sue lemme tell ya. I got this..." Dub was interrupted by the intercom announcing the code blue.

"Oh no, poor old Mr. Tucker again," Sue said as she ran down the hall to help with the code.

Dub waited for the commotion to pass him by and then he stepped into Larry's room. He appraised the situation carefully. Larry was in a room by himself. The other bed remained empty. Larry was snoring peacefully amid a tangle of IV tubes and medical apparatus. A box of latex exam gloves was setting on a small bedside table. Dub pulled on a pair of the powdered gloves from the box and moved closer to Larry's side. Larry continued to drift through his happily drugged dreams. Cato speculatively fingered the syringe with its needle still attached. He picked up the little bottle that was on the table. Its label was filled with words too big for Cato to pronounce, much less understand. What he did understand were the warning symbols that made it very plain that this stuff was pretty powerful. Dub noted that Larry was soundly asleep, and he figured that this drug had something to do with that. His eyes followed the clear plastic tube that led from the hanging bag of medication to Larry's arm. He observed the little port that was used for adding medication to the drip. It was the same port that the nurse had used to inject the pain medication for Larry.

Cato held the bottle up and slid the business end of the needle through the rubber seal just like he'd seen done on TV. He pulled the plunger back on the syringe and it filled with the liquid. He slipped the needle into the port and pushed the plunger all the way in. The morphine began traveling toward Larry's arm. Cato removed the needle, drew in another tube full of liquid and also injected that into the port.

He watched as the liquid slowly continued to flow into Larry's bloodstream. At first nothing happened but Cato stood patiently and waited. He listened to the clattering carts and shouting doctors in the hall. He felt certain that the emergency taking place would keep anyone from taking an interest in Larry's plight.

Suddenly Larry's eye fluttered open. He focused briefly on Cato's face and then the white of his eye showed as it rolled upward. Larry's body shuddered with convulsions, and he turned a distinct blue as his breathing stopped. Moments later he lay still.

Cato carefully replaced the syringe where he had found it. The last fingerprints to be found on the syringe belonged to the hapless nurse. Her fate would be decided by hospital boards and attorneys.

Dub stripped the gloves from his hands, pocketed them and walked quietly from the room and out of the hospital.

CHAPTER FORTY-TWO

Max stood in the doorway hissing and growling. His bared fangs and clawless paws were no defense against Cato's brutal kick. The heavy work boot connected with Max's chest and the cat was thrown against the paneled wall of the camper. Max lay in a crumpled heap, lifeless.

Dub Cato scarcely noticed the little body as he methodically searched Chet's trailer. He found lots of potentially useful evidence, but he had no intention of building a case. He was simply looking for the money. Frustrated, Cato left the camper and began investigating the grounds. A well-worn path led to the concrete structure and another, less obvious path, led into the woods. Dub chose the less worn path which ultimately took him to the practice range. He probed around the firing point, looked at targets and broke open the chained ammo box using a pick that he found in the corner of the shed. In disgust, he emptied the box of cartridges out onto the ground.

He swung the pick over his shoulder and stomped toward the concrete building, cursing under his breath. He found the small door to the structure to be locked. After a tug or two he decided the heavy garage door was also secured.

It required several mighty blows from the pick to break the stout padlock. Dub cautiously pushed the door open. He reminded himself to not underestimate his quarry.

Beyond the doorway was absolute darkness and Cato's keen sense of smell registered the dank air of a seldom used room. Still cautious, he pushed the door fully open and stepped back. Nothing happened. He reached in and found the light switch which illuminated a barren room. The four-wheeler sat under a tarp. Cato stepped inside and perused the ceiling, walls and floor. He noticed the residual paint over-spray on the floor and a few empty paint cans. A careful examination of the four- wheeler revealed nothing of interest. He noted the camo tape, the camo net and the battered boards that were obviously used for ramps.

The well camouflaged trap door completely evaded his usually perceptive eyes. He left the basement and walked around the property. There were no signs of digging where Chet might have buried the money. Perplexed, Cato scratched his head.

He decided to take a direct approach at locating the money. He would wait for Chet to return, and he was pretty certain that Chet would oblige him by producing the cash. Meanwhile Cato walked back to his truck and drove it up to the basement. He entered the building and opened the garage door. He backed his truck inside and closed the door. He would wait in the little trailer until Chet returned.

Dub Cato pulled the Mini-14 from the gun rack in the cab of his pickup. He motioned for Tundra to follow and together they walked toward the door of the basement. Tundra sniffed around the four-wheeler and whined.

"Come on, you've smelled one of them machines before." Cato impatiently said to the dog. Tundra scratched at the plywood and barked.

"Dammit, dog. I said let's go." She obediently followed him out the door and together they walked to Chet's camper.

Once inside the camper, Tundra sniffed indifferently at Max's body and then sat down. Cato helped himself to a beer and he sat on Chet's couch to wait. He rested the rifle across his lap and patiently sipped the cold beer. Dub did most of his hunting from a tree stand.

He believed that if he waited long enough and in the right place, his quarry would come to him.

CHAPTER FORTY-THREE

Bess opened the door before Chet had time to knock. She could see the concern on his face, and she pulled him into the room, closing the door behind them.

"Chet, what's going on?" She stood with her hands on his chest, looking up into his eyes.

He put his arms around her and momentarily lost himself in the simple pleasure of a hug from a woman. He absently stroked her hair and drew in her scent. She responded to his hug but squirmed to know what was wrong.

"Bess, I've got something to tell you about." He began but she interrupted. "Let's sit down, Chet. This sounds serious." He nodded his assent and allowed himself to be pulled to her couch.

"Larry's hurt, Bess. And it's my fault, mostly. And some other people got hurt. My fault, too. We did something and it went kinda bad. Parts of it went real bad, actually."

"Chet, what the hell are you talking about? Just start at the beginning and tell me what happened."

"Well, you see. What I mean is, me and Larry been friends for a long time. We work at the same place, know some of the same people and, ...you know, we're just pretty good buddies."

"I know all that, Chet. What happened? What are you so upset about?"

"We did something, Bess. We've always worked hard and never had anything to show for it. You know what that's like, don't ya?"

"Yeah, Chet. I know." Bess was beginning to suspect her lover was about to share something she might not want to know.

"Anyway, I'm always talking him into doing stuff. You know, get rich quick schemes and shit like that. This time it was a little bigger deal than usual." Chet fixed her with a stern gaze and placed his hands firmly over hers.

"Listen, Bess. What I'm about to tell you is..., well it's about a crime. Maybe you don't want to get involved?"

Bess sat back against the couch. She felt her heart pound in her chest and there was a sick feeling in her stomach. Not again, she thought.

"Listen, Chet. I've really enjoyed being with you and I thought we might have a future, but I can't be involved in anything criminal, Chet. I just can't. If what you're going to tell me is going to make me an accessory, don't tell me. Okay, just don't tell me."

"Over a quarter of a million dollars, Bess." Her eyes widened as he spoke.

"Okay, tell me. What is over a quarter million?"

"Larry and me robbed a bank." Chet spoke matter-of-factly. She gasped.

"No Chet. No way, I don't believe it."

"Yup, we did." In spite of himself, Chet almost sounded proud of his accomplishment.

"When?"

"Yesterday, the Carbontown bank."

"I saw that on the news, Chet. Oh Chet, the guard. He died, didn't he?"

"Yeah, Bess and I did it. He was shooting at us and...well, I shot back. You can't really call that self-defense, but it was.

"What about Larry. What happened to him?"

"We were coming back, and we ran into this old codger. This sonofabitch had a huge marijuana patch in the woods all surrounded by booby traps. Larry got hurt. There were these fishhooks hanging down all over the place and one of em hooked Lar right in the eye." Bess gasped and held her hand over her mouth.

"Right in the eye, Bess. He's blind. Tore his eye right out."

"Oh my God, Chet. Where is he? What going to happen?"

"Hospital, of course. And I don't know. He's pretty messed up right now. In his head, I mean."

"Well, of course he is, Chet. Wouldn't you be?" She demanded.

"Yeah, I guess. Anyway, I don't really know what to do next. We had this plan, but we never figured on anything like this." Chet sat limply on her couch and waited for some reply.

Bess' mind was racing. The lure of so much money. So much money. In the dark recesses of her mind were the nightmare details of the time she'd spent in jail. She just couldn't ever go back, not for money. What those women had done to her was unbelievable, not human. No not even for that much money.

"Chet. Listen. I can't be involved. I, uh, ... well, I did some things when I was younger, and I spent some time in a really bad place. I just can't go back. Not ever."

Chet stood up and wiped his sweaty palms on his pant legs. He felt very alone and confused. Far from his expectations of happiness when such wealth was at hand.

"It's okay, Bess. I don't mean to cause you any harm. I expect you'll keep this between us." The last sentence was spoken firmly with his eyes boring directly into hers.

"Of course, Chet. What I don't know, I can't talk about, right?"

Chet strode from the room and left the cheap door ajar behind him. Bess hurried to the doorway to watch. He didn't turn to look back or even slow down. Chet walked purposely toward his old black Ford.

She bit her tongue. She held her breath. She started running down the rusty steel stairs to the concrete landing below.

"Chet," she shouted just as he opened the door. Chet heard her call his name, but he did not turn. He also did not enter the truck.

"Chet, I know you can hear me. Just wait a minute. Just a minute, okay?" Her voice was restrained to avoid being overheard. It came out as a coarse whisper that carried across the parking lot.

Chet pulled his cap off and dragged his fingers through his closely cropped hair in a gesture of agitation. He stuck the old cap on the back of his head and turned to face the woman who now approached him.

"Chet, come back inside. I was wrong. I can listen. Maybe I can help but I won't do anything illegal. Fair enough?" She looked earnestly into his eyes.

He nodded slowly and accepted her small hand in his callused, battered one. Together they walked up the stairs which were baking in the hot afternoon sun.

Back inside her apartment, she sat Chet down at her dining table. Bess got two beers from her refrigerator and handed one to Chet. He drank most of it in one gulp.

"Another?" She asked as he drained the bottle.

"If you don't mind. I could use it."

"Here, drink this one. I'm trying to cut down." Normally Chet would have declined the proffered beer knowing it must have been her last. Today he really wanted that drink.

"Okay, Chet." She began as he chugged the next beer. "What do you plan to do now?"

"I don't know." He replied after wiping his lips with the back of his hand. "I reckon I need to just go back to work like nothing happened. That was the plan, you know. We weren't gonna do anything with the money for at least a year. Maybe two."

Bess nodded. She'd known Chet long enough to recognize someone with an intense need for immediate gratification. Fat chance, she thought, that he'd really wait a year.

More likely he couldn't wait a week. She kept these thoughts to herself.

"That's probably a good idea. How are you going to explain Larry's injury?"

"Tree limb. That's what the doctors think. At least that's what I told em."

She bit her lip, thinking. Chet looked at her and thought he'd never seen anyone so cute. Those full, pouty lips just begged to be kissed. She awoke him from his thoughts.

"Chet, honey. What can I do to help? Is there anything to do or do you just need to wait?"

"Wait, I guess. Mostly I guess I just needed to talk a little bit. I feel like everything's gonna come crashing down. You know, get caught or something."

"Well, did they see you or get pictures or what?"

"No. I don't think so. We covered our trail pretty good. I kept thinking someone was following but I never saw 'em."

"Is the money safe?" She asked tentatively. Really, she wanted to ask just exactly where all this cash was, but she perceived Chet's slight hesitation when she mentioned the money at all.

"It's safe alright. Plenty safe."

She was aware that he was looking at her with some suspicion.

"I just asked, Chet. That's all. I'm not your enemy, remember? You came to me, right?"

"Yeah, I know. It's just I don't know who to trust anymore. Everything's happening so quick right now." Chet had his elbows on the table and now he lowered his head into his hands pensively rubbing his fingers through his hair.

"I'm going back out to my place, Bess. You're welcome to come." He looked at her hopefully.

"Sure, Chet. But I need to do a few things and take a shower. I'll come out after a while. Couple of hours, okay?"

Chet nodded and got up to leave. Bess wrapped her arms around him and kissed him deeply. She smiled her slow sweet smile and kissed him on the cheek as he left. Now her mind was a turmoil of mixed emotions. Certainly, she cared for Chet but how much was yet to be seen. They'd only been dating for a short while and now here she was in the middle of a mess. Seemed that every time she got involved with someone, it turned out bad.

She walked to her refrigerator and opened the freezer. In the back, under the broccoli, was a baggie with several plump buds. Bess extracted a nice one and stripped away the stem, she crumbled the remaining marijuana into a neat pile on a cigarette paper. She rolled it into a tidy joint which she immediately lit. The dope settled her nerves as she drew the smoke deeply into her lungs. The first joint was gone in minutes and the second one shortly thereafter. Bess wobbled to her bed and lay down. Overhead the ceiling fan hummed and washed her in waves of cool air. She slept.

Chet rolled through town with his eyes darting from street to alley to parking lot looking for...looking for what? Police, he guessed. "Get your shit together, boy." He commanded himself out loud. Instinctively, he knew that guilty people acted guilty and that attracted attention. Being hyper-vigilant could only lead to trouble so he resolved to relax or at least act relaxed.

Chet had left Bess' apartment feeling better. He was certain that she was the person he would spend a long time getting to know. She had accepted his secret and now it bound her to him as surely as a ring. As he drove his mind was occupied with fantasies of taking her to Caribbean destinations, romantic cruises and elaborate dinners out. Before he knew it, he was pulling into his own driveway. His subconscious mind had been driving while he was dreaming.

Normally, Chet was more observant than the average guy. He always took an interest in his surroundings and generally didn't miss much. Today was an unfortunate exception. Chet failed to notice the fresh tracks leading to his basement door. He also got out of his truck without noticing the broken lock on the basement door. He did, however, notice the damage done to the door of the camper. He noticed but it was too late. Before he could react, the door flew open, and Dub Cato stood in the doorway holding the Mini-14 pointed right at Chet's chest. Chet saw Cato's finger tighten minutely on the trigger. He couldn't tell if the safety was engaged or not. He assumed not.

"Jest stop right there. I'm Deputy Cato from the sheriff's office. Keep your hands right where I can see 'em." Cato spoke in his habitual drawl. He paused to spit a stream of residue from his dip of Copenhagen. He absently wiped his mouth with the back of one hand.

Chet stood, speechless. He tried to form words, but his tongue seemed paralyzed.

"I...uh,...I don't know what you want." He blurted.

"I reckon you prob'ly do." Cato replied. Chet stood stock still and tried to think. He couldn't.

"I'm gonna step forward and put these cuffs on you. It'd be best if you didn't so much as twitch." Cato dangled a set of handcuffs from his left hand. Chet's hands were shaking as Cato moved smoothly past him. All the while, the muzzle of the Mini-14 was pointed directly at Chet. Cato quickly snapped one of the cuffs around Chet's left wrist. He laid the muzzle of the weapon against the back of Chet's head.

"Put your right hand behind you." Cato's voice was a whisper that chilled Chet to the bone. He complied and Cato snapped the other cuff on his right wrist.

"Now then, I believe we need to have us a little chat." Cato said equably. "Why don't you just come inside and have yourself a seat."

Chet could smell beer on the man's breath. Something just didn't seem right. Why was this deputy out here all by himself and what sort of law officer would be drinking beer on duty.

Chet involuntarily gasped when he stepped through the door of his camper. Max's small body still lay in an unnatural sprawl. His eyes were open but beginning to glaze. His lips were still drawn back in a silent snarl.

"You killed my cat." Chet started to whirl around in anger, but Cato jammed the muzzle of the rifle into Chet's right kidney, hard. A second, still harder jab propelled Chet into the camper where he fell against the old couch. Dust flew up as his face landed on the coarse fabric. He tensed and lay still as a deep, vicious growl sounded in his ear. The hot fetid breath of a large animal blew against the back of his neck.

Tundra stood poised above Chet and her muscles were tensed, ready for the lethal bite at the base of Chet's skull.

"Out." Tundra drew back instantly at the one-word command issued by Dub. She remained at the alert, waiting for the command that would release her to attack.

Still on the floor, Chet began to tremble. In spite of all his strength and courage, he now tasted true terror. All his senses seemed enhanced. He could smell the animal's breath and musky scent. He could hear her breath and the low growls that emanated from her throat. He could also taste the bitter bile that had come up in his throat. He believed he was about to die.

"I'm here to recover that money you stole." Cato spoke in an undertone, just above a whisper. "I don't much care what I have to do to get it."

Chet was beginning to believe the last part.

"I followed you fellers all the way up that valley and over the mountain. Did you know that?"

Chet shook his head. His face was still pressed into the dusty fabric of the couch.

"Didn't reckon you did. You'uns cut a trail thet a blind man could follow."

Dub sat down on the dinette chair and crossed his legs. He rested the weapon across one leg, still pointed at Chet.

"Turn around. Real slow." Cato's voice was again the dangerous whisper that sent shivers up Chet's spine.

Chet began to move, and Tundra's warning growl caused him to freeze in place.

"Go on. Turn around so I can look at your face."

Chet laboriously shifted his bulk around so that he was leaning back against the couch. He found himself face to face with a huge, slathering wolf that appeared intent on tearing out his throat. She let a low growl rumble through her bared teeth and Chet cringed in spite of himself.

"Mr. Farmer, you may have figured out that I'm not exactly interested in bringing you in to justice. In fact, I don't much give a shit what happens to you." Cato looked Chet directly in the eyes. "You do understand that don't ya?"

Chet nodded, looking first at Tundra's oddly disturbing eyes and then at Cato's small, mean eyes.

"I'm gonna ask you one question here in a minute but I want you to be real sure you understand how serious I am first. That all right with you?"

Chet looked confused. He didn't answer.

Cato snapped his fingers and pointed at Chet's legs. With a blood-curdling snarl, Tundra leaped forward and clamped her powerful jaws around the calf of Chet's right leg. Her huge canine teeth tore through the flimsy fabric of his pants and deep into the flesh of his leg. She bit hard and shook his leg vigorously, as though playing tug-of-war but this was no game. Chet shrieked in pain and fear. He tried to kick her with his other leg, but he was in such agony and terror that his kicks were completely ineffective. The steel of the handcuffs bit into his wrists as he tried to free his arms to defend himself. The attack lasted only seconds before Cato called her off.

"Out." Again, his one-word command caused Tundra to pull back instantly. Chet's blood dripped from her wickedly long teeth and combined with her saliva to drip on the floor.

Chet drew his legs up against his body in a near-fetal position. He was gasping for breath and gritting his teeth to avoid crying out from the white-hot pain. He looked down and could see blood spurting from his wounds and the ghastly white of exposed bone. Her teeth had torn the flesh away from his shin bone. Chet's stomach churned and he fought a wave of nausea that swept over him.

Cato sat silently on the dining chair. Tundra stood poised, waiting for the next command. She was highly agitated; her breathing was rapid and shallow. She had tasted blood and was ready for the kill. It was a little game that she and Dub played often. Every time before it had been with animals but now this pathetically weak human was cowered in front of her. She wanted the kill.

"I reckon we understand each other a little better now." Cato murmured. He eyed Chet's wounds speculatively. They were bleeding profusely but he figured Chet ought to have enough blood to answer a few questions.

"This is your one chance to answer my question. If you answer it wrong..." Cato left the sentence hanging with palpable malice.

"Where is the money?" Cato's voice was just a whisper.

Chet eyed Tundra, her muscles tight as piano strings. He looked at Cato's dead-pan expression. He looked down at his own blood pooling on the floor.

"In the basement." His voice was little more than a croak. Cato nodded. He knew Chet could be lying but didn't think so.

"Let's go look. You show me." Dub motioned at the door.

Chet was incredulous. Surely this mad man didn't think he could walk all the way to the basement. Chet sat frozen in place.

"You either get up and walk or I'll have her drag you there." As if to punctuate Cato's point, Tundra growled ominously.

Chet scrambled to get up. In his weakened condition and without the use of his hands, he fell hard at the edge of the door. He lay stunned for a few seconds and his eyes focused on Max. The poignant tragedy of the death of his cat gave him the anger to get up. He braced one shoulder against the door frame, and he used his good leg to stand up. The throbbing pain of his wound made him lightheaded, and he had to brace himself until the dizziness passed. Chet lurched out of the little camper and into the blazing sunshine. This was the time of Indian summer, and the days were hot and clear. The heavy rains had passed and all around him Chet could hear the sounds of life. Birds were chirping and flitting from branch to branch. He was aware of a fat gray squirrel scampering across his yard, looking for acorns. Chet looked up at the brilliant blue sky with its faint traces of cloud. There was a certainty in his mind that he would never see these things again.

Chet stumbled forward. The shredded flesh of his leg sent throbbing shock waves of agony coursing through his body. He hobbled toward the basement, just barely keeping his balance. Behind him, Tundra followed with hackles raised and fangs bared. She continued to growl ominously.

Cato called her down again. She shrank back but more reluctantly this time. The blood smell and taste had aroused primal instincts that were far older and far stronger than her allegiance to Dub Cato.

"Tundra, out!" Cato shouted and she crouched. The tantalizing smell of blood was overpowering to her, and she began drooling a pink tinged froth. Chet turned and watched her with morbid fascination. He made the mistake of looking directly into her eyes and she instantly lunged.

"Tundra, out. Out, Goddammit!" Cato shouted again. She cowered once more and looked over her shoulder at Cato. He brought his arm down in an exaggerated motion toward the ground. It was his hand signal for her to lie down and stay. She obeyed.

"Don't look her in the eye. Never look a wolf in the eye, it's a challenge." Dub spoke quietly to Chet who quickly looked away from the animal.

Dub Cato had never seen Tundra in such a state. He was uncomfortably aware that his control was minimal at best.

"Get going, show me where the money is and be damn quick about it. This animal wants you bad, and I just may let her have you." Cato's voice was urgent, and Chet turned back toward his basement. His progress was laboriously slow, and Cato grew impatient.

"Hurry up, damn you. I ain't got all day." Tundra picked up on her master's agitation and began to growl again. Chet ignored her this time and continued to hobble toward the basement door some hundred feet away.

Chet tried to think through the fog of the shock that was beginning to set in. He had lost considerable blood and now he was experiencing chills and his vision dimmed. 'Got to keep going.' he thought to himself. 'Think, Chet. Think.' But he couldn't think. In fact, just staying conscious and on his feet was a major effort.

Chet looked down at his leg and saw that the spurting blood had diminished to a steady flow. He wasn't sure if that was good or not.

Tundra continued to follow at a close interval. Chet could hear the constant rumble in her throat, and he glanced nervously over his shoulder several times. In spite of his fear, he couldn't help but marvel at the huge beast following him.

Tundra was indeed a magnificent specimen. Her sire had been captured on the barren landscape of the Northern Canadian tundra.

The huge male had been the alpha male, or leader, of a hunting pack. He wore many battle scars across his snout and one ear had been nearly torn off. This alpha male led his pack in hunting the great American bison, or buffalo. The massive buffalo had few predators on the continent, but the wolves of this pack preyed upon them with some success.

Cato had seen this animal when a hunting buddy of his had returned from an elk hunt. While on the hunt, several of the men had set traps around the area just to see what they could catch. Tundra's father had blundered into the wicked steel jaws of the trap and been caught. His foreleg was broken from trying to escape and he had been beaten into unconsciousness by the hunters.

When Dub saw the animal, he was immediately interested. The proud head had been scarred and battered but the animal still held himself with ferocious defiance.

One of Cato's other friends had started breeding wolf hybrids and Cato thought this might make a good stud. When he approached his wolf breeder friend, the man had flatly refused. No, he'd said. He was trying to breed an animal that could be controlled and if there was too much wolf, you couldn't ever get control.

Dub had persisted and finally the breeder offered one of his less aggressive females for the experiment. Several months later Dub picked out the smartest, most aggressive of the puppies that resulted from the breeding. He named her Tundra after the land of her father.

Chet continued toward his basement. It looked less like a fortress to him now and more like his tomb. The pain in his leg ebbed and flowed with throbbing intensity. He staggered up to the door and saw the lock had been smashed. He pushed it open and flipped on the light switch. The four-wheeler was sitting just as he left it. He was frankly astounded that his tormentor had not found the trap door. Chet leaned and against the door frame. He knew if he revealed the location, he'd soon be dead.

"It's gone. It was right here," Chet croaked in a voice he calculated to sound shocked.

"Don't give me that shit," Cato shouted. Tundra growled deeply and moved toward Chet.

"I'm not lying. Look for yourself. It's gone." Chet pointed to the empty racks on the four-wheeler. Dub leaned his weapon against the door frame and shoved Chet into the basement. Chet stumbled and fell on his bad leg. He bellowed in pain and Tundra instantly attacked. She bit into his still-bleeding wound and Chet shrieked in agony. He writhed and twisted, trying to escape the merciless fangs. His arms were still manacled behind his back, and he couldn't fend off the brutal attack. He managed to land one good kick on Tundra's snout just as Cato called her out. She did not obey. Instead, she renewed her attack higher on Chet's leg, just above the knee. Blood flew and soaked her white muzzle in a gruesome crimson mask.

"Out, Tundra. Out. Out," Cato shouted over and over again but Tundra was lost in the blood lust, and she remained oblivious to his commands. Finally in frustration, Cato booted her squarely under the ribs and drove the wind right out of her. She yelped and retreated to a nearby corner. She watched Cato, waiting for another command.

Chet was left on the floor with blood pooling all around him. He was ashen and shaking, obviously going into deep shock from loss of blood.

"Where is it, damn you." Dub knelt by Chet and shook him by the shoulders. Chet was beyond hearing Cato. He had been so traumatized by his wounds that he simply sat in the pool of blood and rocked back and forth.

"I think you've done just about enough damage." A commanding voice echoed through the basement.

Cato looked up to see Agent-In-Charge O'Conner standing framed in the door with his weapon drawn and aimed squarely at him. Dub sized up the situation and reacted quickly, "Man, am I glad to see you. This is the perpetrator from the bank robbery and ..."

O'Conner interrupted, "I'm very well aware of who this is. Probably better than you can imagine. Now back away. Go on. Move back." O'Conner motioned with his weapon for Dub to move back. Cato moved cautiously back to the four-wheeler and leaned against it. He was confused. His Mini-14 was still leaning against the door frame, and he bitterly wished he hadn't been so stupid as to ever let go of it. He started pondering this situation and what it all meant.

Agent-In-Charge O'Conner moved to Chet's side, cautiously avoiding the growing pool of dark red blood.

"Chet. Chet, it's me, O'Conner." He shook Chet's shoulder and finally slapped Chet on the face to raise his level of consciousness. Chet's eyes registered a blank stare followed by surprise and relief.

"We did it, John. We really did it, man." Chet spoke thickly.

O'Conner looked up at Cato and saw that Cato had heard and had immediately realized what was going on. He raised his service weapon and aimed at Cato's chest, "Don't move. This isn't your business." Cato nodded in agreement. It wasn't his business, but his mind was racing with all the possibilities of how he was going to make it his business.

"I was wondering how those idiots would have known when to hit that bank and how to pull it off. Why, hell, now I know why you sent everybody up and down the interstate. Shit, you set the whole thing up and I just got in the way." Cato scratched his chin and actually chuckled.

"Don't speak again or I will kill you." O'Conner spoke authoritatively and Cato took him at his word.

"Now, Chet. Listen to me Chet." Chet's eyes were trying roll up in his head as O'Conner shook him awake again. "Chet, I'm going to get you some medical attention in just a few minutes but first we have to be sure the money's safe, right? You guys did a beautiful job, and we don't want to lose it, right Chet?" Chet nodded groggily and tried to sit up.

"No, Chet. Just lay there. I'll get you an ambulance but first tell me where you put our money." Chet tried to focus but his brain was starving for oxygen, and he couldn't make sense of what his partner was wanting.

"It's safe, John. Really it is. I took good care of everything. I... except Larry, I guess. Larry got hurt, John. Tore his eye out." Chet started babbling at this point and O'Conner tried another tack.

"Chet, tell me right now. Where is the money?" O'Conner used his command voice and Chet snapped back to consciousness.

"You're standing on it, John. You're right on top of all that money." Both O'Conner and Cato looked down and saw nothing.

"He's lost it. He'll be dead in a few minutes, but I can find that money." Cato spoke to O'Conner in spite of the younger man's warning. O'Conner raised his weapon again, but this time Dub whistled through his teeth. One short, shrill warble sent Tundra bounding across the floor. She leapt and slammed all her weight into O'Conner's body. The weapon discharged with a powerful roar that reverberated through the confines of the basement. The impact of Tundra's body was enough to stun O'Conner and the pistol flew out of his hand and skittered across the concrete floor, away from Cato. Tundra was still under the influence of the blood lust, and she bit savagely at O'Conner's throat. Her immensely powerful jaw muscles drove her fangs deep into his throat and the warm, fragrant blood filled her mouth. She shook her victim violently from side to side tearing the flesh and blood vessels of his neck. Within moments, Agent-In-Charge O'Conner lay twitching on the floor beside Chet. Blood spurted from the severed carotid artery. She continued to hold her victim down, waiting for his body to become still. Millennia of hunting instincts welled up in her brain and she felt the rush of excitement at the kill.

Chet recoiled in fear, and he rolled his tortured body away from the gory scene that was happening right next to him. Tundra watched him over the body of her victim. She still held O'Conner's neck in a vise-like grip of death while deep rumbling growls emanated from her throat.

Cato stood back and watched. He was enthralled at watching his animal kill someone. At the same time, he became aware of an intense burning pain in his right side. He reached down to touch his side and his hand came away wet with blood.

"You fucker. Goddamn you to hell." Cato shouted at the now lifeless body on the floor. The bullet from O'Conner's gun had torn a hole through Cato's side, just above his belt. The slug had expanded, blasting a large gaping hole as it exited his back.

Chet continued rolling and scooting his body toward the door. The sunlight was streaming through the doorway as Chet lapsed into unconsciousness.

Dub pulled a soiled handkerchief from his back pocket and stuffed it into his shirt against the throbbing wound. He was beginning to feel the excruciating fire in his side, and he fought a wave of nausea.

"Tundra, out. Out, Goddammit!" Tundra completely ignored Cato and continued to hold the limp throat of her victim. She snarled a warning toward Dub, and she began dragging the heavy body toward a dark corner of the basement.

"Well, shit." Dub watched in horror as Tundra began tearing hunks of meat from the FBI agent's torso. She was eating her prey in the ancient way of her ancestors. She paused between bites to glare at Cato and to defiantly growl a deadly warning.

Dub held his side and swayed slightly. He looked down at the motionless Chet and wondered, in a detached sort of way, if he was also dead.

The basement was deathly quiet except for the gruesome sound of tearing flesh that came from the dark corner where the wolf was feeding. Dub Cato watched in disgust as the blood from Chet and the huge puddle from O'Conner blended and ran in a sluggish river toward the center of the basement. The gory stream ran to the four-wheeler and disappeared.

Cato looked at the floor in puzzlement. He knew the blood had to be going somewhere.

"Ah, shit. He told us it was right under us." Cato muttered out loud. He moved to the four-wheeler and tried to push it out of the way. It wouldn't budge. He fiddled with the shifter mechanism until he got it into neutral. The big soft tires squelched against the cool, damp concrete with little squeaky noises. Cato pulled away the tarp and the plywood. As the carefully inlaid trap door was exposed, the pool of blood drained more rapidly into the gap between the door and its frame.

"Well, shit again." Cato was disgusted with himself for not finding the hidden spot when he first entered the basement. He knelt down and tugged at the heavy door. The pain in his side left him faint and weak. Cato rested on his knees for a few moments and tried again. This time he succeeded in raising the hatch to its fully open position. He could see the ladder that led down into the pitch-black darkness of the hidden room. There was a cool musty smell of all dark places and Cato felt a nameless fear. It was the fear of dark places and of the unknown. He knew Chet was resourceful and there was a distinct possibility of a booby trap. He also knew the money was down there and that knowledge was more seductive than anything he had ever known.

Dub held his side with one hand and bent down to begin descending the ladder. The blood had poured over the ladder and now it dripped down from rung to rung in slippery, congealing globs. He deliberately placed his feet on the rungs and gripped the bloody frame of the ladder with his left hand. The smell of the blood mixed with the musty odor of the dark hole overwhelmed him and he retched involuntarily. Bile rose in his throat, and he retched again. This time his self-control couldn't prevent the convulsive contractions of his abdominal muscles and he vomited a bitter stream down the front of his shirt. The intense muscular contractions of his vomiting tore the already shredded muscles and tissue of his side. Cato cried out in pain and momentarily lost his white-knuckle grip on the ladder. He fell into the darkness and landed heavily on his back.

Cato fell directly on top of the table where Chet had so carefully crafted his mock-up of Carbontown and its bank. It was also the table where Chet had distributed the money into neatly stacked piles of tens, twenties, fifties and one-hundred-dollar bills. The force of the fall slammed the breath out of Dub, but the piles of paper cushioned the stunning impact. Cato's considerable bulk shattered the legs of the table and the entire structure crashed to the floor with Dub lying senseless on top of a fortune.

He gradually came to his senses, slowly becoming aware of his position on the floor of this dark place. Dim light filtered through the trap door and illuminated the tiny room. Dub gingerly moved his head and looked around. He realized he was in Chet's most secret place. The walls were lined with weapons of every description, boxes of ammunition, and miscellaneous gear that any survivalist would envy.

Dub reached down with his left hand and began to explore his aching body. Miraculously, nothing seemed broken. The hole in his side was hurting with wicked intensity but he could handle that. As he moved his hand over his body, he encountered stacks of paper. He picked up one bundle and held it up in the pitifully dim light. He gasped as he realized he was lying in the middle of a huge pile of cash.

Moaning with the pain of his wound, Cato rolled up onto his knees and surveyed the situation. There was more money on the floor than he had ever seen in his entire life. He grabbed up stacks and bundles of it just to touch so much money.

"Get your shit together, boy." Dub commanded himself. He looked up and discovered the string hanging from the bare light bulb. He raised himself to his feet with some difficulty and tugged on the string. The tiny room was flooded with the harsh glare of the hundred-watt bulb. Cato was again shocked by the sheer volume of the scattered cash on the floor. He picked up the crumpled nylon bags and began stuffing the money into the compartments without regard for the burning pain in his side.

CHAPTER FORTY-FOUR

Against every bit of reason and common sense, Bess left her apartment and drove toward Chet's country home. Her head was pounding, and she was still groggy from the deep, drugged sleep from which she had awakened.

Bess knew Chet was in trouble, but she had developed a sense of self-preservation that told her this trouble could spill over onto her in a heartbeat. Nonetheless there was something about Chet that she desperately wanted. He had the strength and determination of the kind of powerful man that she'd always fantasized about as a young girl. At the same time, he'd shown her warmth and a sense of compassion that she hadn't ever known. There'd been so many men and, God help her, a few women in her life but no one had ever treated her like she was really special.

The road leading to Chet's place was rutted and potholed. She bounced into his yard and killed the engine of her old Escort. The door to Chet's trailer was hanging open. That was very unlike Chet, she thought. With an overwhelming sense of dread, she got out of her little car and walked to the trailer.

"Oh, Max." Bess held her hand over her mouth in shock. Max's crumpled body still lay on the floor. His lips were drawn back into a permanent, silent hiss. She wanted to cry for the little soul that she had stroked and petted so few times. A quick look in the tiny camper revealed that Chet was not there. She stepped out into the sunlight with a sick feeling deep in the pit of her stomach.

"Chet?" she called tentatively, not too loud.

"Chet are you here?" she called a little louder just as she heard a muffled gun shot coming from the direction of Chet's basement. She drew in a quick breath, eyes wide with fear.

She took a step toward the basement and stopped. This was everything she did not want. All those old feelings flooded through her. She'd learned to mind her own business in prison. She'd walked away every time there was trouble. Now here was real trouble and Chet was dragging her right into the middle of it.

"Damn you, Chet." She said under her breath and strode toward the basement door which was also hanging open.

She arrived at the door to the basement and froze. She simply could not make herself go inside. The interior of the concrete structure was dark and forbidding. She heard sounds of movement, and an occasional groan. Just as she was about to enter, there was a muted crashing sound followed by silence. Bess turned away from the door and pressed her back against the wall beside the door. She was breathing deeply and very fast. She had never been so afraid in all her life. Just yards away she could see her old Escort and it looked so good. She knew she could just climb in that old friend, and it would take her far, far away. She looked down at the coarse red soil at her feet. She'd been running all her life and now there was someone who really needed her and all she could think to do was run away.

"Damn you, Chet." She muttered again. "Damn you to hell."

She turned back to the door in time to hear more muffled activity. Cautiously, she peered around the door frame but could see little. She did see a deadly looking rifle leaning against the inside of the door frame. She grabbed it and quickly jumped back outside. She waited. Nothing happened so she peered around the door frame again. She could just make out the form of Chet's four-wheeler when suddenly something thudded on the floor inside. She gasped and jumped back. This was nothing like the shows on TV where the cops just kicked in the door and went for it. She was so scared that she was afraid of wetting her pants. There was another thud and another and finally one more. She peered around the door frame in time to see a person climbing up out of the floor. She thought it was Chet, so she moved into the basement and stopped in horror.

Her eyes quickly adjusted to the dim light, and she could see a huge dog tearing at a prostrate figure on the floor. Dub Cato looked up in surprise at the figure blocking the light coming from the door. He gritted his teeth and held one hand against his side as he finished climbing up the ladder to exit Chet's hidden room. He was puzzled by this female standing in the doorway.

Bess held the Mini-14 that Cato had left leaning against the doorway. She pointed it at Cato. "Get that animal away from him." At this point Bess could only see Tundra worrying the body like a rag doll. She assumed it must be Chet who was actually lying in the shadows next to the door.

With painful effort, Dub stood to his full height and prepared to take command of the situation.

"Look here little lady, I'm Deputy Cato with the sheriff's department. You lay that gun down right now or you'll be an accessory to a felony." He spoke in his most commanding voice. In spite of herself, Bess cringed. She had seen the result of law officers before and she feared their power over her. She swallowed hard and swung the muzzle of the weapon toward Tundra.

"Call him off. Call him off now." She screamed at Cato. Tundra reacted to the aggression in Bess' voice. She withdrew her muzzle from O'Conner's body cavity and coiled herself to attack this new intruder. Bess yanked the trigger and at such close range she could hardly miss. Cato's weapon was loaded with .223 hollow points. A thunderous boom shattered the silence and a foot-long tongue of flame shot out of the weapon's bore. The tiny bullet struck Tundra's skull with an audible smack and blew out the side of the massive head. The huge lupine body slumped over her victim and lay still.

"Goddammit, you shot my dog." Cato bellowed and charged toward Bess. She saw him coming and stumbled backward out the door, trying to escape. Dub closed the distance between them and grabbed the warm muzzle of the weapon. It discharged again, this time blasting a blackened hole through the palm of Cato's right hand.

Bess was horrified. She stood stock still and watched Dub as he looked incredulously at his mutilated hand. He made no sound, he just looked at the blackened hole and the tiny fragments of bone protruding from the top of his hand.

"I'm sorry. I didn't mean..." Bess began but stopped as she saw the rage in Cato's eyes. She took another step back, preparing to run back to her car and escape. All thought of rescuing Chet had left her mind, she was simply trying to escape.

Cato, weak from loss of blood from his first wound and now injured again, staggered forward and sank to his knees. Bess saw his eyes roll up just as he fell forward onto his face with a sickening thud.

Now she was faced with a dilemma. Cato's bulk was blocking the doorway. She would have to step over his body to get to Chet. Cato was still breathing; she could see that. If he came to, she knew she probably couldn't shoot him. It just wasn't in her to kill deliberately.

Bess steeled herself and took a deep breath. She pointed the weapon at Dub's hulk and stepped gingerly over him into the basement.

The smell of blood was overpowering. There was a huge stain on the floor leading to the center of the room where she saw four black nylon packs resting beside an opening in the floor. She turned to the corner of the room where the wolf was collapsed over the other body. Tears welled up into her eyes and she was positive that Chet was dead, but she just had to see for herself. If there was a chance, she thought. Maybe there was the smallest chance that he...

"Bess? Bess, is that you?" A weak voice came from the shadows beside her. She jumped and instinctively pointed the weapon toward Chet.

"Chet. Oh my God, Chet how bad are you hurt?" Bess rushed to his side, afraid to touch him anywhere.

"I dunno. That damned dog got my leg." She gasped in shock when she saw the bone exposed and shreds of flesh hanging from his leg.

"Get these cuffs off me if you can."

"Just lay back, Chet. Let's get this bleeding stopped first." She looked quickly around for anything with which to bind his wound. There was nothing. She tore a strip from the bottom of her shirt leaving her flat belly exposed. She carefully wrapped it around his leg, above the wound.

"Chet, I'm going to pull this tight, honey. We've got to stop the bleeding." She firmly pulled the fabric around his leg and tied it into a knot. The pulsing blood slowed to a trickle. Chet was so far into shock that he scarcely noticed the additional pain.

"Get the key. The key." Chet spoke in a whisper that Bess could barely hear.

She looked around for a key.

"What key, Chet? I don't know what you want." She looked around again in frustration until she remembered being released from her own set of cuffs by detective Hebert so many years ago. He'd used a tiny key that he kept on a clip on his belt.

"Oh, no. I can't, Chet. I can't touch that man." But Chet wasn't listening. He had slipped into merciful unconsciousness.

Bess stood and looked down at Chet. Her heart was breaking at seeing this man in so much pain and so badly hurt. She took a deep breath and cautiously moved toward Cato's unconscious form. She held the Mini-14 at the ready.

Bess knelt down by Cato's prostrate form. She could see his torso moving slowly with each ragged breath. Blood was oozing from the wound in his side and flowing freely from the hole she had blown through his hand. He did not stir.

Bess reluctantly probed his back pants pockets without finding any keys. "Who are you kidding?" She asked herself. What man ever carries his keys in his back pocket, they're always in the front and that was exactly where she couldn't reach. Cato's heavy body was plastered face down across the doorway and she couldn't see any way to move a man that outweighed her by at least a hundred pounds.

She ran back to Chet. "Come on, Chet honey. Let's get up. Chet, get up." Chet did not move or respond. Bess leaned against the wall and slid down to sit beside Chet in absolute resignation. She cried in fear and anger. As the tears rolled down her face, she could see the other fallen man. The huge wolf was collapsed over his upper torso, but she could see the lower half of his body. There was a holster tucked into his pants at the small of his back. Another cop? Maybe he would have the handcuff key she needed to free Chet.

Bess struggled to her feet and wiped her eyes. She glanced briefly at Cato's still form and moved over into the shadows to inspect the other man.

Bess had seen some things in her life. Prison had hardened her, drugs had numbed her, the bar scene had shown her the worst side of people, but nothing prepared her for the sight that awaited her.

Tundra had fed in the way of all wild animals. She had torn out O'Conner's throat and then began tearing at the soft flesh of his belly. Instincts as old as nature itself guided her to consume the mineral and vitamin rich organs of her victims. She had disemboweled him, and she was in the process of gorging herself on his heart and lungs when Bess shot her.

Bess saw the gore and gagged. "Oh, God. Oh, no. Oh, no." She dropped the rifle and lurched away from the spectacle and vomited.

She doubled over heaving and retching. The stench from his torn bowels wafted across her face and she vomited again as she ran toward the entrance. She literally jumped over Cato's silent hulk and landed in the clinging red clay mud and fell to her knees. Fresh air blew across her face and relieved the gut-wrenching nausea, but it couldn't blow away the horror. Bess stood up in the failing light and drew in lung-full after lung-full of clean air. Beads of perspiration covered her forehead, and she trembled all over. Great racking sobs shook her body and she gasped for air. She felt iron-like bands constricting her chest, suffocating her. Bess closed her eyes and focused solely on the next breath of air. Slowly, ever so slowly she gained control of her breathing, and she opened her eyes.

Cato was still immobile on the threshold. No sound could be heard from inside the dimly lit basement. Chet was dying in there and she couldn't will herself to get up and help him. "Get in there." She commanded herself. But she didn't move. The sun was slipping below the horizon and the night things began to chirp, squeak and buzz. Bess took a first tentative step toward the door. She eyed Cato suspiciously but he remained motionless. Only the tiniest movement of his chest revealed that some life remained in him.

Bess moved to a place just beside Cato. She knelt and slid her hand under his belly. He was heavy in a way that only the dead or unconscious can be. Her hand scraped against the concrete until she touched the top of his jeans. Stifling the urge to run, Bess wormed her hand into his pocket and heaved a sigh of relief when her fingertips encountered a set of keys. She tugged at the key ring until she freed it from his pocket. Cato groaned and Bess jumped back with a gasp, but he was still unconscious.

Bess examined the key ring and decided the tiny skeleton key must operate the handcuffs. Stepping over Cato one more time, she moved to Chet's side. His wounds were no longer bleeding profusely. His breathing, however, was very shallow and rapid. In the dim light of the basement, she could see that Chet's normally ruddy complexion was a deathly pale.

"Chet, honey. Chet, I've got the key. Let's get out of here, baby. Chet, come on Chet." Bess fumbled with the tiny key until she got it into the lock on the handcuffs and opened each side. The cuffs slid open with no effort at all, and she breathed a sigh of relief. She let the handcuffs fall on the bloody concrete beside Chet who was completely immobile. Bess shook Chet frantically, but he had slipped so far into shock that he was totally unresponsive. Now she had another problem. Chet was a good-sized man, and she would have to drag him to her car. Cato still blocked the doorway and Bess was positive that she couldn't drag his hulk out of her way.

Bess looked around the basement for anything to use to move Cato and she saw the overhead door. "Damn. Why didn't I see that before?" she said out loud. Bess rushed across the basement and in the darkness, she fell headlong over one of the nylon packs. She landed hard on one shoulder on the cold concrete. After so much trauma, this final hurt seemed so unfair. She wanted to just lay there and whimper, but Chet's condition was worsening by the minute.

"Damn you, Chet. Damn you to hell." Bess staggered to her feet and walked carefully to the garage door. She fiddled with the lock mechanism until she felt the handle turn in her hand and the bars slid out of the door track. She lifted the steel door and fresh night air flooded the basement.

Bess rushed back to Chet and grasped his hands and began pulling his limp body toward the open doorway. As she dragged him past the nylon packs, she stopped briefly to catch her breath. She glanced quickly at Cato to confirm he was still unconscious. He was. She let go of Chet's hands and his arms fell with a sickening plop to the concrete floor. "Oh Chet, honey I'm sorry." Nonetheless, curiosity intervened, and she bent down and examined one of the nylon packs. It was closed with quick release buckles which she unclipped. Bess opened the pack and gasped. She had never seen so much cash in her life. She looked around and spotted the other packs which she also opened. They each contained a similarly staggering amount of money. She looked back at Chet in disbelief. He'd told her about the bank of course. She just hadn't comprehended the magnitude of what they'd done.

Another deep breath and Bess returned to dragging Chet toward her car. She got him to the entrance of the basement and decided to drive her little car right up to the doorway.

She sprinted to the old Escort and fumbled for her keys. The little engine started with less hesitation than usual, and she jammed it into first gear. The path to the basement was muddy after so much rain and the wheels spun as they sought traction. Bess drove right to the overhead door and parked on the concrete apron just in front of the door. She jumped out and left the engine running for fear that it wouldn't start so handily next time.

Chet was lying exactly where she had left him, and she ran to him. Just as she squatted to grasp his hands, she realized that Cato; however, was not where she'd left him. She looked up and froze in horror. Dub had roused himself from his loss of consciousness and had crawled to the Mini-14 that she'd thrown down next to O'Conner's body. Now he sat looking at her with the rifle held awkwardly in his left hand. The barrel rested on his knee and the muzzle was pointed directly at her chest.

"I reckon you got a problem, little lady," Cato said thickly. He was still groggy and disoriented. He could only dimly make out Bess' slim silhouette in the gloom, but he figured she didn't know that.

Bess remained frozen in place. Chet's hands felt so cold. She needed to think her way out this mess and all she could think about was how cold his hands felt. She'd come to love the warmth and strength of those hands and now they were limp and cold.

"You jest bring them bags right over here little lady and..." Cato drifted out briefly. "...and I'll see they don't go too hard on you." Dub's voice betrayed him. Bess realized that if she could delay him just a little while, he would likely collapse again.

"Mr. Deputy, I can help you. I mean, you've lost a lot of blood. You need medical attention."

"Don't you worry your head none about what I need. I told you to bring them bags here. Bring me them bags." Cato shouted and winced. He pressed his right forearm against the wound in his side and his shattered right hand throbbed incessantly. A wave of nausea swept over him, and he gagged but resisted the impulse to vomit. His body failed to cooperate, and another gut-wrenching spasm forced him to lean over and spew a bitter stream of bile and vomit onto the floor beside him.

While Cato retched, Bess tightened her grip on Chet's hands and pulled with all her strength. She rapidly closed the distance to the doorway and Chet's butt and legs thumped over the edge of the concrete. She dropped him unceremoniously as soon as they were out of the building and around the corner. Bess ran back and frantically grabbed the bottom of the overhead door and yanked it down. The heavy steel door slammed down and effectively blocked Cato from being able to direct his fire at them. Nonetheless he did open fire as fast as his finger could pull the trigger. Bess lunged back around the corner and dropped to the ground next to Chet. A hail of vicious little bullets tore through the metal of the door. Fragments of steel and lead showered Bess and Chet but none of the rounds hit either of them directly. Several did hit her old Escort and Bess screamed in panic as one round hit her fuel tank. The fuel from the ruptured tank poured down over the hot exhaust pipe from the still running engine. A white cloud of fuel vapor billowed up from the vehicle but did not ignite. Bess saw that she and Chet were trapped between a potential firebomb and the building. The only means of escape was to drag him in front of the overhead door. If the fuel vapor ignited, they would be burned alive.

Inside the building, Dub Cato was clinging to consciousness. He had expended all twenty rounds in the weapon's magazine. Now he fumbled with the extra magazine that he had taped to the side of the one he'd just used up. His right hand was useless. He thumbed the release allowing the magazines to fall out of the weapon. They clattered on the floor and Cato couldn't reach them without moving. Each time he shifted his body, pain shot through him in such waves that he thought he would surely die. He couldn't hear or see his adversaries outside, but he figured they must be pinned down or else he would have heard a vehicle leaving. The engine from the car was still running and this puzzled him. Had he hit them with his blind shots?

Bess was frantic with fear. She wanted to just sprint across the doorway and be gone. Chet was still unconscious, and his breath was coming in ragged, shallow gulps. If she tried to drag him across, they would both be exposed to Cato's firing and if she left him...well, she didn't want to think about what could happen if the fuel tank went off.

Gasoline was still trickling down onto the exhaust pipe with a frightening hiss.

Another shot boomed through the door and Bess screamed in spite of herself. Cato now knew that she was still out there, but he didn't know where. He was lucid enough to expend his ammunition more carefully. He turned his good ear toward the door and listened attentively. He was waiting for Bess to make a move. She was watching the fuel vapors swirl and eddy. She was afraid to stay where she was, but she was absolutely terrified to try to run the gauntlet of gasoline and gunfire. She had almost convinced herself to try pulling Chet to safety when the engine started knocking loudly and then sputtered to a halt. The only sound was the hissing of the fuel dripping onto the still hot exhaust pipe. Cato waited.

Bess watched the fuel start to puddle on the concrete under her car. The vapor was drifting toward her and Chet, but the puddle of gasoline was running under the door and into the basement. She had seen burn victims before. Of all the ways to die, she didn't want to burn. Please God, don't let me burn, she murmured.

Cato fired another exploratory round, and this time Bess didn't scream. She stood up and grabbed Chet's hands and began pulling furiously. They were halfway across the doorway when Cato fired again. This time he was nearly unconscious, and he'd allowed the muzzle to drop slightly as he fired. The copper jacketed bullet plowed into the concrete in front of her car resulting in a shower of sparks. The gasoline vapor had pooled on the ground and spread all around the vehicle. For Bess, the resulting inferno happened in slow motion. She felt, rather than heard, the blast from Cato's rifle. She saw the shower of sparks and she knew what was coming. The swirling vapors near the ground ignited first with a breathtaking whoosh. The bluish flame spread over everything including Chet who was at ground level. The flames singed his clothing, ignited blades of dry grass and raced toward the puddle of gasoline that soaked the ground under her faithful old car. The pooled gasoline seemed to suck in the blue vapor flames only to blast them out again in a fiery orange conflagration that consumed the little car. Most of the fuel had leaked out of the punctured gas tank leaving a few ounces of liquid and the remaining space was filled with superheated vapor. This vapor ignited within a fraction of a second and it detonated with a thunderous roar that shook the ground and blasted the overhead door out of its track. The concussion and shock wave flattened Bess as she still struggled to drag Chet to safety. Inside the confined space of the basement shards of glass and pieces of twisted metal flew at Dub. He instinctively raised his arm to shield his face from the debris. The metal and glass shrapnel pierced his arms, legs and torso in dozens of ragged but shallow wounds.

After the initial explosion, Dub was stunned but still conscious. He struggled to sit up enough to see the devastation created by the blast. All manner of shredded metal and glass littered the floor around him. The sturdy metal door was a twisted mess of scorched and blackened steel.

The flames had been smothered by the oxygen robbing blast and now the room was darkened by smoke and dust. Outside the doorway, the flames continued to lick at the destroyed vehicle. The tires burned furiously, lighting the area with an eerie light.

The puddle had run inside the basement, soaked into the nylon packs and had pooled under the shelves which held cans of paint, acetone, oil and every flammable sort of product. Dub Cato's relief was short-lived. Bess could hear him shriek as the volatile fumes drifted into the flames and re-ignited. He screamed until he sucked in a lung-full of searing flames.

CHAPTER FORTY-FIVE

Chet had never cultivated any relationships with his neighbors. In fact, he'd discouraged any contact that they'd initiated. Nonetheless, the older couple down the road had taken an interest in Chet's activities, simply out of curiosity. The periodic gun shots were not particularly unusual in the country and definitely not unusual at Chet's place. But the explosion was, and it drew them away from their dinner table to peer out the window. Finally, after discussing what that strange man was doing, they decided to call 911 when they saw the first plumes of black smoke starting to boil up.

Chet's place was well outside the city limits, so the fire protection association consisted of a group of well-trained volunteers. A convoy of pickup trucks with flashing red lights and squalling sirens soon filled Chet's driveway.

Bess had heard the sirens and had seen the flashing red lights in the distance as the firefighters approached Chet's property. The sirens grew louder and more insistent as they approached, and Bess realized she had a decision to make. She carefully laid Chet's head down with a final caress of his hair. It took all of her strength to get up and walk back into the still burning basement. Clouds of noxious smoke blanketed the ceiling, so she got down on her hands and knees and crawled toward Dub Cato. The flames illuminated a charred and horribly disfigured body. The human body, when exposed to such conditions, contorts into grotesque postures and Dub was no exception.

Bess crawled right past Dub with only the slightest glance. The smell of burned human flesh would have sickened almost anyone but she was beyond caring. She kept crawling, trying to avoid the smoldering embers that covered floor. Her hair was blackened with soot and angry red burns covered her hands and arms, but she crawled until she reached the pile of nylon bags. Tendrils of smoke floated up from dozens of small burn holes in the bags, but they were essentially undamaged. She unzipped one of the bags, removed a bundle of one-hundred-dollar bills and tucked it into her pocket.

She then dragged each bag to the edge of the hidden chamber and pushed it over the edge to fall into the darkness with a heavy thud. The door to the hidden chamber was pinned down by fallen debris and smoldering embers. Bess scattered the embers with her foot, using her last ounces of energy to lift the heavy door and drop it into place. Finally, she slid the sheet of soot-covered plywood over the opening to disguise it as much as possible.

Her lungs were burning from the toxic smoke, but she forced herself to begin her crawl back out of the hellish nightmare. Bess emerged into the clean night air, choking and coughing, just as the emergency vehicles arrived at Chet's driveway.

Chet lay just where she'd left him, lifeless. Bess moved painfully into a sitting position and cradled Chet's head in her lap. She stroked his hair and waited for the new day to arrive.

Don't miss out!

Visit the website below and you can sign up to receive emails whenever Boone Lockhart Wilford publishes a new book. There's no charge and no obligation.

https://books2read.com/r/B-A-XSGE-DUHN

BOOKS 2 READ

Connecting independent readers to independent writers.

About the Author

Boone Wilford brings a wide variety of experiences to his stories. He served in the Army after college as a commissioned military intelligence officer, worked in the behavioral health field for several years, owned a dive shop, taught SCUBA diving, then spent most of his working career industrial management. He decided to reinvent himself in his late forties and returned to school and completed a Masters degree in Nursing. He recently retired as an Oncology Hematology Nurse Practitioner.

He and his wife Sabrina make their home in north central Arkansas with their two Australian Shepherds, Mazie and Maddie. They live in a hangarhome with their 1946 Aeronca Champ which they fly to back country strips all through the Ozarks. They also injoy bicycling, hiking, and fly fishing.

Milton Keynes UK
Ingram Content Group UK Ltd.
UKHW040629310723
426074UK00001B/123

9 798223 366607